TALL MAN WALKING

THE ATTIC ROOM

MARIAN SCOTT

TALL MAN WALKING

THE ATTIC ROOM

Marian Gallagher Scott

COACHWHIP PUBLICATIONS

Greenville, Ohio

Tall Man Walking / The Attic Room, by Marian Gallagher Scott
© 2015 Coachwhip Publications

Tall Man Walking, as by Katherine Wolffe, published 1936.
The Attic Room, as by Katherine Wolffe, published 1942.
No claims made on public domain material.

ISBN 1-61646-303-1
ISBN-13 978-1-61646-303-8

Cover: Man in suit © NejroN Photo

CoachwhipBooks.com

CONTENTS

INTRODUCTION
Muses of the Mind: The Mystery Fiction
of Marian Gallagher Scott

Curtis Evans

Detective novels are known for characters' uses of aliases, but the authors who write them often have employed them as well, in the form of *noms de plume*. (The most famous recent example is J. K. Rowling's adoption of the pen name "Robert Galbraith" for her newly-launched mystery series.) A crime writer still enshrouded in mystery today is Marian Gallagher Scott (9 October 1892–8 June1943), who, besides writing prolifically for the pulps, in a ten-year period published, under three alternating pseudonyms, four detective novels: *Dead Hands Reaching* (1932), by Marion Scott; *Tall Man Walking* (1936), by Katherine Wolffe; *The Moon Saw Murder* (1937), by Gail Oliver; and *The Attic Room* (1942), by Katherine Wolffe. Additionally, *Death's Long Shadow*, a final Marian Gallagher Scott mystery novel, was posthumously published in 1946, under the author's Katherine Wolffe pseudonym. Although Scott's second published detective novel, *Tall Man Walking*, received considerable critical praise around the world, the book was never reprinted in paperback and was soon forgotten, like the rest of her fictional work. The neglect of Scott's writing is especially unfortunate in the case of *Tall Man Walking*, one of the finest psychological crime novels produced by an American mystery writer in the 1930s.[1]

Maude Marian Gallagher was born to Benjamin James and Emily Amelia (Van Ness) Gallagher in the small farming community of Wilsey, Kansas in 1892, eight years after the town was founded as a stopping point on the Missouri Pacific Railroad. Shortly after the turn of the century Marian moved with her family to the Kansas state capital, Topeka, where her father owned a drugstore. (Marian's uncle, George B. Gallagher, was a Topeka grocer and her younger sister, Elizabeth Louise, later married a Topeka baker, Samuel E. Weirich.) Marian seems to have led a life in Topeka that, from what little we currently know about her, is not readily distinguishable from that of other young urban Midwest women of her era; yet her artistic muse must have insistently beckoned her even then, on the seemingly endless prairies of her native state, with the promise of a more brightly colored future.

Having graduated in 1910 from Topeka High School and Daugherty's Business College, Marian found employment for the next several years in the capital as a stenographer and court reporter. Although state auditing records list payments made to Marian Gallagher for clerical work done on behalf of the Livestock Sanitary Commissioner and the Kansas Senate, the ambitious young woman had hopes for a future that encompassed something more than mechanically recording the prosaic declarations of attorneys, businessmen and politicians. In addition to performing her workaday typing jobs, Marian regularly attended a class in dramatic expression. One day her teacher, praising Marian's acting ability, urged her to go study at the Lyceum Arts Conservatory in Chicago, under the tutelage of Elias Day, an influential figure in circuit Chautauqua: traveling shows arising out of the nineteenth-century lyceum educational movement that took place in thousands

[1] A 1939 American publisher's blurb claims that Marian Gallagher Scott in fact had "written six novels, published in this country, England, and France." My accounting above only lists three Scott novels, so it appears that there may be three additional, unknown Scott novels that were published, presumably under yet more pseudonyms (or perhaps serialized novels in pulps were counted in the tally).

of small town venues across America and included lectures, ora-
tory, musical acts and performances of famous plays. "At its peak
in the mid-1920s," notes a modern authority, "circuit Chautauqua
performers and lecturers appeared in more than 10,000 com-
munities in 45 states to audiences totaling 45 million people."[2]
Inspired by her teacher's hopeful advice, Marian left Topeka and
typing behind, moving to the Windy City in 1914 and enrolling in
Elias Day's school.

Marian's greatest moment in life up to that time came the next
year when Elias Day chose her to play the female lead in the school's
staging of a renowned Shakespeare comedy, *The Taming of the
Shrew*. The male lead was played by Earl William Scott (1891-1971),
a recent graduate of Nebraska Wesleyan University and the
Lyceum Arts Conservatory who was circuiting the country with fellow "characterist" Bob Mahoney, as the Scott-Mahoney Company.
Marian and Earl became romantically involved and wed at the
Methodist parsonage in Laporte, Indiana on May 21, 1917, when
Marian was twenty-four years old. After their marriage the couple
founded their own acting troupe, the Kenilworth Players (presumably named for 215 S. Kenilworth Avenue, Oak Park, Illinois, their
street address at the time), which for a decade was a fixture in circuit Chautauqua. In the case of Earl and Marian Scott, the handsome pair over the next eleven years would give countless rendi-
tions of the perpetually-sparring Katherina and Petruchio, performing *The Taming of the Shrew* in such seemingly inhospitable
locales as the roughneck central Texas oil boomtown of Caddo.

Marian Gallagher Scott, as she was now known, much later in
life would evocatively detail her circuit Chautauqua experiences
in a 1939 book, *Chautauqua Caravan* (published under the name
Marian Scott), and readers of this introduction are urged to peruse
this fascinating work of social history. However, only at the
close of Marian and Earl's career in circuit Chautauqua—with the

---

[2] Charlotte Canning, "Traveling Culture: Circuit Chautauqua in the Twentieth Century,"
Records of the Redpath Chautauqua Collection, The University of Iowa Libraries Special Collections & University Archives, at http://www.lib.uiowa.edu/sc/tc/.

Earl and Marian Scott as Petruchio and Katherina
in *The Taming of the Shrew*. The Kenilworth Players.
(Records of the Redpath Chautauqua Collection,
The University of Iowa Libraries, Iowa City, Iowa.)

ascent of radio and the automobile the institution had entered a state of terminal decline—did the couple turn to the writing of pulp crime fiction as an alternative source of income. In *Chautauqua Caravan* Marian indicates that she and Earl enjoyed reading pulps while resting from circuits, specifically mentioning their happy discovery, in a cabin outside Woodruff, Wisconsin, of a "tattered copy of *Adventure* tucked back on a shelf," in which they read, much to their delight, a Stephen Chalmers' lost civilization treasure tale, "The Dance of the Golden Gods." Using the slightly disguised pseudonym "Marion Scott," Marian published her first known crime tale, "Folded Evidence," in the October 1927 issue of *Black Mask*. Under this pseudonym Marian would publish a total of three stories in *Black Mask*, while another seventeen tales would appear in this celebrated pulp magazine under the byline Earl and Marion Scott. Writing both jointly and separately, the couple over the course of the Twenties and Thirties published close to two hundred known stories in myriad pulps, including *Street & Smith's Detective Story Magazine*, *Detective Action Stories*, *Mystery Magazine*, *Clues*, *Gang World*, *Thrilling Detective*, and *Top-notch Magazine*.

For Earl Scott writing for the pulps seems never to have served as an impetus to novel authorship, but Marian Scott, following such recent successful examples as Dashiell Hammett and Raoul Whitfield, daringly sought to make the transition, publishing her first crime novel, *Dead Hands Reaching*, with Macmillan in 1932, five years after she had entered the pulp fiction mill. Rather melodramatic in tone and episodic in narrative yet undeniably eventful and exciting, *Dead Hands Reaching* to me very much seems to reflect, as the title suggests, Marian's apprenticeship in the pulps. She wrote the novel, which details the shocking events that follow actress Dallas Gentry's fateful return to Willow Valley to seek a divorce from her wealthy and tyrannical older husband, in Santa Fe, New Mexico, where the couple settled after leaving circuit Chautauqua and became, like a better-known crime writer, Dorothy B. Hughes, fixtures in the city's artistic community. Earl and Marian resided at the wryly-named "Crooks' Nook," a three-room

Marion Scott often made the
front cover of pulp magazines.

adobe cottage on the Acequia Madre, and did all their writing at an office they rented on Sena Plaza. My copy of *Dead Hands Reaching* came from the library of Harry Steeger, founder of Popular Publications, one of the largest publishers of pulp magazines at the time, and is inscribed by Scott herself as follows: "To Popular Publications with all good wishes Marian Scott Santa Fe Aug 30 – 1932."

In addition to its drawing slightly on the author's extensive experience in circuit Chautauqua (Dallas Gentry, we learn, worked her way up to acting stardom from her beginnings in "Tom Willoughby's Repertory Company, touring the South and Middle West"), *Dead Hands Reaching* is of note for introducing New York City police detective Captain Courtney Brade, Marian Scott's series detective in three novels. Observing Brade for the first time, Dallas Gentry is immediately surprised by the cop's sophistication and sensitivity, in a passage that attempts to authenticate the sleuth's sterling credentials as a Golden Age Great Detective:

> Dallas didn't know much about detectives. . . . She rather thought they should be short, heavy men with thick red faces and blunt hands, who wore derbies and broad shoes. . . . Brade was almost as tall as Anthony . . . lean and looked in perfect condition. He was quietly and correctly dressed in gray tweeds. He had very thick, dark-brown hair . . . stained with gray at the temples. . . . He had the strongest, keenest, saddest eyes she had ever seen. They were a curious cloudy gray, rather long and habitually narrowed between crisp black lashes. He smiled and rested a hand on the table's edge. For no reason she could explain, Dallas looked at that hand. It seemed to her that every part of the man was distinctive, individual.
>
> "What a gorgeous ring," she thought, staring at a magnificent Oriental moonstone, set in a massive, hand-hammered, silver mounting. . . . "I wonder why a detective wears a ring like that?"

This crime investigating paragon—a suave study in gray sporting a mysterious moonstone ring that holds, we are tantalizingly
told, "the story of Brade's greatest defeat and mightiest victory"—
would not appear again in another detective novel by Marian Scott
for a full decade. With Scott's second and finest detective novel,
Tall Man Walking, the author separated herself from her pulp past
by using a new author pseudonym, Katherine Wolffe. Although the
title of the book seems a play on *Dead Hands Reaching*, this ambitious and accomplished work is a non-series tale of a much different order from Scott's first detective novel. On the surface *Tall
Man Walking*, which was published in the United States in 1936
by Doubleday Doran's prestigious Crime Club, clearly belongs to
the American tradition of the so-called HIBK (Had-I-But-Known)
novels associated with the hugely popular mysteries of Mary Rob-
erts Rinehart. In the most typical examples of HIBK novels a
middle-aged spinster forebodingly narrates a recent course of dire
events, which might have turned out differently, had the narrator
but known the things she now knows. There has been a certain
male tendency to disparage the "feminine" HIBK novel as what
Julian Symons in his crime fiction study *Bloody Murder* dubbed
fiction written specifically for "maiden aunts" (Ogden Nash coined
the term HIBK in a humorous 1940 poem, "Don't Guess, Let Me
Tell You"), yet in fact the better writers associated with the HIBK
school, such as Rinehart, Leslie Ford, Mabel Seeley and Dorothy
Cameron Disney, enjoyed considerable popularity with both male
and female readers and reviewers and in the last fifteen years or
so an effort has been made within the academic world to revise
modern critical opinion of their work (see, for example, Catherine
Nickerson's 1999 monograph, *The Web of Iniquity*).

Forebodingly narrated by a fifty-four year old New England
village spinster, *Tall Man Walking* in this respect falls squarely
within the HIBK tradition, yet it takes readers into darker spaces
than is customary in this school of fiction. The spinster, local dressmaker Laure Hosmer, explains that she has been tasked with writing an account of the recent rash of murders that savagely struck
Wilromere, "a beautiful little village . . . named after our leading

family, the Rohmers." As described in an unconsciously amusing manner by the prim Miss Laure, Wilromere is a classic tradition-alist village of the sort associated in many mystery readers' minds today with Golden Age English detective fiction:

> Somehow the tide of what is known as progress has pretty well passed us by and I for one am glad. A year ago last fall they oiled the main street and where used to be livery stables are now garages, and a big oil company put in a very nice station with dahlias and cannas blooming in the little square in front. Also the Congregational Church has been painted white. It was red when I was a small girl and I liked it best that way. . . . except for these things that I mention and few others equally unimportant, the town is like I always have known it. The people are old-fashioned, too. . . . I don't mean to imply that we are narrow in Wilromere. No indeed. We are really very up to date. Just last winter the Woman's Culture Club studied a huge book by James Joyce, and Stacey Madden, just back from a season in Europe, gave a lecture on the Art of the Vatican. All of the boys and girls of the wealthier families go off to college and sometimes travel abroad, like Stacey Madden, though she is no longer a girl, goodness knows. She's forty-six if she's a day and I'm sure, though I've never mentioned it to anyone, that her hair has been tinted.

Yet even Miss Laure realizes that, in writing this narrative of criminal violence, she must let her upright mind venture into the midnight alleys where murder lurks, even in old-fashioned villages like Wilromere:

> I closed my eyes, leaned back in my chair and just let my memory go. It was like when you drop a spool of thread and still hold onto one end. The spool rolls

away some place and the thread unwinds, becomes tangled, twisted, tied into knots. Then you're apt to find the spool anywhere. Under the sofa, behind the table, back of a chair. When you go in after it, you discover dust sometimes where you thought it was clean. Maybe you'll run into that coral pin you lost last winter. Perhaps you'll find hateful things like where the mice have been, or a spider has spun a web, so that your skin crawls and you want to back away real fast, not looking much.

That's the way it was with my memory. . . .

The lost spool of thread is a clever image that aptly conveys the unpleasant emotions that are unleashed in certain quarters of Wilromere by the June wedding of David Kaye and Wiletta Owens. When the hateful Wiletta is found stabbed to the heart in her wedding dress more than a half-dozen suspects can be discerned just within her own wedding party. Not for nothing is *Tall Man Walking* subtitled *Murder—with Music by Wagner*. (The subtitle also recalls how Marian Gallagher had once played the wedding march from *Lohengrin* at her friend Agnes Coulter's May wedding in Topeka a quarter of a century earlier.)

"Murder!" writes Miss Laure. "Who of us realized it fully? It was a word we had heard, that we sometimes used, but it was outside our real comprehension, like leprosy or the Black Hole of Calcutta." Yet the citizens of Wilromere come to realize to their mortification that hidden away within the village are its own black holes of hate and bile, which now stand to be exposed under the light of a murder investigation conducted by the novel's apparent detective figure: a mysterious sleuth of the mind, psychiatrist Kenneth Borden (the "tall man" of the title). As another character, Miss Laure's old friend Dr. Marc Wayne, retrospectively puts it to the spinster dressmaker, in the case of the Wilromere murders, the "physical clues weren't the important ones."

Tightly plotted and extremely suspenseful, *Tall Man Walking* twists and turns like an unloosed spool of thread. Part of the appeal of the novel is found as well in Marian Scott's compelling

portrayal of village life in New England, a region that had fascinated the author since she had met her future husband in 1915 and
he had regaled her in his letters with enchanting tales of his circuits with Bob Mahoney in the East. "I lived his accounts of the
snowbound New England villages," Scott recalled fondly in
Chautauqua Caravan. When she finally visited New England in
1922, she found that "the little villages with their quaint, dormer-
windowed houses, their neat squares and time-weathered churches,
were a constant delight."

Critics around the world were similarly delighted with *Tall Man
Walking*. "Why is it that mystery stories in which spinsters play
leading roles are almost invariably good?" queried Isaac Anderson in his highly laudatory review of the novel in the *New York
Times Book Review*. Hundreds of miles away in Middle America,
Todd Downing, himself an accomplished mystery writer, gave a
rave review to *Tall Man Walking* in the pages of the Oklahoma
City *Daily Oklahoman*, praising the novel as "one of the trickiest
and most intelligent yarns of the season, put over without finger-
prints, broken cufflinks or rouge-tipped cigarettes in the way of
clues." The admiring Downing added that "Katherine Wolffe is a name
to be watched in mystery fiction." *Tall Man Walking* also was "warmly
recommended" by nationally syndicated book reviewer Bruce Catton,
who contrasted the novel's mature and superbly controlled narrative
with that of *Danger in the Dark*, a mystery by popular romantic crime
writer Mignon Eberhart that, according to Catton, was fatally afflicted
by the "complete brainlessness of the hero and heroine, plus the
author's breathless, awed style of writing." In Britain and the
Dominions, where the novel was published under the more lurid
(and rather silly) title *Bride of Death*, the critical response was
also extremely positive, with, for example, the *Melbourne Argus*
trumpeting: "As an exciting story of death and crime detection this
book is good; as a skillful study in suspense it is remarkable." In
1937 Scott, in collaboration with Philip Barber, a Yale University
professor of drama and New York director of the Federal Theatre
Project, adapted *Tall Man Walking* as a two-act play, but regret-
tably it seems never to have been performed on stage.

Perhaps daunted by the great critical praise for *Tall Man Walking*—how does one, the author might well have asked herself, follow such a resoundingly huzzahed performance—Scott produced no new "Katherine Wolffe" crime novel for six years. Between *Tall Man Walking* and *The Attic Room* came another non-series mystery, *The Moon Saw Murder*, which Scott published with Macmillan under yet another pseudonym, Gail Oliver, and Scott's impressive non-fiction book, *Chautauqua Caravan*. By the time William Morrow published the second Katherine Wolffe detective novel in 1942, less than a year before Scott's death, *New York Times* book reviewer Isaac Anderson, despite having highly praised the author's *Tall Man Walking* six years earlier, pronounced in his notice of *The Attic Room*: "This appears to be Katherine Wolffe's first mystery story." After merely half a dozen years, Todd Downing's name to watch had become a name that time forgot.

It surely did not help Katherine Wolffe's fading reputation that *The Attic Room*, though entertaining, falls short of the high standard set by *Tall Man Walking*. Evidently for her new novel Scott wanted to retain the sort of middle-aged New England spinster narrator figure that had served *Tall Man Walking* so well (in *The Attic Room* this figure is a fifty-six year old village postmistress, Martha Berry, though she is actually a longtime widow, not a spinster). However, the author shoehorned Courtney Brade, her Great Detective from the Marion Scott mystery *Dead Hands Reaching*, into the novel as well, making a somewhat awkward fit. Brade effectively steps into the shoes of the psychiatrist Kenneth Borden from *Tall Man Walking*, but as an individual personality he seems extraneous to the tale, despite references to his "cloudy gray eyes" and "gorgeous moonstone ring" (how the New York cop comes to take over a murder investigation in a New England village is not adequately explained). Moreover, the novel's non-series characters are altogether more conventional than those in *Tall Man Walking*. Nevertheless, the story is still an enjoyable one and the New England village setting again is well-conveyed.

A little more than a half-year after the publication of *The Attic Room*, Marian Scott died suddenly from a heart complication in

EARL AND MARIAN SCOTT

Hollywood, California, where the couple had moved about five years earlier. At her death Scott had completed more than two-thirds of a final novel, which her husband later finished and published in 1946 as a paperback original attributed to Scott's most successful pseudonym, Katherine Wolffe. The novel, entitled *Death's Long Shadow*, details the last known criminal investigation of Courtney Brade. It is, in my view, the best book in the Brade mystery series and a fitting tribute to the ingenuity of Brade's creator.

Like its two immediate Katherine Wolffe predecessors, *Death's Long Shadow* draws on a New England village milieu, yet it has a more modern feel, as though in its composition the Scotts had been influenced to an extent by the rise in American crime fiction of the hard-boiled style. The novel opens evocatively on a sleeting November evening at a soon-to-be defunct gas station in rural Minnesota, forlornly located by the Chippewa City-Minneapolis highway (I was immediately reminded of the 1940 Edward Hopper painting *Gas*), and then shifts to an isolated cottage where a mysterious hermit woman, Ann Regnas, has been done violently to death. Courtney Brade is soon on the scene—his appearance here is more plausibly explained than it is in *The Attic Room*—and, curiosity getting the better of him yet again, he manages once more to unofficially take over a murder investigation, this one leading to a long-buried past and some dark doings in Reddington, a stern and wintry Massachusetts town.

Marian Scott's depiction of Reddington may have drawn not on quaint New England villages, by which she always seems to have been quite charmed, but rather on her recollections of a dismal winter she spent alone not long after her marriage, when she was conducting a drama class in a small town in central Illinois, Earl being far away on a solo southern circuit. In *Chautauqua Caravan* Scott's memories of that central Illinois town, which she calls "Lovell," are imbued with bitterness over the social exclusion she suffered there:

> It was an old town, as our towns go, and its people
> were clannish, unfriendly, suspicious, to a new-
> comer. They were particularly skittish, where I was

concerned, because I was known to have some association with the stage. Also, although I had "Mrs." Before my name, which according to their lights should have automatically rendered me highly respectable, my husband was not in evidence. No one had ever seen him. With them, seeing was believing. So they stood back, reserved their judgment and some of them turned their heads the other way when I passed them in the streets. . . .

. . . . [I]n spite of [my landlady's] friendship and my class of interested youngsters, I was very lonely those cold, dark months. . . .

More than a year after I left Lovell and managed pretty well to erase it from my memory, I had a letter from the dignified and correct president of the Women's Club, who, during my residence there, had never been at home when I called. She invited me to return and coach a play for them. She was very cordial and pleasantly insistent, naming a handsome sum as compensation. I gathered from the letter that, after a sufficient time has elapsed, they had decided that I was quite harmless after all, and perhaps I did have a husband and was what was generally described in Lovell as a "good woman."

While I was, I trust, properly grateful for their eventual confidence in me, I did not go, and I recalled with natural resentment the only time I had attended one of their churches to be regarded with patent unfriendliness, not one of the large, satisfied congregation bothering to speak to me. . . . It . . . set before me vividly the extreme cruelty of which a small town may be capable.

In *Death's Long Shadow* Marion Scott devised a most engrossing swan song, providing readers a detective novel with both compelling human drama and clever criminal conundrums. Earl Scott, who probably wrote the last four or five chapters of *Death's Long Shadow*, deserves credit as well for so neatly disentangling the intricate plot threads in his wife's tapestry of murder. My only regret with *Death's Long Shadow* is that, the novel being the record of Courtney Brade's last recorded case, we will never learn the story behind the detective's mysterious moonstone ring (which in the novel he twirls with a flourish when making one of his dramatic revelations). The republication by Coachwhip Publications of *Death's Long Shadow* with three other Marian Scott mysteries, most especially *Tall Man Walking*, is an act of due historical recovery that should be applauded by fans of classic American crime fiction.

TALL MAN WALKING

CHAPTER ONE

ISN'T IT STRANGE the things you remember? Sitting here last night, in my low rocker by the window, looking out at the moon on the silver poplar tree, I recalled a maxim I used to see in my copybook when I was a very small girl in the third grade. It said:

Honest confession is good for the soul!

It came before me just as plain, stiff black characters on a shiny white page. How very hard I worked to make my awkward writing resemble it. Last night it held particular significance because of all that has happened since last spring. Anyway, when Marc Wayne dropped in to see me this morning, I told him about it. I added that I should like to write the story of everything that had occurred since the night David Kaye was to marry Wiletta Owens at the home of his adopted parents, Clarke and Caroline Rohmer.

Dr. Marc stuffed his disreputable pipe, got it going and looked at me thoughtfully. "Everything, Laure?" he asked. "You mean you'd write everything?"

I laughed at him. Dr. Marc is always so serious. What could you expect, though, him having married Luella Bell nearly twenty-five years ago and the way she made life hell for him, until the good Lord took her away and gave Marc a chance at peace before the final curtain. So I laughed at him and said,

"Why, certainly, Marcus, I'd write everything."

25

Marc continued to puff on his pipe and look at me from his sad brown eyes that sometimes remind me of the eyes of my old dog Jo who died seventeen years ago come Thanksgiving. He said,

"Well, Laure, I think it would be a fine idea. Give you something to occupy your mind these days and then, who knows?" He paused and I saw dull color begin to creep up his thin cheeks from the edge of his collar that is always a little frayed.

I said, and I guess it was rather snappish, "I can keep my mind occupied, thank you, Dr. Wayne. I've been working at that job for better than fifty years now and never had much trouble. And exactly what do you mean, please, by saying that 'then, who knows?'"

He snorted and his eyes snapped with some of their old fire. "I mean that it might help the case against—" And again that stupid man paused and swallowed and couldn't go on, so I switched my rocker around to face him and finished it up for him.

"The case against the murderer? Is that what you mean, Marc?"

His shoulders slumped. He blinked at me behind his gold-rimmed nose glasses. "That's what I mean, Laure. Course, it's all settled, considering the confession, but what I mean is that the defense might get something out of it that would be beneficial to—"

"The accused, Marc?"

He just nodded, looking so very miserable. Poor Marc! He needed someone to take care of him all these years, and not Luella Bell's constant faultfinding, hectoring, tantrums and general devil raising.

So that's how this history started. Marc and I talked about it until he really got quite excited. He loves detective stories. He said that of course this one wouldn't be so much fun because in the first place we all knew who was guilty now, though heaven can witness that it took a lot of trouble to find out. Then, in the second place, Marc said, it just couldn't be fun because it had brought us all too much misery and heartache. Still, he thought I should do it and he promised to bring me the right sort of paper and lend me his portable typewriter. We fixed up a small table by the window where the red geranium is blooming so gayly and the red-dotted yellow calico curtains give an air of brightness to the room.

Mattie Grisold gave me those curtains nearly three months ago and I bless her for them. I watched the summer sun through them, making golden spots on the floor. I parted them one morning and saw a blue haze over the hills surrounding the valley and knew that summer was on the wane. One dark night I heard rain pounding the roof, and when I looked out next morning the leaves of the silver poplar were drooping. They straightened up some when the sun came out but slowly they turned to crimson, then to brown. Gradually they are falling and soon none will be left and only the bare black branches will show cold under the moon.

This morning when Marc had me all fixed up with the table and the typewriter and lots of nice white paper, he still stayed on, looking worried. He said, "Now you know, Laure, in a detective story you've got to tell everything. You can't hold anything back, remember that."

I just looked at him. "Well, I do declare, Marcus Wayne, what is the use of writing it then? Why not just say So and So was killed on Thursday and So and So on Saturday and So and So did it?"

He wrinkled his bushy brows that are still black in spite of his thick curly hair being nearly white, and explained very patiently,

"It's this way, Laure. Detective stories are written for people to enjoy. They are puzzles and not very many of them are really true, like this one. The pleasure folks get out of them is trying to figure out from the clues given them by the author just who is guilty. They watch the fiction detective working on the case and they try to beat him at it. They try to be smarter than he is, so to be absolutely fair, the reader must have as much information as the investigator has."

"I see that, Marc, and I'll try to do it. But I have the right to withhold information which we have now but didn't have at the time, haven't I?"

"Of course, Laure. You must tell it in sequence, just as it happened."

"And were there so very many clues, Marc? I mean, things like footprints and drops of blood and—"

Marc looked very pale for some reason. He said, "Not very many, Laure. The physical clues weren't the important ones. It was the other kind, the things people said, the way they looked, what they thought—"

"And the lies they told, Marc. They were important. Shall I put in all the lies that were told, just as we heard them?"

"Yes, Laure."

"There were a great many lies, weren't there, Marc?"

"A great many, Laure," he agreed, and sighed heavily, then went on, "You must put everything before the reader but if you're smart as an author, you'll arrange it so he won't know it's important. Do you understand?"

"Yes, Marc, I understand. It's going to be fun, isn't it?" Then right away I wished I hadn't said that, for his poor face got all gray and sweat stood out on his upper lip and he swallowed hard and said,

"Oh, Laure, how can you?"

"Forgive me, Marc. You mustn't think me hard-hearted or cold-blooded, for really I'm not. I'm just as sorry as you that all those people are dead. Why, Marc, some of them we'd known most all our lives, hadn't we?"

"Yes," he said, sounding thick and choked. "We'd known some of them a long time, God rest their souls."

Peter, my big striped tomcat, woke up just then, meowed complainingly and went back to sleep. I don't know what I should do without Peter.

After Marc had explained some more, he left and I started to work.

First, I sat very still for a time, watching the October sun coming through the yellow curtains with the red dots and making bright splashes on the floor. I sat there, rearranging things in my mind, trying to realize myself in the position of an author about to relate the story of tragedy and death that descended on our peaceful little tree-bowered village, beginning with that wonderful moonlight night the twenty-second of June when David Kaye was to marry Wiletta Owens.

I closed my eyes, leaned back in my chair and just let my memory go. It was like when you drop a spool of thread and still hold onto one end. The spool rolls away some place and the thread unwinds, becomes tangled, twisted, tied into knots. Then you're apt to find the spool anywhere. Under the sofa, behind the table, back of a chair. When you go in after it, you discover dust sometimes where you thought it was all clean. Maybe you'll run onto that coral pin you lost last winter. Perhaps you'll find hateful things like where the mice have been, or a spider has spun a web, so that your skin crawls and you want to back away real fast, not looking much.

That's the way it was with my memory. It went along twisted, tangled trails, into dark corners, under heaped-up hates and fears and suspicions. Some of the things I found I didn't want to look at, but since I promised Dr. Marc to tell all the truth, I made myself do it.

I WAS BORN in Wilromere fifty-four years ago, the third of December, and except for short trips down to New York and one once as far west as Chicago to visit Aunt Nellie, I have spent the entire time here. It is a beautiful little village and it was named after our leading family, the Rohmers. Maybe that seems hard to figure out, but it all comes from one of the early members. He was Wild Rohmer and he has lived on in legend to this very day. At first it was Wild Rohmer's Town, then it was, much later, Wild Rohmerville, and finally long before I was born someone had sense enough to keep the significance and still make it sound pleasant, so Wilromere it is.

Somehow the tide of what is known as progress has pretty well passed us by and I for one am glad. A year ago last fall they oiled the main street and where used to be livery stables are now garages, and a big oil company put in a very nice station with dahlias and cannas blooming in the little square in front. Also the Congregational Church has been painted white. It was red when I was a small girl and I liked it best that way.

So except for these things that I mention and a few others equally unimportant, the town is like I have always known it. The people are old-fashioned, too, and still celebrate Thanksgiving and

Christmas with family dinners that last all day and even have quilting parties, believe it or not. And that last phrase I got from David Kaye, who brought it back from college, though where it originated I couldn't even guess.

I don't mean to imply that we are narrow in Wilromere. No indeed. We are really very up to date. Just last winter the Woman's Culture Club studied a huge book by James Joyce, and Stacey Madden, just back from a season in Europe, gave a lecture on the art of the Vatican. All of the boys and girls of the wealthier families go off to college and sometimes travel abroad, like Stacey Madden, though she is no longer a girl, goodness knows. She's forty-six if she's a day and I'm sure, though I never mentioned it to anyone, that her hair has been tinted.

What I mean is that the people of my generation, the Clarke Rohmers, Reverend Grisold and his nice, plump little Mattie, Nora Knightbridge and the Misses Cuthbert, still cling to what we call our traditions. We like to think of ourselves as living in a peaceful sunny harbor, enjoying the quiet and the beauty, while the troubled river that is modern life swirls by outside. That is one reason, I suppose, that after what happened to us all the town will never be quite the same. The barriers did not hold. The river poured into our little harbor, stormy waters dashed high, retreated and left tragedy.

And that brings me to the night of June 22, 1935, at eight-fifteen, when I stood in the east bedroom of Clarke Rohmer's big white house and finished pinning that extra tuck in Wiletta Owens' ivory-satin wedding gown.

It seems odd that Frances, her high-toned maid, couldn't do it, that Wiletta, who had never bothered to hide the fact that she thought me just an uninteresting old maid dressmaker, should have been forced to call me to help her. Of course, I didn't have anything to do with the fashioning of Wiletta's gown. No, indeed, and I don't blame her for it. She had enough money to allow her to put up a fine front, if she could live on her friends enough, and when she knew she had David roped into the engagement, she just continued to stay on at the Rohmers' where she had come for a month's visit, and saved all her money for the trousseau. Also, Caroline Rohmer helped her get her things together. The wedding gown with the high collar and the long, tight-fitting sleeves and the clever side gores came from a very famous designer in New York and it was beautiful.

Wiletta looked lovely in it, though it honestly wasn't my idea of a wedding dress. She stood very straight and slim before the long French mirror, turning this way and that, a frown crinkling her black brows, her pansy-brown eyes bright with impatience, and said,

"Well, that's better. Thank you, Miss Laure. Frances, you should have had sense enough to do that."

Frances' tiny white hands shut in the folds of her black uniform. Her long black eyes narrowed. She was all black and white, that girl. She said, "I am so sorry, madame. I did the same, if I am permitted to say so. Yet you did not approve—"

Wiletta turned her fair head slowly and her soft, rose-red lips went into that hard line which I had always distrusted, thinking of David's temper. She said, "I did not approve, because you were a stupid, bungling fool and took the tuck too deeply. It's all right now, thanks to Miss Laure."

She walked away from the mirror, the satin rustling softly, and sat down before the solid-walnut dresser to run a comb through her shining hair. "See if you're capable of arranging my veil," she said to Frances.

I was going to leave, but she saw me in the mirror and said, "You stay, Miss Laure. Likely you'll have to do it anyway."

I felt really uncomfortable and I saw the girl Frances' face white as flour in the mirror. It was an odd triangular shape, narrowing down to her sharp little chin. Her eyes were long like I've said and black as stove polish. Her nose was thin and quivery, then came that small red mouth, the under lip like a little red button hanging from the upper. Her blue-black hair was pulled down in satiny wings on each side of her face, and on top of it was the small white cap that matched her apron. She arranged Wiletta's veil.

It enfolded her like a cloud. It made her look so lovely that tears came to my eyes and everything in the room looked misty as I stood against the wall, watching. I prayed in my heart, "O God, make her worthy of David. Make her kind and understanding. Dear Lord, please make it that she loves him, that she's not as the Misses Cuthbert said at Aid yesterday, just marrying him for all this money he's come into—"

There was a tap at the door. It opened at once and Stacey Madden drifted in. I'm sure I don't know where Stacey got that drifting air of hers. After all, she was born in Wilromere, just like I was, and though her father was vice-president of the bank and mine only ran the village dray, I don't see that that gives her the right to all these airs. Perhaps it's having been to Europe. Anyway, there she is, thin and burning in pale-green chiffon, her meager arms and her bony neck and shoulders gleaming. She's handsome at that, Stacey is, and certainly those fine schools she attended as a girl and that trip to Europe have given her something. Her head sways on her long slim neck like a flower. Her hair, which I'm sure has been tinted, is the most gorgeous red blonde. It swirls like a ruddy cloud in clever little curls all over her head, coming down to a sharp point in the center of her forehead. Her eyes are gray-green and she holds the lids low, thinking, I believe, that it gives her a mysterious look. To me it just seems that she's too lazy to lift them, but anyway, there she is, leaning against the door, a cigarette burning between her long white fingers, looking at Wiletta over by the walnut dresser in that cloud of exquisite lace.

Wiletta lowers her head a little to glance at her in the mirror. Her pansy-brown eyes showed glints of amber fire, but she smiled sweetly and said, "Hello, Stacey, how's everything?"

Stacey looked white as dust in the soft light. I could see how her thin chest rose and fell and the way her nostrils dilated. I thought, feeling all cold inside, "She hates Wiletta. *She* wanted to marry David after he got his money. She thinks if it hadn't been for Wiletta she'd be sitting here tonight with a veil on her head."

Stacey smiled and said, "Okey-doke, old pal. The orange blossoms are strung, the white doves in place and the guests are panting with impatience to see the articles signed." Her voice had a brittle, tinkling sound and her eyes looked like green ice below the sharp point of her ruddy hair.

Wiletta settled a fold of the lace, slapped Frances' hand away and surveyed herself for a long moment, then she turned, looking full at Stacey. "Well, now, isn't that nice," she cooed, making her mouth all round and sweet. "We won't keep them long, dear." She looked at the small clock on the dresser. "It's eight-twenty. The ceremony is scheduled for nine. That's only forty minutes." She paused, breath making a queer hissing sound between parted lips. She looked straight across at Stacey, not seeming to know that Frances and I were there. She said, softly, "Only forty minutes, dear, and I'll be Mrs. David Kaye!"

I wanted to slap her! That is a cheap, childish reaction, I am sure, but it's the way I felt. That I wanted to lay my rather large bony hand in a hard smack right across her soft flushed cheek. Why? Because of the inflection she managed to put into the words. Because of the hateful, hungry look that glowed in her eyes, of the way her lips sucked in, pressing against her white teeth. Because I *knew* then what I had only feared before—that Wiletta Owens was marrying David Kaye because he was a great, tall shy boy, for all his twenty-seven years. Because he had merry gray eyes that could be so tender and serious at times. Because she craved his youth and his strength, his gentleness and his power. For all of these reasons, yes, but primarily because he had less than three months ago inherited better than a half million dollars!

She was marrying him in less than forty minutes for the same reason that Stacey Madden had wanted to marry him. The same emotion actuated both of them as they looked at each other across the width of that east room heavy with the scent of wedding flowers. I saw hate flick from Stacey's droopy-lidded eyes like heat lightning. Wiletta, I swear, was "crawling" with triumph. Her slim, beautiful body in that fitted satin sheath quivered and I saw the fingers of her left hand curl into her palm, and the lights of the diamond David had given her burned like a hot, white eye.

"Mrs. David Kaye," Stacey said unsteadily. "Congratulations, dear."

"Thanks," Wiletta replied. "I know you wish me joy, Stacey."

Stacey's lips curled like thin, bright snakes. "Of course. Much joy, Wiletta." She straightened from where she leaned against the door, lifted her hand, blew a kiss into the air. "Joy to the victor, whether the victory was won by fair means or foul."

Wiletta went white as the satin against her throat. She rose slowly, hands straight against her sides. "Yes," she said thickly, "joy to the victor. After all, dear Stacey, victory's the only thing that counts, isn't it?"

I don't know what Stacey would have said or done. I do know that I wanted to scream from the beastly tension that filled that room. I couldn't take my eyes from them and I thought miserably, "Oh, thank heavens David doesn't know. I pray he never will know that they stand here fighting over possession of him."

The door opened. Valerie Lane looked in. She said, "Excuse me," then she stopped suddenly, lips parted, and slipped in, closing the door after her. In that moment it was open I heard the fuzzy blur of conversation downstairs, with an occasional high squeal of laughter from one of the Misses Cuthbert. Too bad those Cuthbert girls could never learn to control their laughs. Maida is really worse than Martha and Martha is bad enough.

Valerie was wearing the pink organdie I made for her out of the one she had summer before last. I flatter myself I did a fair job. It had a square low neck and swept the floor with a grand flounce double shirred around the top. The real triumph, however, was the taffeta jacket which Valerie thought she couldn't afford until I talked Bob Martin down at the Emporium into cutting the price a little. It gave her a grown-up look and the gorgeous taffeta bow I'd fixed across the front was delightful. Above it her thin, vivid face, with the dusting of golden freckles across her turned-up nose, her wide, naturally red mouth, her clear brown eyes and the straight line of her dark brows stood out with what was close to startling beauty. Her hair was nice, too, parted in the middle, drawn back and knotted into a big, rich-looking lump on her neck. It came to me then that Valerie Lane might some day be a beautiful woman.

She said, "Excuse me, Wiletta. Caroline sent me to see if everything was all right. If you— wanted—"

"Yes," Wiletta said, tearing her glance from Stacey to look straight at Valerie. "Everything is quite all right, thank you, Valerie, and the only thing in the world I really want I'll be getting very soon now."

"Oh!" Valerie said.

Stacey Madden laughed, holding a match to a cigarette between her bright lips. "She means, dear little Val," Stacey said on smoke, "that very soon now she will be getting full title to, possession of and inalienable right to the person of one David Kaye. The person," Stacey added, "and the fortune."

Oh, heavens, was that a moment! I can still feel the prickle of sheer horror that went over me. I am old-fashioned, of course. I don't understand the mental make-up of women like Wiletta Owens and Stacey Madden, but I always thought that marriage was something sacred. Something to be entered into with prayer. With the prayer that you might make your partner happy, that you might serve him and smooth the rough spots in the road as you went through life. I've read books, naturally, but I never really believed that women talked like that. That they married a man because of how much money he could give them. That they would fight and snarl and spit venom like a bunch of cats in the back alley for possession of what they wanted. I learned a lot that night.

Wiletta's laugh tinkled. "You're absolutely right, precious," she said, looking at Stacey with that queer expression of triumphant crawling. "It's too bad we couldn't both have him and his—fortune, isn't it?" She pushed back the drifting veil. "Well, hats off to the vanquished," she purred. "You made a game fight, Stacey. You almost—hooked him. Of course, being so much older—"

Stacey said, "Stop it! Stop it, you—!" And no matter what Dr. Marc says, I won't print the word that Stacey Madden used. Only her face was suddenly fiery red and Wiletta was white as chalk, crouching back against the dresser, teeth shining between her drawn lips.

"You—you—" she choked, and then something just had to happen.

Caroline Rohmer came in, her orchid taffeta rustling, her silvery white hair like a coronet on her large, fine head. She came like a breath of gorgeous fresh air and before her hate and passion vanished. Only to be hidden, though, as we were to learn later. She began talking brightly and if she sensed something wrong she didn't let on.

"Wiletta dear, you look wonderful. Here, let me fix that veil. It comes a bit too far front, I think." She was immediately bustling, doing this and that. "Your flowers," Caroline said. "Where is the bride's bouquet?"

Wiletta dropped onto the chair before the dresser. Frances, the maid, lifted a large green box from the deep windowsill, extended it. "The flowers, madame," she said through her queer little button mouth.

"Well, we must get them on. It won't be long now, children." Caroline laughed and her large white hands flew as she opened the box. She did her best to inject gaiety into that room and we smiled automatically, but no one really forgot what had happened.

I have only a hazy impression of the flowers. Tiny white roses tinted at the centers, and a few sweet peas, the whole tied together with yards of lacy tulle.

"You carry these," Caroline said, "and this sweet little bunch you are to wear."

"I don't want to wear them," Wiletta said. "I think it's silly to wear flowers."

"Nonsense!" Caroline assured her. "Davey particularly got them for you to wear. See, here's the pin." She held up the bouquet, the pin in her left hand. The light struck her face then and it came to me that Caroline was beginning to show her age. There was a pinched look to her full, sweet lips and wrinkles showed on the soft flesh beneath her large blue eyes. The way she stood, too, struck me unpleasantly. Her fine big shoulders hunched a little, as if she were prepared for attack.

"Oh!" Valerie Lane cried.

Caroline dropped the bouquet. Her hand closed convulsively on the pin as she turned. Her face had a queer gray look under the smooth coating of powder. I thought, "It's the strain of preparing for the wedding—no, Caroline loves festivities. Something's got on her nerves." And it came to me quite suddenly, "She doesn't want Davey to marry Wiletta. There's nothing she can do, though. There's nothing anyone can do."

Wiletta said thinly, "For heaven's sake, what's the matter with you, Val Lane?"

Stacey Madden laughed. How I came to hate that woman's laugh. I think it was the laugh more than anything else that finally made me do what I did, but that's getting ahead of the story.

Valerie said faintly, "I'm sorry, it's the pin—don't you see—it's fashioned like a—blade! See how sharp and long it is. You could kill a person with it." She twisted her thin hands together and rushed on: "I don't mean that, of course, I mean that Davey shouldn't have given it to Wiletta. It's bad luck—to give a blade—"

"Oh," Wiletta said, lowering her head a little. "Bad luck, is it, Valerie?"

"Bad luck?" Stacey echoed. "My *dear* child! What bad luck could happen to the lovely bride?" And her eyes were pale with hate. "Bad luck, indeed!" Stacey said, and inhaled on her cigarette.

Caroline picked up the bouquet. "Never mind, Valerie," she said gently, "that's just an old-fashioned superstition. We're all too enlightened to heed things like that."

Enlightened? I wonder. That means that the old primitive passions are soothed away, doesn't it? And the dark corners are swept clean, the curtains lifted, the sun shining in? In that moment I hoped that Caroline Rohmer was right, but I wasn't sure.

Caroline added, smiling a little, "Besides, Davey didn't have anything to do with choosing the pin, Valerie. The florist just put that in—"

"Isn't that nice?" Stacey drawled. "I wish my florist would include a pin studded with diamonds, whether it's in the shape of a knife or not."

Caroline started and stared at the pin. We all stared at it, dangling there between her fingers. It was a good three inches long, the blade, that is, and the glittering handle added another inch. I didn't know whether they were diamonds or not, though they looked

gorgeous there under the light. The pin proper was fastened behind the blade.

Caroline's nervous laugh broke the stillness. "Well, we won't
argue about that, Stacey. Maybe David did buy it. Men have queer
taste." She frowned at the pin. "Anyway, we can remove Valerie's
hoodoo. All Wiletta has to do is to give Davey a coin before she
wears the pin. That breaks the jinx." She nodded wisely. "I remember that well enough. She just gives Davey a coin—"

Wiletta's laugh sounded harsh and high. She said, "Oh, what
foolishness," and took the pin. "If they are diamonds," she held it
to the light. I saw a vein beating in her throat. She nodded slowly,
looked up. "They're the real thing, all right. And I'll wear the pin.
It would take more than an old wives' tale like that to stop me wearing—diamonds."

And with very steady, strong fingers she fastened the bouquet
of brides' roses at her shoulder with the diamond-studded pin made
like a sword. She turned then, eyes flashing. "Now leave me," she
ordered, "all of you. I need a few moments to—collect my thoughts
before the ordeal."

And that's the picture I carry of her to this very day. Sitting
there in the big, high-ceilinged room with the soft glow of amber
lights showing like yellow flowers on the dark floor, the shadowy
cavern of the mirror behind her reflecting her slim beauty, the jew-
eled sword flashing at her left shoulder.

Valerie Lane went first, an elf like figure in pink organdie. Then
Caroline, in her magnificent orchid taffeta and after that Stacey
Madden, drifting along like a green wave, smoke curling from her
red lips. Frances crossed the room on swift, soundless feet and went
into the bath that connected with the bedroom next door. I started
out, too, but Wiletta stopped me.

"Miss Laure!" I turned, angry to find my heart hammering
against my ribs.

"Yes, Wiletta?"

She sat very still, one arm resting on the chair back, her eyes
dusky blurs in the shadow of her bridal veil. She said, "You don't
like me, do you, Laure Hosmer?"

My lips were dry as autumn leaves. I looked straight at her. "It doesn't matter, Wiletta, if only you're good to David."

She smiled very faintly. The white veil quivered. "You think a great deal of David, don't you, Laure?"

Then it came over me, that queer, faint feeling that I've had once or twice of late, always when I think how much I love David Kaye. It's like waves of something billowing round me, mounting higher and higher, until I seem to be smothering and everything gets dim.

Through the dimness I could see Wiletta very far away, and much nearer, smiling up at me, the face of David Kaye when he was three years old and his yellow-brown curls tangled over his head like curdled sunlight. I saw his gray eyes looking at me, his childish chin quivering. I heard his small frightened voice calling, "Laure—Laure—come help me, please, Laure." And I remembered the day he had been caught in the blackberry thicket behind the house and I had rescued him. Twenty-four years ago! Almost a quarter of a century.

His face vanished and I heard myself saying in my own quiet, neutral voice, "I think a great deal of him, Wiletta. He will be a wonderful man. His wife can make him or ruin him. I'm counting on you to—make him."

I suppose I hoped she would assure me. I dare say I thought in my foolish, middle-aged, sentimental way that she would burst into tears or something, tell me brokenly that David was the eternal light of her life and that she would live only for him. If she had—

Well, she hadn't. She just sat there, the veil making a shadow on her lovely face and suddenly she began to laugh. That bright, tinkling laugh of hers. I hear it yet. She said, "Don't worry, Laure dear. Your David's going into very good hands. I'll—" She caught a quick breath, and her face looked sharp and feline, with eyes narrowed and white teeth shining. "I'll—make him—all right," she said, and then I went out, blood humming in my ears, pounding in my veins, the hall dark before me. It was as if she had plunged that bright-bladed diamond pin into my heart. I knew what she meant. It is given to us sometimes to know things like that, I believe. I

knew that Wiletta Owens would take my David and press him between her slim, nervous fingers like she would a plum. I knew she
would suck the life from him, kill the promise of his mind, blast
the dreams in his heart.

I remember putting my hands before my eyes. I remember
saying very low, sobs in my throat, "Oh, why is this? Why does this
have to be?"

A glimmer of intelligence came to me then and I thought, "Well,
no one *made* him choose her. He loves her, doesn't he?" It didn't
last long. I knew better. Someone did make David choose Wiletta
and that someone was Wiletta herself. Also, I didn't believe he
loved her, but who was I to judge?

I heard them talking downstairs. Maida Cuthbert's laugh! Reverend Grisold's rumbling bass, what I call his pulpit voice, though
he turns it on for weddings and funerals, too, and I heard the im-
ported orchestra tuning violins back in the library.

There was such a flutter of happy excitement there. I could
smell the fragrance of the banked flowers mingled faintly with the
odor of rich cakes from the kitchen. And then before I could move
a bedroom door opened, light shot into the hall, and I saw David.

Sight of him quieted me as it has always done. He was so tall
and strong, with his lean face shaven and smooth, his mouth a little
grim, maybe, because he was nervous. His thick dark brows leveled and straight above his gray eyes. His shirt front made a narrow triangle of white in the soft light of the hall. He smelled of
cleanness and very, very faintly of talcum powder. He stopped when
he saw me, then he was beside me and before I knew what had
happened his arms were around me and he was giving me what he
and I used to call the bear's hug. It fairly cracked my spinsterish
ribs. I said, "Oh—David!" and went all limp against him, and then
he loosened his hold, though still keeping his arms around me and
looking down at me, grinning.

"Laure darling," he said, "I've been wanting to see you. I haven't
seen nearly enough of you of late."

"I'm always waiting, David, you know that. You've only to call me."

He gave me another bear's hug. "I know it, darling." Then abruptly he was serious, too. "Laure," he said, looking down at me gravely, "I want you to remember this always. You were the first mother I ever knew. No matter how far I go from Wilromere and its associations, I'll never get around that or forget it."

And that is what I remember happily of David. Those low, quiet words spoken there in the upper hall of the Rohmer house that June night that David was to marry Wiletta. I know he meant it, bless him, and nothing, nothing whatever that can happen to me in the future can ever take that wonderful certainty away.

We talked a little longer. He made me wish him happiness, as if I could do anything else. He made me lie and say I thought Wiletta was a wonderful person and had I ever seen anything so beautiful and what had he done to deserve her? All the time the laugh and chatter from downstairs came up to us and I sensed a growing excitement in it as the hour of the ceremony drew near. He said, as he left me, "Now, Laure, remember, don't you dare cry. People are always crying at weddings, I know, but don't you dare, Laure, don't you dare!"

Then he was gone, running along the hall toward the back stairs where he was to wait in the library until Jonny Rohmer, the best man, walked beside him along the ribboned aisle, leading through the long double parlors to the altar which had been built at the far end. I wondered how Jonny would get through with it. He is such a shy, nervous boy and I know he was mad about Wiletta himself. But then he and David had grown up together, without it doing Jonny any good as I see it, because the poor child couldn't help but compare himself and see others compare him to the fine, handsome David with all his charm and graces. It's one of the things I'll never understand, that a couple like Clarke and Caroline Rohmer should have but one child and he a poor, trembling weakling like Jonny. But then, the ways of the Lord are inscrutable and so I guess are those of heredity or whatever it is that makes folks what they are.

I started back to the spare room to freshen myself a bit. I just knew that my gray voile was rumpled and my hair was straggling into my eye. In my knitted bag I had some talcum powder, for while I don't hold with women painting their faces, I'm sure a little pure talcum doesn't hurt on special occasions. I have a really nice skin. Of late it's been rather dry and there are very thin lines in it, but it's fine and not coarse and rough-looking like some I know.

The room was very still and a soft wind came in the open window. I could see the great elms around the Rohmer place swaying gently and oh, the moonlight was heavenly. I stood in front of the mirror thinking that this was an ideal night to be married, it being June and all, with roses making the air sweet and the earth throbbing with renewed life. June, the brides' month! I thought back along all the Junes I had known and I remembered one, so long, long ago, when I was nearly a bride, just as Wiletta Owens was tonight. I wondered, standing there before the mirror, looking at my thin face, that no one could possibly call beautiful, what would have happened if I had gone on with it. My life would have been richer, I dare say. I might have had a son of my own, like David.

But I couldn't have loved him any more. David had come into my heart, like a tiny seed blown by unknown winds. He had planted himself there and nothing else had mattered. He had grown into a tall fine tree and the roots of it went deep into my soul. He sheltered me with his love. He made me fertile with his splendor. He *was* my heart, my soul, my life. I remembered that I grew very calm as I stood there. A great peace descended over me. I prayed a little prayer. I said, "Dear God, make everything right for David. Don't let anything happen to hurt him, ever, please. Amen."

After that I felt happier than ever for I knew, as if someone had whispered it to me, that everything would be all right for David.

WELL, THE ROOMS downstairs looked beautiful as I knew they would. I had helped some with the decorations that afternoon. I do things like that for people in Wilromere. Whenever there's something a little odd to be done, or difficult, they say, "Well, get Miss Laure, she'll fix it." And although the florist had sent men out to do most of the work, I had helped with the finishing touches.

I went downstairs feeling much happier than I had in months. Those moments alone in the spare room had done something to me. I saw the people sitting in chairs along the wall, talking and laughing and now and then glancing at their watches. Reverend Grisold was maneuvering up and down the line, beaming and benevolent, his red face shining with good nature, his bald dome fairly radiating cheer. He's been in Wilromere for nearly twenty-five years now and we all love him. He takes all our troubles and joys on himself. He attends to all the marriages and he christens the new babies and, God bless him, with his fat, kind hands he closes the eyes of those who have gone into eternal sleep. I don't see how a man could be more saintly than Brother Grisold though he doesn't make any fuss about it. So that night I looked at him and my eyes filled with tears of happiness just at seeing him bowing and beaming and mopping his shining bald head.

And there was Clarke Rohmer, tall and fine, with his nice blue eyes and his Roman nose and his white mustache so stiff and fierce, yet a gentler man never lived in spite of his mustache. I saw them all as I came down the stairs. My friends, people I had known mostly since childhood. I knew them all. Their weaknesses, their meannesses, and they had them, of course. Also, their bigness, their unselfishness, their fineness. There was one alien there. Kenneth Borden. I scarcely knew what to think of him, though he was always pleasant and courteous. But his strange, light blue eyes had a disconcerting way of seeming to look straight through you and when I talked to him, which I had done infrequently, I felt that he knew entirely too much about me. I understood that he was some kind of a doctor, something to do with the minds of people who are sick. There is a name for it, but I never can remember it. He had been staying with the Rohmers for nearly a month now and had spent a great deal of time tramping over the spring countryside with Jonny.

Caroline came toward me, rustling with taffeta and excitement. "It's only a few minutes now, Laure. Everything's all right upstairs, isn't it?"

I smiled into her worried face. After all, she and Clarke had legally adopted David twenty-two years ago, so he was just the same as their own son and naturally they were concerned over his wedding.

I said, reassuring her, "Everything is all right, Caroline. I don't know how it could be any better."

She sighed with relief. "I'm glad. I've been nervous tonight, all day for that matter, Laure." Then she smiled with that quick charm that makes you forget she is close to sixty and weighs too much. "This wedding business." She shook her large white head. "Well, it will soon be over. Stacey—" She paused, frowning. "Of course, Stacey is Wiletta's bridesmaid. They'll come down the stairs together. I sent her up a few minutes ago. She went up the back way. Did you see her?"

I told her I hadn't. Wiletta was to have but one attendant and she *would* choose Stacey Madden.

Caroline stood there uncertainly, saying things under her breath, like she was running over a list. "Ceremony at nine. Supper at ten-thirty. The children leave for the station at twelve-ten—catch the train at—" She looked up. "Laure," she said, sounding breathless, "do run up and see if the girls are ready, please. You know how Wiletta is. I believe she'd enjoy holding up the ceremony. Just tell them it's only a few minutes now before the music starts."

I left her whispering directions and started back upstairs. It was about ten minutes to nine. The buzz of excited conversation rose with me, seeming to gather intensity the higher I climbed. It was like waves of heat rising, and it made me feel dizzy. There is a landing halfway up the Rohmers' stairs and as I paused there for a moment to get my breath I heard a rustle of taffeta and organdie and looked up to see Valerie Lane coming down. She came very fast, rushing past me like a small, hot wind. I started to say something, but sight of her face checked me. It was flushed and tear-stained. Her brown hair looked disheveled. Her little taffeta jacket was wrinkled. Oh, she looked so small and tragic and frightened.

I just stood there looking after her, while fear closed on my own heart like a cold hand. Something which I had suspected for a long time became a certainty in my mind. Valerie loved David Kaye! I'd sensed it, but I wouldn't face it. I doubted if David knew that Valerie was alive in that sense at least. I knew he liked her, but thought of her as a child, a nice, brown-haired, small girl to be teased and petted and forgotten. But Valerie had grown up this last winter. Trouble had had something to do with that. After her father's death, after she took that job in the bank, well, Valerie had grown up overnight.

I glanced down just in time to see her flit across the wide hall and disappear through the front door, then I went on with my errand. Up ahead of me a door closed softly. I stopped, hand against my foolishly fluttering heart. The hall was very dim, there were only softly shaded lamps here and there and it was very long, but I had a flash of green like a bright wave that leaps up and disappears.

I said to myself, "That was Stacey coming out of Wiletta's room. Everything's all right then. I don't need to go in." But just the same I went on down and as I reached the door here was Stacey coming toward me from the side hall up ahead. She walked in her drifting way, except that it wasn't quite so graceful and lacked its usual floating effect. There was a suggestion of jerking about her. It increased the angles of her thin body, so that she looked rather like a mechanical doll on wires. And it was the strangest thing, but before she reached me I could hear her breathing. That was jerky, too, harsh, almost gasping, as if she were choking.

She met me just as I got to Wiletta's door. She paused, looking down at me. "What do you want?" she demanded, and again I was conscious of her uneven breathing.

I said, "Caroline wanted me to see if everything was ready. Everything all right."

Her laugh stopped me. It was sharp and hard and I'll swear there was no mirth in her shadowed eyes. "Oh yes," she said, "everything's ready, Laure. Everything's all right, quite all right."

I adjusted my glasses to look at her. A curious impression came to me then, looking at Stacey Madden in that dim hall. She was so pale. Her face looked so thin and washed away and her green dress gave it a strange, unearthly tint. I might have been looking at her through water. Clear, cold, green water, with Stacey Madden lying drowned beneath it. She made a queer gesture and her thin hands clutched at her heart.

"What's the matter with you?" she asked harshly. "You look as if you'd seen a ghost. As if someone were—walking on your grave, Laure Hosmer."

I said sharply, "Stop that foolishness. That's fine talk for a wedding night. I have no ghosts to see, Stacey Madden, and when I'm in my grave I care not who walks over it." Yet I couldn't stop trembling. I couldn't get over thinking of Stacey floating under green water, her face washed so white and cold. And though I fought it desperately, I thought of myself lying in a narrow grave in the village cemetery. I remembered the black fir trees under the moon and the neat little mounds all covered with green in summer and white with snow in winter. Fear of death came on me then, for all I've lived my life as a God-fearing woman, and never missed a Sunday at church only that winter my neuritis was so bad.

Stacey said contemptuously, "Do all old maids look like that at weddings, dear Laure?" Then, before I could answer, she tapped on Wiletta's door. At the same moment the strains of the wedding march started downstairs and Stacey's hand fell as if it had been stricken with paralysis.

I remember how ghastly was her attempt at a smile. "Happiness to the bride," she whispered, then she said, "You knock, Laure. She wouldn't open the door for me."

I didn't bother to knock. I opened the door and called "Wiletta! You're ready, aren't you, dear?" and wondered how I could call her dear, considering everything.

Then I went in. Stacey followed me. The music swelled louder. The voices were drowned. I remember how the lace curtain billowed out in the breeze from the open window.

"David will be starting very soon," Stacey said at my shoulder, "he'll be coming to meet his bride—" Her voice trailed away to a trickle of sound. It died to silence. I felt her standing behind me and I felt again the fear of death. I was looking at Wiletta. She lay face down on the mulberry-colored rug, like a broken flower in the midst of drifted snow. The snow, of course, was her white satin wedding dress, the cloudy veil that heaped around her. She lay with her head turned to one side so I could see her wide-open, sightless eyes. She was beautiful, even in death.

The diamond-crusted sword pin had killed her. It had been plunged into her back, on the left side. It had gone in to the very hilt. I remember how the diamonds glittered in the light. Blood made a small portion of the veil soggy, stained the white satin. I couldn't move for a time. I kept hearing Stacey's jerky breathing. I saw her drowned face in the shadowy mirror opposite. It was twitching crazily.

A woman screamed. It was Frances, the maid. She had come in from the bathroom. She stood there, screaming. The music downstairs stopped with a jarring discord. There was a terrible moment of silence. I remember the little bouquet of brides' roses, dabbled with blood, crumpled on the floor beside Wiletta.

The music started again almost at once. It ran like an undertone through all that happened right afterward. I guess those boys were used to all sorts of things occurring maybe and kept on playing regardless. The leader said later he did it to quiet people, hold back panic. It worked, too. At least there was no panic, though maybe the kind of folks there had something to do with it.

Clarke Rohmer came first. I heard his strong, swift steps pounding up the stairs and he called, muffled like, "What's wrong? What's the matter?" Then he was at the door. I opened it for him. I remember how the light struck his face, showing his eyes bulging and his mouth sagging beneath those fierce mustaches. I wonder if he had a premonition of what had happened.

Behind him came Brother Grisold, Mattie puffing at his heels. Mattie wore the same old brown foulard she'd appeared in at weddings for the last twelve years. It's a wonder to me how it lasts. I've made it over at least five times. Silks nowadays don't wear like that.

Next was Caroline and oh, I pitied her. She's such a good woman. Why should so much trouble come into her life? Jonny is enough, goodness knows. Dr. Marcus Wayne came shouldering his way through the press at the door to drop to a knee beside Wiletta. His hands moved swiftly, surely. I have always admired Marc's hands. I think he should have been a great surgeon, but Luella Bell spoiled that, though maybe I had something to do with it, too. I wonder if *all* our sins are counted against us at the Judgment Day?

Dr. Marc rose slowly. He hitched his right shoulder in that quick, nervous way. He said, "There is nothing I can do. Wiletta is dead!"

It was just then, of course, that David appeared at the door. The crowd parted to let him in, though I think at first they huddled together in an instinctive effort to bar his entrance. They all liked David. They wanted to spare him the sight of his bride in her white, blood-stained veil.

But that could not be. There Wiletta lay, dead, in her wedding gown and there, just inside the door, stood David, with the folks backing away from him as if they were afraid of him. He seemed in that moment to be very much alone. More alone than that day his mother died, leaving him among strangers without even a name. In his helplessness then there had been many kindly hands reaching out for him. They experienced no difficulty in reaching him either. David, the infant, had not lacked for love and care. Now they wanted to help him, but they could not get to him. He stood isolated among us all, cut off from our sympathy, beyond our love.

The room was very still and the strains of music came softly from below stairs. David asked harshly, "Wiletta is—dead?"

Oh, who would answer him? Dr. Marc did, of course. He said: "Yes, David." Just those two simple words. "Yes, David."

David went slowly to where she lay. He stood a long moment looking down on her. Then, without a word, he turned and walked over to the window, with his back to the room. He did not speak again for a long time.

I heard clamor in the hall, where the fifty or sixty guests were milling at the stairs. There came a sharp, clear voice. Kenneth Borden's.

"Please, folks, keep back, won't you? There's been an accident. Miss Owens is—ill!" He hesitated before that last word and I wondered if he, too, had a premonition that Wiletta was dead. The troubled uproar died. People surged on the stairs, hesitated, descended slowly, talking in frightened, uncertain voices. I heard Maida Cuthbert's high laughter, quickly silenced.

Then Clarke Rohmer said, his deep voice quivering, "My God, this is terrible. This is—"

Caroline silenced him with a hand on his arm. "Yes, Clarke. Let's see what we can do. You are sure, Dr. Marc, that there is nothing—" Her brave voice shook.

Dr. Marc shook his gray-maned head. "Nothing, Caroline, we'd best call Sheriff Birket. It's—murder!"

We all stood so quiet when Dr. Marc said that. There was a moment of unrealizing blankness, when everybody looked at everybody else and the faces of our friends were abruptly the faces of strangers. Murder! Who of us realized it fully? It was a word we had heard, that we sometimes used, but it was outside our real comprehension, like leprosy or the Black Hole of Calcutta.

I saw Jonny Rohmer just then, a slim lad, narrow shouldered, thin-chested, with hands that are never quiet. He has a nice face, but it is weak and his blue eyes are vague and always a little frightened. He stood just inside the door, looking at Wiletta. There were tears in his eyes. His lead-pencil fingers were plucking at the black bands on his trousers. I was afraid he'd start laughing. That would have been more than anyone could have endured. That Jonny Rohmer, whom we all knew had hopelessly loved Wiletta Owens, had seen her lost to him and won to David— Well, we couldn't have stood it if Jonny had laughed.

All the time the music went on downstairs, bright and gay, and seeming very far off. I have always appreciated that orchestra leader's good sense in continuing to play.

Clarke Rohmer mopped his wet face. He looked at Frances, Wiletta's maid. "Do you know—what happened?" he asked. "Who did this?"

It was really a very childish question, so simple and direct, that way. Clarke didn't understand in that moment the twisted strands of hate and frustration that lay behind that deed, or he wouldn't have asked Frances Cosette that plain question.

The girl stood by the bathroom door. I don't believe she had moved an inch since she first stood there and screamed. She said now, "I do not know, sir. She sent me away. She said she wished to be alone. I went to my room. I stayed a little time. I came down again. I thought perhaps she would allow me to assist her right at the last. I saw the ladies," she indicated Stacey and myself, "talking outside her door, so I went there," she motioned over her shoulder through the bath to the spare room adjoining. I came in—I saw—" She lifted her tiny hands, pressed them against her red button mouth, stared at us over them, blankly, shaking her head.

"The pin," Stacey said very low, "the pin killed her. Val Lane said it was bad luck."

And then I remembered Valerie and wondered where she was.

"Hush!" Caroline said, her face all gouged and sagging. "There's no sense in talking like that, Stacey."

After that was silence and no one knew what to do, while the music kept on downstairs. Then a very quiet voice spoke and I saw that Kenneth Borden had entered the room. He said, "If I may offer a suggestion?" and paused, while all eyes turned toward him. He went on, "Mr. Rohmer, you must call the local authorities. It is a job for them." He stood very easily, beside Wiletta's body. He glanced down at it with that light of speculation in his eyes which always seemed so shocking to me. Just as if he were considering the whole thing as an interesting scientific problem. I wonder if he was.

"After that," he said, "there is nothing to do but wait until they get here. Of course, no one must leave the premises."

We realized then that he thought someone in the house had murdered Wiletta. I dare say we had known it all along, but his saying it just that way made it worse. It explained, I guess, why we had all looked like strangers a while ago.

David hadn't said another word. I see him yet, standing by the dresser looking through the open window where the curtains billowed, to the white wash of moonlight outside. What was he thinking? That this was to have been his wedding night? That Wiletta should have been his bride by this time? That now she would never be? That she was only a crumpled bit of uselessness lying there in her white satin. My throat ached and my eyes felt as if they would never close. I wanted to help David. I wanted to comfort him. I had a terrible moment when I thought, "Oh, perhaps I have been wrong all along. Maybe he *did* love her. Maybe she would have made him happy."

Clarke Rohmer said, "Stacey, you found Wiletta? You and Miss Laure?"

Stacey nodded. "Yes. Caroline sent me up the back stairs saying it was nearly time for the ceremony." She shut her red lips hard. "I came across Valerie Lane in the back hall and stopped to talk to her a moment. She was crying."

David turned from contemplation of the moonlit garden and looked at Stacey. "What made Valerie Lane cry?" he asked.

"I don't know," Stacey returned slowly. "I'm not sure, that is, David. But she was in a state. She was all huddled down in the window seat and she had a fit of near hysterics. She talked wild and crazylike. That she wasn't worth anything in the world, that no one needed her. That she'd be best out of it." Stacey shrugged. "Things haven't been easy for her," Stacey said, and disposed of Valerie Lane, although she did add, "I tried to talk some sense into the child. I advised her to get outside if the sight of you marrying Wiletta was too much." Even at a time like that Stacey couldn't refrain from being hateful. What she meant was too plain to miss and David's gray eyes held a momentarily startled look. He didn't say anything. I knew that Stacey had guessed what I had when Valerie passed me on the stairs.

"So she went downstairs," Stacey related. "And a few moments later I came along the hall here and met Miss Laure outside the door. We came in together. That's all."

Clarke looked at me. I said, "Yes, Stacey met me outside the door and we came in together, like she says." I wanted to add that I was sure Stacey had been in this room before she came toward me from the side hall. I remembered that flash of green I had glimpsed, the conviction that had come to me that Stacey was just leaving. I kept thinking of the hateful scene I had witnessed between Wiletta and Stacey earlier in the evening. Of the way they had faced each other, claws unsheathed. I kept quiet, though. Something inside of me made me keep quiet then.

Kenneth Borden said, "How long has she been dead, Dr. Wayne?"

"A very short time," Dr. Marc said. "Less than an hour."

Caroline spoke, her voice thin and edged with hysteria, "I left her such a little time ago. We all left her. She said she wanted to be alone. She was all right then. She was so beautiful and—proud." Caroline looked across at me. "You were the last, weren't you, Laure? You were the last to come out?"

"Yes, Caroline. Wiletta called me back as I was opening the door."

"What did she want?" Mr. Borden asked, looking at me from his queer, seeing eyes.

"She accused me of not liking her," I said.

Mr. Borden smiled with his thin, mobile lips. "Well, did you like her?" he inquired.

I felt them all looking at me. I was terribly frightened, but I have always tried to tell the truth. I said, not letting my eyes waver, "I do not understand women like Wiletta, and I cannot really like people without understanding them. I told her when she asked me that whether or not I liked her did not matter. It only mattered that she would be kind to David."

"And of course she would have been that?" Kenneth Borden asked. "She assured you of that, I dare say."

And then I told a lie, or something like a lie. There was no use trying to make them see what I had seen in Wiletta's face, all thinned and hungry and feline. I nodded after a pause. I said, "Yes, she assured me of that, Mr. Borden."

Clarke Rohmer said, "I must get downstairs, call Shad Birket." He shook his big head. "Oh, this is terrible. It's terrible. What shall we do? Shad won't know what to do. He's only one of the home folks like the rest of us. He won't know what to do." He started toward the door, walking awkwardly, his feet shuffling along the mulberry rug.

David said, "I'll go," and went after Clarke, laid a hand on his shoulder that sagged and trembled. David said, his voice unsteady, "Let me go, Clarke. Let me do this."

Clarke paused, lifted his big head, looked at this tall man whom he loved as his son, and his rugged, handsome face quivered and broke so that it was pitiful to see. Even his fierce mustaches actually seemed to droop. He said, "Oh, David, my boy, I am sorry. So sorry, David, lad."

And David said harshly, agony in his eyes, "Yes, Clarke, I know. Thank you, Clarke."

Those two men stood there in the room's center and were alone so far as the rest of us were concerned. It wasn't hard to see how much Clarke Rohmer loved David Kaye, or what David Kaye thought of Clarke. David should have been Clarke's son, really. It always seemed to me that somewhere outside our mortal ken a mistake was made and Jonny, poor, weak Jonny, was delivered to the Rohmers through error. David should have come to them instead of Jonny. I guess something like that struck Jonny, too. I was so sorry for him. He was white and trembling. His blue eyes looked almost mad. He stared at his father and his foster brother and I believe he hated them both. David most of all, perhaps. That's what made him say what he did. It was such a foolish thing for him to do.

He said, "All very touching, very touching indeed. Accept my condolences, David. It's a great loss to us all, to you particularly, I suppose, but Wiletta was not for you. I told you she was not for you. You didn't deserve her. You weren't fine enough for her. She was like gossamer. You would have soiled her, broken her—you—you—" His voice rose shrilly. "Oh, I'd rather she be dead than your wife! It's better this way. Better, I say. Better that she should be dead—"

Borden was beside him, a hand on his shoulder. "Easy, son," he said. "Easy does it. Let's get a breath of air."

And just then downstairs a woman screamed. I know it was Maida Cuthbert. She wouldn't have any better sense than to scream at a time like that. It broke the spell. It sent us scurrying into the hall. It heralded the advent of fresh tragedy. The group on the stairs parted like waves before the sharp prow of a steamer.

Up the stairs a man staggered. He held something in his arms. It was Shad Birket, the sheriff. I thought, "Well, we won't have to call him, anyway. He's here." Then I saw what he carried. A limp, pitiful bundle of dripping pink organdie and taffeta. Valerie Lane! She lay in his arms like wet seaweed, her head drooping backward, her face colorless, eyes closed, hair loosened.

Shad Birket was breathing heavily. He said, "I fished her out of Wilromere Lake. Just happened to be walkin' along, lookin' for old Barney. I brought her here because I knew Doc Wayne was here, and Caroline would take care of her. It's Val Lane—poor little Val—"

Shad isn't usually a loquacious man. His conversation is what could be called sparse, but fear and pity loosened his tongue tonight. He stood there on the stairs, holding Val in her dripping pink organdie, begging us to do something.

I remember that I thought how foolish it had been for me to talk her into buying the pink taffeta. Also I remembered that old Barney was Shad's twenty-two-year-old gray horse, who was always straying off somewhere. Then Shad took a deep breath and came on up the stairs, carrying Valerie.

David met Shad at the top of the stairs, took Valerie from him. "Dead?" he asked.

Shad mopped his lean tanned face. He was wet to his waist and water dripped onto the waxed floor. "I don't think so," he puffed. "I saw her when she went in, had some trouble getting her out." He pointed with a thick, gnarled finger at a red bruise on Valerie's right temple. "She must have hit her head there when she dove. I think that's why she's unconscious."

Dr. Marc had a finger on the girl's wrist. "Get her somewhere in a hurry," he ordered. "Caroline?"

"Here," Caroline answered in her quiet way, just as if nothing out of the ordinary had happened, and opened the door to the spare room next the one where Wiletta lay in her white satin. I went in with her and the doctor. I heard Clarke Rohmer speaking to Shad as the door closed. After that I was busy for quite a time helping Marc with Valerie.

Shad had been right about the bruise. She had evidently struck her head when she jumped into the lake and the blow had stunned her. We got the water out of her lungs. Caroline, assisted by Matilda, one of the maids, heated blankets.

Dr. Marc gave her a hypodermic, sat for quite a time beside her, watching her frail breathing, fingers on her pulse. He looked up at me once, across the bed. His face was lined and weary. He said, "Poor child. She's not had even breaks, Laure."

"No, Marc. Her mother was flighty and worthless, her father a no-account. She was born into poverty, but she had something. She's as fine and true as one could wish. She's everything good, Marc."

"Yes, Laure. She deserves the best. I thought, once old Jim Lane was gone, when she got that job in the bank, when she began going places, well, I hoped things were adjusting themselves for her. Now this!"

I didn't say anything. My heart was too heavy for Valerie. I could have pointed out to Marc that things don't adjust themselves so easily sometimes. That for a sensitive child like this unpleasant memories were too deeply etched on her mind to be easily erased. Yet I had never thought it would reach the point where Valerie would try to kill herself!

The orchestra stopped playing about this time, and I was sorry. It seemed that with it missing we would at once be conscious of what had happened. That the music had somehow held at bay the complete realization of the tragedy of that June night.

Marc said suddenly, looking at me across the slim line of Valerie under the blankets, "Laure, when you left Wiletta, was she normal? Was she all right?"

I thought a moment before I said, "As far as I could tell, Marc. I never knew when Wiletta was normal, if she ever was."

He grinned mirthlessly. "You didn't like her very well, did you, Laure?"

"No, Marc, I didn't." I knew I could be honest with him. "I tell you I didn't understand her. I don't understand Stacey much better, though I've known her so long it's a little easier. But when I heard those two women quarreling tonight—" I stopped, too late.

Dr. Marc leveled his bushy black brows and regarded me thoughtfully. "Quarreling, Laure? What about?"

"Oh, nothing. I'm sorry I mentioned it, Marc."

"That won't do, Laure. You can't hold things back now. Why were they quarreling?"

I remembered that likely Shad Birket would get it out of Frances anyway and Marc was my friend, so I told him. "It was hateful," I added. "They made me think of two cats, Marc, baring their teeth and snarling."

He straightened back in his chair, frowning at Valerie's quiet face. "This is bound to be nasty, Laure. We mustn't lose our heads. We mustn't start running wild, accusing here and there and everywhere. Things that looked innocent enough at the time now take on an ugly significance. We must be careful, Laure." It was almost like he was pleading with me. And I knew as well as I knew my name that dear, honest Marc had something on his mind. Something that in the light of Wiletta's murder held significance.

"That's why I didn't want to tell you about the quarrel, Marc. Why I'm sorry I mentioned it. Just because Stacey wrangled with Wiletta is no sign that she murdered her."

Marc bit his underlip. "Of course not. Naturally not. Murder! My God!" He ran nervous fingers through his thick hair. "Why, no one in this house *could* be a murderer, Laure!"

Again he was pleading with me, begging me to reassure him that our safe little world couldn't crumble like that. "We know all these people, Laure, we've known them always. Don't you understand that one of them *couldn't* have murdered Wiletta Owens?"

"One of them did," I insisted stubbornly.

He couldn't get around that. We were silent a time. Caroline and Matilda had left us. We heard low voices in the hall, the hushed purr of cars on the drive downstairs. The wedding guests were departing. I wondered how Shad Birket had got on with his questioning. Marc asked suddenly:

"Why did Valerie try to kill herself, Laure?"

"Loneliness," I answered. "Grief over her father's death last winter. She loved him in spite of everything. She's always been high-strung, emotional."

He stared moodily at the light. "Yes. I dare say that's right. Then the excitement of the wedding, an emotional strain. Valerie was all mixed up in the preparations, wasn't she, Laure?"

I told him yes, Valerie had been over every evening for two weeks, talking over the plans with Caroline and me, making suggestions about little things, helping out wherever she could. I built up quite a case to account for Valerie's attempted suicide.

He asked suddenly, "Was she in the room when Wiletta and Stacey had that set to?"

"Part of the time, Marc. She heard some of it. She was the one who said that the diamond pin was bad luck. That David shouldn't have given it to Wiletta. Caroline tried to laugh the notion aside, said all that Wiletta had to do was to give Davey a coin before accepting anything with a blade, so the blade wouldn't cut their friendship."

"Huh!" Marc grunted, then smiled grimly. "I guess she didn't do it, Laure. Wiletta didn't have a chance to give Davey a coin. Oh Lord!" He rubbed his forehead again. Then he said, "This is murder. Someone here did it. Well, you know Shad Birket. He's a nice chap, but this is out of his class. Of course, Borden is here."

"Kenneth Borden? Why, he isn't a detective, Marc. He's a doctor, isn't he?"

Marc considered me through narrowed eyes. "He is a psychiatrist, Laure. Do you know what that means?"

"I think so. It's a doctor who knows about people's minds, isn't it?"

"Yes, that's about right. Well, that's Borden, and he's plenty good. And while he isn't a detective in the regular sense, he has done some remarkable work with the police on several cases and has a very high unofficial standing with them. He's made a very thorough study of abnormal psychology. He understands a lot about why people are queer, and why they do the things they do."

I thought this over a bit. "Will he work on this case, Marc? Will he try to find out who murdered Wiletta?"

"I don't know, Laure. Certainly some expert assistance is needed. I feel that Borden would be the man to give it, but—"

"He doesn't seem like a detective to me, Marc," I interrupted. "I can't imagine him going around hunting clues, picking up pins and cigar stubs and measuring footprints."

Marc smiled. "Borden won't do that, Laure. That will be Shad's work, that is, if there are any pins and cigar stubs to pick up and any footprints to measure. What Borden will do, if he does help out, is to look inside people's brains, analyze their emotions, their reactions, and find out who had the moral capacity and after that the opportunity to murder Wiletta Owens in her bride's satin."

"Oh," I replied, digesting this new notion of a detective. "He can do that, you think?"

"He's trained to do that sort of thing, Laure. Look inside people's minds, I mean, understand why they do the things they do."

"That maybe accounts for the way he looks at one, Marc. His eyes seem to go right through you. Is he a close friend of Caroline and Clarke's? Where did they meet him?"

Marc didn't answer for a moment, for just then Valerie stirred, moaned and slipped back into unconsciousness. He bent over her, eyes anxious. Then he looked across at me. "No, Laure, he is not a close friend of the Rohmers. I mean, that's not why he's here. He's here in his professional capacity."

I guess I looked rather blank, for Dr. Marc said, "It's Jonny. You know, you can't help it, but the boy's queer. Not definitely off or anything like that, but he's full of inhibitions, repressions. He was such a weakly lad, Laure. He never could get out and tear around with the other kids. It drove him in on himself. Then, of course, David didn't help."

"You can't lay Jonny Rohmer's queerness on David, Marcus Wayne, and you know it. It wasn't his fault that Jonny—"

"I didn't mean that, Laure. But Jonny was an only child. He resented it when David came. That resentment grew with the years. Then when David grew so strong and fine, when he played football and took the high-jump contest, Jonny grew more introspective and resentful. He's twisted now, Laure. Clarke and Caroline talked it over with me last winter and we decided to get Borden. We didn't want Jonny to know about it so Borden agreed to take his vacation down here as a guest, study the lad, try to get next to him, untangle the kinks. Jonny likes him, I believe, and doesn't suspect a thing. I haven't told another soul about this, Laure."

I said gravely, "Thank you for telling me, Marc. I hope it helps Jonny. He's lonely and unhappy and bewildered. He was in love with Wiletta—"

I paused uncomfortably.

"Wiletta was bad for him," Marc agreed quietly. "She excited and tormented him. She built up all that fantasy about being a strand of gossamer or something." He grinned sourly. "Borden tipped me about that. She was—" he hesitated a moment, shutting his lips hard—"she was a vicious woman, Laure. There's no getting around it."

I said, "You heard how Jonny talked to David, Marc."

"Yes. I don't like to think about it, but we must, Laure. We must consider everything—" His lips made a dry, clicking sound as he stopped.

"Marc, you don't think, you aren't suggesting—that Jonny—killed Wiletta!" The words turned me cold. I added, trying to make it sound better, "If he loved her, he wouldn't kill her. He wouldn't kill something he loved, Marc."

Marc said, "That's a logical supposition, Laure. That Jonny, loving Wiletta, wouldn't injure her, but remember he's not logical, not normal. His words to David prove that. He said, 'Wiletta was not for you. You weren't fine enough for her. You would have broken her—it's better this way—better that she should be dead.' Do you see, Laure?"

"Yes, Marc, I see. But it isn't true. It isn't possible—"

Marc said, as if the words were forced out of him, "I was in the lower rear hall about a quarter to nine, Laure. I saw Jonny coming down the back stairs. He was shaking like he had a chill. His face was dough-white. I saw his lips working—heard him muttering to himself. He went into the library without seeing me."

I said weakly, "Oh, Marc—" And just then Valerie opened her tired brown eyes and looked at us. Slowly her glance went from my face to Dr. Marc's, over the shadowed room to the window where the pale moonlight shone. She drew a deep, shuddering sigh. Tears ran over her white cheeks. She said faintly, "Why didn't you let me die? Oh, why didn't you let me go—when I—wanted to?"

She began to sob brokenly.

THERE'S NO USE going on in detail about that horrible night. We weren't used to murder, you know, and no one reacted, professionally, as you might say. We were just bewildered, frightened folks who had lived simply and rather uneventfully and the murder of Wiletta Owens stunned us. We only had Shad Birket to do the investigation and though he did the very best he could, the case was too much for him, just as Dr. Marc had predicted. Shad worked hard to do his duty, at that.

He made himself forget that these people were his friends and neighbors, and that one of them had committed murder. I learned afterward that he got them all together in the library and did a rather good job of questioning. To the very best of his ability he found out where everyone was at approximately the time Wiletta met her death.

To the best of his ability, I say, because some of the people involved lied to him, as was to be expected, and Shad, the kindly, simple soul, didn't have the perception to know they were lying. He got their stories, though, and tried to divide truth from imagination to get at the heart of it. When he had learned all he could, he allowed them to go home.

For the rest of that night, the house was in ghastly confusion. I stayed, and Dr. Marc stayed and the lights burned all the time and people were coming and going and the telephone rang almost constantly. Out of the whole mess very little was learned. Valerie's attempted suicide, of course, added fuel to the flames of our bewilderment. Most of us shrank from accepting the obvious conclusion, that the girl, temporarily unbalanced, had returned to Wiletta's room, stabbed her, then huddled down in the window seat in hysterics until Stacey Madden's sharp words had sent her into the night, thinking to end her life in Wilromere Lake. We just couldn't allow that premise, not then, at any rate. We couldn't adjust our stunned minds to the possibility.

They laid Wiletta's crumpled body on the bed and Dr. Marc covered it with a sheet. There wasn't anything in the room to help us. They figured that Wiletta had been stabbed while she was seated before the dresser. That she had risen, turned a little and fallen forward, dead almost before she hit the floor. Dr. Marc said the vicious little blade had pierced her heart and that whoever jabbed it in that way had known pretty well where to strike.

I remained with Valerie in the spare room, lying on the couch and trying to sleep toward morning, but not making a success of it.

It was about seven and I was lying there looking at the sun edging the drawn blind and hearing the birds singing joyously in the maple trees, when Matilda knocked. She brought me a breakfast tray with coffee, toast and some of Caroline's wonderful grape marmalade. Valerie was asleep. Matilda looked at her like she was frightened of the poor child and whispered to me, "They're all up and about, Miss Laure. Mr. Borden, he's having breakfast in his room. He asked me to find out if you'd come and see him for a little. He wants to ask you some questions, I think." Matilda's whisper was sibilant and her large, protuberant brown eyes rolled. She is a plain, good woman who has worked for Caroline Rohmer for close to twenty years. Nothing fussy or frilly about Matilda Combs.

I sighed and began to arrange my hair. "Yes, Matilda, I'll go and see him, though I can't tell him very much."

Matilda stood at my shoulder; her lips looked gray and pinched. She said, "It's terrible, ain't it, Miss Laure?"

"Yes, Matilda. Too terrible for words."

"To think," Matilda hissed in my ear, "that it was on her wedding night and her in white satin and a veil and all. The veil makes it seem worse, don't it, Miss Laure?"

I didn't want to talk to Matilda, yet I felt sorry for her and right at first it wasn't possible to talk of anything else. Besides, it occurred to me that I might learn something from Matilda.

"Poor Mr. David," Matilda went on, shivering in her limp pink gingham. "Oh, poor Mr. David. Do you think he'll—kill himself—or something, Miss Laure?"

The comb clattered from my cold fingers. "For heaven's sake, Matilda, try to use a little sense! Mr. David is too well balanced, too sensible to do anything so mad and—wicked." I leaned against the dresser, staring at Matilda, and my heart pounded so it hurt.

In spite of myself I asked, "You don't know anything—you haven't heard—seen anything—"

"—that made me think he might, Miss Laure?" Matilda drew a long breath. "No, I really ain't, but I read a story once where a fine young man did just that thing, and him being so in love with Miss Wiletta—"

"Do you think he was, Matilda?"

She made her eyes big and round. "Why, of course, Miss Laure. If a man marries a woman, or sets out to, of course he's bound to be in love with her." Which explained Matilda's logic. She went on earnestly, "Besides, I heard him say so. I heard him tell Mr. Jonny—" Matilda stopped, looking frightened.

I said impatiently,

"You heard him tell Mr. Jonny what, Matilda? For heaven's sakes, get it out."

She jumped nervously, looked over her shoulder at the sleeping girl on the bed. "Well, it was just yesterday," she said hoarsely. "It was in the garden behind the lilac hedge. I'd gone out to cut some flowers and the two young gentlemen came up on the other side. I couldn't help hearing." She sighed and smoothed her ample hips. "It was terr'ble," she whispered.

"What was terr'ble?" I snapped.

"The things Mr. Jonny said to Mr. David, Miss Laure. Why, that poor child, Jonny, course he will always seem like a child to me, well, he just said such awful things. He accused Mr. David of taking Miss Wiletta away from him. He said David had always taken things he wanted. He said if it hadn't been for David coming in here like a—like a—" she gulped, but went on bravely—"thief in the night, everything would have been all right."

I didn't want to listen but I couldn't move. That big, strong, homely woman held me with the force of her earnestness. She went on, "It made me sick to hear Mr. Jonny talk like that. Mr. David, he tried to reason with him, but it wasn't no use, and finally Mr. Jonny got all crazy like. He said he'd rather see Miss Wiletta dead than Mr. David's wife. That David didn't love her anyway, and David got mad then and that's when he said he did love her, but

Mr. Jonny, he—" Matilda's eyes were popping—"struck Mr. David," she finished on a gasp of dismay.

I said weakly, "Oh, Matilda, you dreamed all this!"

She frowned at me a moment, then she laughed. It was a harsh sound, not at all like Matilda. "Oh, I wish I had—I wish to the dear Lord I had, Miss Laure, but that's the way it happened. Jonny hit David and David just stepped to one side so the blow only grazed his chin. And then Jonny began to curse—oh, something sinful, and said that he couldn't even hit a man and do a good job. I felt terrible sorry for him, Miss Laure. He was almost—crying!" Her own eyes were blurred with tears on that. "Poor Mr. Jonny," she said brokenly. "Poor Mr. Jonny. Why, I remember, Miss Laure, how when he was only a little shaver, he used to come running to me, all trembling like and sobbing and begging me to tell him he was as good as David. He'd show me his poor, skinny little arms and want me to tell him his muscle was developing. Oh, poor Jonny."

And oh, poor Jonny was what I was thinking also, as a little later I knocked on Mr. Borden's door. I had fixed my hair nice and smooth the way I always wear it, in a little flat knot on top of my head and looped down over my ears. I guess it isn't very stylish but it seems sensible to me and I've always worn it that way, so I guess I always will. Mr. Borden had on a real nice-looking dressing gown or whatever they are when men wear them. He was sitting in a chair by the open window with his breakfast on a table in front of him.

He is a tall man and very lean, with shoulders a little stooped like he's done a lot of studying in his life. He has a long pale face with a big nose and wide mouth with very strong-looking lips. His eyes are that pale blue I've mentioned and his hair is thick and blond, with a reddish tinge in it. It stands up most disorderly all over his head and his eyebrows are so black and heavy that it makes him look very queer. But he has a nice smile when he wants to use it. I felt a little afraid of him after what Marc had told me, but he got up when I came in and placed a chair for me and asked me if I'd have a cup of coffee.

I thanked him and said no, then I sat down and waited for him to question me. He wanted to know if I minded if he smoked his pipe. I said of course not and he got it going. All the time I could feel him watching me, even when he seemed to be looking at his pipe bowl.

He said all of a sudden, "So far as we can ascertain, Miss Laure, you were the last person to see Wiletta Owens alive, except for her murderer."

"Maybe I was," I told him. "I don't know."

"Well, none of us know. All we can go on is what people say, and no one admits being in there with her after you and Miss Madden and Mrs. Rohmer left about eight-thirty."

I just waited, feeling rather light in the head. "Between that time," he went on, "and approximately five minutes to nine, when you and Miss Madden found her lifeless body, someone entered that room and stabbed her!" He tapped his pipe stem thoughtfully.

"Yes, I guess that would be right," I agreed.

"That only leaves twenty-five minutes," he went on, "which isn't very long, but plenty long enough."

"Yes sir, I guess it would be, Mr. Borden."

He stared at me in that disconcerting, direct way for a moment, then he said, "When you left Miss Owens, she was herself in every way? Nothing had occurred to upset her? There hadn't been any friction, anything of that sort?"

Oh dear, there it was. It had to come, of course, but I wished he hadn't asked me. I said, "She was all right as far as I could tell. She seemed perfectly all right."

He crossed one long leg over the other. "What was the nature of the argument she had had with Miss Madden a little earlier? You needn't mind answering. I've heard about it. I just want your version."

It made me feel a little better to think he'd had it from someone else first, so I told him about it. I tried to tell it just as it happened. I worked hard not to let my dislike of Stacey Madden color my story and I think I succeeded.

When I had finished, he didn't say anything for a time and I grew uncomfortable with the sunlit silence all around me. He said at last, "Well, that tallies very well with what Frances Cosette told me." He grinned suddenly and I felt a little more relaxed. "Miss Madden and Wiletta Owens all but had a hair-pulling bout over young David, didn't they? They both wanted him and Wiletta was the winner."

"Yes, that was the way it was," I said wearily. "I don't understand things like that, Mr. Borden. I don't understand women acting like that, ladies and all."

His grin widened. "Ladies, Miss Laure, react to much the same stimuli as those who are not ladies, sometimes. Did you see Miss Madden between the time she left the room and when you met her at the door?"

"No sir, I didn't. I saw David for a few moments in the upper hall. I saw Mrs. Rohmer, downstairs. She sent me back, you know. Those were the only two I really saw, the only two I talked with." I gasped audibly, remembering that moment on the landing.

"All right, Miss Laure, what is it?"

"I did see Valerie Lane for just a moment. She passed me as I stood on the landing. She went on downstairs and out the front door."

"Ah yes," he said slowly. "Valerie Lane. Well, what did you say to her when she passed you?"

"I didn't talk to her, Mr. Borden."

"She was in a hurry?"

"She seemed to be. She had been—crying."

"Yes. Miss Madden found her crying near the back stairhead, sent her outdoors. That's when she went past you, I dare say." He made marks on the chair arm. "As nearly as we can find out, Valerie Lane didn't go downstairs after she left Wiletta's room. You've been with her all night. Can you add anything to what we already know?"

"Oh, Mr. Borden, the poor child is all unstrung. I talked to her, I just had to. She was so hysterical over what had happened—"

"Did you tell her about the murder?"

"Oh, heavens, no. Dr. Marc said nothing must disturb her in the state she was in."

"Mrs. Rohmer didn't tell her, did she?"

"No, no, no. Valerie was still unconscious when Caroline and Matilda left us."

"Then how," he asked, "did Valerie Lane know Wiletta Owens had been murdered? She left the house before the crime was discovered. She was carried back unconscious. How would she know, Miss Laure?"

I forced myself to sit very still. "Why, I suppose she heard them talking—she came back to consciousness in a little time, you know. She must have heard—"

"Maybe she did," Kenneth Borden agreed drily. "Yes, maybe she heard someone talking."

I said, trying to hold my voice steady, "Now look here, Mr. Borden, you're not for a moment to think that little Valerie Lane did this terrible thing. You're not to have any such foolish ideas as that. It's insane. It's ridiculous—why, Valerie Lane—she couldn't— she wouldn't—"

"Kill a woman?" His sharp tones clipped through my protests. "Wouldn't she? In a moment of emotional stress? When everything she longed for all the twenty-three years of her life is brought to a shining climax for the benefit of that same woman? You think she wouldn't because you are acquainted with her outer self. Because you know her face and her smile and the color of her eyes and the way she dresses her hair. Yes, but do you know what lives in her mind? Do you know what secret dreams she cherishes? What fears, longings, hates and hungers consume her secretly? No, you do not, Miss Laure.

"We all wear masks and they are usually common enough and fairly pleasant. They conceal effectively our real selves, which are frequently ugly and twisted."

His brilliant eyes were narrowed to bright slits of light. He said softly, "Take myself, for instance. You see me. You talk to me. You eat at the same table with me, yes, but do you know me? Do you have any idea what sort of a man I really am? You do not, because I manage to keep the real man hidden from you. We all have the instinct for cover. We want to hide our nakedness. That's why we wear clothes. We are bound to conceal the deformities of our minds, too, the stark ugliness of them sometimes, so we clothe them with commonplaces and show that to the world."

He stopped, and I was conscious of his quickened breathing, the tense rigidity of his lean body. I must have been hypnotized. I couldn't move for looking at him. I saw his long, pale face, his big nose, his thin lips, his light eyes, those dark, stormy brows.

I thought, "No, I *don't* know you, Dr. Borden, or Mr. Borden, or whatever you are. I don't know you at all."

He asked abruptly, "You don't really know Valerie Lane, do you, Miss Laure?"

"Maybe I don't, Mr. Borden, the way you set it out. Just the same I've *thought* I've known her for every one of her twenty-three years. I helped take care of her when she was a baby and I've watched her grow up, and in spite of everything, I still think it's impossible for her to have killed Wiletta Owens."

"She was on this floor," he said, "from the time she left Wiletta's room until she passed you on the stairs, just before you found the body. She could have returned to that room—" He paused, frowning at me. "Miss Madden told me," he stated, "that Wiletta fastened the bouquet on her shoulder with the pin while you were all in the room. Is this correct?"

"Yes."

"How do you suppose the murderer got it off to use as a weapon? The material of the gown wasn't torn, so the pin wasn't jerked off. Can you offer any suggestion as to that?"

I smiled at him and felt my tense face relax. "Why, I'd say it was quite simple, Mr. Borden. Wiletta was what you might call fussy. She had a time getting her gown to suit her. She had her veil rearranged half-a-dozen times. Don't you think it possible that after we all left she removed the pin to set the flowers at a different angle? Isn't that possible?"

"Yes, it's perfectly possible. And while she was doing it, the murderer entered, picked up the pin and stabbed her?"

Oh dear, his words brought the whole ghastly business back to me. I could just see Wiletta taking the flowers off, laying the pin on the dresser, holding the bouquet in her fingers, frowning down at it, at the spot where it should go.

He said abruptly, "What does Valerie Lane have to say about her attempted suicide?"

I started violently. "Oh, the poor child pretends it was an accident. She admitted that she was very unhappy, that all the festivity and celebration made her terribly lonely. She did sit down in the window seat and she did cry a lot. Stacey Madden came along and talked to her. Valerie said she just had to get outside. She left the house and went down to the lake. It's not very far from here, you know. Just a piece down the road. She claims she got dizzy. She says she remembers falling, she tried to save herself—"

"Do you believe her?" he asked.

I couldn't take my eyes from his. They had a curious power of holding your gaze. It was hard to lie to him, too. "Do you believe her?" he questioned again.

I had to tell the truth because I knew I couldn't successfully deceive him. "No," I said miserably. "I think Valerie tried to kill herself."

"Yes," he agreed, "I think so, too, Miss Laure. She tried to kill herself because she knew that Wiletta Owens was lying dead there in her room with the blade of that beastly pin in her heart. Because she knew that she, Valerie Lane, had thrust it there and that—"

"No!" I cried, and suddenly found myself on my feet. "That's not true. You have no right to say that. I'll prove it's not true. That child shan't suffer for what someone else did. I tell you she didn't kill Wiletta—she didn't—"

I felt his hands on my shoulders. He pushed me back into my chair. He looked pleasant and quite cheerful again and he said, laughing a little, "There, there, Miss Laure, don't get excited. The girl's not going to be arrested before noon. I was principally interested in getting your reaction." He sat down and poured two cups of coffee. This time I didn't refuse.

He said, "There's no doubt but that you are convinced of her innocence, and I believe you're a good judge of character, Miss Laure. However, we can't cross Valerie off our list yet." He took a drink of the hot liquid, then he looked at me sharply. "Since you're so sure she didn't do it, have you any suggestion as to who did? Can you help me?"

I was weak as a kitten. After all, I'm fifty-four and the strain of the night had told on me. I drank some coffee and it made me feel better. I said, trying to hold my voice steady, "I'm sorry I gave way like that, Mr. Borden. Of course, I haven't any suggestion to give you. I can't throw suspicion on someone who might be entirely innocent."

He set down his coffee cup. "If the person is entirely innocent, the suspicions won't hurt him."

I sat very still, staring at the spot of yellow sunlight on the floor, hearing a hushed clatter from downstairs where the wedding decorations were being removed. The flowers would be wilted and drooping. It would be a blessing when they were gone. Their heavy fragrance filled the place. It reminded me of a funeral and at that notion it was all I could do to keep from breaking into hysterical laughter. It came to me that the roses for Wiletta's wedding could very well grace her coffin.

And then, before I knew it, I was telling Mr. Borden about having seen Stacey Madden coming out of Wiletta's room last night! If there had been even a shadow of a doubt in my mind before it was gone now. I just knew I had seen her! She had gone to the cross corridor, ducked out of sight, then appeared again, pretending to be just arriving. I told him how white she had been, how she had jerked and how her breathing had sounded so queer. I just told him all about it, because he had assured me that if she was innocent, knowing things like this wouldn't hurt.

He sat very still, forgetting to draw on his pipe. At first I was very nervous, but gradually I forgot that, and was leaning forward, talking straight to him, trying to make it all very honest and clear.

I ended, "That's the way it was. I'm sorry if I've done anything wrong. It's the truth I've told you."

"Thank you, Miss Laure," he said. "You have done exactly right. Mrs. Rohmer sent Stacey Madden up the back stairs to this floor at about twenty minutes to nine. You met her at the door of Wiletta's room at five minutes to nine. There're fifteen minutes in there, during which time she talked briefly with Valerie Lane. Obviously some of those fifteen minutes are unaccounted for." He sipped his coffee, replaced the cup. "Miss Madden has an explanation, of course. She claims she knew it was too early to call Wiletta so she just dropped into one of the bedrooms in the cross corridor, sat down and smoked a cigarette. When she came out she saw Valerie, talked with her as reported, went on and met you."

He frowned at the sunlight. "Unfortunately," he concluded, "there is no one to substantiate her story."

"It isn't true," I said soberly. "Stacey isn't telling the truth. I saw her come out of Wiletta's room—"

"Why should there have been any doubt in your mind about it?" he interrupted. "The hall was dim, I know, but—"

"I was thinking about Valerie," I told him truthfully. "My mind was busy and my eyes weren't just at that moment. I caught a flash of something green at Wiletta's door. I thought, 'There's Stacey.' It vanished very quickly around the corridor turn but not before I had seen her red hair, recognized her. When we found—Wiletta, I didn't want to believe it. I guess I tried to make myself think I wasn't sure."

He nodded. "A natural enough reaction. An unconscious shrinking from something unpleasant."

"Yes," I said.

He tapped out his pipe on the ash tray at his elbow. He grinned at me engagingly and I thought him suddenly very charming. He said, "I believe you would make a good detective, Miss Laure."

Well! Think of that! I started to tell him I really wouldn't be good at it, though I did have a habit of noticing things, but he interrupted,

"Look here, suppose you and I work on this together. I had a talk with Clarke Rohmer and David this morning and they asked me to help out. Naturally, they want it cleared up. They shrank from importing foreign aid, though they were considering it when I came on them." He began filling his pipe again. "I'm not an orthodox detective, Miss Laure, but I've worked some with the department up in town. I talked with them over the telephone and they're willing for me to do what I can."

His pale eyes narrowed hard on me. He said slowly, "I've a feeling it's my sort of a case, that the clues we find are going to be, well, shall we call them mental?"

I was trembling with excitement. I said, "You mean that someone who was—crazy—did it?"

He frowned, then grinned meagerly. "That's too general a term to describe it," he stated. "What I mean is, the best way to find the murderer of Wiletta Owens is by walking through people's minds, observing what lives there, what hides in shadowed places."

Oh! That just sounded terrible to me. I had a ghastly impression of this tall, thin man treading silently through my brain. I declare I felt a heaviness in my head, like he was already there. He went on quietly,

"So I'm taking unofficial charge, Miss Laure. Shad Birket's doing the routine stuff, though I'm afraid it won't get him far. I'm here at the Rohmers'—" He paused and I said soberly:

"I know why you're here, Mr. Borden. Dr. Wayne told me. I hope you don't mind. Marc and I are old, old friends and we are both very fond of Jonny Rohmer."

He studied me curiously a moment then he nodded. "Wayne doubtless knew what he was doing when he confided in you. You've known him a long time, then?"

"Marc Wayne and I attended the third grade together, Mr. Borden, and you know that was a long time ago. We grew up together. Went to picnics, husking bees, they really had them then, you know, and at one time we were—" I stopped, feeling deep color flood my tired face. Whatever made me get on that subject at a time like this? But once you knew Mr. Borden, it was easy to talk to him. You found yourself telling him things you really hadn't remembered for a long time.

"Yes, Miss Laure, you and Dr. Marc were—go on, please."

"Well," I said, "if you must know, at one time we were engaged to be married!"

His eyes crinkled. "That's interesting. You won't mind my asking why you didn't conclude the arrangement?"

"It was David Kaye," I replied quietly.

"David? He came into the picture about then?"

"Yes. You've heard his story, haven't you?"

"Not entirely. I understand that the Rohmers adopted him when he was very young."

"He was five," I told him, and found myself staring at the sunlight and looking back over a long vista of years. "A woman came into this town twenty-seven years ago the eighth of last February, Mr. Rohmer. She took a room in old Mother Grainger's house, giving her name as Mrs. Wendle. Two days later, David was born and his mother died. When we tried to check up on her, find relatives to notify, friends to advise, we were helpless. The woman was a mystery and her identity died with her. They used every means at their command, the people of this village, but there was no trace of where she had come from, who she had been. So there we were with a tiny baby on our hands, whose name we did not even know, because we felt sure the name she gave was not her own. I took the baby when he was four days old. I cared for him until he was five years of age. Then the Rohmers took him."

"You were willing to give him up?" Mr. Borden suggested. "He had grown a burden—too much—?"

"David a burden!" I remember yet how my throat ached when I said that. "David was my life, Mr. Borden. I only let him go because I realized that they could do more for him. Educate him. Care for him as I never could because I am really very poor. They were sweet about it. Caroline didn't try to persuade me. She just laid it before me, let me think it over. I thought it over for a week. I realized, partially, at least, what giving him up would mean. I knew also what letting the Rohmers have him would do for David, so he went to them twenty-two years ago. I was wise, wasn't I?"

He said gently, "You were brave and unselfish, Miss Laure. I know David loves you dearly and appreciates what you did for him."

It was nice for him to put it like that. I know David loves me. I wonder if anyone can appreciate what giving him up meant. I told Mr. Borden then, "Marc and I were engaged when I took David. I can't explain it, really, perhaps I cared too much for the baby, Marc was young, I was unreasonable—we quarreled because I insisted on keeping him. Marc went away for a while. He married, all in a hurry, you know. Then I lost David—I lost everything, Mr. Borden— but I'm not sorry, really."

I thought of the young Marc I had loved. Of the tired, worn man I knew now. Of his spent ambition, his ruined dreams, wasted through the years he had put in trying to combat Luella Bell's eternal nagging. Oh, how are we to know what is wise, what is best? If Marc and I had married . . .

I said, "The rest of the story is recent. David's father was discovered eventually. He was a cold, proud man who never forgave his young wife for running away, following a bitter quarrel, hiding herself until the baby was born. He came to see his son once, I'll never forget it. David shrank from him. He readily agreed to the Rohmers adopting him, yet when he died last year—"

"He made David his heir," Mr. Borden finished for me.

"Yes. At least he left him a great deal of money. If that had not happened, if David had just continued to be the David we had always known without all that money, well, perhaps things wouldn't be as they are now. I don't believe Wiletta Owens would have wanted to marry him, fine as he is, if he had been without that money. Stacey Madden wouldn't have fought for him—"

"Yes, it added attraction, no doubt," Mr. Borden said. "Thank you for telling me this, Miss Laure. I understand things better now. It helps me to realize why Jonny is as he is today." He leaned toward me, eyes serious. "Since you understand why I'm here, you'll see that I'm concerned in more ways than one, but principally on account of my patient."

I nodded. He smiled rather grimly. "Did Wayne also tell you that he saw Jonny sneaking down the rear stairs a short time before Wiletta's body was found?"

"Yes. He was much upset about it."

And abruptly I knew that Kenneth Borden was also. He said quietly, "Jonny must be handled carefully now. It's been a terrific shock for him. If the process of adjustment is too difficult—"

He paused on a quick breath. I looked into his strange, pale eyes and a coolness came over my body. I asked, "You mean he might—lose his mind—go—"

"Crazy?" Mr. Borden smiled. "That word is used in a very general sense, Miss Laure. The uninformed say someone is crazy when his reactions vary from those usually accepted as normal. Strange things live in the subconscious. They come to us sometimes in dreams. They move us to seemingly inexplainable actions. They make us do things from which we shudder. If they can be discovered, recognized, brought into the open, subjected to the sun—" His quiet voice trailed to silence. I thought of the spool of thread that rolls into the shadows and is lost. Of the dust, the spider webs, the mice!

He said very quietly, "That's what I was trying to do with Jonny Rohmer. Bring out his fear of failure, his nightmare of inequality, his hatred of his foster brother—"

"Oh!" I gasped.

"What?"

"I wish you hadn't said that."

"Said he hated David Kaye? He does, you know."

"No, I can't believe it. They're like brothers. They grew up together. They had everything alike. Shetland ponies, bicycles, boxing gloves, college education—"

"Yes. And David rode his pony like a Cossack, did tricks on his bicycle, won the local championship boxing contest, forged ahead at college." His voice slowed, remaining there in the air, suspended between us. I had to finish from the fund of my own knowledge.

"And Jonny never could learn to ride. He was afraid. He was awkward on his wheel, fell off, broke his leg. He didn't do very well at college, didn't have any fun, lagged behind in his studies and oh, those wretched boxing gloves. His poor arms were like pipestems. The muscles wouldn't develop. He used to come to Matilda Combs, crying and begging her to tell him his arms were getting big. Yesterday he quarreled with David behind the lilac hedge. He told him he'd rather see Wiletta dead than David's wife. He struck at David and missed. He was nearly crying when he said he couldn't even hit like a man. Oh, poor Jonny Rohmer!"

I saw Mr. Borden's face through a mist of tears. I hadn't honestly intended to say all that, but it just came, anyhow. He leaned back, crossed his legs.

"Who told you that last?" he demanded.

"Matilda Combs, the maid."

He continued to stare at me. "You're not to mention it, understand? If you work with me, you're not to tell things."

"I may talk to Dr. Marc, mayn't I?"

"Wayne? Yes, that's all right. He's safe, but no one else."

"Certainly not. Is there anything special I can do?"

His black brows drew down in a frown. After a time he said, "You're in a peculiar position here, Miss Laure. The folks trust you, as witness Matilda. I talked to her and learned nothing. Your cue is just to be yourself. Let people confide in you as they have always done. Find out all you can and don't tell anything. You are particularly to win Valerie Lane's confidence." I guess he saw something stubborn in my face for he smiled and shook his head. "Now, none of that, if you're going to help me. You must play fair and not allow your preconceived ideas of people to influence you. Go into it with an open mind. Agree?"

I rose. "Yes, I agree. I'll do it to the best of my ability."

AND THAT IS HOW I became a detective! I can't say that the commission Mr. Borden gave me brought me much satisfaction, however. It was all too close to home. There could be no thrill of victory if I did help to fasten the crime on someone, because it was bound to be someone I was fond of. I thought over the possible suspects as I went slowly downstairs that morning.

Valerie Lane! I loved the child. Jonny Rohmer! A boy I pitied with all my heart. Son of a man and a woman I deeply admired and cared for. Stacey Madden! Now, there was something. I stopped on the landing and thought some bitter thoughts. They were to the effect that if someone had to pay for the crime I almost found it in my heart to hope that it would be Stacey. I didn't like her. She did no good in the world! Why couldn't it be Stacey? Then I reflected what Mr. Borden would say to ideas like that and forced them from my mind. Just because I, personally, couldn't see any reason for a person living was no reason why he should suffer. Yet it always seemed unfair to me when the strong, the good, the worthy are taken and the worthless, the vicious, the useless left.

The house was very quiet. It had a chill, dead feel for all the day was bright and sunny. The fragrance of the wedding flowers still lingered, though, thank heaven, they were all gone except that in corners stray petals drifted now and then, stirred by a soft breeze.

A quiet, haggard Caroline was looking after things, superintending the removal of the decorations she had arranged with such happiness. David and Clarke had gone somewhere in the car. I saw Jonny crossing the lawn, a thin, nervous figure with touseled hair and sunken eyes. I turned from the sight of his tragedy.

I met Dr. Marc coming in to see Valerie and went back upstairs with him. We found her sitting up in bed, nibbling at toast. She was very quiet, and answered his questions apathetically. She had apparently suffered no serious physical effects from her experience, though Dr. Marc was worried about her. I could see that. Very gently he brought up the subject of Wiletta's death. Valerie sat white as a snowdrop, great dark eyes blank, and retold the story she had told me during the night. It ran smoothly, convincingly, certainly. She had not returned to Wiletta's room. She had cried because she was lonely when everybody was so happy. Stacey hadn't helped the situation when she advised her to get outside if she couldn't endure the sight of David marrying Wiletta. Valerie didn't say so, but we saw that she thought, from Stacey's hateful remark, that everyone knew that she was hopelessly in love with David. Shame, confusion, loneliness, all those emotions had lain behind her wish to end her life. I thought, without wanting to, of Mr. Borden's statement that we didn't really know anyone.

Matilda met us as we came out. She said Frances, Wiletta's maid, was in hysterics and would Dr. Marc please go up to the girl's room on the third floor and give her something to make her sleep. Marc sighed and said yes, he'd attend to it.

I went home for a few hours in the middle of the day. There was Peter to feed, of course, and my geraniums to water. The town lay breathless under the hot sunlight. A pall of horror shrouded it. People talked in hushed tones. Curious eyes followed me, but no one attempted to question me just then. Reporters had been out that morning, I learned. Mr. Borden had talked to them and sent them away, if not satisfied, at least temporarily silenced.

Wiletta had been an orphan, without relatives or many close friends. She was to be buried in Wilromere. The funeral was to be Thursday, two days after the one she had selected for her wedding.

As I opened the gate leading up to my neat little white cottage with the honeysuckle growing over it, I saw Stacey Madden coming toward me from town. She had on a handsome fawn-colored crepe with a wide-brimmed straw hat to match. Her thin, pointed face looked very white with the geranium red of her lips, the glow of her gray-green eyes standing out sharply in contrast. She hurried to meet me. I didn't want to talk to her, but I remembered what Mr. Borden had said, so I waited.

She leaned on my gatepost, looking down at me. "Well, Miss Laure, how are things at the house of tragedy?"

"Just about what you would expect," I told her, disliking her intensely.

She smiled and swung her little bag against the post. "Why so somber, Laure dear? It strikes me there's a great deal of hypocrisy about all this."

I said unsteadily, "You're a heartless woman, Stacey Madden, and if that's all you have to say, I don't want to talk with you."

I opened the gate but something in her eyes held me. They were narrowed and the gray was all gone, so that they looked green like ice. The shadows of the maples with the sunlight streaming through gave me again that shocking impression of seeing her face through clear water. I do declare, the heat of the morning was suddenly breathless and I felt weak.

She said, speaking slowly, "Be yourself, Laure. You hated Wiletta as much as I. You didn't want her to have David any more than I did. Any more than Val Lane, than Caroline Rohmer. Clarke didn't like her. He told me so a week ago, the poor lamb. Yet all of you act so shocked, so stricken, so horrified." She lounged lower on the gate, put her face close to mine. "I think, Laure, that whoever lodged that pin so neatly in Wiletta's heart did a damned good job. So do you. Why don't you be honest and admit it?"

I said, speaking with difficulty, "Taking human life is wicked. Who are we to be judges of what is best?"

She laughed at me, green eyes glittering. "Horse-feathers!" she said. Oh, some of these modern expressions! "Tripe," she added. "I wish I knew who did it."

Something made me say, "Sure you don't, Stacey?"

The nervous jerking of her body stilled. The shadows played across her face, like shifting water. Her eyes were for a moment curiously sunken.

"No," she said, "I'm not at all sure I don't know who did it."

My heart thumped against my ribs. Down the street the Laughlin boys were playing ball. Their shouts came to us faintly. She added, "I'm sure of one thing, though, Laure," and waited.

"Yes? Sure of what, Stacey?"

"Sure that there is one person in the house who *does* know who did it!"

"Who?"

She stirred, examined the snap of her handbag. Her bright lips smiled. Her eyes were shadowed and burning. She looked straight at me. "Have you talked to Frances Cosette, Laure?" she inquired.

"Frances, the maid?"

"Of course."

"No. Why?"

She straightened, brushed a tendril of hair from her cheek. "Oh, nothing, perhaps, except that Frances saw the murder committed!"

Before I could speak, she was sauntering away down the sun-splashed street, her slim body swaying like a lazy wave.

Oh dear! What a time that was. No one normal. Everybody saying things they didn't mean, everybody lying, evading, inventing. I don't for a moment believe that Frances Cosette saw Wiletta killed, but I do believe that that morning Stacey Madden thought she had.

I WAS BACK at the Rohmers' by four o'clock. The brief time spent at home had comforted me a great deal. Peter was so glad to see me and the geraniums did need water. I changed into my gray print and packed a few things into my little bag because Caroline had asked me to stay on a few days.

I kept thinking about what Stacey had told me. That Frances had seen the murder committed. It sounded crazy at first because I remembered Clarke asking the girl right there in the room if she knew who had killed Wiletta. If she had known she would have told, wouldn't she? Which shows how naive I was at that stage. I have learned since that people have queer reasons for withholding information at times.

I wondered if I should tell Mr. Borden or if I should try to talk to Frances myself. I put my toothbrush, comb and kid curlers into the bag, along with a few other things I wanted from the bath cabinet, locked the house and went back to the Rohmers'.

There was no one about when I arrived, so I went through the cool, quiet hall, up the stairs and to the little room at the end which I always occupied when I stayed there. Memory of Stacey's statement bothered me.

I listened outside Mr. Borden's door and didn't hear a sound so I marched straight across to the door leading to the third floor and mounted the stairs. Frances' door was unlocked. I opened it very softly, looked in. She lay in bed, and she was asleep. It was not a sound sleep, though. She tossed, whimpering. Her thin face was drawn. Her little red button mouth tight and pale. Her shining black hair was in two long braids over the pillow. I watched her a while, wondering if I should waken her. There was a glass half full of water on the table and a box containing, I supposed, the sleeping tablets Dr. Marc had given her. I decided against trying to talk to her then. If she had taken the medicine, she would be dopey if awakened. He certainly hadn't given her much of a dose because she slept so poorly. So after a time I left her. If she did know who had killed Wiletta, well, she'd still know when she wakened.

I went down to the first floor. There were sounds of activity from the kitchen. Somewhere as I crossed the hall I heard the nervous tap of a typewriter. I knew it must be Jonny because he had a little portable which he kept in the library and used quite a bit. I crossed the living room and looked in. Sure enough, there he was, the poor lad, sitting before his little desk in the corner. He jumped like he was shot and I know the door made only the tiniest sound when I pushed it.

His gray face was so haggard. There in the shadowy coolness his eyes looked strange and brilliant, like the eyes of an animal glimpsed sometimes at night. He dropped back when he saw me. I said, "I'm sorry, Jonny. I didn't mean to startle you."

He glared at me a moment, then wiped his damp face with that queer, jerky gesture. He said, "Who wouldn't be startled? People sneaking up behind! Peering, prying!" He fought for control. I didn't like what I saw in his eyes. He tried to smile. "Forgive me, Miss Laure, I'm just jittery. Will you come in?"

I went toward him and he watched me suspiciously, his thin body tensed. I said, "Jonny, you like me, don't you?"

Well, now I'm not what Mr. Borden is, a psychiatrist! I don't pretend to understand how the human mind works. I don't know anything about the subconscious, or inhibitions, or repressions.

Usually if I've got something to say, I just say it. I did that time, and it's curious the effect it had on Jonny Rohmer. Maybe they weren't as smart as they thought and he knew more than they suspected. Anyway, he blinked at that direct question, then he relaxed in the most wonderful way and suddenly he was smiling at me, the Jonny Rohmer I'd known one time a good many years ago.

He said, "You bet I like you, Miss Laure. You used to give me bread with strawberry jam on it."

I laughed and sat down beside him. "That's fine. I thought you did. Liked me and trusted me."

A curtain came over his eyes which had been momentarily clear and normal. "I don't trust very many people," he said sullenly.

"Well, I don't either, for that matter, Jonny. I trust you, though, and I believe you'd trust me."

He watched me suspiciously. "What you getting at?" he demanded.

Maybe the good Lord guided me then, or maybe it was just because I didn't know any better, but I said, "I want you to tell me honestly what you were doing upstairs last night about a quarter of nine." And the moment I said it I was frightened to death. I thought of all Mr. Borden had done to heal this boy's sick mind, of what the tragic effects of my blunt question might be. I think I held my breath, half expecting Jonny to turn into a raving maniac before my very eyes. He didn't move, however. His face was quiet, too, and his pitiful eyes looked straight into mine without flinching.

He said, "I'll tell you, because you'll understand, Miss Laure, and I know you won't laugh at me."

"No, Jonny, I won't laugh at you," I promised.

Even at that it was hard for him. He said, "I was in love with Wiletta. It was a hopeless love, Laure. I was not good enough for her. I knew it, and I was content to worship from afar. Something died inside me, I think, when David bullied her into accepting him as a husband. I tried to be honest about it with myself. I tried to believe she'd be happy with him. I couldn't, but there was nothing I could do about it. It came over me as I waited there in the library last night, that I'd have one last word with her. See her once more just as she was, before—"

His face flushed painfully. He began gnawing at his underlip.

I sat very still.

He went on, "Before she became David's wife. I wanted that picture to carry with me, so I went upstairs. I didn't want anyone to see me and laugh at me. I went very quietly. I got to her door. I stood there, listening for sounds of her—"

In spite of myself, I said, "Yes, Jonny, yes, go on, child."

He passed a shaking hand across his eyes. "I was a coward. I couldn't let her witness my misery, my failure, so I just turned around and went back. I felt worse and worse the farther I went. I wanted to drop through the floor, thinking that I'd failed even in that."

He stopped speaking, sat listlessly staring at the typewriter, lips twitching. So this was Jonny's story of why he was sneaking down the back stairs about the time Wiletta had been killed. Was it true?

I left him a few minutes later, still sitting before the typewriter, with a wastebasket half full of crumpled sheets of ruined paper.

I DISCOVERED that Stacey had come straight to the Rohmers' from talking to me that morning. She and Caroline had discussed things for a while, then Caroline had lain down to try and get some rest. Stacey was too highly keyed for that. I wondered sometimes if the woman ever did rest with recourse to heavy opiates. She was prowling around the house from cellar to garret, it appeared. I ran into her once or twice but always saw her coming and avoided her.

The more I thought about it, the more I realized that I should tell Mr. Borden what Stacey had said about Frances having witnessed the killing. So about six o'clock, when I saw him come in from the grounds and go upstairs, I went after him. He admitted me at once, offered me a cigarette which left me breathless for a moment, until he laughed and said, "You should try one, Miss Laure. Burning tobacco is a splendid method of relaxing."

I couldn't believe that, thinking of Stacey and of how she smoked almost constantly. Anyway, I said no I didn't care to learn at my age, then I got it out, all in a burst of words. He was standing before the window smoking and he did not look at me as I talked. But I saw his black brows come down in a straight, hard line, then he turned slowly, facing me.

"Why didn't you tell me at once?" he demanded.

I felt rather fluttery. "I'm sorry. I guess I didn't really believe it."

He said impatiently, "You are not qualified to judge, Miss Laure. Remember that, please. You say you went to see Frances yourself?"

Oh dear, I was frightened. "I just looked in, Mr. Borden. She was sleeping so I didn't bother her. That was several hours ago. Also I talked to Jonny—"

"We'll let Jonny rest for the moment," he said, "and see Frances. Want to come?"

I didn't really want to but I didn't dare show it or let him think I was nervous, so I said, yes, I'd like to come.

We went out, met no one, crossed to the stairs and went-up to the third floor. It was almost dark up there for there are heavy vines over the window and the sun was on the other side. It was very still, too, and I could hear the maple boughs scraping against the roof.

"Which is her door?" Mr. Borden asked.

I pointed, not being able to say anything, I was that nervous, thinking maybe we'd learn a lot before we left. We did, too. Mr. Borden tapped. There was no answer and I suggested that she still might be asleep. He grunted, looking worried, then he opened the door.

The little room was very dim. The dormer window showed a pale oblong of dusk and a sweet, cool breeze came through the starched curtains. He went in, crossed to the bed, walking softly.

"Yes, she's asleep," he said under his breath, and bent over her. I remember that I stood by the door and I saw his tall form stiffen suddenly, though he didn't straighten. He just stayed there, bending over Frances on the bed until I found myself chewing my under-lip from nervousness. I guess I wouldn't make a good detective, after all. I don't like moments like that.

He said suddenly, "Turn on the light, Miss Laure."

I'd been waiting for him to say that very thing. I pressed the switch. A little shaded lamp beside the bed sprang into a rosy glow. I crossed over, paused beside him. "She's sleeping soundly now," I said.

He straightened, then, slowly, "Yes," he replied. "Very soundly. She's dead."

CHAPTER THREE

I DIDN'T SAY ANYTHING. I couldn't. I just looked at Mr. Borden. It seemed strange to note that he was trembling. Somehow I thought that a man like that would be above ordinary weaknesses, yet there he stood, looking down at Frances Cosette, and he was shaking all over.

I made myself look at Frances. It wasn't easy but I had to do it sometime. She was at peace now, head back, eyes closed, lids blue, and her queer little button mouth sagged open so I saw her very white teeth and pale tongue.

Suddenly I began crying. It wasn't because I felt any particular grief over Frances' death. I hadn't known her, really, but it all seemed so wicked, so strange and cruel that it should be necessary to take life like that.

"Stop it!" Mr. Borden snapped.

I did at once. He said, "How long ago were you here?"

"I—I got back here by four. I went to my room, then I came right up here."

"And she was alive then? There isn't any doubt about it?"

"No. She was sleeping poorly, tossing and moaning. I know I thought Dr. Marc hadn't given her a very heavy sedative or she would have slept more soundly."

"Wayne gave her a sedative?" His eyes flashed to the empty glass on the table.

"Yes. Matilda brought word this morning that Frances was in hysterics and asked Dr. Marc to give her some medicine. I didn't

85

see him after that, but here—" I picked up a small white envelope—
"this is the kind he uses. I suppose the medicine was in this."

Mr. Borden examined the empty envelope. I asked, trying to
keep my voice steady, "How did she die? What caused it, Mr.
Borden? Was she—"

"Murdered? I don't know." He pulled the covers down a bit,
exposing Frances' bright red-silk pajamas. It seemed to me that it
was almost sinful to meet death in a getup like that. He laid a hand
on her cheek. "Recent," he muttered. "Wonder what Wayne gave
her?" He looked at me suddenly. "Go downstairs and phone him,
will you? Ask him to step right along up, please. Don't make any
fuss about this. They'll have to know but we'll try and make it easy."

I was glad enough to get out of that small, shadowed room. I
ran downstairs, hanging onto the polished banister so I wouldn't
fall. I was shaking all over when I reached the telephone in the
lower hall. I got Dr. Marc at once. His voice had a very comforting
effect.

"Marc, will you come over to Caroline's at once, please. Right
away, in a hurry." I kept my voice low and tried not to let it get all
quavery. I said, in answer to his question, "Yes, yes, something's
happened. Don't ask me, please. Just come fast."

"Be there in ten minutes," he snapped, and as I replaced the
receiver, turned to see Caroline standing half way down the stairs.
She had on her powder-blue crepe and it looked very nice for all
her face was so tragic. She came slowly toward me. She said, "What
is it, Laure? What has happened?"

I remembered what Mr. Borden had said about making it easy,
but what could I do? I tried to think of the best way of telling it, and
while I hesitated her fear grew. She clutched my shoulders, actually
shook me; Caroline is a big, strong woman and I fairly rattled. "Tell
me what it is, Laure!" she demanded. "Tell me! Tell me!"

She released me then and I slumped back against the wall. "It's
Frances, Caroline. She's—dead." There came a stifled sound from the
shadows back of the stairs and suddenly Stacey Madden was there,
rising from a low stool and coming toward us. "What's that you
say, Laure Hosmer? Frances dead! You mean that? You mean it?"

I thought she was going to shake me, too. I felt quite helpless between those two tall women. I just nodded. Caroline choked a sob. Her eyes were wide and frightened. "Laure! Please tell me, please talk, won't you? How did it happen? What caused it?"

Stacey laughed. Oh, dear, how could she? I do believe that woman had no regard for human life, including her own. She said, before I could speak, "Isn't that too bad? Now Frances can never tell who murdered Wiletta. Oh, what a shame. What a shame!" But for all her laughter, her eyes haunted me. There wasn't any mirth in her eyes. I still see them sometimes at night, when I can't sleep. She was a strange woman and there was much evil in her. There had been, at one time, I believe, a capacity for much good, too, but something happened along the way that ruined that.

Caroline just looked at her, turned without a word and started up the stairs. I remember how the skirt of her blue crepe swished around her very shapely ankles and that the heel of her right slipper was slightly run over.

Stacey took a cigarette from the little black case she always carried, then, oddly enough, she offered it to me. I shook my head impatiently. She lighted hers, inhaled deeply and said,

"You'll come to it, old dear. You'll seek solace in tobacco before this is over."

I didn't bother to answer. Instead I said, "Stacey, what did you mean by saying that Frances saw Wiletta murdered?"

Smoke drifted from her quivering nostrils. "Just that, Laure. Frances looked in through the bathroom door and saw who it was who jammed that blade into Wiletta's heart."

I just couldn't believe it. I guess she read the doubt in my eyes. She shrugged her thin shoulders. "Well, the wench said she did but she got cautious and wouldn't give details."

"Good heavens, Stacey Madden, if the girl knew that, why on earth didn't she tell it at the time? Why did she stand there in the doorway and scream like a ninny, then insist she didn't know anything about it?"

"I wouldn't know," Stacey drawled, "what exact motives actuated Frances in that particular. The screaming act was simple. She had to *appear* surprised, of course. Maybe she intended to black-mail the murderer. Maybe she was afraid to tell. Her own position wasn't too sweet. Wiletta treated her like hell and she hated her mistress most royally. Ask any of the servants."

I was listening for the sound of Marc's car. Presently I heard it thumping up the drive. I said to Stacey, fear cold on my heart, "Did you tell anyone else what you told me? That Frances knew the murderer? Did you, Stacey?"

She studied me a time in silence, her eyes green in the gloom. I heard the car door slam and Marc running up the steps. She said, just before he reached the door, "Yes, Laure, I told Valerie when I dropped in to see her, and I told Jonny Rohmer."

DR. MARC CAME IN just then. He was bareheaded and his linen suit was wrinkled. He asked, "Well, Laure, what is it this time?" and tried to smile. I turned away very quickly so he wouldn't see the tears in my eyes. Sometimes the sight of Marc Wayne is more than I can endure. He looks as if there is something in life that was very vital to him, which he has completely missed. Usually he is just a quiet, courteous small town doctor and a very good one, too, but again all that vanishes and I see him clearly. Those are the times I can't stand to look at him.

"It's Frances Cosette, Marc. Come with me, please." I started up the stairs. He came behind me. Stacey followed, smoke drifting over her shoulder.

We found Caroline on her knees beside the dead girl. She was crying silently and stroking the poor, cold hand. Caroline is like that. Her heart is big enough to encompass the world. She should have had at least ten children to hover. Instead of which there was only poor, twisted Jonny, and David, of course.

Marc looked quickly at the bed, then at Borden. Mr. Borden said, "Looks like an overdose of something, Wayne. What did you give her?"

Marc set his satchel on a chair beside the bed. Caroline got heavily to her feet, moved away. Stacey and I stood near the door. Dr. Marc made a few swift movements with his hands over the dead girl. He did not answer Mr. Borden's question then. Instead, he spoke over his shoulder, "Wait outside, will you please," and we went slowly into the hall, closing the door.

I remember how peaceful the grounds of the Rohmer place looked as I stood by the window. There was a rosy sunlight over them and the willows were all green where the little river ran. I heard children laughing down in the village, the distant honk of an auto horn and somewhere a cow was lowing mournfully.

I thought back over my life in Wilromere. Remembered other springs that had come and gone. Bright, hot summers and long, sweet autumns, blue with haze and fragrant with the drift of leaf fires burning. I saw myself then, like someone who is set up on a stage, to be looked at. I saw a thin, stoop-shouldered woman with gray hair and a plain face, blue eyes and a mouth that I guess has become rather pinched with loneliness through all the years. It's odd that I thought so much about myself just then, in the light of all that had happened. Perhaps that is the reason I did it, though. I was trying to understand my relation to events, discover exactly what I was to do and why, what I had done and why, make sense out of it.

I didn't succeed very well, but when the door opened and Dr. Marc looked out, I know that I was calmer. Those few minutes reflection there by the vine-shadowed window had helped a lot.

Dr. Marc said, "Laure. Mrs. Rohmer, Stacey, will you come here, please?"

Immediately my temporary peace was shattered. I went slowly toward that door, not taking my eyes from his face. He stepped aside to allow us to enter. Mr. Borden stood by the foot of the bed. His eyes looked almost white with excitement. Between his fingers he held a crumpled piece of paper.

Marc said, "We have found something which seems to explain a lot. We thought you should know." He looked at the paper Borden held. Borden said:

"This was thrust under the girl's pillow. I'll read it to you. It names the murderer of Wiletta Owens."

Caroline sank to a chair. I heard Stacey's sharply drawn breath, caught a glimpse of her pale, strained face, then Borden was reading:

"I killed Wiletta Owens because I hated her. I thrust the knife into her heart when she asked me to fasten the bouquet on her shoulder. I know it is sinful to take human life, but she was a cruel, selfish woman. She destroyed everything she touched. I do not regret what I have done. I do not care to live any longer, though, so I am taking the easiest way out."

Borden's strong voice stopped. His eyes went slowly over our faces. He said, "It is signed, 'Frances Cosette.'"

Well! Did that hand out a jolt! And that last expression just shows what all this has done to me. It's another one that David brought back from college.

It was Stacey Madden who broke the breathless silence. Stacey laughed! Believe it or not, Stacey Madden laughed. She said, "So that's settled, isn't it? How convenient," and started toward the door.

"Just a moment, Miss Madden."

Stacey turned slowly, looking at Mr. Borden. Moisture showed at the edge of her ruddy hair. "Yes?" she inquired. "It does solve the mystery, doesn't it?"

Borden's pale eyes were narrowed on her face. I got again the impression that he was studying an abstract and rather interesting problem.

"Perhaps, but we won't hurry, anyway. You told Miss Laure, I believe, that Frances knew the identity of the murderer. That correct?"

"Yes. This seems to indicate it, doesn't it?"

He disregarded that last. "How did you get that information?" he demanded.

"Well, I found her throwing fits in here this morning and asked her what was the matter. I knew she wasn't broken with grief over Wiletta's death. She talked a lot of tripe, and out of the mess I got it that she had gone into the bathroom through the spare room, peeked in on Wiletta just in time to see the gory deed done. I thought at the time she was balmy and making a play for attention. Later I decided she was talking straight."

"She wouldn't tell you whom she had seen?"

"Not a chance. I don't pretend to understand her play." Stacey looked curiously at the dead girl, glanced across at Borden. "Do you?" she asked innocently.

He smiled faintly. "Not entirely. The supposition is that Frances murdered her mistress, as indicated, then ended her own life?"

"That would be my opinion," Stacey admitted languidly.

"There are objections to a ready acceptance of the theory," Borden stated, watching her closely.

"Yes?" Smoke drifted through her parted lips again. "Such as?"

"We are wished to believe," Borden told her, "that Frances took an overdose of the sedative Dr. Wayne left her. Unfortunately for the theory, the sedative was perfectly harmless and could not under any circumstances cause death."

I remember how blood flooded Stacey's face, receded, leaving her too white to be real. She didn't move though, except to lift the cigarette to her lips again.

"What killed her?" she asked.

"Veronal, perhaps. We're having the slight residue in the glass analyzed."

"Couldn't she have had veronal in her possession?"

"Yes. Sufferers from insomnia frequently use it. Dr. Wayne, who has attended Frances once or twice in a minor way, assures me, however, that according to her own statement she was an excellent sleeper."

Stacey shrugged. "That doesn't mean anything. People frequently lie about things like that."

"Possibly, though it seems rather pointless. Would you do it, Miss Madden?"

She shook her bright-maned head. "Not a chance. I'm the world's worst sleeper. I can't remember when I've slept decently without—" She paused on a quick breath.

"Veronal, Miss Madden?" Borden asked.

The long, thin hand holding the cigarette lowered slowly. She stared at him with an expressionless face.

"You do use it, don't you?" Borden insisted.

Her eyes were terribly alive. They burned like banked fires. "Yes, Mr. Borden, I use it regularly. What effect exactly are you endeavoring to produce?"

"Only a very general one," he assured her. "I am pointing out the possible inconsistencies in the alleged confession and apparent suicide."

"There are others?"

"One at least which strikes me forcibly."

"You wouldn't mind stating it?"

"Not in the least." He tapped the crumpled paper. "The message, including the signature, was written on a typewriter. That fact automatically makes it worthless. I hesitate to believe that a smart young woman like Frances wouldn't have realized that fact."

"In the stress of intense emotion," Stacey said, "many facts might escape one's attention."

"Exactly. However, the one fact that cannot escape our attention just now is that any one of a number of people in this house could very easily have typed this message."

Stacey's eyebrows lifted. "Yes? So simple as that? There is a typewriter here?"

A moment of aching silence. I felt fear creeping round that room. Then Caroline, poor, dear Caroline, said on choking sobs, "Yes, yes, there is one here. It belongs to Jonny. It is in the library."

And like a flash of lightning on a dark night came to me the ghastly memory of Jonny Rohmer crouched above the little portable in the library! It struck me like a heavy blow in the solar plexus. Breath went out of me. I didn't know I said anything, but I must have, for Mr. Borden glanced at me sharply. I wanted to die just then! Why hadn't I thought of it before, why hadn't I remembered it? But things were whipped from my brain those days. And I was not the only one. None of us reacted normally.

Mr. Borden said, "Yes, Miss Laure? What have you remembered?"

My throat was so dry and tight I couldn't speak. I dare say I looked queer, for Dr. Marc made a half motion to come to me, but Stacey Madden spoke. She said, in that soft, drawling voice I hated,

"I think I know what Miss Laure has remembered. The half hour she spent with Jonny in the library this afternoon when he was at the typewriter."

Caroline rose to her feet, swayed unsteadily, dropped back. "Stacey!" she choked. "What are you saying?"

Stacey regarded her coolly. "Nothing, dear, that isn't true and nothing very terrible at that. Jonny spent considerable time at his machine. Anything strange about that? He's writing poetry, I believe." And her light laugh tinkled.

Mr. Borden was watching me. His eyes questioned in such a way that I had to answer. I said, "Yes, I did talk to Jonny while he was at his typewriter this afternoon."

"Did you see what he was writing?"

"No. When I came in he jerked the paper out, crumpled it up and tossed it into the wastebasket." "Hm!" Mr. Borden said, which might mean anything.

Caroline rose. "I'm going downstairs," she said.

"I can't stand this, I can't endure—" She pressed one large white hand across her eyes, turned toward the door. She stumbled in reaching it. Her shoulders sagged.

"Yes," Mr. Borden agreed, "we'll all go downstairs. We must call What's-his-Name, Birket, the sheriff, too. Wayne, will you attend to that?"

Dr. Marc said yes, he'd call Shad Birket at once. He began fumbling with the covers, trying to pull them over the dead girl, and I stayed to help him. Marc is usually very clever and deft with those fine, steady hands. I suppose he had pulled coverings over many dead faces in his time, but tonight he fumbled and I helped him, while the others went out.

When that pinched white face was hidden Marc sighed and looked across at me. "What's the answer, Laure?"

I held my glance steady before his. "Maybe we'll never know, Marc. I wish, almost, that we might never know. That everything would just stop now. That this would be the end. That nothing more would happen."

"That can't be, I'm afraid, Laure. This can't be the end. It's like when you start a rock rolling down a steep hillside. It breaks flowers, it dislodges other rocks, it starts an avalanche." He looked so serious, Dr. Marc did. "The rock was started last night when Wiletta Owens died. You can't halt the avalanche now, Laure. Not until it reaches the very bottom, not until it comes to rest at the foot of the hill."

I had never known Marc to be allegorical before, which just goes to show the condition we had reached. I said, with what I hope was plain common sense, "If we found the murderer, things would stop, wouldn't they?"

He considered this a moment, then, "Well, at least, Laure, there wouldn't be any more deaths." And I knew that he meant that even if the murderer was caught, the effect of what he had done would go on and on destroying and bruising and spreading ruin. If it should be proven against Jonny Rohmer now! Oh, I just couldn't contemplate that. I said, my voice all quivery,

"Marc, Jonny didn't do this. You know he didn't. Marc, we must prove that Jonny didn't, we must, we must!"

He came slowly around the bed and stood beside me. I saw his dear, kind face, his gentle eyes. I smelled the fragrance of good tobacco along with that faint suggestion of antiseptics that always clings to him.

"You didn't really see what Jonny was writing, Laure?"

"I did not, Marc. I didn't give it a thought. I just went in to talk to him."

"What did you talk about? You'll tell me, won't you?"

"Yes. I'll tell you, Marc, because Mr. Borden said it would be all right to talk things over with you."

He smiled faintly. "You're helping Borden, Laure?"

I felt my cheeks color. "Yes, he asked me to, but let's go into the hall, Marc. I don't like it in here."

Without a word he opened the door and we went into the dim, quiet hall and over to the window where I had watched the sunset. It was nearly dark outside now and I saw the tall trees moving softly in the evening breeze. We sat down on the sill. All the windows in the Rohmer house have those wide, comfortable seats. I told Marc what I had learned from Jonny. About why he had gone upstairs last night and what he had done.

He listened, with his far-away eyes on the shadowed garden where a night thrush was singing. "It's possible, Laure," he told me when I had finished. "It's a perfectly possible reaction for him to have. Also," he stirred uneasily, "it could be a deliberate lie. Something he figured out in his sick mind, knowing that he would be questioned sooner or later."

"Stacey told him what she claims Frances said," I remarked miserably. "If Jonny did—if he could have done that—killed Wiletta—and Frances saw him—" I stopped from sheer dismay. Marc leaned toward me.

"Yes, Laure?"

"Stacey said when I asked her why Frances kept the knowledge to herself, that maybe Frances figured on blackmailing the murderer!" I whispered. "I didn't think then, it didn't occur to me—if it was Jonny, Frances might have thought she could get some money from him."

Marc nodded. "Yes, that's possible. If Jonny did kill Wiletta, if he thought Frances knew, well—"

I laid a shaking hand on his arm. "Marc, do you think veronal did it?"

"I'm quite sure of it, Laure. It's used frequently as a suicidal agent. Generally speaking, it takes a lot of it to do the trick, but the girl was suffering severely from shock when I visited her this morning. Also she had a rotten heart. Under those circumstances—"

I said through stiff lips, "Is there any—do you know—about any in this house?"

He nodded gravely. "Caroline always keeps a supply on hand. She hasn't slept this last year, Laure."

I recalled the shadows under Caroline's fine blue eyes and I sat silent a time, looking down at the white blur of the snowball bush below. My tumbled thoughts finally formed themselves into words. I can hear myself yet saying to Dr. Marc:

"Then Jonny could have obtained the veronal, written the note, gone to Frances' room—"

"She was sleeping when you were there, Laure?"

"Yes, very uneasily. I wondered why you didn't really put her to sleep."

"It was because of that tricky heart, Laure, that I couldn't take chances. I only wanted to quiet her." He pushed at his heavy gray hair. "If we are to entertain that notion, well, how did Jonny give her the tablets?"

"Well," I suggested, "suppose he just went in, saw her like I found her, perhaps, suppose he saw the half glass of water on the table—"

"There was half a glass of water on the table?"

"Yes. I remember it distinctly. Suppose he dropped the tablets into that and went away? Suppose she wakened, drank the water, maybe putting in one of the tablets you left, not thinking, not knowing—"

Marc stood up. "Let's get downstairs, Laure. After all, this isn't really doing any good. We're only surmising and it can lead us anywhere. It could have happened as you say. I told the girl she could take the remainder of the tablets during the day if she needed them. Let's get downstairs now."

I followed him, walking slowly, because the stairs were thickly shadowed. Light came to meet us as we descended, along with the hushed, tight murmur of voices. I tried to think that the house was just as it had always been, an island of additional safety in the quiet harbor. But I knew better. The harbor wasn't pleasant any more. The safety was gone. Somewhere among us walked one with blood on his hands. The rock had been started from the hilltop. It was still pursuing its way of destruction toward the bottom. I shuddered to think what we would find there.

I guess we were both very busy with our own thoughts. Anyway, I started nervously, and Marc jerked up sharply when a door opened almost directly before us on the second floor.

Valerie Lane was looking out. She was very pale. Her brown hair hung like a cape over her shoulders. Sight of her brought my thoughts from Jonny Rohmer. Made me remember that Stacey had also told this girl before us that Frances Cosette, the maid, claimed to know who had killed Wiletta Owens.

Marc went straight to her. "What's this, Valerie? Didn't I tell you to remain in bed today?" He pushed her gently back into the room. I followed. She allowed him to guide her to the bed. She sat down, pulling a sheet over her pajamaed legs. She looked very small and frightened.

She said, "I don't want to stay in bed any longer. It makes me nervous. And what's going on, anyway? There's so much running up and down stairs and when Matilda brought my broth she was all atremble, but she wouldn't tell me what was wrong. I can't stand it any longer. I want to get up. I'm not sick. I'm going home. I won't stay here!" Her voice kept rising, getting tighter and higher. Bright spots burned on her cheeks. She saw Marc make a motion toward his satchel. She cried wildly, "Now don't you give me any more of those pills, Marc Wayne. I won't take them, I tell you I won't. Nor a shot in the arm either." She hugged her thin little body with her slim, tanned arms and shook herself defensively. "Now you tell me what's wrong," she insisted.

Marc knew when to talk and when to be quiet. He studied that hysterical girl and made up his mind. "It's more trouble, Valerie. Frances Cosette took an overdose of sleeping medicine and died as a result. That's why everyone is so upset."

Valerie's arms loosened, hung limply at her sides. Her mouth quivered, but she did not give way completely.

She said in a queer, small voice, "She was murdered, wasn't she?"

Marc moved uneasily as he sat on a chair beside her. "We hope not, Valerie. We hope that it was accidental—"

Valerie shook her head. "No, I don't believe that, Marc. She was killed because she knew who stabbed Wiletta. Stacey told me. I believe that is why she was killed."

I had my say then. "Frances left a note, Valerie, confessing the murder of Wiletta. She wrote that she did it herself and was committing suicide."

Valerie's great dark eyes met mine. They were pitiful in their confusion and terror. "I don't believe it," she whispered. "Frances didn't do it. I don't believe it."

Marc said, "Why are you so sure, Valerie, that Frances didn't do it?"

Valerie looked at Marc. "Wiletta was killed between eight twenty-five and five minutes to nine, wasn't she?"

"Yes. Laure saw her alive at eight twenty-five. At approximately ten minutes to nine—"

"I know," Valerie interrupted. "Well, during that time, Dr. Marc, I sat all by myself in the window seat at the end of this hall. I sat there looking down into the garden. It was bright moonlight, you know, and I saw Frances standing by the sundial smoking a cigarette. I saw her plainly and I had no trouble in recognizing her, from her uniform. None of the servants here wore black and white like that, you know. You remember, Laure, she went into the bath when Wiletta sent us away. Well, she came out of the spare room just after I sat down out there. She went down the rear stairs and a moment later I saw her by the sundial. I watched her. She looked so trim and—pretty. Even when Stacey came along and talked to me I still saw Frances standing down there smoking. She was there when I left to go outdoors." Valerie leaned toward us, dark eyes intent. "Don't you see? She couldn't have killed Wiletta. She couldn't even have *seen* who did."

And that, if we could accept Valerie's story, settled that point.

I DO NOT ATTEMPT to justify what happened concerning the death of Frances Cosette. There must have been an understanding among the principals in that tragedy, yet we certainly did not reach any agreement through discussion. Everyone, however, acted as if it had all been worked out and settled.

Clarke Rohmer and David arrived almost simultaneously with Shad Birket, the sheriff. Mr. Borden took them into the library, the three of them. I was there also, and told them quietly what had happened, then he led the way to the little room on the third floor.

I can see their faces yet, standing out from the clustering shadows. I remember how Shad's eyes popped, how his mustache quivered. I remember Clarke's haggard face. And David! There wasn't much change noticeable in him when he looked at the girl who had been Wiletta's maid. It was like the shock of Wiletta's death, left no room for further emotion.

Clarke was the first to speak. He said, looking at Mr. Borden, "She died from an overdose of—something, you say? It was—suicide?"

Mr. Borden laid the crumpled note on the table. They read it, all three of them, bending over it, wordlessly. I won't admit that Mr. Borden or anyone else actually lied about the facts. He presented them. He told them that the sedative Dr. Marc had given the girl was harmless. He added that in his opinion and that of Wayne death had resulted from an excessive dose of veronal, which had proven fatal, due to her leaky heart and the shock of Wiletta's murder.

He told them that Dr. Wayne stated that the girl claimed to be an excellent sleeper. He told the absolute truth as far as he went. He did not go all the way. Thinking it over at this late date, I am still not entirely clear as to his motive in withholding certain points. I am not clear as to why any of us did what we did. We felt, all but Clarke and David and the sheriff, that Frances Cosette had been murdered. We knew, at least I did, that Frances Cosette had not written that note on the typewriter, but all of us kept still. Was it because we sensed that was the best way to reach a solution of the mystery? Could it have been merely an instinctive attempt to smother fear? Was it our pitiful endeavor to re-establish and save what was left of the peace of our harbor? I don't know. But we did it.

Shad Birket, more power to him, seized on the "confession" as a drowning man is alleged to grab a straw. He accepted it without question, at least as far as we could tell. What he really thought, what he feared, recoiled from, I shall never know.

The sheet was drawn again over the face of the dead girl and we left the little room. Clarke established communication, by telephone, with a sister of Frances Cosette in New York. She did not

appear to be deeply shocked, grieved or particularly surprised. She
asked him to make the necessary arrangements about having the
body shipped. Reporters got wind of the second death as a dog
smells carrion. Three of them arrived that evening. Clarke Rohmer
and Mr. Borden received them in the library. I was not present.
Shad was there, too, of course. His presence lent official sanction
to the affair. Their interest centered on the "confession" and apparent suicide. How convincing it was to them, I don't know, for I
definitely did not read newspapers during those days.

We gathered around the supper table at eight-thirty. It is never
dinner in Wilromere except when Stacey Madden is hostess. After
all, Stacey has been around. She was there tonight, too, like a white
flame burning against charcoal. She wore a black lace dinner dress.
It clung around her like wet, dark moss. It is uncanny how all
through those horrible days I thought of Stacey in connection with
water. I have never considered myself at all clairvoyant.

We did rather well, everything considered, I think. We all ate
something. We talked quietly, rather normally. Clarke said he and
David had been over to look at Lucius Farraway's farm which Clarke
had considered buying. They discussed the price. David thought it
too high. Clarke agreed but added that the soil was rich and the
location excellent.

Valerie was with us, too. She wore the ivory boucle dress she
had knitted with such pains last winter. It was almost exactly the
shade of her skin. Her hair shone like satin. Her eyes were fever-
ishly bright and the long lashes could not dim them. I'll never forget that meal. It lives in my memory like something etched in fire.

When it was finished, we separated. The universality of food,
the tangible quality of linen and china and silver had formed a bond
which held us together. While we sat around the table, soft with
the shine of yellow candles, while we tasted soup, toyed with salad
and broke bread into bits, reality was held back. We sat in a
charmed circle, eight quiet people, weaving a spell. Our conversation was the incantation we chanted. The pleasant food was the
offering we laid on the altar and the candlelight, mingled with the
smoke of the men's cigars, was the incense that rose from that altar.

Then the meal was ended. The chanting ceased. The offerings were ended. The incense died and we pushed back our chairs, drifted from the room, no longer safe from the specters that crowded round us, the horrors and gibberings of our own consciences.

A little later I went onto the veranda. It was a still, breathless night. The moon was hidden by clouds. The air smelled hot and sweet. I stood very quietly by the great white pillar at the far end and that is how I heard David and Valerie talking.

They met accidentally just below me, David coming up from across the lawn, Valerie rounding the corner from the back of the house. I heard them coming. I knew David's walk, even on the grass. I glimpsed his tall figure. I heard Valerie's quick, nervous patter on the gravel. They stopped suddenly.

Valerie gasped audibly. David said something under his breath and for a moment he was silent. Then, "Oh, Val, that's you, isn't it? Did I startle you?"

"Yes. I didn't see you, hear you."

"Where were you going, Valerie?"

"I don't know, David. I couldn't remain in the house. I wanted to get away from the house."

David said after a pause, "Yes, I understand that."

"I'd like to go home," Valerie told him, "but Caroline insists that I stay."

"I think you should stay, Valerie," David said. "I should like you to stay."

"You, David?"

"Yes, Valerie."

"That is kind of you. Thank you."

David laughed a little. It was good to hear him laugh, even though it did not sound just right. He said, "You are the one to be thanked, Valerie, if you remain."

Then they did not speak for a few moments and I could feel them there below me in the scented darkness, standing against the high porch, quite close together. When Valerie's voice came next I scarcely recognized it.

"David!"

"Yes, Valerie."

"I want you to know—to believe—that I'm—sorry, David. It's hard to say—to make you understand—"

"I understand, Valerie."

"I—David—you believe me—I—did not—kill Wiletta!"

Oh! I shut my teeth hard. I closed my eyes. I stood there so quiet and listened to that child make her pitiful statement. "I did not kill Wiletta!"

I heard the queer, choked sound David made. I sensed his movement. He said, "Valerie, please, don't say that. I don't believe—I never thought— I—"

"Mr. Borden does," she told him.

"Borden! My God!"

"Yes. He believes I killed Wiletta. I see it in his eyes."

David said, trying to be calm, "I am sure you are wrong. Borden could not believe that, knowing you."

"He doesn't know me, David. And that thing—I tried—to do—"

David took her small cold hands. I knew they were small and I was sure they were cold. "Valerie, dear, why did you try that? Why did you want to die?"

Her words were a thin wail. "I was so alone. There were lights all around me. People were laughing. Music playing—and I was alone. I've always been alone, David. Suddenly I could stand it no more. I wanted to die—I wanted to forget that I was alone—"

David said very gently, "Valerie, you must not feel alone any more. I am your friend. You need never be alone." I think he put his arm around her, stroked her shining hair. I am sure his eyes looked beyond her head to the gray shadows of the garden. I know he must have thought of Wiletta.

He said suddenly, "This is all nonsense about Borden. Frances Cosette—she—killed—"

"No," Valerie spoke very quietly. "Frances did not kill Wiletta, David."

"Then what . . ? That confession—"

Valerie laughed. It was not a comforting sound from one so young. "The confession is a forgery, David. Listen, I will tell you something. I didn't dare tell Laure or Dr. Marc, but I will tell you."

"Yes, Valerie, tell me."

"They think only of Jonny's typewriter. They believe that that is the only one in the house. There is another."

"Another? Who has it?"

"Mr. Borden!" Valerie said.

And just then the door opened, light shone across the veranda, and Kenneth Borden strolled toward me, smoking a cigar. His coming made me dizzy for a moment, and when I had regained control the two below the veranda had gone. He saw me in the light from the door, paused beside me. He stood tall and dark, his cigar a red eye glowing at me impishly. I caught now and then the white flash of his teeth as he talked.

"Alone, Miss Laure?"

"Yes, Mr. Borden."

"Enjoying the evening?"

"Enjoying isn't exactly the word."

He frowned down into the darkness of the garden. "No," he muttered. "I dare say not."

I was silent, thinking of what Valerie had said. Mr. Borden had a typewriter. Well, what of it? Any business or professional man might have one.

I said suddenly, "Mr. Borden, do you believe that the confession of Frances Cosette was written on Jonny Rohmer's typewriter?"

He didn't move for a moment, but somehow I felt that the question had startled him. Then he turned his head slowly. "I know it," he replied quietly.

I shivered for all the night was so hot. He said, "I know something of type, Miss Laure. I have made comparisons. It was written on Jonny's machine."

"Did he—write it?"

I could feel him looking at me. I couldn't actually see his eyes. They were dark blurs in the pale outline of his face, but oh, how I could feel them. He said slowly, "I don't know, Miss Laure. I don't know yet, for sure."

"Have you talked to Jonny, Mr. Borden?"

"Yes."

"What does he say?"

"That he did not write it, of course."

"But he was writing—something—when I came in."

Mr. Borden stirred. I think he smiled faintly in the darkness. "Jonny admitted after a time that he had been trying to compose a poem in memory of Wiletta."

"Oh," I said.

"Yes," Mr. Borden agreed. "It sounded reasonable, knowing Jonny. I regret"—he tapped ashes from his cigar and they fell in a bright shower over the railing—"that Jonny thought it necessary to burn the entire contents of the wastebasket before I could examine it."

WILETTA WAS BURIED on Thursday. It was one of those unseasonable days that come sometimes in early summer, holding, strangely enough, a definite hint of autumn. Oh, this business of funerals! Six months ago I should not dared to have said it, but I say it now. They are heathenish. They are relics of the Dark Ages. The solemn words, the sobbing music, the dismal tread of heavy feet. Wind crept across the hills. The sky was overcast. There were dashes of cold rain. The bright green leaves, the flowers of summer looked out of place. It was in reality a bleak October day that Wiletta Owens was laid to rest in the Wilromere cemetery.

We all stood around on the thick, damp grass while Brother Grisold read the last words. Then the Cuthbert girls, who, up to this time had stood quietly enough, began singing. It was entirely their own figuring. Maida told me after with tears in her eyes that she thought it would be a beautiful touch. Just to have their voices coming out like that in a hymn which might bring comfort to the bereaved.

I could cheerfully have choked her. Beautiful touch, my eye! It was horrible. I remember the gasp that went over the little group. I remember—oh, that I could forget—David's gray-granite face, his fixed, expressionless stare. Caroline, poor soul, broke into stifled sobs. Brother Grisold grunted, fidgeted and cleared his throat. Clarke Rohmer looked as if someone had suddenly thrust a knife into his heart. Of course, I don't know exactly how one would look if a knife were thrust into his heart, but I believe it would have been like that.

Then there was a horrible stillness and through the thin gray air the voices of the Cuthbert girls quavered on, breaking now and then, gurgling a little, and finally, thank God, ending in silence. Brother Grisold said something more that was considered appropriate, the flower-laden coffin, resting even with the ground, sank a little. We turned away. We went stumbling, like blind people, toward the cars parked outside the gates.

Stacey Madden walked beside me. Her face looked pinched and faintly green. With her dark gray suit she wore a dull green scarf. She did not look at me. Her eyes were straight ahead and I wondered, glancing at her, what she saw. It could not have been pleasant. Her thin lips twitched in what had come to pass for a smile with her. She said,

"Well, that's ended, Laure. David is safe, isn't he?"

Oh, what a woman! I looked at her quickly. "Safe from—Wiletta, you mean?"

"Of course that's what I mean. He's fair prey now for—some of the rest of us."

We had reached the gates. The others were outside. I stopped, looking up at her. "Stacey," I said, "a devil lives in you, I do believe. How can you talk so, with her—who was to be his bride—there in the ground—"

She laughed at me. The wind whipped her green scarf past her colorless face, hiding it for a moment. The scarf was chiffon, and again I had that strange impression of seeing her face drowned in green water.

"Yes, a devil lives in me, Laure," she admitted, and though you wouldn't believe it, she tapped out a cigarette and lighted it there at the very gates of the cemetery. "A devil lives in all of us," she added, mocking me with her feverish eyes. "What shall we do to cast out the devil, Laure?"

She blew smoke in my face. I heard the purr of motors as the cars drove away. I had told Caroline that I would walk home.

Stacey's car was parked just beyond where we stood. She said suddenly, "Let's take a ride, Laure."

I didn't want to but something made me do it. I am thankful that I did. It was a smart car, a rich olive green with lighter green trimmings on the body and wheels. It had a long thin nose and the fittings inside looked like silver though I don't suppose they were. I don't know much about cars.

Yes, a devil lived in Stacey Madden, surely. She drove like the devil. She almost looked like the devil, sitting there beside me, so thin and taut, her head thrust forward, lips set, eyes glittering. Wind whipped past us. The countryside flashed by like something seen in a dream. I was scared silly. Good heavens, I could only hang on and try to keep from screaming. David takes me for rides occasionally but when I am along he drives sensibly.

At last, as if some of the frenzy had spent itself, Stacey slowed the mad pace. I relaxed a little and opened my eyes. I had faced death in those miles and I was not ready to die. Nor am I yet for that matter.

Stacey sat back and exhaled slowly. Presently she began to talk. She sounded more like the Stacey I had known twenty years ago. I almost enjoyed myself. She talked about her trip abroad last year. Told me some of the people she had met, the places she had seen. Twilight deepened over the stormy landscape. We had left the highway at the crossroads and were following a leafy lane that led eventually back by the lake. It was a fairly good road and Stacey drove slowly now. I felt the wet leaves of the hedge around me, heard the nervous twitterings of birds as we passed.

We came out at last into what seemed like open country after that trip through the hedge lane. There lay the quiet green meadows, dark with moisture. There was a faint tinge of angry crimson in the west and just ahead lay the clear water of Wilromere Lake. Stacey nosed the car close to the edge, shut off the motor and lighted a cigarette. She looked out over the quiet lake, to the low line of hills beyond, and I saw in her face all the weariness and futility of her unhappy life. I felt sorry for Stacey Madden then, though later that pity was driven from my heart.

She said at last, "Allow me to be philosophical, Laure. Our lives are like dim paths leading through the woods. Sometimes we glimpse the sunlight for a moment and are happy. Mostly we walk in the shadows and know not the light." She looked at me and a trace of her old impish humor flashed in her green eyes. "All our lives are leading to what, Laure?" she asked.

Well, now, I don't know how to express myself very well. That's why I hesitated about writing this story, but Marc said just to tell it as it happened and not bother about flourishes. But when Stacey asked me that, I for once had a burst of eloquence. Afterward I felt quite foolish about it but at the time I said, solemnly enough:

"We are put in this world, Stacey, to accomplish some purposes. I don't know what your reason is for being here. Mine, I believe, is to help people. Help them to be happy and to live as they should. I try to do that. I always have. No matter what it costs me, I believe that is the purpose of life. I believe that is where our lives are leading—to the completion of that purpose, whatever it is."

She looked at me so strangely. Her face shone white in the dusk and I had a curious feeling of fear, but it passed. Then abruptly her face was all broken up and quivering. She looked like an old woman. She said in a voice I scarcely recognized, "I wish I could believe like that, Laure, but I can't. To me, there is no purpose in life. It leads nowhere—nowhere." She turned then and stared out at the gray waters of the lake, stirring faintly in the evening breeze. "Nowhere," she repeated as if to herself, "except to oblivion."

Then the moment was gone. She shook her shoulders impatiently, tossed her cigarette out the open window, lighted another and was at once the old cynical, scoffing Stacey.

"Well, Laure," she said in her thin, bright voice, "I've solved our little mystery."

Heavens, did that give me a jolt. She didn't give me a chance to speak. "I won't say who killed Wiletta, but I'll give you something to think about for a time." She laughed and snuggled deeper into the seat.

"I'll tell you a story," she began, laughing at me from her green eyes. "I've never told another soul in Wilromere, or any place else for that matter. Wiletta Owens and I were old—acquaintances, before she ever came to our fair village."

"What?" I leaned forward, staring at her.

"True as true," she said, and I could not tell whether she mocked me or was serious. "I met her in Cairo three years ago. She was staying at Shepheard's. I was visiting friends. We met at a dinner. She was not Wiletta Owens then."

I couldn't say anything. I just sat and looked at her. She was quivering all over like an electric current was running through her. She studied the tip of her cigarette with narrowed eyes. I could see her thin, bright lips working.

"When Wiletta arrived at Wilromere," she continued, "and I met her officially at the Rohmers', she lost no time in getting me to one side and throwing herself on my mercy." Stacey laughed and I shivered, thinking there was no mercy in her. She said, "Well, I didn't care. I saw no reason for spilling—then. At any rate, I kept still." She glanced at me sideways, lifted her hands, showed a magnificent emerald set in old gold on her thin finger. "Wiletta gave me that," she stated, "to keep quiet. After all, I have my own code."

Oh, dear, dear, what a lot I learned about people in those days. She sat there smoking, looking out at the lake until I could stand it no longer.

"Well, aren't you going to tell me, Stacey? Are you stopping now? If Wiletta Owens wasn't Wiletta Owens when you knew her, who in time was she?"

"I'll give you three guesses, Laure," Stacey said, laughter running through her voice like a bright thread.

"Fiddlesticks! Of course I couldn't guess. I just thought she was always Wiletta Owens. I knew she was an old friend of Clarke and Caroline."

"No," Stacey interrupted. "Clarke and Caroline had never seen her before she came to visit them. Caroline had been a girlhood friend of her mother. That was the connection. She wrote them from New York, they invited her down. That's all."

"Oh," I said, digesting this bit of information. "Well, what about it?"

"Nothing particularly. Wiletta came here under her own colors. That's all right. She came, she met David, she liked him, who wouldn't, but she was after money. Money was her god. She had to have it. She didn't seriously consider marrying David until after he received his inheritance. The moment that broke, David was her prey. She went after him, tooth and nail."

"Well," I snapped, "she wasn't any worse than you, Stacey Madden. You were after him tooth and nail, too, and Wiletta just beat your time, that's all. Why couldn't you have been a good loser?"

Maybe I should be ashamed of myself for that outburst, but I'm not. It wrecked me after a while, the way those women fought and clawed for possession of David Kaye and his money. I was shaking all over from nervousness and dislike of her and she just sat very still, looking straight ahead. Then slowly she turned and her green eyes went into mine. She said,

"You and I grew up in this town, Laure Hosmer. We went to school together, but we were never friends. You never liked me and I never liked you. You're too—pure—or something. You aren't human. You always looked at me like I was—soiled." Her tight voice broke. I saw her thin hands clenched in her lap.

I started to reply, but she rushed on: "It's bitter for you, I know, that I tried to get David Kaye. You think of him as your son. You think that I'm old enough to be his mother. Well, I'm not. I'm more than ten years younger than you—"

That's not true. I'll just register that fact right here. However, it doesn't really matter. It wasn't age alone that made me afraid for David where Stacey Madden was concerned.

She said, "I'm not a good woman, not according to your narrow, hidebound code, but I'm honest, Laure, and I'm a fair fighter. I'll warn before I strike, like the rattlesnake. I'll sound my challenge, then I'll do anything I can to get what I want. I'm telling you now, Laure, do you hear me?—I'm telling you this moment I'm marrying David Kaye! Wiletta tried and failed. Now it's my turn and I'll succeed! I'm giving it to you as a warning. I'm letting you see my hand. You can't stop me. You needn't try. It will be better for you if you don't! Let me alone. Let me have David. I can get him. I can catch him on the rebound while he's still dazed and groggy. He never loved Wiletta. He doesn't love me but I'll make him think he does and I'll be fair with him. I'll take care of him and his money. I'll be a proper wife for him. Maybe I'm too old to give him children, but he won't miss them. I've plenty else to give him, Laure, and there's something in a boy like David marrying a woman who's old enough to know her way around. There's something to be said for wisdom and—experience, in the building of a happy marriage."

She was pleading with me. I know it now. I didn't realize it then. She sat there beside me in the gloom of the little car beside the lonely lake and pleaded with me to let her have David. I felt all cold inside. My heart seemed to stop its beating. I thought for a moment I would die, just sitting there with the wind whimpering across the lake and Stacey's voice in my ears.

I didn't want Stacey to marry David. I prayed that something would happen so she couldn't. I believe I must have known that she could do it if something didn't happen to stop her. She had power, that woman. It was the power born of determination, of the relentless pursuit of something she wanted, and she wanted David.

Abruptly I felt very tired and old and my shoulder started aching so that I knew my neuritis was coming back. I sensed the futility of trying to arrange people's lives for them, though honestly I've never really wanted to do that. I thought that maybe my little philosophy about life was all wrong. That perhaps after all I wasn't put here to help folks. That maybe I'd do better if I'd just let them alone and allow them to go their way.

I said, and it sounded pretty simple, after Stacey's outburst, "I hope you don't succeed, Stacey. I do not think you would make David happy."

I felt her go limp beside me. I heard her broken breathing. I knew almost without looking that there were tears on her cheeks. I didn't feel sorry for her then, however. We were enemies, open enemies from then on.

She didn't try to argue with me. She had stated her intention, she had warned me and she had pleaded with me. She had nothing more to say just then but I had. I asked her suddenly, "Who was Wiletta Owens, if she was not Wiletta Owens?"

"Oh," she said, "I'd forgotten about it. It's not really important. It didn't have anything to do with her death. A man doesn't stab a woman just because he was at one time married to her and she divorced him, not even if she's going to marry another man. He doesn't do that, you know, Laure."

I was shaking like a leaf. She didn't believe what she was saying. Her eyes mocked me and her brittle voice strung through with crazy laughter. I remembered her saying, "Well, I've solved our little mystery, Laure," not fifteen minutes ago. I said, "Who are you talking about, Stacey Madden?"

"About Wiletta Owens, of course. She's been married and divorced. When I met her in Egypt she was married, though her husband was not with her. It was unfortunate that he was to have attended her second wedding, wasn't it? It must have been a blow to both of them when they met."

"Stop talking riddles! Tell me whom you mean? Who was her husband?"

I remember the queer little pause that followed my words, how they seemed to hang in that clear, cool air there between us. And I remember the gaunt heron that rose, flapping, from the water's edge.

Stacey turned the key in the ignition, started the motor.

"Dear Laure," she crooned, "I didn't mean to upset you so. When I met Wiletta in Cairo three years ago she was Mrs. Kenneth Borden!"

CHAPTER FOUR

EVERYTHING WENT BLACK for a moment. I was completely stunned. I had no thought, no feeling, not even one of surprise, as Stacey's words echoed in my ears. "*Wiletta was Mrs. Kenneth Borden.*"

And right after that I heard little Valerie Lane saying to David, "They think only of Jonny's typewriter. They believe that that is the only one in the house. There is another! Mr. Borden's."

The import of what Stacey had told me shot like brilliant light across darkness. Everything seemed clear to me. I saw with new eyes. I heard with new ears. Stacey must have been watching me, though I wasn't aware of it.

Her cool voice broke through my tumbling thoughts. "There's nothing to it, really, Laure. Just a coincidence that they should have met here under the circumstances in which they did."

Coincidence! The word had a pitifully inadequate sound. She said again, "Wiletta secured her divorce in Paris that same winter. I never saw her again until I met her here two months ago. I've told you about that."

I started to say something, but my voice shook so that the words wouldn't form and Stacey interrupted me. "Don't be silly, Laure. I know what you're trying to get out. Kenneth Borden is an important man in his line though he isn't generally known outside professional circles. I'm sure he was thoroughly glad to be rid of Wiletta, who was no earthly use to him and doubtless a big expense." Came her tight laugh again. "Now I can't make myself think

112

that a man like that, a brainy, levelheaded person like Kenneth Borden, is going to stick a pin into his divorced wife's heart, just because some other unlucky wight is set to get her."

I felt her watching me. I was conscious of her green eyes on my face, though it was dark now and with the lights off I really couldn't see her. She was arguing against the possibility of Kenneth Borden having killed Wiletta, though I hadn't said one word since she gave me the astounding news. And right then I wondered *why* Stacey had told me. Why had she picked me as a confidante? Was she afraid? Was this her way of combating suspicions against herself? Did she think I would rush back to the Rohmer place, shouting the news? Did she hope in the resultant excitement and confusion to figuratively make her own escape?

I found my tongue at last. "No, Stacey, it doesn't seem like Mr. Borden. It would have been a silly thing to do, after all. Besides, he must have an—alibi—for the time Wiletta was killed. He doubtless was in sight of twenty people all the time in the crowded rooms downstairs."

I heard her quickly drawn breath. "He wasn't," she stated. "I know he couldn't have done it, really, but just the same, Laure, I made some inquiries. I flatter myself I was rather clever about it, and I checked up rather thoroughly. *Kenneth Borden most certainly was not in any of the downstairs rooms at the time that Wiletta Owens was killed!*"

Oh, mercy me! I just made myself sit still. I held my voice steady. "Well, where was he then?"

"I don't know. I can't find anyone who saw him, and I've worked at that, too." A match flared in the soft gray darkness of the car. Stacey's face stood out sharply as she lighted a cigarette. "If we wish to—surmise," she said, "we might say that he had gone by the back stairs up, as the Germans put it, entered Wiletta's room and—well, offered to arrange her bouquet for her!"

Blood slowed in my veins. Oh, that horrible picture of Wiletta unfastening the shining pin from her shoulder! Would people ever stop reminding me of it?

"That's just surmise, Stacey. You can imagine anything. It isn't hard to think of any one of several people doing that very thing. Offering to pin Wiletta's bouquet into place on her shoulder."

"Yes, it's surmise, Laure, and there are any one of half-a-dozen people who might have done it. Valerie Lane is the most likely, if you're going to count Borden out."

"Nonsense! That child. She couldn't kill anything."

Stacey laughed. How I hated her laugh! "No? Be your age, Laure. Realize emotion. Try to comprehend the tumult that rages sometimes in the human breast over what is erroneously called love. Look at Valerie. Consider her eyes. Regard that strong, stubborn, passionate mouth of hers. Think of her meager, restricted life, of the freedom she must long for. Look at her! Study her honestly, intelligently, then tell me if you dare that she could not have done it."

I locked my fingers in the silk of my skirt. I refused to do what she told me. I refused definitely to consider for a moment that Valerie Lane had killed Wiletta Owens. I *knew* better.

"Then," Stacey went on, "there's our young friend, Jonny." She must have felt me shiver for she laughed softly and said, "He's an excellent candidate, Laure. The case against him is so good, he's so well fitted for the part emotionally, mentally and morally, that it's a waste of words to talk about it. And he was upstairs at the time. You know that, don't you?"

"Yes," I replied dully, "I know that." I didn't take time to wonder how she had found out about that. My poor brain was whirling. I'd gone over all this so many times of late. She went on, almost as if she were enjoying herself,

"Jonny's definitely balmy, Laure, you know that. He's not in an institution, though maybe he should be, but we all know about him. How he hates David. How he imagined himself in love with Wiletta. She played him for a sucker. She made him think she was God or something. All that tripe about her being too fine for David. About David soiling her! My eye!" And Stacey's laugh gave me a queer, sick feeling around the heart.

"And Jonny went sneaking up to Wiletta's door that night. Oh, I know about it. I've a nose for news, Laure. I didn't see him go into the room. You didn't, I dare say. I suppose he has some line worked out to explain why he was there, but as the detective stories say, he had motive and he had opportunity."

I couldn't stand it any longer. I couldn't sit there and let her build up that case against Jonny Rohmer. I said, through lips that were so stiff they ached,

"So did you, Stacey, have motive and opportunity. You hated Wiletta Owens. Remember, I heard the quarrel you and she had, I heard it. You hated her. You were in her room. You left it just as I came up the stairs. I saw you. I saw your green dress, then you came back and pretended to be surprised when you saw her dead—you—just as well as Jonny Rohmer, had motive and opportunity."

Oh dear, just writing about it tears me to pieces. I feel again all I felt that night by Wilromere Lake when I came out in the open and accused Stacey Madden of having killed Wiletta Owens!

I remember how still she sat, yet I could hear her fluttering breath, feel the quivering that ran through her thin body without seeming to move it. Her face was close to mine. I could see her green eyes burning. I thought, "She could kill me. She is strong enough. She is so much stronger and taller than I am. She could kill me, throw me into the lake—no one would know—"

She said, "Clever Laure! So you saw my green dress as I left Wiletta's room, did you?"

"Yes."

Breath whistled between her teeth. "You haven't told anyone, have you, Laure? You've kept it all to yourself, this bit of information?"

Cold sweat prickled along my spine. I said clearly, "No, I haven't kept it to myself, Stacey. I told Mr. Borden, because he made me see it was my duty to do so."

"Oh," Stacey said. "He did, eh? Your duty? Of course, Laure, of course."

I felt, rather than saw, her thin hands curl themselves into talons there on her lap. I saw the winking eye of the emerald Wiletta had given her to buy her silence. Fear was cold around my heart. I imagined it as a hand, as Stacey's hand clutching my heart, squeezing out my life, with the emerald winking in the faint light.

"Yes, I told Mr. Borden," I heard myself saying, "so there's no use in your choking me to death and throwing my body into the lake, because he knows, and if you—"

Her sudden wild laughter stopped me. She hunched back in the corner of the seat and I swear that her face was absolutely expressionless. It's not right for people to laugh without their faces moving. When you laugh, your eyes crinkle and your nose quivers and your cheeks do things, but not Stacey's that night. The crazy peals of laughter echoed all around me, filling the gray twilight, filling the quiet world, but Stacey just sat there with her face immovable and abruptly she stopped laughing and I saw tears in her eyes.

"I won't kill you, Laure," she choked, "though I have no doubt that I could if I tried. You're little and skinny and though you've a certain wiry strength, I'm more than a match for you. I'm really very strong. I've danced and ridden horseback and played golf and I'm like a piece of steel, you know. So it wouldn't be at all hard for me to strangle the life out of you and forever close your gossiping lips about seeing me come out of Wiletta's room. For I was in there. I admit it. I'm telling it to you now and I'll tell you why I went. Simply because Caroline sent me. She said to me, downstairs, 'Stacey dear, run up and be sure Wiletta's ready. You know how Wiletta is.' So I did. I went up the back stairs and because I had a few minutes to spare I dropped into Caroline's sitting room and smoked a cigarette. Then I came out. I passed that sniveling little Lane brat in the window seat. I told her to get on outdoors if she couldn't endure the sight of Wiletta marrying the man she was crazy about. Then I left her and went to Wiletta's room. I went in without knocking. She was lying on the rug just as we found her, you and I, Laure, less than five minutes later. She was dead. I left the room. That's when you saw me. I went round the corridor, then I came back and met you. Now you have the story. That's how I found Wiletta Owens when I went to hale her to the altar. She was lying in her crumpled white satin, with blood on her veil, God rest her, and a diamond pin in her heart."

The broken panting words stopped. Silence ached between us. I thought, "She's telling the truth. That's the way it happened—that's surely the way it happened—"

Stacey said, hoarsely, "You believe me, don't you, Laure?"

I looked into her gaunt white face in the gloom, caught the writhing of her thin bright lips. I said, "No, Stacey, I don't believe you. It's a silly story and I do not believe a word of it."

After all, I had never liked Stacey Madden. Since girlhood we had been enemies. There was a definite feud between us now. We were fighting over David Kaye, just as she and Wiletta had fought, though the motive on my side was different, the Lord knows.

"You don't believe me?" she whispered.

"No."

She shrugged, sat back. "Sorry, old dear. It's the way it happened. It's my story and stick to it I will."

"Why didn't you tell it at first? Why didn't you admit you'd found Wiletta's body before you and I went in?"

"My God," she said on a long, slow breath. "You're not that silly, Laure. You just can't be that dumb. Should I admit I'd been in there? Should I lay myself open to suspicions, questions, grilling? I should not. I say as little us I possibly can. I keep my skirts clean, Laure. In the first place, I've told you and I repeat it," she hesitated, went on carefully, "that I don't give a damn about seeing the murderer of Wiletta Owens caught. Call me ruthless, if you like. I am. I have no proper respect for the law. It can rot for all of me. I'm glad Wiletta's dead. I'm glad she died before she married David. I say, more power to the hand that killed her. I'd help whoever did it, if I could. I'd help him, Laure, understand that?"

I couldn't take my eyes from her face. Her frankness fascinated me.

"You can't mean that, Stacey," I said quaveringly. "You just can't mean that."

"No? Try me and see. If you know who did it, tell me, see what I'll do to help him."

"Good heavens!" I gasped. "How should I know who killed Wiletta?"

Her laugh tinkled. "You have a nose for news, Laure, and you have a damned good intuition. I think you're helping Borden on this business, which is a big laugh, but just the same, I'm making my offer. Find out who did it, bring the dope to me and see what I'll do to help him clear himself."

"If the murderer of Wiletta is discovered," I told her sharply, "he'll go to the electric chair. He'll pay with his own life for the life he took."

"Horse-feathers!" she said. "I'm for him a hundred per cent. I'd like to give him a medal or something." She paused, drew a long, shivering breath and her hands came out, curled, toward me. I went dizzy for a moment when those cold, strong hands closed on mine.

"Let it rest, Laure. The law's satisfied. They have Cosette's confession, her—suicide. Let it rest. Why poke and probe among the ashes? Think of Caroline, of Clarke, of all of them. Let them sink back into their comfortable grooves. Go on with life that leads nowhere. Let them enjoy it while they can. It's over soon enough for most of them, Laure. Why aren't you satisfied?"

"I am satisfied, Stacey," I replied, and my voice sounded dull and hollow. Oh, that I could have been. That I had been content to let the ashes rest until they cooled and went gray above the graves they covered. I wish I could have spoken truly that night when Stacey and I sat in the car at the edge of the lake. I wish that I could have meant what I said, when my lips formed the words, "I am satisfied, Stacey."

I WENT HOME that night. Much as I like Caroline and Clarke Rohmer, much as I pitied them in their trouble and confusion, I could no longer remain in their house.

My own small cottage welcomed me. Peter meowed his pleasure and the red geranium seemed literally to prick up its drooping leaves when I returned. I dusted up a bit, unpacked my bag and hung my clothes in the closet. Then I fixed myself a bite of supper in the kitchen, Peter, in his usual chair, opposite. Peter is such a handsome cat, gray and black striped, with a proud white vest. He is very large and his eyes are deeply intelligent and understanding.

I said, "Well, Peter, things have changed since you and I dined here the last time, less than a week ago," and then I laid a bite of cold canned salmon on his small plate.

He burst into mellifluous purring, reached up one white paw, lifted the fish to the chair and solemnly devoured it. Then he wiggled his whiskers and regarded me hopefully.

I poured my tea. Rain had come with dark. I heard it slashing against the window. I thought, "There go my Lady Hamilton roses, and me working so hard to get them started." The tea was refreshing. My kitchen, so clean and orderly with bright print curtains and nice faded rag rugs, looked very pleasant to me.

I said to Peter, "Wiletta Owens is dead and Frances Cosette is dead and the law is satisfied because Stacey says so. We can let it rest now, Peter. There's no use digging in the ashes any more, old friend. It's all settled." My cup clinked against the saucer as I set it down. Peter made comfortable purring noises and lifted his right paw a little as he blinked. It is a sure sign that he is content but hopes to be more so. I gave him another bite of salmon.

"It isn't settled," I told Peter. "There're more things going to happen, little cat. When human life is taken, wilfully, whether it's murder someone can be punished for or legalized murder like war, something has to happen to really settle it. Someone has to pay. A man or a woman or a country, Peter. Don't make any mistake, little cat, someone has to pay." Then I thought of a text Brother Grisold had used in a sermon recently, "Vengeance is mine, saith the Lord. I will avenge."

I got all cold thinking about that and wondering what the vengeance of the Lord would be for Wiletta's death, for Frances' murder. The windows were black behind the bright curtains. I heard the rain thumping on the roof, the kettle singing on the fire. I thought of Wiletta who had worn white satin for her wedding, and now garbed in plain white crepe, lying in a handsome box lined with shell-pink silk, so deep under the dark earth in Wilromere cemetery.

I remember that I bowed my head on my arms on the white-and-red-checked table cloth and tried to pray. I said, "O Lord, forgive whoever did that thing. Wash the blood from the hand that thrust that diamond pin into her heart. Make David happy and don't let Stacey have him. Keep David from Stacey, Lord—"

Steps pattered across the front porch. I heard them deep in my heart before I heard them with my ears. I didn't move. I just sat there, with my head on my arms. The front door opened. It is seldom locked. Everyone comes into my house without knocking. I heard hurrying steps along the hall, the kitchen door was open. I looked up and saw Stacey Madden standing there. Rain ran in rivulets down the gleaming surface of her silk raincoat, made her green silk scarf a sodden string. Her face was set. Her ruddy hair was a tangled mass of curls. She was deathly pale, yet excitement burned through her like a bright flame. She said, "Well, Laure, I've done it, though heaven knows I didn't mean to. I had to come and tell you. I thought you'd be interested—"

She groped for a chair, sank into it. Her eyes closed for a moment. She looked so thin and wasted and again I had that horrible impression of looking at her through water. The raincoat was green and it seemed somehow to color her face.

"What have you done, Stacey?"

She said, "I spilled my in'ards to Kenneth Borden, Laure, God help me, and oh, it was worth it, it was really worth it, Laure."

I waited until I was sure my voice was steady. "Will you have a cup of tea, Stacey? You look done up. Have you been running?"

"Yes, I've been running and I'll have some tea, Laure, dear," and she brought out a cigarette and lighted it. Peter glared at her, eyes black, then he jumped down and ran away, tail lashing indignantly. I made fresh tea. The rain was getting worse. There was wind behind it now. I was glad that my house was so tight and comfortable.

I poured Stacey a cup of strong tea. She looked at it a long time. I wondered if she hoped to read her future in it, though you must have leaves to do that, and there are no leaves in the tea I pour. Then a smile quirked her red lips, she drew a small silver flask from the pocket of her raincoat and before my very eyes she poured whisky into the tea, drank a long draught and let the cup clatter into the saucer. I was afraid she'd break it, and it was my best Haviland too. I don't believe she'd have cared a penny's worth, if she had.

She said, "That's good. Lace it a bit. Whips up the old blood stream, Laure. Try it. Take a taste of tea laced with White Horse."

I could actually feel how white my cheeks were. I said, "Why will you put into your mouth an enemy to steal away your brain?"

"Oh, my God!" Stacey said. "You spout moralities like a Sunday-school teacher, Laure Hosmer. Haven't you any blood in your veins? Don't you ever feel anything except about helping people or trying to save your soul? Don't you know what it is to—love someone? To feel all weak and sick with love for—someone, Laure? Haven't you ever been on fire with wanting someone—so that you burned like fever and ached with chill at the same time? Don't you know what it is to waken in the night, Laure, and feel—feel—someone beside you—someone's arms—"

"Stop that! I won't listen to such talk! I don't understand what you're saying, Stacey Madden. I don't know what you mean! I'd die of shame this minute if I had depths in my mind like that. If I allowed thoughts to live inside me that did to me what your thoughts do to you—"

"What thoughts live in your mind, Laure?" She leaned forward across the table, scorching me with her burning green eyes. "Not in your topside mind, Laure. Not in the mind you know and look at every day. The one that causes you to put up watermelon pickle in the fall, attend church bazaars and make over someone's old brown foulard. Not that mind, but the one underneath. The one that's hidden and deeply buried, whose portal is guarded. What lives down there, Laure? Do you know? Are you aware of what stirs beneath the surface? Aren't there desires, longings, hates, ambitions that wiggle there like worms in a cesspool? Don't they slip past the guardian now and then, come to you in dreams? Haven't you felt them, sensed them, smelled them, Laure?"

Her brittle words fell like hot pebbles. The very air seemed to crawl with the horrible things she suggested. Worms in a cesspool! I felt sick. I wanted to scream and run away where I would never see Stacey Madden again. I thought the only thing that would haunt me would be her green eyes, her thin bright lips, her gaunt burning face.

She relaxed suddenly, sitting back, eyes closed, like a dead woman. I couldn't speak. My lips were like clay. I heard Peter complaining at the back door. I got up, went across, opened it for him. He started forward, stopped, back arched, one paw lifted, whiskers taut. Oh well, cats never do like the rain. Yet when he turned around, slithering for his corner, when he looked up at me with his great green eyes that were so like Stacey's, I began shivering violently and wondered what he had seen out there in the dark.

Stacey said, "Forget it, Laure. I'm balmy, like Jonny. Come and sit down. Smoke a cigarette with me, that's a dear. Please, for old time's sake."

There was something in her tired voice, something in her beautiful haunted eyes that made me feel faint, and I tell it to my shame, that I sat down opposite her across the red-and-white-checked table cloth, in my own decent kitchen, and as God is my judge, I smoked a cigarette!

Stacey said, a little later, "I didn't mean to mention it to him, Laure."

"You mean Mr. Borden?"

"Yes. I had dinner at the Rohmers', a ghastly affair. I expected to see Jonny start chewing the table cloth any moment. David looked like the devil rode his tail and that milk-faced Valerie Lane—"

"Valerie is still there?"

"She is," Stacey said, and her thin lips folded in a tight hard line. "She's got her cap set for David, Laure, if you're interested in knowing. She's so sweet and simple, like hell! And she's fastened onto him like a leech. She'll never let loose until—"

"Tell me about Mr. Borden," I interrupted.

"Oh, that! Well, it was simple. The subject of marriage came up at table. A most appropriate topic of conversation, don't you think? And once they got onto it, they couldn't get off. It was like a witch's feast or something. Caroline sentimentalized over her wedding day. Clarke got fairly weepy thinking of it. They asked me when I was going to celebrate mine. And then the devil possessed me and I looked at Borden and said, 'Do tell us about your wedding day, Mr. Borden.' And then, Laure, there was a queer little pause, with the air prickling and the lights going dim before me. He just sat so still and in the candlelight his face was gray. It looked wet, too, and his eyes had a queer sunken look. Everyone stared at him, the dumb brutes, myself among the rest. Clarke said in his 'big-top' voice, 'Why, Borden, I didn't know—I didn't understand—you never told me—' and just then he pushed back his seat and smiled. He looked a hundred years old, Laure, and he said, with his voice sounding normal enough, 'I'm sorry, Miss Madden, I can't tell you about my wedding day. You see, I've never had one.'"

Stacey paused and I saw that she was shaking like a leaf. I waited, not able to say anything, remembering that if Stacey had told the truth, the woman who had been Kenneth Borden's wife was buried now in Wilromere cemetery.

She poured more whisky into her cup, not bothering this time to put in any tea. She drank it at a gulp. Her eyes were very bright. Red spots came on her white cheeks. She looked very beautiful and she was like a woman turning to flame.

"That was all at dinner, Laure, but later I was in the breakfast room, alone, and he came in. I knew as soon as I saw him what he wanted. He came straight up to me. He said, 'What did you mean by that remark at dinner, Stacey Madden?' And then, Laure, it was the devil again, but I just looked straight back at him and said, 'I wanted you to tell us about how you married Wiletta Owens when she was sweet sixteen or something, out in sunny California.' I thought he would die, Laure! I never saw such a look on a man's face. I know it will come to me at night when I can't sleep."

She crouched forward over the table, thin hands clenched against her heart which must have been pounding from all the liquor she had taken. Her eyes went round my peaceful little kitchen and they were the eyes of one damned. She said,

"Oh, Laure, that's why I came to you. You're so solid, Laure. You're so sensible and—decent. I want you to help me forget how Kenneth Borden's eyes looked when I reminded him of his wedding night. I haven't any fear of God in my heart, Laure. I'm not afraid of God, or death or the devil. I've known them all, too many times, but I can't go on living unless I can forget how he looked when I told him about Wiletta. He loved her, Laure. He must have loved her more than he loved life or hoped for salvation. I read it all in his eyes. How much he had loved her. What he had suffered when she went to pieces on him, what he must have felt when he met her at Rohmers', as David's promised wife. And then, Laure, I saw what he suffered when she died. That was the hardest to take. I couldn't hold my eyes on his. I had to look away. I looked down at the shadows under the table and I know my teeth were clicking. He said, 'She told you this?' I said, 'I met her three years ago in Cairo. She was your wife then, that's how I know.'

"Sweat ran in trickles down his thin face, Laure, when he asked me, 'You haven't told anyone else? You haven't mentioned this to anyone?' And I was afraid, Laure, so I lied. I always lie when I'm afraid. I said, 'No, I haven't told a soul about it.' He drew a deep breath. His shoulders straightened. His face was once more just the face of a man we both know. All the rest was hidden. He said, 'That's decent of you, Stacey Madden. There's no use further complicating things by dragging this out. May I depend upon you to continue to keep my secret?' And he held out his hand. I had to take it, Laure. It was strong and warm and there were queer prickles running from it into mine. I only nodded. He smiled at me and said, 'Thank you,' and out he went, closing the door very softly behind him.

"I dropped into a chair and the silence deepened all around me and I felt Wiletta in the room with me and I saw Kenneth Borden there, too, looking at her. I heard what he said to her, what she said to him, how she laughed at him and mocked him.

"And I grew afraid, Laure. Afraid that I was going mad! That he had planted something in my mind, like the seed that springs into a vine that chokes and destroys. I felt vines growing through my brain, sending out little tendrils, choking the life out of my brain. I couldn't stand it any more. I said I'll go and see Laure. She's levelheaded. She's got her feet on the ground. She puts up watermelon pickles and makes over foulard dresses and she doesn't have vines growing through her brain, choking her. So I came, Laure. You'll have to help me. You'll have to talk me into forgetting what I discovered. What I saw in Kenneth Borden's eyes tonight— Oh, Laure—help me—help—"

And abruptly she was sobbing, fingers locked in her bright damp hair. She laughed through the sobs, too. She talked like a crazy woman. I looked deep into her heart that night. I saw what lived in her mind. I struggled to keep cool, to keep my feet on the ground, to help her as best I could. Most of all I had to shut my thoughts away from what a menace she was for David. I couldn't even consider the possibility of her winning David Kaye.

She was quieter after a while. Dr. Marc has told me since, that what ailed Stacey that night was that she was just plain crazy drunk. I dare say he is right, but it was a terrible thing. She stayed until nearly eleven. She dozed some in front of the little fire I kindled in the parlor. She didn't sleep so much as she just seemed to slip into periods of unconsciousness that she must have been grateful for. But they didn't last long enough. They didn't give her sufficient peace, poor soul. She sat up at last, her face all drawn and ravaged. She said, "I'm going home, now, Laure. I'm not going back to Caroline's. I told her I wouldn't be back. I want to go home."

I didn't think she should go home alone and I said so. I didn't believe that she was in any shape to spend the night at her big gray house on the hill with only that queer South American negro woman servant as company. She wouldn't listen to me though. It was like talking to a tempest. For all Stacey seemed so quiet, for all she spoke so coherently and sensibly, I got the feeling that she was like a raging, billowing wind, careening through the night toward destruction.

When I saw I couldn't talk her into remaining with me or going back to Caroline's, I helped her into her green silk raincoat, gave her her bag and scarf. We walked to the front door. The rain had stopped, though water still dripped from the trees. The town was all abed. A few lights twinkled and old man Eggleston's Rover dog was baying over across the hill, but otherwise it was quiet.

I went with her to the front gate. I said, "Want me to walk home with you, Stacey?"

"No, Laure, thank you. You've helped me a lot, just listening to me. I'll tell you what's the matter, Laure, I'm drunk. Do you understand me—drunk?"

I said, "That's all right, Stacey, you'll feel better in the morning. I wish you'd stay here with me."

"No, Laure, I want to go home. I'm going to take a walk first though. It's a wonderful night. It's so quiet and black. The blackness is like a cloud all about me. I'll walk a bit and let the fumes burn out, then I'll go home and tumble in. I'll sleep well tonight, Laure. It's been so long since I've slept well. Tonight it will be different. I'll sleep soundly tonight, Laure."

"Good night, Stacey. Don't walk far. Sure you're all right?"

"Quite okay, old pal." She let her hand fall from the gatepost where she had been steadying herself.

She smiled down at me. "Drunk as Christmas," she said thickly, and laughed low in her throat. "It helps, though. Helps to forget, Laure. When you get so you can't forget, try a shot or two of rye. Helps you to forget—"

I don't know why I did what I did then. Surely she was in no condition to be pestered, but I caught her arms, I held her for all she was so strong, I pulled her toward me. I said, "Helps you to forget what, Stacey? What do you want to forget?" And I thought of Wiletta lying in her crumpled satin with a diamond-studded pin in her heart. "What would you forget, Stacey?" I whispered.

She didn't tell me, of course. She was too far gone. She laughed crazily, she reeled out of my hold, she started to sing. She talked about the time when she was a little girl here in Wilromere and of the things she had dreamed as she lay under the maple trees in spring. I guess Stacey had poetry in her soul and maybe getting it all twisted and warped like was what made her what she was. Maybe memories of when she had been a girl here in Wilromere and of these dreams under the maples was what she wanted to forget that night. Anyway, she left me standing there by the gate, and she walked unsteadily down the black tunnel of the silent street and disappeared from my sight. I stood looking after her for a long time, and listening to the tree toads making queer whirring noises over my head, then I turned and went slowly into the house.

Peter was waiting for me at the door. He rubbed against my skirt and meowed in welcome. That cat must have kissed the Blarney stone one time. He is always so affectionate when he wants a saucer of cream just before bedtime.

It must have been two o'clock when I wakened. Now, I'm not in the least nervous. I've lived alone in my little white cottage for better than twenty-seven years and it would be strange if I got jittery now. Yet that night when I opened my eyes and looked straight into the darkness, I was afraid. I felt my heart beating like the mill motor and blood raced through my veins like a spring torrent.

It was very quiet. I could feel the quiet all around like still cool water lapping me. Then little sounds made themselves felt. A tree limb scraping the roof. The drainpipe dripping very softly in the kitchen. And Peter's purring! My word, what a thunderous purr that cat has. He must have sensed me rousing and wakened, too, for there, from his basket at the foot of my bed, I could hear him purring. It was comforting somehow. It tied me to the sane, safe world I've always known. It helped me to forget worms crawling in a cesspool!

Then I heard someone crossing the front porch!

I sat up. I reached for my kimono. I found the matches I always leave on the table beside the bed. If someone came to my house at two o'clock in the morning it was because I was needed and that was that.

I lighted the lamp. I don't have electricity in my house. Lamps do well enough for me. I picked it up and went into the hall. The steps had paused before the door. There is a glass in the upper half, a clouded sort of glass with the picture of two dogs romping through clover worked into it. I have always thought it very nice, but tonight I wished that it was plain, so that I could see through it and recognize whose white face it was that looked in at me.

But the romping dogs got in my way with their big silly paws and plumy tails. Beyond their eternal play I could see a white face, but whose it was, I could not tell. I suppose I was what David calls groggy from sleep, but actually those wretched dogs seemed to move and roll over and bounce around like rubber balls, obscuring my sight of the face.

Well, I just opened the door. I never did believe in standing and staring at a letter, wondering who had sent it. I opened the door and there, the Lord help me to forget, was Jonny Rohmer. The lamp nearly dropped from my hand. He was white as flour and his eyes appeared perfectly black and sightless. His blond hair was plastered to his head with wet. His silk shirt clung to his thin body and his white linen knickers hung like Monday's wash.

I said, "Heavens above, Jonny, where have you been and what's the matter?" I stepped aside and he came in, staggering a little. "It's raining again? You've been walking in the rain?"

He leaned against the wall. "No, Miss Laure, it isn't raining."

I set the lamp on the stand table. "Well, then, where did you get so wet? What in time have you been doing?"

"I fell in the lake, Miss Laure. I didn't want to go home like this. They think I'm nuts anyway." His face jerked crazily. "Maybe you don't know it, but they think I'm nuts, Miss Laure, and if I go home all wet like this and they find it out, they'll—oh, I don't know, but they might—"

"We'll fix that," I told him, picking up the lamp. "You come right along into the kitchen, young man, and help me build a fire. Then we'll make you a cup of hot tea and dry out those clothes of yours. It's a fine pass, I'll have to admit, when a boy like you goes skiooting around at night and tumbles into the lake. My word! What would your mother say. Now you come along and help me and don't stop to argue."

I kept on talking, scolding him, and fussing around him and he came into the kitchen and stood there dumbly while I built up a fire and set the kettle on. I worked hard and fast. I'm not naturally slow, Brother Grisold says I'm like a human dynamo when I start to do anything, but that night I went faster than ever. I had to do it so I could shut the sight and sound of Jonny Rohmer out of my mind. I didn't want to give myself an opportunity to think what this escapade of his might mean.

I said, "Now get out of those clothes," and I ran into the bedroom and brought out the lovely Chinese kimono Caroline gave me last Christmas and which I have never worn. I said, "Now peel off your duds and put that on and don't bother to be foolish. Go into the hall there, if you're too bashful to undress before me, though the land knows, Jonny Rohmer, I'm old enough to be your mother and I've bathed and dressed you a thousand times. Maybe you don't remember, but I have. When you had poison ivy so bad when you were eight years old, well, I just stripped you and smeared you all over with that grease Dr. Marc gave me. Now get along with you."

But he didn't go. He just started taking off his clothes right before me. He peeled off his shirt and I saw how thin his chest was and how skinny his arms. Then he slipped off his trousers, showing his white legs in the blue-silk shorts. He picked up my kimono and put it on. He was very serious about it. He sat down with the folds of it all around him, took off his white shoes and set them in the oven.

"Here, don't do that," I snapped. "They'll curl like Maida Cuthbert's hair when she puts on those fancy fixin's she brought home with her." I set the shoes under the stove where the heat was not so intense.

Peter appeared, stretching and yawning, regarded us gravely, then strolled over and humped his back against Jonny's bare leg. Jonny looked down at him. "Hello, kitty. Nice kitty. Hello, Peter." He sat there, all hunched over, Peter rubbing against his bare leg.

I put tea in the pot, poured water on it. "I'd like to have a shot of scotch in that," Jonny said. "You haven't any White Horse in your private stock, have you, Miss Laure?"

I nearly dropped my Willow pattern teapot. His idiotic question reminded me of Stacey and how only a few hours earlier she had sat here in my kitchen drinking tea laced with White Horse.

"No, I haven't any whisky, Jonny, and you know it. Now drink that and tell me what in Tophet you mean by wandering around at night and falling into the lake!"

He just sat there looking at the stove top and I heard again the silence creeping into the room and the tree branch scraping against the roof.

Finally he said, "I couldn't stand it, Miss Laure. I went to bed at ten-thirty. They all got on my nerves. My God, I couldn't take it. It got so they didn't look like the people I knew. Mother and Dad and David and Valerie and even Borden, who is usually so steady. They looked like strangers. I found myself staring at them, wondering, 'Now who is *that* woman?' and 'Where have I seen that man before?' See? They weren't real to me, Miss Laure, they were all strangers."

"Yes, Jonny, I know. It seems like that sometimes, but they're really your folks, you know. They're your friends."

I don't believe he heard me. He went on like I hadn't spoken. "So I went to bed. I undressed and put on my pajamas and lay down on the bed and pulled the sheet up under my chin. I tried to go to sleep. I thought, 'Now I'll just lie here quietly and then I'll drop off to sleep.' The longer I lay the more wakeful I was. I saw those strangers in my room. I heard them talking. I didn't know any of them, though they wore familiar faces. I said to myself, 'Now that's really Mother and that's Dad. And there's Valerie in spite of her face being so queer.' " He drew a shaking hand over his eyes. "I figured it out after a while, Miss Laure. I decided that I was seeing them really as they were for the first time. That I was looking through the semblance of themselves that they put on for every day wear and seeing them truly as they were." He brushed wet hair from his forehead.

"Drink your tea, Jonny. Here, let me give you some fresh."

"I couldn't take it," he said, not heeding me. "I got up. I dressed and sneaked down the back stairs. It wasn't until I was outside that I thought that all my life I'd been sneaking around, going out the back way. Afraid of being seen, of being heard, of not being able to take it.

"It was raining some but I didn't mind. I walked and walked and thought about so many things. Principally, I thought about myself and then I thought about Wiletta and how she had died, just as she was about to marry David."

He paused, breath catching in his throat. He turned slowly, looking at me with his strange blue eyes. He said, "It came to me, Miss Laure, that it was God's will that Wiletta should die. God made it that way, so she wouldn't marry David. I saw it all so clearly. It was better for Wiletta to be dead than David's wife, so God put the thought of murder into—someone's heart—he strengthened the arm that struck—he had it done to save Wiletta."

I couldn't move. I believe I expected to see Jonny Rohmer struck dead before my eyes for his horrible blasphemy. I sat there, staring at him. His face got all dim and sort of luminous as I looked. It seemed to disappear completely and then it came back and it was not the face of the boy I'd known for twenty-five years, but the beautiful face of a man I'd never seen. It was almost like the face of Christ that I see on the Sunday-school cards. That terrified me. It seemed blasphemy, too. I felt cold and shriveled and I couldn't feel my heart beat or blood in my veins. Then something moved my lips. They opened without my volition. It was almost like a miracle.

I said, "He had it done to save David," and my voice was loud and clear and ringing in that quiet little room.

Peter meowed softly from his basket. It broke the spell for us. Jonny was Jonny again and I was I. Perhaps when his face looked so beautiful to me, in that moment when it was all dim and luminous, mine had looked queer to him, too. Maybe if I'd seen the real Jonny then he had seen the real Laure Hosmer.

"No, no, no!" he said, his voice sounding all strangled and thick. "It can't be that. It can't be—" His thin hands were twisting at my Chinese kimono, his lips were white and stiff. He scrunched back in the chair and kept saying over and over, "No, no, no—not that! Not that!"

Well, I came to myself then. I guess I've got a pretty good store of plain old horse sense tucked away in my head some place. I'll admit that the happenings of the last week had thrown us all off which maybe accounts for things I thought, and things I believed I saw, but just the same when the pinch came, I got hold of myself.

Jonny was in a bad way. It wasn't any time for vagaries and seeing faces that weren't there. I got up and pulled my wrapper closer around me. "Now Jonny," I said, "you just snap out of it" (another of that boy David's expressions) "and drink yourself that hot tea. Then you climb into your clothes and get along home. Hurry now, no foolishness. And while you're drinking I want the rest of the story of how you happened to tumble into the lake. I won't tell on you, child," I grinned down at him. "You know I never let you down, Jonny, so come along, now, drink your tea and tell me all about it."

He took the cup I handed him. He drank the tea obediently but he didn't speak for quite a while. I kept on talking. Just simple, homely things that we both knew about and gradually whatever it was that possessed him seemed to lessen its hold.

He said at last, "Well, Laure, it isn't much of a story. The night and all the rest got hold of me, I guess. I kept walking like a loony, and I got to the lake. I went along the bank for a while, watching how black the water was and thinking the strangest thoughts. About stories I'd like to write, if only I believed I could, and letting the lines of poetry that dance in my head all the time just come out and form themselves into verses."

He drew a long slow breath. His face was quiet then and there was in it a shadow of latent strength. "Gosh, it was swell," he said to himself. "And anyway, before I knew it, like a moon-struck calf, I just up and walked right off the Point into about seven feet of water."

He looked up at me and there was sudden humor in his eyes. "Imagine it. Can't you see how nutty it looks? What a cockeyed story it would be to try and make anyone believe. That I just walked into the lake. Lord!"

He shook himself, set down the teacup, stood up. "But that's the way it was, Miss Laure, and the shock of the cold water brought me around mighty quick. I never could swim very well." He glanced away and I saw dark blood creep up his thin face. "But I'll tell you, Miss Laure, I learned more about it tonight than in all my life before. I had to swim to get out. So I did. I swam about fifteen yards, believe it or not, to the old boathouse piling, and I pulled myself out. Then I came here."

I said, relief bringing laughter to my voice, "Well, child, it's nobody's funeral but yours, if you fall into the lake—" Then I stopped, biting my lip and wishing someone would kick me good and hard. For how nearly it had been Jonny Rohmer's funeral and why would I mention funerals anyway, and why did he stand there like a ghost, staring at me, his face twitching like he wanted to laugh, crazy like.

"Funeral!" he said. "My God, Miss Laure, haven't we had enough funerals around here of late? Haven't we dug enough graves? Funerals?" And then he did laugh, a high shrill laughter that chilled me like an icy wind and I thought:

"I'm here alone at three o'clock in the morning with a madman. I'm here with him, alone. Jonny's mad—he's mad—mad—"

There came a sharp knocking on the front door!

A voice called, "Laure—Laure—"

Life flowed through me again. David Kaye! David's voice would rouse me, I believe, if I lay under six feet of earth. I turned, stumbling over Peter's basket, made for the front door. It opened before I reached it. David came in, like a strong spring wind.

His gray eyes were black in his pale face. He said, "Laure, darling, I'm sorry to startle you. I'm looking for Jonny. Caroline's frightened. He went out some place. We can't find him—I thought—"

The words died in his throat. His quick upward glance centered on the kitchen door behind me. His eyes widened, his jaw dropped.

"Good night!" he gasped, and I turned to see Jonny standing there, his thin body wrapped in my gay flowered kimono, looking at us.

David said, "Where in hell have you been? Your mother's scared to death. What the devil do you mean roaming off like this in the middle of the night—"

"What the hell's it to you?" Jonny asked, and came slowly toward us, walking exactly like a Roman senator I saw once in a movie, holding the kimono around his lean stomach, like a toga. "Why the hell shouldn't I go where I please, when I please, how I please? What's it to you, anyway? What you snooping around for, checking up on me? Am I six years old? Am I a child? Or am I a grown man, who can take care of himself—?"

"You're a grown man," David told him, lips thinned, "but you act like a six-year-old. Maybe you've got brains stored in your cranium but you damned well never use them. Why do you have to go sneaking down the back stairs and out the side door, like—like—"

"A coward?" Jonny asked, and I heard his harsh panting breath. "That's what you mean, isn't it, David? That I'm a coward and a washout, a flat tire, a punctured balloon. That's what you think. It's what you've always thought, ever since the first day you came into my home, stole Mother and Dad away from me, pushed me outside their affection, took everything for yourself. Everything, do you understand? You got the best room. You got the biggest bicycle. You had the finest clothes. You—always you, David! You, taking everything! You, claiming the world as your inalienable right, David the conqueror. David the magnificent!"

"Shut up," David rasped. "You're talking like you're drunk!"

"I am drunk!" Jonny stated. "I'm drunk with power, David. I've found myself. I know myself. I know what I'm worth. I see you in your true light and you don't dazzle me any more. You marched ahead like an invincible conqueror and I crawled like a slave. And then you were stopped, David. There had to be a check put to your progress. You claimed the world, but you couldn't have Wiletta. She was not for you. God wouldn't let you have her, so He killed her. Do you understand? He killed her. It was the arm of God that struck Wiletta down, took her away from you. She lies six feet under ground now, David, where you can never have her. I'm closer to her than you are, David. You never knew her soul. You only saw her beautiful body and that's gone. That's rotting in the grave, but

her soul, her shining soul is free and it lives with me—with me—
with me—!"

His voice was a thin scream. He'd forgotten all about the Chinese kimono when he raised his arms and it fell around his scrawny body like a flowing robe of splendor. He stood there with his hands clenched, his arms above his head, his face lifted, and screamed his madness into the night:

"She lives with me! Wiletta is mine! My bride! My eternal beauty, my salvation. Through Wiletta I shall find salvation. She comes to me in the silence—she guides me—she lives in me—! Forever—forever—"

Abruptly the light of him went out. His arms dropped. The hands hung limply, fingers uncurled. His head lowered. He stared at us from dull eyes. He shook his head once or twice, he took an uncertain step forward. He fell with a crash to the floor. He lay motionless.

I thought, "This is the end. His heart has broken. Jonny is dead—"

And once again on that memorable night I heard someone on my porch. It was Kenneth Borden. He came in without knocking. He was bareheaded. Water dripped from his clothing. He looked as if he were drowned, but his eyes were strangely quiet and sane.

He leaned against the door. He looked at us slowly, Jonny last. "So here's where he is," Borden said. "I've been hunting for him. I missed him two hours ago. I've been searching for him. So here is where he is."

"Two hours ago you missed him?" David asked. "Caroline only discovered he was gone twenty minutes ago. She was worried. I started out to trail him. I saw the light here and—"

"Two hours," Borden repeated. "I've been watching the boy, you know. He's had me worried. I don't mind admitting it. I found he was gone and I trailed him to the lake, but I got there too late."

David frowned and brushed at his damp hair. "Too late? What do you mean, Borden, too late?"

"Eh?" Borden asked, like one rousing from deep thought. "Oh! Well, it's bad news again. It's Stacey Madden. She was in the lake. I got her out. I was too late though. She's dead."

And then, distinctly, I saw Stacey walking toward me. She came in bright sunlight that shone on her ruddy hair, on her quiet happy eyes. She looked straight at me. She smiled. I heard her voice so clearly in that quiet hall. She said:

"I'll sleep well tonight, Laure. It's been so long since I've slept well. Tonight it will be different. I'll sleep soundly tonight, Laure."

DAVID SAID, all choked and thick, "Stacey dead! You mean—Stacey Madden drowned herself in the lake?"

"Drowned herself?" Borden repeated. "Oh no. Her own green scarf was around her neck, knotted like destruction. She's been murdered."

"Oh!" David said, and breath whistled between his gray lips. "Murder again, eh?"

"Yes," Borden agreed and looked at Jonny Rohmer. "What's the matter with him? How'd he get here in that rig?"

"I don't know," David told him. "I was talking to Laure when he appeared in the kitchen door, looking like the Rajah of Punk, or something. All he needed was a turban." David's voice cracked. I thought he was laughing, until I looked at his face. Borden bent over Jonny. That was the first time that I fully realized that he was a doctor. There are certain ways a doctor does things.

David did not move from where he leaned against the wall near the door, and he held his eyes on Jonny. I believe that in that moment David saw a number of things clearly. That he knew the truth of what Jonny had said in his mad tirade, that he saw and understood how, unintentionally, he was guilty of the charges Jonny had made.

He asked hoarsely, "He's not—dead?"

Borden rose slowly. "No, though lights are out for him now. He may slip away without regaining consciousness. He may return to live out his days in insanity. He may, God willing, come back—a different man."

David straightened then. He came slowly toward Borden, shoulders slumped, hands hanging limply. "Let's quit stalling. You believe he killed Stacey Madden, don't you, Borden?"

A quiver went over Borden. He looked straight at David. His face was old and tired. I imagine that was the way Stacey had seen it in the morning room. He said, "He was there, David, there at the Point where Stacey went in. I found his tracks in the mud. I found this." He dragged a handkerchief from his pocket. It was mud-stained and wet. In the corner were Jonny's initials. We recognized it at once. Jonny was always particular about his handkerchiefs. Borden's eyes left David, came to me.

"How does he happen to be here, Miss Laure?"

Oh, what could I do? Does anyone have a suggestion as to what I could have done in that moment? There was Jonny sprawled like one dead on the floor, dressed in that ridiculous kimono. There were his wet clothes hanging behind my kitchen stove. What could I do except tell Mr. Borden that Jonny had come to my door, saying that he had been wandering around thinking crazy thoughts and had fallen in the lake? As I talked I saw how unutterably silly it sounded. I remembered Jonny with a trace of laughter in his voice, saying to me, "Can you see what a cockeyed story it would be to try and make anyone believe? That I just walked into the lake?"

How could I make them understand the power I had glimpsed like a flash of sudden sunlight on Jonny's face when he spoke of the stories he wanted to write, of the lines of poetry that danced in his head and how in that solitary pilgrimage through night and darkness they had formed themselves into verses and he had, for a tiny space, known peace?

I couldn't get any of that across. All I could do was to repeat the plain, ugly facts. Jonny said he had fallen into the lake. He had asked me to help him dry his clothes before going home. Topping those facts was another. Stacey Madden had been choked with her own green scarf, thrown into the lake. Stacey Madden had talked to Frances Cosette, who claimed to have witnessed Wiletta's murder. Stacey said Frances wouldn't tell her who did it, but had that

been the truth? Had Stacey known who murdered Wiletta? Had
Stacey died, as Frances had, because of that knowledge?

I know those thoughts were in all our minds as we stood there
in my little hall near morning of that June day and looked at Jonny
Rohmer. Borden said, when I finished,

"Well, let's get him home, David. He needs care. I met the night
watchman on my way here. I sent word to the sheriff by him. That
end of the thing is being cared for. Let's look after Jonny."

So I dug up a small camp cot I had in the woodshed and they
laid Jonny on it, still in my flowered kimono. I spread a blanket
over him and David and Mr. Borden carried him back to his home.
I saw their tall forms disappearing along the graying street.

I did not move for a long, long time. It was cold as I stood in
the open doorway. Peter slithered, purring, around my ankles, but
I did not heed him. I thought of the avalanche which had started
with the loosening of a single stone. Which was still pursuing its
deadly way toward the foot of the hill.

I thought, "If Jonny dies, it will kill Caroline. It will break
Clarke. David will never be the same again. He will blame himself
for Jonny's death. All through his life he will carry that terrible
burden. That he came into Jonny's home, that he usurped Jonny's
place, that he crushed Jonny beneath his own strength."

They rounded the corner before the jail and passed from my
sight. I went into the hall and closed the door. I dressed and built
up the fire again. The kitchen was haunted for me that morning.
Stacey laughed in the silence and Jonny looked at me from every
corner. I saw his limp white shirt, his silly looking linen knickers
on the dryer behind the stove. I set his muddy, warped oxfords in
the windowsill. I remembered him as a small boy one Christmas
day racing up to my door, with a basket of fruit from Caroline. How
he ran to get there ahead of David, who had already arrived with a
fruitcake. Always Jonny plunging ahead, trying to beat David,
always Jonny exerting every ounce of strength in his frail little
body, only to see David walk past him on the homestretch, without effort, head high, eyes shining, unconquerable, in his strength
and assurance.

Oh, my heart was heavy for the two boys I loved. David was my life, of course. I think sometimes I only live because of David, but I loved Jonny, too. I took down his shirt and folded it. I lifted his knickers, smoothed them on the table, felt something crackle under my fingers.

I stood there frowning at the wrinkled linen garment, then I slipped my hand into the right rear pocket and drew out a folded piece of paper. My fingers were quite steady as I opened it. There were lines written in a swift flowing hand, gay, dancing lines, kicking up their heels in the face of tragedy and disillusionment.

I read,

> Darling Ken:
> Please don't be an ass. We tried and failed, so hooray for the one who wins, and that's David. Once I'm safely married to him I don't care what he finds out about us, but I'm counting on your well-known chivalry to keep the lid on until the fatal words are said tonight at nine. After that I'll have some time for you, precious. We might manage to be very good friends again. I'm sure this pitiful cry for quarter is not really necessary, but you avoid me so thoroughly, and look at me so queerly in a room full of people, I must make it.
>
> Come and see me for a few minutes, won't you? I'll be alone just before the fatal wedding march starts. I'll get rid of everyone, so drop by, old pal, and let's take off a very brief trial balance. I'd like your approval of my gown, too. Remember the one I wore on that other wedding night? Oh, what silly things we were, with dreams of eternal love and endless fidelity.
>
> Cheerio. I'll be waiting for you. Just for a few minutes, please.
>
> Wiletta.

I groped behind me for a chair. I sat there and looked at the note I had found in Jonny Rohmer's pocket. The note which Wiletta had written to her former husband. In that moment I thanked the dear Lord that Wiletta was dead and not David's wife. Maybe it was wicked, but I couldn't help it. Everything seemed justified then and I knew I had been terribly right about her.

But where had Jonny come on the note? I knew that he spent a good bit of time in Mr. Borden's room. Even when Mr. Borden was out Jonny used to sit in the window seat and read, waiting for him to return. I remembered Jonny saying, "I couldn't take it. They were all strangers to me. Even Borden, who is usually so steady." Had the discovery of this note been back of the boy's frenzy last night? Had his uncertain world toppled when he found this letter in Borden's room? No wonder he hadn't been able to sleep. Small cause for surprise that ghosts had driven him into the night. I knew that Jonny had clung to Kenneth Borden as the one stable and unchanging thing in a world of shadows.

I folded the note and put it into my purse. I wrapped up Jonny's clothes, I fed Peter, pinned my Paisley shawl around my shoulders, for the damp air was chill, then I went again to the Rohmer house.

It was a still dark morning. The leaves were heavy with moisture and there were small black pools in the sunken places of the brick walk. You have to go down Main Street from my place to get to the Rohmers'. Of course, everyone knew what had happened in the night. Old Walter Watson, sweeping off the walk before his store, stopped me.

Walter is a big heavy man and there is a cataract growing over his left eye. He always wears a white apron around his fat middle when he cleans up in the morning. His head is bald and shiny with just two or three strands of hair crossing the dome like straggling roads across a desert.

He said, "Well, Miss Laure, the ways of the Lord are inscrutable, as Brother Grisold pointed out in last Sunday's sermon." And I could feel his one good eye probing into mine like a gimlet. Walter always did like his gossip.

I guess I was rather snappish, being tired and all. I said, "It's not for me to say, Walter Watson, but I don't see that the Lord's had much to do with what's been going on in this town of late. It's comfortable to have the Lord to blame for things, but it looks to me just like plain downright cussedness," and then I pulled my shawl tighter and went on in a hurry, hearing him puffing and grunting behind me.

The big stone house of the Rohmers looked very quiet and sad that morning when I approached it. I saw Dr. Marc's Buick parked in the driveway and Phil Lester, the boy from the drugstore, came up on his wheel, just as I arrived, to deliver a package of medicine. He was bursting the buttons on his blue jeans with curiosity but precious little satisfaction he got out of me. Matilda was not so easy to shake, though.

She was waiting in the hall, imposing in pink starched ging-ham and she took the medicine from me when I came in. She started up the stairs, then she stopped and looked down at me over the banisters.

"Oh, Miss Laure," she said in a breathy whisper, "when will the judgment of the Lord cease to lay heavy on this house? When will the tribulations cease?"

"Not while decent, sober women, who should have more sense, stand around and whimper," I told her, being heartily sick of all this moralizing, "and you get along upstairs with that physic or whatever it is, Matilda Combs. Then you tell your mistress I'm here and ready to do whatever I can."

Her brown eyes flashed. Her lips set. She was real mad, always having considered herself better than a common servant, which she is, though heaven knows they're good enough, I guess. She started off, then stopped again. She leaned down real low, glaring at me.

"It's well enough for you to talk so sharp," she said, "but there's them that could talk, too, if they would. I guess I know a thing or two and them that—"

I said, "Come here, Matilda," and, after she gasped a moment, she came slowly down the three steps and stood before me. She looked bad, Matilda did, and there were brown patches under her eyes. "Now, let's have this," I snapped. "What do you know? Come out with it!"

She squirmed uncomfortably. "It's nothin'," she said sullenly, "and I'm not one to be gossipin' about my betters."

Then I had an inspiration, having known Matilda for close to fifty years. I said, "There are no betters of yours in this house, Matilda, you who have served so faithfully and rendered such a fine account of yourself. Trouble and death are here with the people you love and if you know anything, it's your duty to tell it. Now, I'm waiting."

The flattery worked. Poor Matilda never had enough nice things said to her, though Caroline has always treated her as a friend. But the brown eyes filled with tears, the plain, pleasant face worked and she caught my cold hand in her strong, calloused one.

"Oh, Miss Laure, I want to do what's right. I can't bother Ma'am Caroline with it, her with her trouble and all, but ever since I heard, ever since I knew about Miss Stacey—"

She stopped, gulping like a fish. "Yes, Matilda," I urged, "go ahead and tell me. Of course you don't want to bother Ma'am Caroline. What is it you've been thinking since Miss Stacey died?"

She sucked her lips in until they pressed blue and cold against her white china teeth. "It was what I overheard in the morning room, Miss Laure, and the Lord strike me dead if I tell a lie about it."

I said softly, "Go on, Matilda. Whom did you hear talking in the morning room, and when was it?"

She glanced around, her eyes frightened. "It was last night, after dinner, Miss Laure, and Miss Stacey was talking to—Mr. Borden."

"Oh," I said, thinking, "Well, I know all about that and I'm not sorry that Matilda overheard it, too."

She caught my hand again. "I started to go in, when of a sudden I heard Miss Stacey say, laughing that way she used to, 'Maybe the letter Frances Cosette left was written on Jonny Rohmer's machine. Maybe it wasn't. It isn't the only typewriter in the house, you know.' And Mr. Borden—I hadn't known who she was talking to until he spoke—he said, 'No, it isn't the only one. I have a Remington Portable myself, Miss Madden.'

"Miss Stacey was quiet for a moment, like him saying that had surprised her, then she said, real soft like, 'And Jonny Rohmer wasn't the only one to stand outside Wiletta's room the other night, either.' 'No,' Mr. Borden told her, his voice sounding very queer, indeed, 'the murderer stood outside her room, Stacey Madden, and the murderer—'"

"Then, Miss Laure," Matilda said, looking at me very seriously, "there was the queerest silence. I could just feel it prickle along my spine with Mr. Borden stopping in the middle of a sentence like that. Miss Stacey broke that silence. She said, 'There's where you're wrong, Kenneth Borden. The murderer of Wiletta Owens did not stand outside her door.'"

Matilda drew a long shivering breath and brushed a hand across her lips. "I heard someone coming then, Miss Laure, and I had to leave. I didn't mean to listen, so help me, but it's worried me a lot and I don't know what it means. What did Miss Stacey know? What did she mean when she said, 'The murderer of Wiletta Owens did not stand—'"

"Hush, hush, Matilda," I broke in, trying to tie my scattered thoughts into some sense. "We don't know what she meant and I guess we'll never know now. You were right in telling me instead of Ma'am Caroline—"

She caught my shoulders in her strong brown hands. "He did it," she whispered hoarsely in my ear. "That man. That Mr. Borden. I just feel that he did it. I can't get it out of my head. He killed Miss Wiletta, he poisoned that girl Frances, he choked Miss Stacey—"

Upstairs a door slammed. Matilda drew back, lips blue. I heard Dr. Marc speaking. Thought of his quiet strength sustained me then. I said, "Look here, Matilda, you're talking like a fool. You keep your mouth shut and don't go round accusing gentlemen like Mr. Borden—" Then I thought of the note in my pocketbook which Wiletta had written to Kenneth Borden so shortly before her death. I pushed that knowledge aside. I said, "Now get along and fix up some breakfast, like a good soul, and don't speak of this to anyone, do you understand, not to anyone?"

I went past her up the stairs, stumbling a little in my excitement and hurry. Matilda followed slowly, carrying the blue wrapped package of medicine in her hands. She wouldn't talk to anyone else, of that I was sure, but oh, what a lot she had suggested to me. Evidently Stacey hadn't told me everything she and Borden had discussed there in the breakfast room. "Jonny Rohmer was not the only one who stood outside Wiletta's door," Stacey had said, and Borden had answered, "No, the murderer—" The words went over and over through my brain as I climbed the stairs. "The murderer stood there. The murderer stood there—"

I met Caroline coming out of Jonny's room. She wore a crepe kimono over her nightgown. Her heavy gray hair was in a braid down her back. She stopped sharply, stood there staring at me, then she moaned real softlike and I was beside her with my arms around her, and she was sobbing on my shoulder. Such long broken sobs, the kind that seemed to tear her poor body to pieces. No tears with them either. All dry and rasping as she twisted and turned in my hold.

Dr. Marc came out just then. He took it all in with one quick look. He said to me very quietly, "Get her to lie down, Laure," then he went downstairs as if just telling me to do it was like having it done.

I did it, too. I wonder yet how I managed to get that frantic woman into bed, but I succeeded. Maybe just because Marc expected it of me. He came in and gave her a hypodermic and presently she was lying quietly, heavy lids closed, breathing evenly. Marc watched her for a time, then he stood up and our eyes met. I did not allow mine to waver. There seemed nothing much we could say. I remember how gentle and kind his eyes looked and how deep were the lines in his face.

"You look like you could stand a sedative yourself, Laure," he told me.

I caught sight of my face in the mirror and was shocked. How trouble changes us. I'd always been just an ordinary-looking woman, I suppose. My quiet life hadn't made many marks on my face. Now it was gouged and ravaged so that I scarcely recognized it. The night that was past had put a definite blight upon me. I'll never lose it entirely.

He said, "Jonny's in a coma. Borden's with him now. We've sent for a nurse. I'm making some calls I can't pass up, then I'm coming back. We're thinking of getting Harrison down from town. He's a specialist in this sort of thing and Borden feels he'd like to have him."

I said, "Yes, we want to do everything, everything, Marc. Jonny has to be saved. We can't let him die or—"

He smiled crookedly. "It might be better, Laure. He's locked away from us now and there's none of us, not Borden or Harrison or any of them wise enough to say how he'll come back. It might be better if he didn't come back—"

"Yes, Marc, it might. I'd rather see him dead than—insane. It seems to me that David might blame himself for it. David learned a lot last night—he might think he was responsible—"

Marc's face twitched as he turned away. "Always David, Laure. It's always David with you, isn't it? It's been David since the very first." He went out then without giving me a chance to answer. I was too tired to feel anything much, but I'd caught the pain in his voice, the old, old pain that I sensed there twenty-seven years ago, when he ran away from me to marry Luella Bell.

I laid a light blanket over Caroline's feet and left the room very softly.

SOMETHING MADE ME halt outside Jonny's door. I wasn't at all sure that I should go in or if I would be allowed to. While I hesitated David came out and nearly ran straight into me as he turned toward the stairs. He stopped with a startled grunt and frowned down at me. Oh, he looked terrible. His face was all gray and thin and his eyes were sunken and feverish.

"Oh, hello, Laure," he said thickly. "Glad you're here," and he started on.

"David!" I caught his sleeve. "David, wait a moment. Tell me—"

He stopped and I could feel him trembling under my touch.

"Tell you, Laure? What is there to tell? You heard the indictment read there in your own hall this morning. You know, as you must have known all along, just what my coming here did to Jonny. He lies in there now, the mind, the spirit, all but the very life gone out of him. It will be a blessing if he dies so that years of hopeless insanity will be spared him, and it's all my fault. I did it! I went romping along like a big-footed Newfoundland, stepping on sensibilities that were finer than my own, taking everything I wanted. I stole and cheated and failed to play the game, and I've killed Jonny because of it. I've ruined his life and his mind and—"

"David!"

He stopped, like turned off mechanism, at my command. He stood there, trembling, looking down at me, and I saw the agony in his eyes. I said, and the Lord gave me strength for it, "David, you took nothing. What you received of admiration, of affection and praise came to you by right, as the rain comes to the earth in spring. There is in you something that attracts good things. Some people have that power and for it they should not be praised or blamed. Because of it you will always be successful and have power to make folks love you and to accomplish the way your destiny is written. Jonny does not have it, but he has other forces in his makeup that can bring him as certain happiness. He must be taught, he must learn to develop what he has and not allow his soul to corrode with envy and hate for the gifts the Lord gave you. You took not one whit of the affection his parents had for him. The difference in what you received and what he had are entirely in his imagination. To escape his own weakness, he has taken refuge in hate of you. He uses you as an alibi for his own failure. He escapes the reality of his individual lack by dwelling on your gifts. Now stick out your chin, lift up your head and forget it!" I drew a long breath and added, "Snap out of it, *pronto!*"

Well! Dr. Marc told me afterward I had read that young man a most excellent lecture in elementary psychology and added that it wasn't so very elementary at that. It did the work, though. David blinked at me like a frog in a thunderstorm, wet his lips, fumbled at his collar, swallowed and said,

"Gosh, Laure! I didn't know you had it in you! And while you're probably making it all up to make me feel better, it does help," and then he turned quickly and was gone, running along the hall to his own room.

I went all limp after he had left and leaned against the door. It opened and I nearly sat down, only Mr. Borden caught me. He helped me inside and into a chair. He was grinning for all his face looked so white and tired.

He said, very low, "Bravo, Miss Laure. Good work! You handed it to him straight. He needed it. He was in a mill race, going round and round, getting nowhere."

I saw then that the room was very dim, the curtains drawn and a light burning low on the bedside table. Jonny lay there, eyes closed as if he were asleep. He breathed heavily. I looked at him once, then at Mr. Borden.

"I couldn't take it," I told him. "I couldn't stand there and let David talk that way about himself. It just came to me some way. I just knew what to say and I said it."

He nodded and sat down across the table from me. I saw his long strong hand fumbling nervously with one of Marc's prescription pads which he had forgotten.

"You said it right," he told me. "You analyzed the situation perfectly. When Jonny comes back to us he's due for a long course of careful training in fastening his interests and creative abilities upon something beside himself."

I looked at Jonny's colorless face and closed my eyes a moment. "When Jonny comes back to us." The words had an ominous ring. I glanced at Mr. Borden. "You think he will come back—to—us?" I asked, not very steadily.

He frowned at his fingertips. "I think so," he said, half to himself. "It happened as I feared. The adjustment was too difficult, his train left the track, ran wild. The current is shut off temporarily. With time and care and—intelligence, I believe he's bound to get on the rails again, this time I trust headed for the proper destination."

Well, that was comforting. We were silent for a time and the only sound was the soft drip of water from the maple leaves against the window.

Then again something stirred in my mind. I thought, "But the murderer of Wiletta, and the— others, is not known yet. When Jonny comes back—he'll have that to face. What chance will he have at adjustment with that before him—"

I began trembling and heat went over me in quick blasting waves. I looked at my hand lying on my lap, a thin veined hand, with callous spots worn from my thimble. I wondered about it and how it had belonged to me all these years. I thought of all the tasks it had accomplished, small and large, and how it might yet bring order out of the chaos that surrounded us, if it were guided by intelligence. The hand lifted, seemingly of its own volition, went to my pocketbook on the table and rested there.

I thought, "Now, Laure Hosmer, consider well what you are about to do. Look at it from all angles. Try to understand the ultimate outcome if you go ahead and open that black leather purse."

Whether or not I considered it, I can't say, but I did open the purse. I took out the letter I had found in Jonny's pocket and laid it, folded just as it was, before Mr. Borden, who sat opposite me across the table. I didn't say anything. I just laid it there.

I didn't even look at him but I sensed that the movement of his hand stopped and that he sat very still, eyes on the letter. He said at last, a queer hushed sound to his voice:

"Where did you get that letter, Laure Hosmer?"

"I found it in Jonny's pocket, when I folded his trousers to bring over here."

Still he did not touch it. It must have been very familiar to him that he should know so well what it was.

"You have read it?" he asked.

"Yes."

He picked it up. He turned it slowly round and round in his strong sensitive fingers. I looked at him then. The shaded lamp threw a circle of dim radiance on his face. It was gaunt and harsh and somehow terrible.

"So you believe," he inquired quietly, "that I killed Wiletta?"

The question staggered me. I felt my heart jump, sending blood pounding through my tired body, so that I was, for a moment, strong and sure. I lifted my head, turned a little and looked straight at him.

"I believe, Mr. Borden, that you killed Wiletta," I said, in a voice I hardly recognized as my own.

He looked straight back at me. I couldn't see his eyes very plainly for the way the light was, but I got that uncomfortable feeling that he was looking through me as if I were a clear, bright window-pane.

"You'd like to hear about it?" he asked slowly.

"Oh, I don't know—I don't know. You tell someone else. You tell the sheriff—tell Shad Birket—don't tell me—"

He laughed gently and his face was sagging and tired. "You mean I should make my confession to the proper authority, Miss Laure? That it?"

I couldn't speak. I could only nod. He shook his head. "You must know about it," he told me. "I engaged you to help me in this investigation and you have worked too well. Now you must bear the consequences. You must hear my confession."

I shut my hands tight in my lap. My lips felt stiff. I didn't want to hear what he called his confession. Thought of it filled me with a shivering, sick terror. I thought of running for the door, getting into the hall, back to my room, somewhere in silence and safety, away from this very quiet man with the strange pale eyes and that curious quirking smile to his white lips. But there was not strength in me, the Lord witness. I tried to get up. I put every ounce of determination I possessed into the business of rising to my feet, but for all of that I sat there, motionless, across the table from Mr. Borden, and did not move.

He lighted a cigarette. The scratching of the match made a sharp sound in the silence, but there was no fear of Jonny wakening. He was off somewhere in a world of his own, happy, I trust, making lines of poetry into verses, writing stories that had hummed in his head for years.

Mr. Borden said, "Wiletta Owens was my wife for five years. As she suggests in this timely little note, the venture was not a success. We need not go into that. She divorced me, went her way. I went mine. We met here, after a long period, entirely by accident, if you will concede that there is such a thing as accident in human relationship. I had not the slightest intention of interfering with anything she planned to do," he frowned at his cigarette, "though I sincerely pitied young Kaye. I purposely avoided her. There was no point in reopening old wounds." I saw the quick movement of his lips and the way he shut them hard. He went on, "It was like Wiletta to wish to talk to me. I gave her no opportunity alone, which accounts for the note you found. Then came the night of the wedding."

He paused, eyes narrowed, looking back to that wedding night. I looked, too. I could not help it. I saw it all again. The lighted house, glowing like a great Christmas tree. The cars on the drive, the people crowding in, good friends of the Rohmers, and of David, and of mine, come to wish happiness to the bridal pair.

I saw Caroline in her orchid taffeta with her snowy hair piled high and the lovely old-fashioned amethysts glowing against her full throat. I saw little Valerie Lane in her pink organdie with the big bow across her breast and, God help me, I saw Stacey in her green chiffon, like a cool wave floating through the halls.

"Wiletta must have slipped this note under my door," Mr. Borden continued, not looking at me. "I deduce this because if she had arranged for one of the servants to do it, we should have heard about it. At any rate, I found it there, about six o'clock when I came up to dress. I had no intention of going to her room, of course."

"But you did go?" I asked.

He stroked his chin thoughtfully. "Yes, I went, Miss Laure. We will not at this time enter into any attempted analysis as to why I went. Sufficient to say that I went. Perhaps I wished to see her in her bridal gown as I had seen her once before. Possibly I was merely weak in my human emotions, or it is possible that I wished to plead with her to use young David gently."

"David!" I exclaimed, hunching lower in the chair. "Oh, what that woman would have done to David!"

He looked at me curiously. "You see it, too, Miss Laure? You saw it all along? You felt what Wiletta was?"

I tried to remember that she had been his wife, that he had loved her at one time, but it was no good. I felt my face get dark when blood rushed into it. I said, trying to keep my voice steady, "Yes, I felt what Wiletta was. I knew what she would do to David. I prayed with all my heart that something would happen so they could not—"

"Be married?" he asked. "Well, something did, Miss Laure. But let's get on with our confession."

I said, "I don't want to hear it. Tell it to Birket—not to me—"

He paid no attention to my plea and I'll admit by this time that some of my shivering horror had left me and there was in its place a growing curiosity. Call it morbid if you like, but from then on I would not have left if I could. I wanted to know. I wanted it from his own lips.

"I stood outside her door," he continued, gazing, narrow-eyed, at the ceiling. "I heard her moving inside. I called, 'Wiletta— Wiletta' very softly. She must have recognized my voice for she said, after a moment, 'Yes, come in' and I opened the door and went in. She was sitting by the dressing table, looking into the mirror. I can see her face yet reflected there as she lowered her head to see me as I approached. She looked very beautiful, Miss Laure, with the white veil around her head like a cloud, and her eyes like stars. It was momentarily hard for me to remember what a menace she was to David, to the world at large, what a really beneficial thing it would be to—"

"Kill her?" I whispered. "You knew that you would kill her when you went in?"

"I wonder," he mused seriously. "I wonder if I knew, when I opened that door and walked into the room that I would kill Wiletta Owens? That is too difficult a question for me to answer, Miss Laure. Let it rest for the moment. Possibly it will come out as the story progresses."

"I believe you did," I told him. "I believe the idea came to you as you stood there looking out at the moonlight!"

"Possibly," he said. "You are possibly right. At any rate, I know it was clear in my mind when I stopped behind her. She said, not turning her head, but looking at me in the glass, 'So you came back. Well, I'm not sorry. I want you, among other things, to help me fasten this ridiculous bunch of flowers.' Then I saw, Miss Laure, that the little bunch of posies lay on the dresser and that the pin was beside them. She said, 'I can't get it right. Frances is too stupid to do it. You do it, dear. Here, you fasten them in place,' and as if the Lord worked on my behalf, Miss Laure, she handed me the pin and herself held the flowers against her shoulder."

I shut my lips hard. Oh, it was so realistic, the way he described it. I could just see Wiletta sitting there before the mirror, I could actually hear her saying, 'Here, you fasten them—'

"I took the pin," Mr. Borden said in his quiet, unemotional voice, "and I started to fasten it into the silk. She leaned forward a little and then I knew what I would do. I thrust the blade of the pin into her back. Something guided my hand. I felt the blade rip through the satin. I felt the quick gasp of agony she gave, the quiver that shook her body at the swift, terrible pain. Her hands came up, the flowers dropped. I stepped back. She rose to her feet. I can see her yet, with her face twisted, her eyes black with surprise. She tried to cry out. I saw the muscles in her throat working, but she made no sound that carried outside that room. She took a step or two, then she slipped down, all in her white satin, and lay there, twitching a little but not for long. I saw the blood seep through the satin and dampen the veil. I saw the flowers lying beside her clenched fingers. As I looked, the fingers relaxed, the twitching stopped. I knew, before I left, that she was dead."

Oh, dear Lord! I thought I should faint. The room got dim all around me and there was a roaring in my ears. I thought, "What will they say when they hear this? Clarke and Caroline and David and—"

Mr. Borden did not appear disturbed. There was a queer sort of intensity about him, as if he had concentrated his mind on accomplishing some purpose and intended nothing to interfere. I suppose a confession of murder would be somewhat of a strain, at that.

He said, crushing out his cigarette, "So that takes care of Wiletta. It was really very simple. I went out and into the hall. I went downstairs. I met one or two people, but naturally they thought nothing about seeing me."

I asked faintly, "How did you feel? How did it seem to have killed—someone? Were you frightened? Did you think that you would one day have to pay for the crime, or were you borne up by the knowledge that you had done a good deed? I've often wondered what it would feel like to have murdered someone."

"Have you, now?" he asked. "Well, that's interesting, Miss Laure. I should say that a person of your type would never give a thought to the violent taking of life."

"Only as a means of saving someone you love from danger," I told him seriously, remembering how I had almost definitely wished that evening by the lake that something would happen to Stacey.

"Yes, I understand," he assured me. "Well, as to my feelings, they were not complicated. I was not frightened; I was, to the contrary, definitely elated and yet strangely peaceful. There was in my mind no thought of paying for any crime, for I did not consider that I had committed a crime. I felt as if something outside myself had guided me, Miss Laure, and there was for me no sense of personal accomplishment."

I thought this over a time while the soughing of the maples came softly through the slightly opened window and Jonny Rohmer lay so still in the big carved bed. Then I said, my brain rushing ahead over all that had happened, following Wiletta's murder,

"And Frances? You—killed her—too?"

He shrugged, a little wearily, I thought. I wished intensely that someone else could hear this confession along with me. Suppose he denied it afterward? Why was he telling me, anyway? He interrupted my thoughts.

"Yes, I killed Frances Cosette, too, Miss Laure. Once you take a life the next one is easier and the girl was dangerous. She claimed to know who had killed Wiletta. You can see, I trust, that there was nothing else I could do. As soon as I found that out, I made my plans. I knew Dr. Wayne had given her sleeping tablets that morning, so I got some veronal out of the bath cabinet and when the house was quiet and no one around, I went up to the girl's room. She was tossing in uneasy sleep. There was a half a glass of water on the table beside her. I dropped several of the veronal tablets into the water, then very quietly I went away. You may think that it was not a very sure way to commit murder. That she might not drink the water at all and that if she did, the veronal might not kill her. But again, something told me to do it that way. I reasoned that sooner or later she would waken, be thirsty and take a drink. That is exactly what she did and you and I found her dead."

There was a potency about that man that had the power of re-creating moments for me. I remembered so clearly when he and I walked into that quiet little room. How he went at once to the bed, bent over the dead girl, then called to me to turn on the light. Oh, it was terrible, sitting there, listening to it, seeing it all again. A weakness grew on me. My feet and hands felt like ice. I thought that icy water was creeping around me, higher and higher and when it reached my heart I would die.

"You wrote the note on your typewriter?" I asked him.

"No," he said. "I wrote it on Jonny's typewriter. I found him typing in the library. I talked to him for a time, then I left. I came back later and he was gone, so I wrote the note then. I put it under the girl's pillow where I knew it would be found and appear that she had stuffed it there."

I asked, out of horror that made me sick, "Didn't you think what might happen to others? Didn't it occur to you that Valerie Lane, Jonny or Stacey Madden might be involved in your net of crime, might pay the penalty for what you had done?" He narrowed his pale eyes at me. They were burning like white flames and there was a dark spot in the center of each one where the pupils were tiny points.

He said, "I did not think of that when I killed Wiletta. When I realized how many people, of whom I was genuinely fond, might be involved—well, it was a bad time. I determined to prove them innocent if it was the last thing I did. I worked at it. I thought that the confession Frances was supposed to have left would clear the slate. I expected exactly what happened, that the sheriff would accept it and the matter would be closed. I thought the chapter was ended when Frances 'confessed' and 'committed suicide.'"

"But it wasn't?" I whispered. "There was Stacey. Stacey knew something? Stacey knew who killed Wiletta?"

He crossed one long leg over his knee. "Shall we leave the motive for Stacey's death alone for the immediate present?" he suggested. "I believe I can make it all plainer to you if we take that up last. I have not the slightest objection, however, to outlining to you the method by which Stacey met her death."

"Well, that's obvious," I said. "You found her drunk and out of her senses and she stumbled and fell, striking her head, then you jerked her green scarf around her throat, choked her into unconsciousness and pushed her into the lake."

He frowned at me. "Miss Laure," he protested, "you are not clairvoyant, are you?"

I guess I looked guilty. I said, feeling rather foolish, "Of course not, but it couldn't have happened any other way. She was drunk when she left my house, staggering drunk and crazy as a coot. She could scarcely keep to her feet. You were wandering around hunting Jonny and you met her by the lake. She liked to walk there. The rest is just—well, I guess I just guessed it, Mr. Borden."

He smiled crookedly. "That's the usual explanation of real clairvoyance. That's the common-sense method of brushing aside such remarkable insight as you have just displayed. You know one or two pertinent facts and you 'guess' the rest. Well, that's the way it happened. It was not difficult to murder Stacey Madden for all she was a strong woman, because she was thoroughly and completely pickled. Did she take on the load at your house, Miss Laure?"

"Yes, she did, Mr. Borden, but not with my approval. She brought the liquor with her in a flask. She was crazy when she got there, talking like a wild woman. That's when she told me about her conversation with you in the morning room."

"Oh, I see. Yes, she would have, at that. Stacey Madden was a remarkable woman in many ways, Miss Laure. I sincerely believe she knew all along, or had a very good idea, as to who had committed the murders. I believe she honestly tried to help cover up for the murderer because she wanted him to escape, he having done her a very good turn in disposing of Wiletta."

"Yes," I said, "and giving her a chance at David. She was set for David, Mr. Borden. She told me herself, the day of Wiletta's funeral, that she was going to get David, no matter what I did or thought. She warned me, I'll say that for her."

"She did?" Mr. Borden asked, looking at me curiously. "Well, well, I didn't know that. It makes a few points clear that have bothered me. It supplies rather thoroughly and completely the real motive for her murder. You know I told you I wanted to leave it to the last."

"Yes, I know you told me that but I don't see how it supplies the motive."

"You don't?" He picked up a cigarette, lighted it carefully, then took it from between his lips and frowned at it.

"Well, you see it's like this, Miss Laure. It wasn't difficult to understand why you killed Wiletta, who was to marry David. It wasn't hard to see why Frances had to go, by the method I've outlined, but I couldn't quite get your reason for finishing off Stacey. To be sure, I believe she suspected you. I think she did everything in her power to help you cover up. She worked hard to implicate Valerie Lane, she didn't even spare Jonny. She built up a tentative case against me and it was all so that you, the real killer, should go unscathed. She had a curious, twisted sense of loyalty to one who had done her a good deed."

I sat very still, looking at him. His face stood out sharply against the dark folds of the curtains, its lines and hollows picked out by the lamp. I thought, "The man is mad. The world is mad. I'm in a room with a madman. I'm in a world with mad people—what shall I do? Shall I scream? Screaming won't do any good. One could scream and scream and scream and it wouldn't do any good—any good—"

He said, still looking at me, "I did stand outside Wiletta's door, Miss Laure, and that is why I told Stacey Madden that the murderer did not do so. I stood out there while Wiletta was killed. I heard the sound of your muffled voices as you talked. I heard the choked cry she gave when you stabbed her. It was blurred by the noise from downstairs and I did not attach significance to it then. When I knew she had been murdered, well, anyone might have been in there with her. Valerie, Stacey, even Jonny Rohmer. As I left Wiletta's door and went toward the back stairs, I saw you come out of the spare room.

"When Stacey Madden told me last night, 'Wiletta's murderer did not stand outside her door' I realized that she had the same knowledge I had. The murderer of Wiletta Owens certainly did *not* stand outside her door because *you* were her murderer and you entered her room through the bath from the spare room. Jonny, wandering around on his lovesick mission up here, saw you go into the spare room. I saw you come out. You killed Wiletta to keep David from her. You killed Frances not only because you feared she knew your secret, but because in her death and 'confession' you believed you saw a way to divert suspicion from those you loved. You killed Stacey Madden not from fear of her possible knowledge, but because again, you wanted to protect David from what you thought was a danger. You killed them all—you—"

And then I could stand it no longer. I remember getting to my feet. The room was black and I saw destruction before me. I fought against giving way. I said to myself, "If you just hold on someone will come. This nightmare will end—"

The blackness increased. It was shot through with orange lights. I heard waters thundering around me. I felt the icy waves creeping toward my heart. I let loose of everything. I gave up trying to be brave. I embraced terror. I screamed and screamed and screamed. I can still hear the echoes of my own screams, like the harsh metallic clang of lances striking in combat.

KENNETH BORDEN looked up as the door opened. He laid the bulky manuscript on the table beside him, smiled rather wearily in welcome. "Hello, Wayne. I've been expecting you." He glanced briefly at the neatly typed pages beside him.

Dr. Marcus Wayne looked at them, too, back at the other man. His lips compressed. He set his satchel on a chair by the door, tossed his hat beside it and came to the table where Borden sat. The dusk of a stormy November day closed in around the big Rohmer house. The room was pleasantly warm from the open fire that danced on the hearth. Dr. Wayne said, "Well, you've finished it?"

"Yes, just. Remarkable document, don't you think?"

Wayne sat down, brought out his pipe, turned it carefully between sensitive fingers. "God help me, Borden, I can't judge it. I can't do anything about it. It was all I could do to make myself read it. You must remember, you must understand that—" His voice thickened. He cleared his throat angrily, laid the empty pipe on the table.

Borden said, "Yes, I understand. You thought a great deal of Miss Laure, Wayne. You can scarcely look at the matter calmly."

"Calmly!" Dr. Wayne stared at Borden a moment, then he jumped up and began a nervous pacing. "Calmly," he said again, and laughed. "Look here, Borden," he turned suddenly, frowning down at his companion, "when I go down there every morning, when I see her sitting there so happily, with that big fat tomcat asleep in his basket, the yellow curtains at the window, and that red geranium blooming—when I talk to her, when I see her just as she always has been, apparently, then when I think, when I realize—"

He couldn't go on. His thin tired face worked. He muttered something incoherent under his breath. Borden said gently, "Yes, Wayne, I know. Yellow curtains don't belong over those windows and a red geranium shouldn't look out at bars—"

"No," Wayne said harshly, "yet I thank the Lord she's as comfortable as she is. It wasn't hard to get those little concessions for her, the cat and the rocker, the geranium and the yellow curtains good Mattie Grisold made to hide the cell bars. And she seems quite happy. She laughed and joked about writing this story. Every day when I went in she greeted me enthusiastically with her report of its progress. Wouldn't you think, Borden, doesn't it seem reasonable that she'd have a conscience? That she'd suffer for what she did—that ghosts would haunt her—?"

Borden rose, a tall thin man, with stooped shoulders and a wide, tolerant mouth. "Take it easy," he advised. "Don't let it get you, Wayne. You and I both understand the world of shadows where Miss Laure lives. You, as well as I, can trace clearly the years of thought processes which resulted in her turning mass murderess."

"Yes," Wayne said harshly, "I can trace it. I can understand it when I set it off by itself and look at it, but by God, I don't get it— I can't get it—"

"That," Borden told him, "is because you allow the personal element to intrude into your reasoning faculties. You have known Miss Laure since childhood. You loved her, you still love her. And you cannot divorce the woman you love from the woman who stabbed Wiletta Owens to death."

"No," Wayne admitted. "I damned well can't."

"I can," Borden told him. "I can set her off and look at her impersonally. I can see her intense maternal instinct balked of natural outlet, fasten itself like powerful tentacles around the infant that came into her life twenty-seven years ago. I can see her as a woman to whom a man is important for only one thing. To give her children. For that she loves him, until the children come. Then his importance vanishes. The children are all that count. The man is pushed aside. He lives outside her world of reality, which is composed entirely of her devotion, her abnormal absorption in her children. You are lucky in some ways that you never married Laure Hosmer."

Marc Wayne stared with tired, unseeing eyes at the cold gray dusk outside the window.

Borden went on, "The infant David came to Miss Laure, and you, as a possible mate to give her children, ceased to be important. David sufficed. For five years she had him, then by a tremendous self-sacrifice, she gave him up. Physically he was gone from her, but mentally, emotionally, she still held him close. She cherished him in her heart and mind all those years, Wayne, and he crowded out everything else. All her real ability, and she has plenty of it, all the energies of her mind, were transformed through hungry necessity into love for David. Behind the murder of Wiletta lay first Miss Laure's fierce jealousy of any woman whom David loved, or who would take David from her. Perhaps if Wiletta had been worthy—" This time it was Borden who paused and stared at the darkening windowpane.

"Yes," Wayne said slowly, "if it had been little Valerie Lane. If David had known then what he knows now—"

Borden looked at him quickly. "Yes? David is coming to his senses? He is finding his balance?"

Wayne nodded. "He spends a great deal of his time with Valerie. He's young, you know, and Valerie, well, she's offering him the real thing. One of these days there'll be another wedding here—"

He stirred suddenly, looked away.

"I'm glad," Borden said. "Does Miss Laure know?"

Wayne shook his head. "No. David goes to see her regularly. She is so happy when he's there. It breaks his heart every time he sees her, but he takes it on the chin. He feels, I think, that she is his real mother. He understands better than I do, why she did what she did."

Borden tapped the manuscript. "Miss Laure wrote faithfully," he commented. "She displayed an almost uncanny ability to get the facts right, to present everything, and yet cover cleverly." He smiled thinly. "Under happier circumstances she might have been a successful author."

"Yes, she did a good job. She put in all the—clues." Wayne's lips twisted in a mirthless smile. "She tells how she went into the spare bedroom, what she thought when she looked into the moonlight, how peaceful she was when she came out. If you're to consider it as a straight story, all the reader has to do is to remember that the spare room connected by a bath with Wiletta's room. Consider her stated feelings about Wiletta, about David—"

"Yes," Borden agreed, "and that neat touch about her 'taking the things she wanted from her bath cabinet at home.' That was the veronal, of course. She knew then that she would murder Frances. She did exactly as I outlined to her when I named myself the murderer. She simply dropped the tablets into the half-filled glass and went away, confident that Frances would awaken and drink it. She wrote the note on Jonny's typewriter when she returned to the living room as I indicated. I dare say she did not realize that a typewritten confession would be worthless and she did not fully understand how she was implicating Jonny."

"She was," Wayne said, "strangely unsophisticated in some things."

"She was not, after all, a professional murderer," Borden pointed out with a trace of grim humor. "I picked her almost from the first merely by what I saw in her of abnormality. I realized she was quite capable of the crime with her unused passions, her repressed emotions. Of course, I did not actively accuse her even in my own mind. I simply considered her as I considered the others.

As events developed, she grew in importance. In each killing she had opportunity. Of her motive I was never in doubt, really. That is why I asked her to help me. I wanted to study her at first hand, analyze her, try to understand her."

Wayne sat down, picked up his pipe, replaced it. "Well, you did it," he commented. "You studied her, analyzed her, just as you would a beetle stuck on a pin."

"If I had crystallized my study and analyzations earlier in the game," Borden told him, strolling over to lean on the mantel, "at least one life might have been saved. I was too slow in my reactions. I accepted the surface picture of Laure Hosmer, a religious, kindly spinster, who lived decently and went about doing good. All the rest, all this consuming maternal instinct, all this buried hunger of years duration, was hidden from me. It is a common mistake, but one which I should not have made."

"I knew her for fifty years," Marcus Wayne said slowly. "And I couldn't have guessed—I did not see—"

"We do not see," Borden said, "until some additional strain is put on the mental mechanism and the control slips. I was mortally certain that Laure Hosmer was guilty after Frances Cosette was killed. Do you remember the note, the alleged confession? Well, in it, Miss Laure gave herself away. She wrote, 'I know it is sinful to take human life, but she was a cruel, selfish woman. She destroyed everything she touched.'" Borden flicked ashes from his cigarette. "There spoke the consciously religious person, 'It is sinful to take human life.' The next line Frances *could* have written. 'She was a cruel, selfish woman.' Speaking of her mistress she might have said that. It was," Borden said, smiling faintly, "a rather common impression concerning Wiletta Owens. The last line, 'She destroyed everything she touched' is Miss Laure entirely. Miss Laure speaking of David. She was convinced that Wiletta would destroy David; to save him, she destroyed Wiletta herself. It was the false note in the letter. Frances Cosette might have and probably did hate her mistress poisonously, but it was not because of anything which Wiletta destroyed."

"Yes, I see," Wayne agreed. "When you set it out like that it seems clear. Generally speaking, though, I'll have to admit that the clues on which you based your accusation of her were pretty flimsy."

"Clues? Accusation?" Borden's black brows lifted slightly. "I had no clues. I worked myself into Laure Hosmer's mind and walked among her unconscious thoughts. Did you think I found footprints, cuff links, cigarette stubs and presented her with them?" He shook his head. "I was convinced in my own mind that she was guilty. I allowed her to accuse me, noting her eagerness to accept the opportunity. I admitted nothing when I asked her if she believed I had murdered Wiletta Owens. I asked her if she would like me to tell her how it was done. Then, while she sat, practically paralyzed, I outlined to her the way I believed *she* had committed the crimes. I dwelt on details, I presented it before her eyes for her to contemplate and the contemplation was too much for her. It was, I suppose," Kenneth Borden said thoughtfully, "a rather terrible kind of mental third degree. It is, however, the only way by which we would have obtained her confession."

Dr. Wayne mopped sweat from his brow. "Yes, and now she's coming up for trial in December, only a few weeks away. Laure Hosmer will face trial for murder before the year ends."

Borden's face twitched with quick pain, straightened again. He said, "Yes, she'll stand trial for murder, Wayne, but there's not much question as to the outcome." He glanced at the manuscript. "Any one trained in mental sickness has but to read that story to see, to understand. Laure Hosmer will not pay for her crimes, not the way you think, at least. She is, of course, hopelessly insane."

Dr. Wayne said thickly, "You'll testify to that? You'll go on the stand and testify?"

Borden shrugged. "I'll be called as a witness, certainly. I believe my professional standing is sufficiently good to permit my testimony as to her mental condition to bear some weight. Then, of course, Harrison is coming down for the defense. He's a headliner. They'll listen to what he has to say."

They were silent for a time, each busy with his own thoughts. Dr. Wayne said at last, "Poor Laure, how carefully she labored at writing that wretched story. How seriously she took what I said to her about the author being morally obligated to present all the facts. A blind man should be able to tell from those pages that she was the murderer."

"Yes, Laure played fair, you'll have to admit that. I remember one line. It was about Stacey. Laure said, 'I grew to hate her laugh. I think it was her laugh more than anything else that made me do what I did—'"

"I remember that," Borden stated quietly. "She kept referring also to the way people brought back the picture of Wiletta seated before her dressing table, with the bouquet in her fingers. She pleaded, 'Won't they ever stop reminding me of that. I can see her yet—'"

Wayne nodded, eyes on the smoldering fire. "Also, there's one more thing I recall. It's right at the last, when she's hearing your 'confession.'" He smiled grimly. "She said, answering her own question to you as to whether you knew you would kill Wiletta when you supposedly entered her room, 'I believe you did. I believe the idea came to you as you stood there looking out at the moonlight.' Remember that?"

"Absolutely. It was a clue, in a way, at that. Of course, if she accepted my statement that I stood in the hall outside Wiletta's door, there was no way I could look out at the moonlight. She was, naturally enough, reliving her own experience. She stood in the spare room and looked out at it, decided what she would do and entered through the bath, to kill Wiletta."

"Also," Wayne stated, "the details about Stacey's murder. The part Laure claimed she guessed."

"Exactly," Borden cut in. "She supplied me with a number of important points. I found a bruise on Stacey's temple, but assumed that she had struck a rock when she fell or was pushed in. Miss Laure told me clearly, 'You found her drunk and out of her senses. She stumbled and fell, striking her head and then you jerked her green scarf around her throat, choked her into unconsciousness and pushed her into the lake.' That, of course, was exactly the way Laure murdered Stacey. She followed her when she left her house and acted as indicated, after which she returned, went to bed and was roused by Jonny's arrival. Jonny's story was absolutely truthful. He simply mooned around and fell into the lake. Stacey's scarf caught in a buried root, kept her body floating, but Jonny missed it entirely when he swam to the boathouse landing. From a careful checking of the time, I am sure it must have been there then."

"Jonny Rohmer," Dr. Wayne said, a quick light in his tired eyes, "is making a remarkable comeback, isn't he?"

Borden nodded appreciatively. "It's marvelous to watch. I dropped in on him up in town last week. He's a different chap since he got that assistant editorial job on that sporting magazine. It isn't much of a job but oh, Lord, what it's done for him! For the first time in his life he's sure of himself. He realizes his own importance. He's confident and happy. He's not afraid or ashamed and he's writing every spare moment he can manage. He's headed somewhere, Wayne. He'll bear watching."

"Thank God!" Marcus Wayne muttered, then he added, "He and David understand each other now. They're really brothers. There'll be no more friction there."

Borden went back to the table. "You know, Wayne, we all are guilty of bromides. I'm satisfied that the reason bromides exist is because they're so damnably true. They're facts that have been demonstrated so many, many times that they have to be accepted."

"Meaning what, exactly, Borden?"

"Well, for example, that one about it's an ill wind that blows nobody good. God knows, I don't advocate mass murder as a satisfactory way of straightening out a number of problems, but whether you like it or not, consider the number that were straightened out in this case. First off, David is saved from Wiletta." He nodded definitely, his pale eyes hard. "That was a good day's work, Wayne. I won't mention poor, unhappy Stacey Madden, who, as you know, was a drug addict and lived in an eternal hell. I like Miss Laure's picture of Stacey walking toward her there in the hall, after I announced her death, head up, eyes quiet and shining, the sun all around her. We'll not go so far as to say it would be a kindness to release some people from life, but we'll agree, I think, here just between ourselves, that Stacey Madden is better off dead than alive."

Marcus Wayne nodded slowly. "Yes, knowing all I did about her, I'll heartily agree with you there. I'm old-fashioned enough to believe in another chance and I hope next time Stacey gets better breaks."

"The greatest good that comes out of the tragedy," Borden continued, dropping into his chair, "is the saving of Jonny Rohmer's reason, and the understanding that has grown up between him and David. Think what it has done to Clarke and Caroline Rohmer. It's like sunshine just to see Caroline smile when she mentions her two boys. The way Jonny was headed, in spite of all I could have done, he'd have been in an institution before the year was out. You realize that."

"Yes, and now he's healed," Wayne said. "Laure told Stacey her mission in life was arranging things for folks, helping to make them happy. That no matter what it cost her, that was her mission, that was why she was here." He lifted his head slowly. His fine dark eyes held for a moment a strange, mystic look. He said softly, "Maybe she was right, Borden. Maybe she did just that—moved on to her appointed end—straightening out tangles—making people happy."

Borden stared back at him, his thick black brows drawn in sharp thought. His own eyes were oddly startled, as they answered something in the other man's.

"That's a hell of an idea, Wayne," he muttered. "That a person was born, destined to take three lives just to make others happy. It's a hell of a notion."

"Yes," Wayne agreed, shaking himself like a man waking. "It is a hell of an idea. Let's not entertain it any longer. It might lead to dangerous conclusions."

"It might. One of us, you or I, might decide that we were destined for something like that. We might start out to set things straight, by removing someone—" His voice trailed to silence. They sat very still, looking at each other in the fire-lit silence.

"Let's drop it," Wayne said. "It's uncomfortable. After all, we know so little about each other—about anyone—"

"Yes," Borden agreed, reaching for a cigarette. "Let's just go on looking at folks on the outside. Let's not try to see too clearly what lies underneath except at such times as we can, through training and understanding, bring about a cure." Marcus Wayne did not answer except by his silence. They continued to sit there, looking at the fire, while outside the big house a cold November wind whimpered through the leafless maples and over the dark expanse of Wilromere Lake the thin sliver of an icy moon rose slowly.

THE ATTIC ROOM

Chapter One

I<small>T WAS EXACTLY</small> fifteen minutes to six on as fair an August morning as ever dawned on Alder Valley that I rounded the turn of the woods path leading over the shoulder of Alder Hill and got the biggest shock of my life.

Up to that time, of course. In the days following I received a series of jolts that made the first one seem like a light pat on the wrist, but, as Lars Knowlton says, you only appreciate things by contrast or by comparison, and at five-forty-five of that particular August morning in 1938 I had nothing of a similar nature to use as a standard of measurement.

I was always one for early rising. The way of my life had made it necessary. It has grown to be a habit, and in it I have discovered much of value.

I have witnessed many dawns in Alder Valley; seen bright stars blink out in the blackness of a winter sky, watched day break over an autumn-tinted world, the tremulous beauty of a spring morning—and before this August morning I had watched many another summer day born into the long procession of the days. But there had never been another quite like this.

I was up at half past four because, having finished my preserves the day before, I wanted my cucumber pickles ready for canning when I left the post office that afternoon. It was a real boon when Arthur Wakefield, who went to Congress nearly twenty years ago, got the post office appointment for me, and that none of his successors had seen fit to suggest a change. What it pays isn't large, but it is steady, and enough for me to live on and lay by a little.

There are those in Alder Valley who pity me for a lonely, footless woman, but their sympathy is wasted. I have lived long enough to know how to make something out of what I have, and my life is neither barren nor empty.

I have my cozy cottage at the end of Evergreen street. I am fond of my five rooms and the attic place which is my own special retreat, and where I am writing this history. Before this morning of which I write, no one save myself and Ratsy, my fine striped Thomas cat, had ever set foot in it. There are memories of others about it now, and with those memories some that are painful, much that is pleasant. With the passing months they have mellowed, yet without difficulty I can see those who came, remember the way of their coming, and how it was I took them to the attic place.

Lars Knowlton was here, his homely inspired face pale in the growing light of that autumn morning, and little Nesta Fortune with her bright squirrel eyes, her tight brown curls, and that fragrance of expensive rose perfume that always went with her.

Claribel Fortune could not leave her bed of self-imposed invalidism, and I went to her in the big sunny room at the Fortune home, and felt my heart grow sick, for I thought she would die before my eyes.

Young Shane came also, that tall, dark boy with the riotous, sooty hair, the laughing, far-visioned eyes that have haunted me since I first looked at the tiny black and white baby Claribel brought back with her from Italy twenty-four years ago.

And there was Mary Morningstar, she who was Mary Dawn for all the years she was gone from Alder Valley, traveling the world to sing before kings. For before that terrible illness that struck her on the South American tour, Mary Dawn was one of the world's great contraltos. But Mary and I have been friends from the time we wore pigtails, and, say what you will, Mary Morningstar will always be for me the most wonderful woman in the world.

A man was here also, and his presence lingers most vividly of all. A quiet man, with gray eyes that reminded me of rain against the slanting side of Alder Hill and dark hair touched with silver. When first I saw him I little thought to serve him sandwiches and coffee in my attic room, but during those days I did many things I had no thought to do, and I have never known another man like Courtney Brade.

But all this is getting far ahead of that August morning when I went early to gather herbs along the woods path over the shoulder of tall Alder Hill and came, sharp and sudden, upon the body of the man with the small gold ring in his left ear.

It was dim in the woods and very quiet, except for the rustling leaves, the almost soundless whirring of insects where a shaft of sunlight pierced the green gloom.

The man lay squarely across the path, and I all but stepped on his hairy hand with the blunted, broken nails. I might have thought him asleep, head resting on his arm, sunlight touching his dark, unshaven cheek, his thick, greasy-looking hair stirring with the passing of the dawn wind.

But for all he lay so naturally, the discarded pack marking him as one of the many peddlers who visit our countryside every summer, I knew even before I caught the reflected light in his wide-open glassy eyes, the stain of blood between his shoulders, that he was dead. And just then the bushes opposite parted and Lars Knowlton shambled out, a light rifle held awkwardly in the crook of his arm.

I've known Lars since he was knee-high to a duck, as I have known most of the younger generation in Alder Valley, having lived there all of my fifty-odd years, and never in my memory had I seen a firearm in his hands.

He looked shock-headed and unkempt as usual, and his long, homely face was white, his queer, mis-mated eyes wide and blank like he'd been looking at the sun for a long time.

I could believe that Lars would spend hours looking at the sun, for he says it is the center and origin of life, but there wasn't any sun worth speaking of yet, so I just relaxed, let my basket thump to the ground, and said in the weakest, most foolish sort of voice, "Good morning, Lars. Out early, aren't you?"

This, to Lars, who wanders all night over the hills, knows which way the streams flow, and where the wild birds build their nests. And then I said, he standing there staring at me with his odd, blank eyes, "Hunting, Lars?"

That brought him round. He shook himself like Evinrude, my ten-year-old police dog when I give him a bath, shuddered violently. I thought, "Lars! Lars would no more murder a wild thing than he would a human being!" but I couldn't take my eyes from the gun.

He said in his slow, unmusical drawl, "No, Mis' Martha, not hunting," and drew a big, finely molded hand across his eyes. "Who," he asked, motioning to the dead man, "is that?"

"I don't know, Lars. He's been shot, hasn't he?"

He separated himself from the elderberry thicket, squatted beside the man. He has a great shock of sunburned hair, one lock always boggling into his right eye. His bushy brows are sunburned too, jutting from his craggy face to form deep, shadowed caverns.

He is just a big, homely wight, seeming dull in spite of his years at college, until he looks at you out of his eyes that don't match.

Then you know that a powerful intellect dwells behind that bony exterior, that Lars Knowlton may be what most of the villagers say— crazy as a coot; or what the little man with the pointed beard named him when he looked at those ugly, nonunderstandable pictures Lars painted—a genius. He lifted his head slowly, squinting up at me.

"Murdered, Mis' Martha. Shot from behind clean as a wild goose flies."

"Yes," I said weakly. "Who is he?"

"Don't know. Saw him in town yesterday, selling things. Fake Oriental rugs, strings of beads—junk! See, here they are." He motioned to the pack, a bulky thing, fitted with leather straps for carrying. "Look, everything's scattered. It's been opened!" In the growing light I saw the ground littered with small rugs, gaudy beads, a small, inscrutable Buddha, a horrible little brute with wide, expressionless face, plump hands resting on his knees, eyes fixed in endless meditation. Only they did not seem fixed as the eyes of the

Buddha should be, being of glittery red stones that in the brightening sunlight blinked and darted with uncanny life.

The woods were stirring all around me. A fresh breeze sent the tree tops swaying, the undergrowth rustling. A blue jay screamed raucously, and a woodpecker thumped at a lusty trunk, disinterested in death. I cried suddenly: "Lars! Where's the gun?"

He jerked up, staring at me dazedly. "Gun?" he repeated stupidly.

I felt absolutely dizzy. I pride myself on the accuracy of my observation, and I knew that when Lars stepped from the elderberry tangle he had carried a rifle in the bend of his arm. It was a slim, beautiful thing with a blue steel barrel, a tiny silver plate shaped like a shamrock leaf set on the stock. I'd seen it fall from his hand when he knelt; remembered it lying there, the light on the silver leaf and now—it was gone.

The spot where it had rested was empty save for sodden brown leaves, and an invisible spider had already swung the lacy mystery of a web from the bushes' edge.

Lars saved my tottering reason by saying, "Oh, yes, the gun?" At least he admitted that he had carried a gun. "Why, I don't know where it is—guess I dropped it."

"Yes, you dropped it," I said shrilly, "right there beside you and it's—it's gone."

Lars rose with surprising swiftness, his eyes, suddenly sharp and powerful, flashing to the spot I indicated, then without sound he slipped into the bushes and I was once more alone in the clearing except for the dead man with a small gold ring in his left ear. The stillness throbbed round me, and my heart was a painful thing in my side. I wished I was somewhere else, that I'd let Evinrude come; if Evinrude had been here no one could have crept up behind the screen of bushes and sneaked that gun out of sight.

"Well," I argued angrily with myself, "someone *did* do that, didn't they? Guns don't just dissolve into thin air." And then, over to my left, along the path that twisted round the hill, came a lusty whistle, a lilting Irish air that shifted into song, a clear strong baritone singing "Oh, for the sound of the Kerry dancers." The next moment the singer came into view around the turn, a tall man in baggy tweeds tucked into well-worn, laced boots, flannel shirt open at the throat, battered felt hat jerked over one eye, a rifle crooked most professionally in the bend of his right arm.

I just stood there looking at him, he not seeing me yet; his head lifted, eager eyes roaming the sun-lighted tree tops. I thought, "He's not hunting, too much noise. He stole that rifle—no, if he had he wouldn't come marching back."

He stopped suddenly across the clearing, something hypnotic in his pose. It was as if everything about him that could cause motion had been magically arrested, and his eyes, I somehow knew, were focused with a terrific intensity on the dead man.

Then his head lifted and from under the tilted hat brim he looked at me. The upper part of his face was shadowed, so I only saw the jut of his nose, the sharp, clean line of his chin, the quirk of his wide, whimsical mouth beneath a close-cropped dark mustache.

He said, "Who are you, please?"

I said, "Martha Berry, postmistress in Alder Valley. I was going herb gathering and found this man." I paused, realizing the quiet quality of his voice, wondering why I had so naturally answered him.

He continued to look at me and in that long, comprehensive regard I felt that he gathered everything possible to learn from visual contemplation. My light print dress, dew-drenched to the knees, my straw hat gone, my black hair so thickly threaded with gray these last years, loosed from the heavy knot in my neck.

He set the rifle against a tree and I saw at once that it was not the one Lars had carried. He bent swiftly, laid a finger to one side of the bloody spot on the coat, touched the dead man's arm. "Dead about eight hours," he muttered, and I decided he was a doctor. "Shot," he said again, entirely to himself. "Fairly close range, pack rummaged." He flicked aside crumpled fabrics, rattled cheap beads, paused, considering the hideous little Buddha, then his eyes ranged over the damp ground on either side of the path. He straightened.

"Let me see your shoes," he ordered, and dumbly I lifted my right foot, displaying my stout, uninteresting oxford.

In that moment I hated flat-heeled shoes and wished I had been the kind of woman who belonged in delicate, stream-lined, high-heeled things, the kind Mary Morningstar wore and that made her look light and poised, ready for flight. No one in Alder Valley wore shoes like Mary's, ordering them as she did from a firm of importers in New York.

He said, "Thanks. Now who in the neighborhood wears shoes with heels like that?"

He pointed and, as though strong chains drew me, I walked round the dead man, followed the line of that long, brown finger and saw in the rich mold the print of Mary Morningstar's beautiful heels! The inner line, curving to a shallow half-moon, gave the heel the outline of a shield.

I pride myself on my control. I didn't know who this remarkable person was, strolling out of the woods to the tune of "Kerry Dancers" and taking charge of everything, but I did know that no mortal man was going to make me say aught to injure Mary Morningstar.

I was very still bending there, hands clenched against my knees. Hot blood stained my cheeks, my throat ached, everything went dim and I knew that something terrible was going to happen, something much worse than just finding a dead peddler on the hill path of an August morning.

He laughed and I straightened sharply. It was such a delightful, friendly sound. I turned, looking into his eyes, and that was the time I remembered autumn rain across Alder Hill, saw that his hair was tinged with gray at the temples, and that he was older than I had thought.

He said, pleasant lines crinkling his eyes, "Okay, Martha Berry, unclench your loyal hands and keep the name of your friend to yourself. It won't be too difficult to find who favors such foreign heels."

He turned quickly, I with him, and saw Lars Knowlton by the elderberry thicket, a wet leaf tangled in his sunburned hair. Lars said, "Spooks, Mis' Martha. Someone sure sneaked the gun—" He saw the stranger and stopped, prominent Adam's apple flopping frantically.

The brown man said in that casual, friendly way, "Now who would have sneaked the gun? And where did you lay it, young man, that it could be taken?"

"Dunno who took it," Lars said, that way you think him dim-witted, "but I laid it right there when I came on Mis' Martha, and ten minutes later it was gone."

"What were you and Mis' Martha doing those ten minutes?"

"Looking at this citizen, deciding who he was."

"And who is he?"

"Don't know his name. He's a peddler. Saw him in town yester-day."

"And during this time your gun was taken without your seeing or hearing anyone?" the stranger asked.

"The wind that comes after dawn was blowing," Lars stated sleepily, "and we were entirely concentrated on the dead man. It wasn't my gun," he added as an afterthought, and the man in tweeds glanced up quickly.

"No? Could you describe it?"

"A rifle. Can't tell you the make because I don't know anything about firearms. It was light, and nice to look at."

The stranger nodded, glancing at the small puncture in the back of the peddler's light coat. "If it wasn't your gun," he questioned softly, "whose gun was it?"

"I wouldn't know," Lars drawled, and for a moment his sleepy eyes opened wide and I saw the brown man's head jerk forward in surprise. Then he took out a case and, without moving his eyes from Lars' face, lighted a smoke.

"Where'd you get the gun?"

"Found it, back in the woods, at the foot of Tan Top Rock where someone fell last night running in the dark."

The man grunted softly, and his gray eyes widened slightly.

"Interesting. Would you care to tell me how you deduce all this?"

"I don't deduce it," Lars said. "In order to make a deduction, it is necessary to have for consideration, an unknown quantity from which to draw certain more or less logical conclusions. In this case, everything was known to me by the simple process of ordinary observation. Vegetation was destroyed by the passage of hurrying feet. Indentations made by large, flat heels in the soft mud when the man walked rapidly changed to circular impressions that could only be formed by the toes of the same shoes when he broke into a run.

"It was night because the sun would soon draw moisture from the impressions. It was dark because last night was moonless, and no man with any sort of light, or any real knowledge of the woods, would head a straight course for Tan Top and come so near crashing to death on the road below. I *deduce*," he smiled slightly, "that when he fell he lost the gun and was too dazed or frightened to stop and find it."

Well, now I ask you! There was the Lars I knew. That same Lars the villagers called "crazy as a coot," who painted those weird pictures and was named genius by a great art critic, who played divinely on a cheap old fiddle, roamed the woods at night, and knew things about the stars. Lars, who went away when he was eighteen and somehow, in spite of poverty and aloneness, worked his way through four brilliant college years.

The man in brown tweed sighed and seemed to come back from far away. "Keen observation, young man. I stand corrected on my use of the word 'deduction.' Now what did you find on the trail of whoever stole the gun?"

"Tracks of tennis sneakers leading to the clearing the other side of the hill where they were lost on the rocks."

"Tennis sneakers? Obviously a different man from he who ran last night."

"No," Lars corrected him patiently. "Obviously the *same* man—from length of stride, similarity of weight, gauged by depths of impression making allowance for the difference in a headlong run and a very careful walk. Undoubtedly the same man. He just changed shoes."

"Yes," the stranger agreed softly. "Of course. He merely—changed shoes. That is simple."

"Entirely," Lars agreed, and seated himself comfortably on a stump.

The brown man leaned against a tree, hat tipped low over his eyes, let smoke drift through his nostrils and stared unseeingly into the green depths of the woods. He asked suddenly, "What's your name, young man?"

Lars told him, and after a little silence, asked, "And yours, sir?"

"Eh? What?" He frowned at Lars, then grinned. "I'm Brade. Courtney Brade. Out from the city, bit of vacation. Staying at the Chesterworth place beyond the hill."

His name didn't mean anything to me, but Lars said, "Not much of a vacation, Captain, stumbling on a mystery like this."

"So you know me, eh?"

"Yes. Followed all your cases I could locate."

"Flattering," Brade said, not looking exactly displeased, and added quickly, "Out here I'm just an ordinary citizen, Knowlton, and my only duty is to report the matter. After that, it's up to the sheriff."

Lars grunted. "Anse Grubber's sheriff, and picking up speeders on Bonnyville Pike's about his limit," and then we all turned as heavy steps crunched along the path coming up from town. I looked up to see Bennet Calder swing into view around the turn.

I have seldom been so glad to see anyone. Bennet Calder is an institution in Alder Valley, lawyer and adviser to all the families important enough to need advice. He had charge of the Fortune money while old Amos lived, they being close friends, though Calder was much younger than the fine, grim old man pretty Claribel Wyndham had married close to thirty years before.

After Claribel returned from Italy, bringing her husband's body for interment in the Alder Valley cemetery, and his six months' old son, born after his death, she had just up and taken affairs away from Calder. Not such a good idea to my way of thinking, for Claribel was a flighty, scared little thing and she'd managed to get rid of that substantial fortune, though no one knew exactly how she'd done it. It was plain that there'd be little enough for Shane and his bride.

Things like that went through my head as Bennet Calder stalked up the path, his handsome, ruddy face flushed a deeper red from the climb, the fringed white hair under his panama hat blowing in the breeze.

"Oh, Mr. Calder," I cried, and he stopped suddenly, steadying himself on his ebony cane, blinking into the shadows.

"Mis' Martha! You startled me! What are you—?" his voice trailed away as he saw first Lars on his stump, then Courtney Brade leaning against the tree. Then his glance lowered and he saw the man with the gold ring in his ear. His blue eyes popped wide and his white imperial wobbled until I thought it would fall off.

"Why—why—what's this? What's happened?" His eyes went helplessly from one face to the other. "An accident? This man, he—he appears to be—"

"He's dead," I said flatly. "I found him, then Lars came, and this is Captain Brade, Mr. Calder." I hated the way my voice sounded, so thin and shrill in the sunlit silence. My knees were like water, and I actually wanted to cry, a woman of my age! And all because Bennet Calder had unexpectedly happened in when my nerves were stretched tighter than I knew.

He removed his hat, mopped his moist pink face, said, "Captain Brade?" with a curious upper inflection as if he expected Brade to immediately state his business and background.

Brade nodded. "Glad to meet you, Mr. Calder. Spot of mystery here. The man's been murdered!"

"Oh, my God!" Mr. Calder said in a deep, dismayed voice, hand trembling as he set his hat over his white, abundant hair. "Murdered?" he repeated. "Oh, come now—"

He stepped closer, balancing his rimless glasses in place, peering curiously, lips sucking in and out with his uneven breathing.

"As I live!" he muttered. "So he has! A man can't shoot himself in the back."

"Correct," Brade said. "Know him?" He grasped the stiffening shoulder, pulling the body back so the face was fully exposed. That was the first real view I had had of the dead man.

He looked about forty-five, handsome in a coarse, swarthy sort of way, with wide, black eyes, full, reddish lips, big, strong nose. An evil face, evil in some way I could not define, as though the man had known every sort of unpleasantness, tasted all that was bad and destructive.

"Know him?" Mr. Calder gasped. "Heavens, no! Never saw him—though, wait, he might be the fellow who was in town yesterday, peddling trinkets. I didn't see him, but Nesta, young Mrs. Fortune, mentioned him to me."

"Look out!" Lars shouted, and swooped forward, pushing Mr. Calder aside, lifting something from the damp ground where the body had rested.

Brade eased his unlovely burden to the ground. "What is it?" he asked, and held out a palm.

Lars hunched there, fingers tight locked, face white as flour in the green gloom. His eyes had a dazed look, as if he had received a tremendous shock. I thought he would refuse to give Brade what he held, but slowly he straightened and extended his hand, showing a small round object that glinted metallically in the shifting light. I had only a glimpse of it as Brade took it. It might have been a button or a little pin.

Brade turned it slowly. "Hm! Right under the body."

"Under the hand," Lars corrected. "He must have held it in his hand when he was shot."

"What is it?" Mr. Calder demanded irritably.

"Well, what is it?" Brade asked and gave it to him.

Again silence while Mr. Calder examined it. I thought, "Well, *what* is it? Why doesn't someone decide?"

Mr. Calder said sharply, "You might know, Mis' Martha," and his hand trembled as he passed it to me. "What is it?" he asked, and shivered visibly in the hot August morning.

But I was as bad as the others. It was such a confusing thing, slightly smaller than a dime, of a dull, rich looking metal engraved with a beautiful 'G' in old English script. I turned it over. A tiny fragment of leather clung to the mechanism of the back.

I said, "A snap! A clasp off—a—"

"Glove?" Mr. Calder said breathlessly, and sopped at his wet face. "The fastener off a leather glove!"

"I'm not so sure," I told him, angry because his eager interruption had destroyed my impression.

Brade took it, turning it slowly in long, brown fingers. "Large for a glove, don't you think, Mis' Martha?"

I couldn't tell. I was terribly confused and still angry because I knew I should be able to place it. I looked at Lars. He stood back in the shadow of the elderberry thicket again, and he might have been a tree trunk for any movement. I thought suddenly, "Lars knows! Lars recognizes it!" Then I met his dazed, uncomprehending eyes and decided, "He's not sure. It's shocked him. He hasn't tied it up."

Brade said, "Jerked from its moorings. Stout brown leather." He fingered it carefully, not looking at it. "Too heavy for a glove—whale of a yank to get it loose." He glanced at Lars. "How about it, Knowlton? Ever see it before?"

Lars started, mopped at his face. "No," he said harshly. "Haven't the faintest notion what it could be."

Brade smiled without much mirth. I thought he felt as I did that there was too much vehemence in Lars' denial. Yet I could not believe that Lars actually recognized it. It seemed rather that it suggested something to him, something startling which he could not entirely connect with facts in his possession.

Mr. Calder spoke, voice thin and fibrous. "Let me see it again, Captain Brade." He bent over it, breathing heavily, considering it with his thick, soft fingers, returned it. "Still think it's off a glove," he muttered unsteadily.

"Maybe," Brade agreed, slipping it into a pocket. "Heavy type of glove for an August night." Then he said abruptly, "Let it rest. We'll hit the connecting link. Knowlton will remember," the faintest smile quirked his lips, "just where he's seen it."

Lars opened his lips, shut them stubbornly, slumped down on the tree trunk.

"You were saying, Mr. Calder," Brade suggested, "that this man was mentioned to you by—"

"Nesta Fortune," Mr. Calder replied eagerly. "She mentioned a peddler."

"Yes, he is a peddler," I said. "There's his pack. It's been robbed."

Mr. Calder peered across at the rumpled canvas pack. "So it has. Robbery is doubtless the motive."

"Certainly nothing much has been taken from the pack," Brade pointed out reasonably. "I doubt if it could hold anything more than what lies beside it."

"Money? Did the fellow carry money? Have you investigated?"

"No," Brade admitted. "We were going to call the sheriff before—"

"Am I mistaken," Mr. Calder asked, "or is this Captain Brade of—?"

"Yes," Brade snapped. "I'm from Headquarters. Nothing official in my position here, however."

Mr. Calder smiled. "But surely, Captain Brade, you won't refuse your services. Our law officers are quite unprepared to deal with this. I would consider it a personal favor," he bowed slightly. "I hold something of a position of public trust and I know I'm speaking for my fellow citizens—"

"Sorry," Brade interrupted curtly, "the local boys will have to do the job. I'm on vacation, damn it!" Then abruptly he smiled. "Don't want to be unpleasant, but I get a craw-full of murder in line of duty. However, it's only the smart thing to do—" He dropped to a knee and in the swiftest, most efficient way, did what I believe is called fanning the man's pockets.

I watched in complete fascination. He didn't seem like the same man who had come out of the woods singing "Kerry Dancers" a while back. A policeman! A detective! No wonder I'd answered his clipped, incisive questions so readily. I noticed then that there were lines in his face, his mouth was grim; that his strange gray eyes could remind me of the barrel of that mystery gun that had been stolen from under my nose.

"Well, here's the line-up," he stated, motioning to the motley collection; bits of string, newspaper clippings, stray coins, a dirty envelope, a shabby bill fold. "Eighteen cents in cash," he commented. "Robber, maybe." He opened the wallet. Bills spewed out and spilled on the ground, one atop the other like soiled, green-gray snow—fifties, half a dozen twenties. "I conclude," Brade said dryly, "that robbery was not the motive."

"Unless," Lars suggested, "the murderer was shooed off before he could collect. He was bad scared, you know. All but broke his neck at the Tan Top; dropped his gun and all."

"What's that?" Mr. Calder demanded. "What're you saying, Knowlton?"

There was no love lost between them. Mr. Calder thought Lars a good-for-nothing lout; Lars considered Mr. Calder a sanctimonious old hypocrite. From the sullen glare in Lars' eyes I thought it best to relate that part of the story, and Mr. Calder listened carefully, nodding in approval.

"Excellent deduction, Knowlton," he admitted grudgingly, and Lars said angrily:

"No deduction about it. Just simple observation."

"Exactly three hundred and fifty dollars," Brade interrupted, and closed the fold over the replaced bills. "Mr. Calder, take charge of this, please."

Mr. Calder started to protest, reconsidered, accepted the fold, penciled a brief receipt and the captain thanked him with a nod.

"Now the letter," Brade said, studying the envelope. "Foreign post mark, badly worn. He must have carried it—why, the thing's over a year old! It come from," he bent nearer the light, "Bariloche, Republica Argentina." He hunched against the tree, eyes half closed. "Bariloche," he repeated softly, "Bariloche."

"What's it say?" Mr. Calder interrupted, but Brade just sat there motionless, eyes blank with concentration.

"That's it," he announced suddenly. "Bariloche, South American prison, Black River district—" he glanced at the dead man. "You might have been there, my lad," he muttered, then fell to studying the address. "Pietro Donelli, care of somebody or other, Italian name, can't make it out, New York City address. Yes, you could be Pietro Donelli," he said again, and it made me shiver that way he had of talking to that sodden thing, then he drew out a frayed sheet of paper.

"Why would he keep it all this time?" he asked of no one in particular and spread it out to read aloud:

> Pietro: I do not warn again. For what you have stolen from me, for the confidence you have once betrayed, I shall exact death. You cannot travel far enough, hide close enough to the earth you desecrate, to escape. There is only one chance. Silence, eternal and complete, would earn for you your worthless life, but I know you well enough to realize that you are unable to resist the golden lure, so this is to say goodbye to one I was so blind as to call in an hour of black despair my friend. Death will find you many thousand miles from where I write, for always I hold in my mind, in my lifetime of darkness, the thought of death for you.
>
> Angelo Marquand.

An amazing letter! Utterly fantastic! Only Brade's quiet, emotionless voice gave it any reality. Mr. Calder held out a hand. Brade gave him the letter. He blinked at it, then said indignantly, "Why it's written in Italian!"

Brade's eyes crinkled faintly. "It would be, naturally. Donelli and his one-time friend, Marquand, were Italians I take it, though Marquand smacks of French."

Mr. Calder looked at him with new respect, returned the letter.

"It's preposterous," he complained. "Men just don't write letters like that."

"Not the men we know," Brade pointed out. "You must make allowance for the dramatic Latin temperament." He stared thoughtfully at the dead man. "This, I conclude, is one Pietro Donelli, who at some time did a death-deserving injury to one Angelo Marquand, for which Marquand promised, a year ago, that he should die 'many thousand miles' from Bariloche, Republic of Argentine, where it is entirely possible that Marquand is serving a life sentence. He speaks of his 'lifetime of darkness,' promises to hold in mind the thought of death for Pietro, thinking about it being perhaps about all he can do." He shrugged. "Well, it certainly worked, for last night Pietro Donelli came to his death most definitely."

"What's that?" Lars demanded, and pointed to a folded paper beside the dead man. It must have fallen from the wallet, for otherwise we would have noticed it before.

Brade picked it up, a soiled newspaper clipping, studied it in silence then slowly looked up. "Is there not," he inquired, "a young man in this community named Shane Fortune?"

My heart flopped. Claribel's handsome, restless boy—

"Recently married to a Miss Nesta Cramer?" Brade continued and extended the clipping. "Here are their pictures. A handsome pair. I wonder why Pietro Donelli cut it, along with the announcement of their marriage, from a newspaper of June 25th, this year?"

Well, that was something! Mr. Calder glanced at the paper, lips compressing into a worried line, passed it on to me. I didn't want to look at it. If it really was the picture of Shane and Nesta Fortune this ugly business was no longer a general problem, but at once definite and personal to all of us in Alder Valley. That picture formed the link. There had to be some reason why Pietro Donelli, from far away Argentine in South America, should cut it out and carry it in his pocket, some reason why he was lying there in the sun-flickered shadows of the hill path with a small, dark puncture between his shoulders.

My eyes blurred as I looked at the young, eager face of Shane Fortune. A handsome boy if ever one lived, with more than masculine beauty in his dark, vital face, more than just the fire of youth in those splendid, stormy eyes.

The present faded, voices grew faint, years went with them, and I stood again one spring morning in the big sunny bedroom where Claribel Fortune, two years the wife of Amos, and ill almost from the hour of her marriage, sat up in her wide bed.

"Oh, Martha, Amos is going to take me to Europe! The doctor thinks a sea trip might help. Think, Martha! Europe! France—Italy!"

They went for six months, stayed nearly two years, and Amos never again looked on the little leafy town he loved. For he returned in an expensive steel casket and was laid in the old, fir-shaded cemetery in the shadow of the great Fortune shaft, and to fill his place, Claribel, more fragile and intensely frightened than ever, offered us a small, black and white boy, a brief six months old.

That boy's face, strong with youth, ravaged with some inner unrest, defiant, strangely lonely, looked back at me now from the cheap newsprint found in the pocket of a murdered man on the hill road. Beside him was his bride, she who was Nesta Cramer and who a blind man, deaf in both ears and stricken dumb from birth, would know was never meant for him.

From a long way off, Calder's voice reached me. "I cannot offer any explanation, Captain Brade. Nesta, the younger Mrs. Fortune, mentioned having seen a peddler, said she hoped he came round; she wanted to buy one of the Buddhas she'd heard he was selling."

"Maybe this was the one she wanted to buy," Brade suggested, and lifted the hateful little red-eyed god.

I couldn't stay any longer. It was insufferably hot, and flies buzzing lazily along a ray of slanting sunlight set my head to throbbing with their racket. I wasn't interested in dead peddlers, policemen from the city, or crazy letters from South America. I was just plain Martha Berry, widow of Mat Berry, who'd been dead these twenty years; postmistress at Alder Valley with my job to be attended to. At that moment Courtney Brade said, without seeming to look at me, "You must be tired, Mis' Martha. Why don't you run along and look after the morning mail? I'll drop in to see you later, if I may." He glanced up at me then from where he squatted on the ground, and I thought I'd never seen kinder, more understanding eyes.

"I'll go," I said weakly. "Here's the picture."

He rose, took it from me. "Thank you, and you wouldn't have any idea why Pietro Donelli would be carrying this picture, Mis' Martha?"

It was very hard to lie to Courtney Brade. You could figure out a splendid story when he wasn't there, but when he stood opposite and just looked at you, well, all at once you knew that nothing really mattered except what was true.

Not that I had to lie about the picture. I didn't have any notion. Not really. All I had was a tumbled confusion of misty scenes and uncertain impressions, memory of voices I had heard down the years:

Claribel laughing; Claribel crying and saying, "Martha, if anything should happen to Shane; if anything took him from me, I'd die."

Mary Morningstar, standing beside my tea rose in the garden, poised in that way that makes her seem ready to fly, saying,

"Wherever did Claribel Fortune get that beautiful, dark boy, Martha? Claribel, with a son like Shane!" And her low laughter had made it seem not only ridiculous, but utterly impossible, that Claribel should really have Shane for her son.

I remembered things like that. Many things—little, unimportant, worthy only to be forgotten—and here I stood on the woods path looking at a man who asked a simple question, and what could I tell him?

I said, "I'm sorry, Captain Brade, I haven't any notion why he, that man, should have been carrying this picture."

He didn't believe me fully; but then, he knew so much about people, how their minds and emotions work, that he was never surprised when they tried to deceive him. He just nodded. "Thank you, Mis' Martha. Now run along. I'll be seeing you later."

CHAPTER TWO

IT WAS QUARTER PAST eight when I turned into Evergreen Street from Bailey's pasture, which you have to skirt to get to the hill path. It was warm but the backbone of the summer heat was broken, and through the brilliant sunlight was already a tinge of autumn.

Evergreen is the main residence street of Alder Valley, long and wide, and lined with many tall, sharp-pointed, green-black firs. Behind the worn, uneven, old stone walk are most of the fine, important homes.

They are old, too, very large, with sometimes three stories of great rooms and winding halls. People thought large thoughts when they built their first houses in Alder Valley, and they all had, or expected to have, large families and many friends.

I walked fast, wanting to get to the post office and look after things, although I knew Linda Barstow, my assistant, would have taken care of the mail. And then, just as I got opposite Claribel's house, there was Nesta Fortune, all frothy and bright in a gay print dress, fussing over the late roses behind the fence. I had never liked Nesta Cramer. If I had allowed myself I could have hated her, but, as Lars pointed out, hate is a corroding emotion and hurts no one so much as he who indulges in it. Lars does say the queerest things.

Nesta looked up, bright eyes dancing at me over the top of the white pickets. "Good morning, Mis' Martha," she chattered, sounding exactly like a sharp-toothed brown squirrel when you walk under his bough.

"Good morning, Nesta," I said, and made to walk right on, but she leaned on the fence, crooking smooth, brown arms around the pickets.

Her brown hair laid around her small, pointed face in neat artificial curls, and her slim brows arched above her bright, yellow-brown eyes, which moved continually when she talked. She had a small, very red mouth; her teeth were as white as popcorn, pro-truding just a tiny bit in front—not enough to disfigure her pretti-ness, but surely enough to remind me of a squirrel.

Nesta was like a squirrel when it came to hoarding things, too. I always imagined she had a secret place where she stored what-ever she could get her bright-tipped fingers on, packing them tight and hard within its dark interior, never, never to release them. This was the girl that Shane Fortune, with his faraway eyes and lonely hands, had married.

She said, "You're late this morning, Mis' Martha."

As if it was any of her business! "I went herb gathering," I snapped, and she looked at my empty basket and laughed.

"Not much luck," she mocked, then, "Wherever is Mary Morningstar?"

That halted me. "Why, I don't know. Where should she be? Home, I suppose."

Nesta shook her tightly curled head. "Should be, but isn't. What's more, she's been out all night." She swung backward, hang-ing onto the pickets, laughing. "Think of it! Mary Morningstar! Our famous diva!"

"Nesta!" I snapped, longing to slap her. "It's scarcely proper for a girl like you to even suggest anything unkind about a woman like Mary Morningstar. Why, you aren't even—"

I checked myself, startled at what I'd meant to say. She stopped swinging, and in the shifting light and shadow of the lace vine her face was thin and cruel. Her red lips tightened and drew back from her popcorn teeth.

"Not fit to buckle those Parisian pumps of hers," she said softly. "That's what you mean, isn't it? Okay, darling. She may be tops to you, but to me she's just a worn-out, third-rate yodeler. And, if you want to know, someone was here looking for her yesterday and she wasn't here like she'd told Daisy she would be; and last night Shane and I strolled over and she still wasn't there; and this morning early I dropped by to take her some posies, and she hadn't been there all night because I looked into her bedroom, and—"

"You're a hateful little snoop, Nesta," I cried, too angry to speak clearly. "What business is it of yours if someone did come looking—" I couldn't go on. Something cold settled round my heart, so I was sick and dizzy in all that summer brightness.

Nesta picked up her scissors and began brutally snipping the rose stems. "It isn't any of my business, Martha Berry, only if you see her, tell her that a queer, dark man with a gold ring in his ear wanted to see her."

"Nesta," a man's voice called, and Shane came down the winding, aster-bordered path. He and Nesta had been living with Claribel since their return.

It was good to see him, tall and fine, his dark head high, shirt open at the throat, showing his strong, tanned neck. He always moved as if he were on springs. When he was a youngster I used to say he had wings on his heels. He saw us and waved in greeting.

"Mis' Martha!" He reached across the fence and I gave him my cold, trembling hand. He squeezed it hard. Shane and I were old friends. I thought he didn't look as happy as a bridegroom of three months should. His face was thin, and there was even a greater restlessness in his eyes. He said, "Run up and see Claribel, honey. She's in a bad way."

Well, Claribel was always in a bad way, poor dear. Old Doc' Wentworth, dead these many years, once told me that she was scared to death before she was born and had never outgrown it. He was about right at that. I have never known a person who lived in such a constant and unending state of total terror as poor Claribel Fortune.

I said, "What's the matter with her, Shane? I mean, in particular?"

I had my own special theory about what ailed Shane's mother, a most unchristian way to regard her aches and pains and that tricky heart that kept everyone around her in a state of nerves and unending attention.

His face settled into tired lines. "Oh, something upset her last night. Don't know what it was. Once she's upset she can't talk about it. Doc' Sloan was here twice. This morning she can scarcely lift her hand." His eyes met mine in hopeless pleading. "Go and see her, Martha," he begged, and I nodded and passed through the gate he held open for me.

I talked to Bessie in the lower hall. Bessie has been with Claribel since she was a bride, and that's a time ago. She's a loyal soul, placid and strong as a horse. She wears her hair, grown gray now, in a little bun at the back of her neck, drinks tansy tea in the spring, and believes in infant damnation. But she is a peach where Claribel is concerned.

She said, "I don't know what struck her, Mis' Martha. She was real good yesterday. I ran over to get a quilt pattern from Mis' Douglas 'bout four, and she was down stairs in the sittin' room, readin'. When I come back she was in bed, takin on somethin' terrible. Said she'd rather die than live, tellin' over and over how she never had any-thing anyway, and what she had would be took from her."

"All right, Bessie," I said, recognizing Claribel's regular act. "I'll run up. She's not asleep?"

"No'm. She just lies there, that little and frail, starin' off at nothin'. She's only alive when Mr. Shane is with her, poor soul. He stayed with her most of the night."

I was halfway up the stairs, stamping hard I fear. I thought that Claribel just actually developed her shakes and vapors to keep that fine, dark boy beside her, and if that's a cruel thing to say may I be forgiven as likely don't deserve it.

I never saw exactly why she was so anxious for him to marry Nesta except that Nesta and Claribel were pretty good friends, and maybe she thought if he married a home-town girl he'd stay right on in Alder Valley instead of getting out and being what he was intended to be from the beginning.

I didn't bother to rap. I'd walked into that room too many times in the last twenty-six years to bother about formalities. She was lying flat as pancake batter on her wide, fragrant bed, and did not open her eyes, but said in a ghost of a voice, "Shane, darling—"

"It's not Shane," I snapped, and she reared up, eyes enormous in her porcelain face, then collapsed with tears draggling from under her lids that seemed so thin the blue of her eyes showed through.

I stopped at the foot of the bed and sudden fear came on me. I knew in that moment how sinful it is to judge another, thinking of all the unkind things I'd told myself about Claribel Fortune: how she'd only married old Amos for his money, then got sick because she didn't want to be a wife to him; dragged him to Europe to satisfy her whims, it being the death of him; of how many times I'd accused her of pretending to have heart attacks so Shane wouldn't leave her.

I said, "Claribel, you're ill! Let me call Doc' Sloan," and panic thickened my voice for I truly thought Claribel would die before my eyes.

One hand lifted, she motioned me beside her. I sat on the edge of the chair. The bed smelled sweet, the room smelled sweet. Claribel smelled of lavender. The skin of her throat was like paper, covering thin ropes of throbbing veins. Her hair spread over the snowy pillow like a misting of golden rain, and I said, tears heavy in my eyes, "Claribel, what's happened? What is it, Claribel? Tell me, tell Martha," and took her hot little hand, so dry it seemed to rustle in my hold. Her fingers curled round mine like tendrils of a vine you try to tear from the wall, and I thought then that if Shane should go away and have a life of his own it would be like tearing Claribel from the tall, strong wall she had grown fast to. Without Shane she would surely die.

She said, "Mary! Where is Mary Morningstar?"

"I'll find her, Claribel. You're not to worry. I'll find Mary for you."

Her fingers loosed. Her lids lifted. "Tell her to come," she whispered. "I must see her soon."

I pressed her hand, laid it on the blue silk quilt and started a cautious backing, tiptoeing in that sunny room filled with the sweetness of the drowsing garden, the liquid song of a wild canary in the branches of the tall old cottonwood.

She said, "Martha!" and I stopped as if she had shouted. Her eyes opened, she lifted to an elbow, resting her cheek on her hand. "Martha," she whispered, "have you heard—Is there any news— Has anyone found—?" The frail voice trickled to silence, she just lay there resting on her hand, looking at me.

I cannot say what happened to me in that moment. It was like something outside of and beyond myself spoke with my voice, for I said very quietly, "Yes, Claribel, they found the dead man on the woods path. He is only a no 'count peddler, and no one will worry much about what happened to him." Then I was out of the room, stumbling down the stairs into the shadowed front hall, seeing, through the open door, old Henry plodding along behind his lawn mower, and Mrs. Fisher across the street, airing her woolen blankets against the winter.

Only I really didn't see anything except Claribel's face, suddenly broken and twisted with such tremendous relief that it was like a handkerchief wrung out of water, tears pouring down her cheeks as she slipped back and lay quiet on her wide, fragrant bed.

I stood there hanging onto the newel post, thinking that I must go right away and find Mary, knowing that I was waiting until Shane and Nesta wandered on to another part of the yard as I could not meet them just then.

To my right yawned the great front parlor, so cool and restful looking that I went in and stood before the wide, clean fireplace where a clump of sweet wild grasses stirred gently in the breeze from the open window.

That was a grand place to be on a stormy winter night, and I remembered well old Amos Fortune in his high-backed chair, a fine old man who lived well each day that came and trusted in some power higher than himself for the unknown future.

He was not at all like his younger brother, Ezra, who, so many years ago, had started out in the world to conquer it to his own liking. He never came back, but it was said he had made a pile of money in mining out in Arizona and lived fine and high, not trust-ing to any power but himself. Ezra was gone now, same as Amos, and no one knew what he had done with his money, or cared, I guess, unless it might be Claribel, who had somehow wasted what Amos left, and maybe would have liked a share of what Ezra had made.

I looked at the portrait of Amos over the mantel, and his deep-set, quiet eyes gave me a steadying look. Then my glance lowered and rested on something just below the edge of the somber dark frame. I looked at it a long time before realizing what it was. The light was dim and I did not see too clearly that morning, but when I picked it up, turned it slowly, set it down again, there was no doubt about its identity.

It was the exact duplicate of the hideous little red-eyed Bud-dha I had seen lying on his back, glittering up at the morning sun-light, beside the woods path on Alder Hill.

Chapter Three

I didn't see a soul on my way to Mary's house, which was the abandoned old Shields place until she came back five years ago, bought it and made it her home.

There is a high trimmed hedge around it now, and over the top you see the brown gables of Journey's End. I wondered sometimes why Mary chose that pretty, fanciful name; wondered if, after all her years of brilliant, crowded life, Mary Morningstar could call this old brown house in its sun-checkered garden the end of the journey and be content.

Sandra, the Russian wolf hound, lifted her long, triangular head and growled, then rose with joy that was tempered with the dignity she never loses and loped down to meet me.

Mary belongs with a wolf hound beside her, as she belongs always on slim, high heels, standing on a hilltop somewhere, head lifted, looking at far white clouds. I cannot understand why at least one of the many artists who have painted her portrait failed to catch that quality about her. If I had been an artist that is how I should have pictured her, but then I'm not an artist. I'm just plain Martha Berry, postmistress of Alder Valley, and many folks would say I'd best keep my mind on more practical things.

I patted Sandra's handsome head, opened the screen door and stepped into the hall. It was like stepping into another world, a place compounded of mystery and beauty and the essence of all the things each of us has longed to know and experience all our lives.

I can't explain why it is that way. It is so simple, and though Mary's furnishings are different from those of the other houses in Alder Valley, you can't lay it to that. You never think about that marble head in the corner being something rare that belongs in a museum in Italy, or that old, dim painting occupying a place of honor in some famous French gallery. You don't really notice the Oriental rugs thrown carelessly on the nice dull floors, or the curtains at the windows in the long, low living room that are of such queer, coarse stuff with odd crescents and stars and pyramids appliqued on them in gorgeous colors.

Mary's house is like that all over, beautiful, distinctive and satisfying. Mary is like that too, and just then I heard her low laugh behind the closed door of the living room, remembered why I had come and was so glad she was there I cried in sudden frenzy:

"Mary! Mary! Mary Morningstar!"

The laugh was checked so the house seemed very silent, then I heard her heels tapping the floor and she opened the door, light streaming into the hall from the French doors giving on her eastern terrace. She stood there with the sun behind her throwing her hair into gold-brown radiance, and the shadows on her fine, thin face made her seem like something carved out of marble, only rich and beautifully pliant.

She said, with that upward lilt to her unforgettable voice, "Martha! My dear! Will you come—?"

"It's Claribel," I said breathlessly. "She's calling for you. She's terribly ill. It's that man, that horrible man with the gold ring in his ear who was looking for you, and was murdered—"

My throat closed as if a hand had suddenly clutched it. I stood there stupidly while the color drained from Mary's face and the life went with it, so she was just then old and ruined. Without a word she slipped quietly to the floor and lay as one dead.

A voice said from just beyond her, "Don't be alarmed. She's only fainted, Mis' Martha," and there was Courtney Brade crossing to bend beside her.

He lifted her easily, laid her on the low, pillow-strewn divan, under high windows where the English ivy made a dark, delicious shade, and she looked small lying there, though I had always thought of Mary as tall and strong and intensely alive.

It was the first time I'd ever seen her with her eyes closed and it's strange what happens to the face when the eyes are out. It's featureless somehow—like when I walk into my comfortable sitting room in a winter dusk. I recognize the chairs, the sofa, the center table, the rug, but they are only shadows to me until I light the lamp. It was like that with Mary's face.

I saw her strong dark brows, the fineness of her nose, the width of her pale lovely mouth, but I could not understand the lines eaten into her flesh, the terrible weariness of her thin cheeks, the helpless, defeated look to her closed lids.

I thought, "It isn't Mary? Not the Mary I know." And then, "I've never really known Mary! She's a stranger!"

Brade said, "Sit down, Mis' Martha. You look plum tuckered out."

The homely phrase was so odd, coming from him, that I looked up helplessly and then dropped into the chair he placed for me.

"Too bad you don't smoke," he said, lighted a cigarette and sat down on the end of the divan close to Mary's slim, high-heeled gray pumps.

"Mary," I choked, "we should—"

"Let her alone," he interrupted. "She's received a shock. Jangled nerves need a holiday. Why bother her?" And that seemed just then highly intelligent. He gave me no time for reflection. "You know, Mis' Martha," he continued, eyes crinkling in amusement, "when I was a youngster, I always wanted to live in the country. It remains one of the unsatisfied desires of my life. We all have them. I'll bet you always wanted to live in the city."

"No," I said. "I tried it once and I don't like it. I was born in Alder Valley, married here, and here I hope I'll be when I die."

He nodded understandingly, staring at his cigarette. That was the first time I noticed the moonstone ring, glowing in the light like a pale, blue-tinged sun, and I could not take my eyes from it.

"Yet if Mat Berry had lived you might have gone," he suggested. "Mat was a restless sort, ambitious, with far-reaching plans."

I shut my lips hard. No one ever spoke to me about Mat. They thought they were being kind by ignoring what they considered my life of tragedy tied to a helpless, crippled man, but that is because they could not know the love between us, or the gorgeous years we spent together. I did not bother to wonder how Brade knew, but felt my heart leap and tears sting my eyes, and realized how lonely I had been because no one ever talked to me about Mat.

I said, "He had plans, Mat did. He would have gone far. He was a forward-looking man."

Again he nodded. "And if you hadn't married him you might have gone on with your school teaching. You were a splendid teacher. I know. I can tell by your eyes, that are level and direct and clear-seeing."

I felt color sweep over my lined face. A splendid teacher! No one had ever called me that except Mat, and he in different words.

"Teaching was easy for me," I said. "Their minds were so thirsty. Those youngsters—Lars Knowlton, Shane Fortune, Sadie Clemmons, all of them."

"Well, your Lars Knowlton is a genius. Young Fortune I haven't met, but with his background he should have gone far."

"How could he?" I choked, throat tight. "His mother ill, clinging to him, frightened, only living with him around."

"Like that, eh? Not equal to the general business of living?"

"I guess not," I told him dully. "I don't see how she had the courage to have her baby far away like she did, but old Amos was sick and couldn't be moved."

"Oh, so the boy wasn't born here?"

"No. In Rome, I believe. He was six months old when she got here with him."

"I see. And did you say this man with the gold ring in his ear was at the Fortune home yesterday, asking for Mary Morningstar?"

"Yes. So Nesta said. It's what upset Claribel so badly they had to have the doctor twice last night." And then suddenly I was on my feet, facing him with such black fury in my heart, he was startled and rose to stand before me.

"So that's the way you work," I choked. "You act friendly, pretend to be interested in me—in Mat; tell me I was a splendid teacher, get me to liking you, trusting you, because I'm tired and everything, and then you—you—"

The room went all dim and I couldn't talk any more. I knew suddenly that I was a tired, plain old woman, the best of life behind; in front, a long corridor of empty days. Brade stood very still looking at me, that light pucker of concentration between his brows and I never hated anyone so intensely.

"I won't talk to you," I cried. "Who are you anyway? What right have you to be snooping around? Who asked you to solve anything? Why don't you go back to your city and do your detecting where it's needed? We don't need you here. We don't want you!"

He flicked his charred cigarette into a tray. He said, "No, I guess you don't at that. Want me, at least. But I'll tell you one thing, Martha Berry, and you can take it or leave it. Detecting is my job and I do it with everything I have. Don't get me wrong. I'm not a judge. I don't pass on the motive behind murder. I represent society and the law that society establishes in its effort to maintain itself. Transgressors of law must compensate, pay their debt to the society they have outraged. In order to pay that debt, they must be apprehended. That's my job and I do it. I'll use any means that come to my hand, within my individual code of ethics. If I outrage personal feelings, I'm sorry, but I do the job. Now will you sit down like the straight-shooting sort you are and tell me what you know about Pietro Donelli's visit to Claribel Fortune, why it upset her so and why he was looking for Mary Morningstar?"

"No," I said flatly. "I won't!"

"That's splendid, Martha," Mary Morningstar said, lifting to an elbow, "and I appreciate your loyalty, but I've listened to Captain Brade's masterly presentation of ethics, and I feel that we should co-operate with him. Won't you sit down, please, stop glaring at each other, and hand me a cigarette?"

I flopped into the chair. Brade opened his black and silver cigarette case, Mary accepted one; he held a light for her and sat down near the foot of the divan.

She drew herself up on the pillows, Mary again with her eyes open, though she looked terribly tired. "We really haven't much choice, Martha," she added. "Captain Brade is here officially. Sheriff Grubber has put him in charge of this affair."

"He would," I said nastily. "Anse Grubber'd be glad to get anyone to do his work for him."

Brade's glance was like a slap in the face. "That's not true and you know it," he said quietly. "But let it pass. Knowlton got to a telephone after you left, located Grubber, and he got there in a hurry. I didn't want the job," he gestured briefly. "I wanted my vacation—"

"Captain Brade and I," Mary interrupted with a faint smile, "were enjoying a very intricate game of 'guess why, what, and who' when you came in, Martha. He told me of the death of an unknown man on the hill path last night. Just why he thought I should have knowledge concerning it, I can't quite say. Frankly, his interest put me on my guard. Now, however, I'll answer any question you wish, Captain Brade."

"Thank you," he said comfortably. "That's much better. Now do you know why this man Donelli was searching for you? You won't deny that he was, I suppose?"

"Oh, no. My maid reported his visit on my return, explaining that she had sent him to the Fortunes, as I had said I was calling there."

"What time was he here?"

"About four o'clock. I had been gone possibly half an hour."

"Where did you go, and why did you not call at the Fortunes as you had planned?"

She said, eyes level, "I just didn't want to, after I had started. It was one of those days when I felt I couldn't do justice to Claribel's ailments."

Brade smiled slightly. "So you did—what?"

"I circled back here, came in the lower garden gate at the rear, picked a huge bouquet of late flowers, walked to the cemetery and placed them on my mother's grave."

Brade considered his ring carefully. "You stayed there quite a time?"

"Yes. It was beautiful and very quiet. I am not one to weep about graves, Captain Brade, but it is a sorrow that I shall always bear that I was far away and thoroughly engrossed with my own affairs at the time of my mother's death. Placing flowers on her grave is poor compensation, but sometimes I must do it."

"And then?"

"When I left I was ashamed that I had allowed selfish motives to keep me from being kind, so I decided to call on Claribel anyway."

Brady's brows lifted imperceptibly. Mary said: "I got to the house a little before six. It was deserted, so I wrote a note in Claribel's room, and left."

He glanced at me under lowered lids. "Will you tell me, Mis' Martha, what time Donelli called at Fortunes asking for Miss Morningstar?"

"Right at four-fifteen," I said sullenly. "Nesta didn't tell me, but Bessie, Mrs. Fortune's maid, said so when she told me about the Buddha Nesta bought, on my way out."

"The Buddha?" Brade asked. "Similar to the one we found beside the path?"

"Identical. It's standing on the mantel in the living room."

He thought this over for a moment. Then, "We may conclude, I think, that Donelli went directly to the Fortunes after leaving here. Reverting to my original query, Miss Morningstar, why did he want to see you?"

Mary laughed. "Captain Brade, I haven't the slightest notion, except that I am troubled a great deal by people wanting to sell me things. I'm really quite helpless to resist them."

It was true. Mary was a prey to every sort of wandering huckster with a pack on his back. She had plenty of money, and her sympathies were easily touched. She would buy the most ridiculous things, patent vegetable slicers, spot-removers, silver polishes, because, as she said, she felt so sorry for anyone who had to make his living that way.

I breathed a deep sigh of relief, then Brade said, "Possibly, but that doesn't fully explain how the imprint of your shoe heels were found in the wet sod beside Donelli's body, Miss Morningstar."

I'd have lifted straight out of my chair if I'd had the strength. Mary gave a sharp, involuntary start, and her face held again that queer, bloodless look.

The fingers closed round the smoking cigarette lowered slowly until they hung, white and lifeless, over the edge of the divan.

"My heel prints!" she whispered. "Mine? There beside that man?"

"Yes," Brade assured her, in a voice that made me think of Ratsy purring over canned salmon. "Your heel prints, Miss Morningstar."

She was motionless, looking at him, completely and totally dismayed. At once all the pleasant, easy story she had told was for me a clever and well-thought out fabrication without a grain of truth. The silence of the room grew oppressive. Neither of them moved as they sat there facing each other; Brade stretched out comfortably, long legs crossed, head lowered; Mary so limp she'd have collapsed if the divan hadn't supported her, completely at his mercy, not because of what he had said but because of some hidden knowledge of her own that sent her defenses crashing.

From down in the kitchen, I heard black Daisy singing in her throaty contralto, "He don't plant 'taters, he don't plant cotton, and them that plants 'em is soon forgotten," and I have never liked "Old Man River" to this day.

The shrilling of the telephone was like a sharp cry.

Mary said, unsteadily, "Martha, will you answer, please?"

I went into the hall, closed the door behind me, placed the receiver against my ear. I said hello, and Nesta Fortune's brittle tones reached me, "Mary? Is Mary there?"

"I'll call her," I said and Nesta chirped:

"Oh, Mis' Martha! I just wanted to say good morning and ask Mary if she'd heard about the excitement, you know, that man that was—"

I placed the receiver on the table and stared out at the brilliant sunlight over the golden asters where bees buzzed and one gorgeous purple butterfly dipped and circled like a bright, blown leaf.

So Nesta knew about the murder. It was likely all over town by now. I went into the living room. Neither of them appeared to have moved or spoken during my absence. I said: "Nesta wants to talk to you, Mary—this thing we're discussing."

She nodded, rose slowly and went out, closing the door. Brade stood up, stretched, walked over and deliberately opened the door a small crack so that Mary's voice came clearly. He turned, looking down at me. "I use any means within my code of ethics," he said softly, and smiled through the hard-set grimness of his face.

Mary said from the hall, "Sorry I wasn't in, Nesta. Thanks for calling. The flowers were lovely." Then, after a pause, "Yes, I've heard." And her sentences came at short intervals, punctuating Nesta's chattering.

"Peddlers are always hunting me. No, I didn't see him. Where were you all when I dropped by around six?" There was a longer interval when I gathered that Claribel's absence was news to her daughter-in-law. Then Mary said: "I'm sure it will be straightened out soon, Nesta. What? Last night?" I caught her quick gasp. So did Brade. "Why, I was here of course, and by the way, Nesta, next time you call, if I'm out, there's make-up in the dressing room on the first floor. Save you the trip upstairs."

There was laughter running through Mary's voice like a thin silver thread. She had evidently learned from black Daisy of Nesta's meddling excursion to the second floor.

I said to Brade as Mary replaced the receiver, "Aren't you going to close the door?"

"Oh, no," he said, relaxing in his deep chair again. "I'm against subterfuge generally, Mis' Martha, totally against it."

Mary did not seem to notice that the door was unlatched. I saw at once that the telephone call had given her time to rally her scattered forces for further defense, for I felt definitely that Mary was on the defensive, fighting desperately against Brade's courteous and entirely ruthless probing.

He remarked as she sat down, "You weren't really home last night, were you, Mary Dawn?" for the first time giving her that lovely professional name that she had used so long.

She lighted a cigarette, blew a cloud of blue smoke. Her face is elfish when she puckers her mouth like that and lifts her amber-brown eyes to watch the smoke disappear.

"No, Captain Brade, I was not home. I was on the point of telling you about that when the telephone called me."

He settled lower and gave the impression of grunting in satisfaction, though he didn't utter a sound.

Lars Knowlton once said that Brade had a marked sadistic strain in his make-up or he would not so thoroughly enjoy threading his way through the confused mazes of people's minds, bringing to light things that had best been left hidden.

After I came to know Brade well I did not entirely agree with Lars. I think it was more the satisfaction that a fine workman feels when he has accomplished a designed result through his own painstaking and careful manipulation.

And I have thought, at times, that he all but purrs when he gets information he wants.

Mary said, "I make no apologies for what I shall tell you, nor offer elaborate explanations. I can only say that my difficult professional life has left its mark. When I gave it up—"

"Why," Brade interrupted carefully, "did you give it up, Mary Dawn? I have lived for years in hope of hearing you in one of my favorite roles."

She flushed with that bright beauty that always comes to her at mention of her singing; then the color died and she looked gray and very tired. Again I thought about defeat.

"Because I cracked up in a big way. I can't explain those things exactly. I am strong enough now, but—" she turned, eyes narrowed on the shadowed ivy, "I shall never sing again," she said in a queer, breathless voice that made my heart ache.

"Pardon me," Brade said, with that gentle courtesy he could so easily assume, and waited until she was ready to go on.

"I was restless yesterday," she said suddenly. "The house, the town—everything was too much. I had to get away. You know what I did in the afternoon. I returned here about seven, got my car, left a note for my maid and started out to drive. I drove for hours. No place in particular. Just to be moving, seeing the countryside flash past, the moon over the fields, feel the wind in my face."

She stretched her arms high in a long, swift gesture of free-dom. Mary Morningstar never belonged long in one place. Hers was the way of the wide world to wander forever. I know that often she felt prisoned.

"Then I came to the foot of Alder Hill. It was very lonely, and very beautiful and I parked my car, started up the path—"

I saw a vein beating in her throat like something alive, and could not put into words the thought that was in my mind.

Brade asked, "This was about what time?"

"Exactly half-past two. I looked at my watch, glad there was no one to worry about me. I went into the woods, stopping several times to listen to the night sounds, smell the wet earth. I sat down once, smoked a cigarette and thought about a number of things, and then I went on—"

The exquisite voice slowed, Mary not looking at us, but at the shadows of the ivy on the latticed window above her head.

"That is how," she stated, "I came on the body of the man. I said I would make no apologies. I do not. I stopped, too terrified to move. I thought he was sleeping, then I saw, somehow, that he was dead, and I turned and ran, and ran—to my car and kept on and on driving. I reached home at eight-thirty this morning, less than an hour before you came, Captain Brade. That is all."

Brade turned the moonstone ring slowly. There were sounds in the street now, distant voices. Brade said: "You can add nothing, Mary Dawn? You saw no one, heard nothing?"

"Nothing. I only did what I have related."

"You will pardon my insistence on detail," he suggested. "You approached from the north, up the path on the side of the hill to-ward town, the one Mis' Martha used this morning?"

"Yes."

"And you did not go very close to the body? Say three feet?"

"I do not understand distances in those terms, Captain Brade. I came close enough to see that the man was dead. I stood there for possibly a minute and a half, though it seemed hours, hanging onto a branch, then I turned and ran as hard as I could for the car."

"You didn't circle the body? Walk around to the other side?"

"Heavens, no! Why should I do that?"

"I don't know, but since the heel prints clearly indicate that you did exactly that you must have had a reason."

Mary's hand clenched slowly, relaxed. Her head lowered. She looked at him, straight and hard, and I have never seen a more bitterly hostile face. Then slowly she rose.

"Captain Brade," she said, and he stood also. "I have given you a truthful account of my actions last night. To that account I have nothing to add, nothing to change. You may make what you will of it. That, I take it, is your job."

He took his hat from the table. "I thank you for your patience with me, Mary Dawn. I regret to say that I do not believe a word you have said, except that you *did* go to the woods path last night. Yes, my job is to make something out of what you have told me. I shall do that to the best of my ability."

He crossed to the door, went into the hall and the next moment we heard his steps on the gravel path. I heard also, the sound of his whistle. Yes, it was the "Kerry Dancers."

Neither Mary nor I moved until the front gate clanged, then Mary turned. "Martha," she said, voice dry and hard, "what is that man doing here? In this town?"

"He's vacationing at the Chesterworth place," I told her. "He was strolling in the woods this morning and came on him, that man, and I was there—"

"You found him?" She asked, sagging to the divan.

I looked straight at her. "No, Mary. *You* found him at half-past two this morning when you were wandering over the face of the earth."

She stared at me dumbly for a moment, began to nod her head, gently, monotonously.

"Yes, Martha, I found Pietro Donelli."

"Mary! Did you shoot him?"

She cried out at that, hands lifted against her throat. Over them she looked at me, lovely Mary Morningstar who couldn't kill a chicken if she was starving.

Mary Morningstar couldn't! Not the Mary I knew. But that other Mary, the one I had glimpsed behind that blank, suffering mask that was her face when her eyes were shut, that Mary I did not know.

That was the Mary who had run away from Alder Valley one bitter winter night with seven dollars in her pocket, and a coat with an imitation fur collar around her thin shoulders. She had starved and all but begged in Chicago and New York, worked in restaurants, washed dishes at lumber camps, worked with a tawdry variety show, and God knows what else, all for the chance to train that precious voice. That was the Mary who had gone away that black January night, me crying like a ninny when I came back from walking to the cross roads with her where she had arranged for a ride into town with Pete McGregor, the milkman.

That was long ago, and between that night and this bright day was a trail of victory built out of defeat, success won over unbelievable odds; one of the great voices of our times; and the glitter and beauty of the opera in Paris, London, Rome, New York.

She had come back to Alder Valley with that defeated look in her eyes, glimpsed only in flashes that you couldn't really believe. I didn't know all that had happened to Mary in those in-between years. I didn't know that other Mary, or what she might do.

Her voice came to me from a long way, "Martha, what did Claribel want of me that you were in such a state when you came?"

"I don't know, Mary. I was talking to Nesta, and Shane came out and begged me to go to her. Mary, as I live, she looked—well, I thought she would die while I stood there."

She twisted at the folds of her light wool skirt. "Shane worries a lot about her, doesn't he?" she asked pathetically.

"Well, who wouldn't? After all, she is his mother. His father he never knew."

"No," Mary said, "his father he never knew. But I must go and see Claribel, Martha."

"Yes, Mary, you must go." I stood up, groping for my basket which I had clung to so foolishly all that amazing morning, and it with not a green leaf in it.

Mary rose too, looking slim and young with her nice straight legs and long aristocratic feet housed in those fine pumps with the high heels, and suddenly I remembered those heel prints beside the track on the hill path and what Brade had said about not believing what she said, and then I saw she hadn't answered my question.

"Mary," I asked, looking straight at her, "where were you, really, last night? That story—"

"Martha Berry," she said, head high, "that story was the solemn, blessed truth, and you must believe it." Her voice broke. Her hands came out in a swift, imploring gesture. She caught my arms, strong, hot fingers biting into my flesh.

"You've got to believe it, Martha," she said, eyes frantic. "Tell me you believe it. No one else will. The town, that man Brade, no one else—but *you* must. You must help me, Martha, help me make them believe it. Tell them you saw me there, that you *know* I was there, that—"

"Mary Morningstar," I said flatly, "you're crazy as a loon! A man's been murdered and you're insisting you found his body, and ran away like a ninny without reporting it."

"I was that upset, Martha. Think what it meant, coming on that—thing, his heavy dark face, thick lips, that black, greasy hair, that little flat gold ring in his ear—"

Well! Mary *had* been there! She might have guessed that Donelli, an Italian, was dark, but she wouldn't know about his *heavy* face, his *thick* lips, his hair, and, most of all, she wouldn't know that the ring in his ear was *flat* instead of *round*.

"All right, Mary," I said, "I'll believe that you were there, but I'll have to believe too, that you didn't just take a look and run, for I saw those prints, and they're on the *other* side from where you said you stood. And you haven't told me yet, Mary, whether or not you shot him."

Her hands fell. She stepped back, suddenly white and quiet, and just then a man's voice sounded from the path, and Mary whirled, eyes like light, head lifted in that indescribable way. "Shane!" she said on a queer, high note. "Shane!"

He heard her, for he took the steps in one long bound, crashed into that quiet, shadowed room like a spring wind, bringing the freshness of the morning with him in the rumpled darkness of his hair, flare of his open collar, the healthy color that showed like low fire beneath his tan. I swear he didn't even see me. He only saw Mary.

"Shane!" she said again, and went toward him, hands out.

"Mary!" He caught her hands, looking into her eyes in a way I had never believed possible.

They stood there like that, hands clinging, eyes lost, and I felt the room go dim and dizzy and struggled to catch my breath for in that way they came together, light blinded me and I saw.

Oh, well, men have always loved Mary Morningstar. She suggests everything they've ever dreamed of, maybe. When she was a skinny, flat-chested girl with no color, quiet and far away inside herself, never saying much, all the boys of the town and county were in love with her. I could understand in a way, why Mary had never married. With all the males in her vicinity drawn to her like bees toward honey, how could she find one, just one, out of the swarm to care for? I knew all this watching Shane Fortune that morning, but this, this was different. This couldn't be! Then Mary said, "Martha's here, Shane." Their hands fell apart, he saw me, and immediately everything was as it had always been.

He said, "Hello, Mis' Martha. Thank you for visiting Claribel. She's sleeping now."

"I'm glad, Shane. I'll be going now, Mary. You'll go see Claribel, won't you?"

"Yes," she promised, her voice alive with its golden lights and shadows again, "and thank you for coming, Martha."

And so I went out, along the gravel path, into the hot, dusty street. I was very tired. My head throbbed and my stomach felt queasy. I kept my eyes on the toes of my stout, flat-heeled shoes and watched the little puffs of white dust they kicked up.

It was just like I stood outside myself somewhere and watched myself go down that hot, dusty street, a tall angular woman with square, bony shoulders and thick gray hair straggling from under a shabby brown straw hat with a few silly yellow flowers on one side.

I saw my skinny arms, my big, strong hands, my flat chest, my pancake hips. I knew that my face was lined, my throat corded. I knew every angle and hollow of my hard, lean body and that never in all my life could I stand like an up-pointed lance on a high hill, watching white clouds go by. Never wear high heels and lift my head so the light made delicate planes of shadow on my face. Yes, I was very tired.

Chapter Four

THE TOWN WAS HUMMING with the news. Clem Hoskins, Bill Winthrop, Abe Underhill, and all the rest of them had come out of their stores, buzzing like flies around a frosted cake. Old Flora Makepace was there with her Paisley shawl around her fat shoulders, wide, thin-lipped mouth yammering for all to hear.

They would have liked me to stop and talk. I'm sort of an institution in Alder Valley, I guess, and they knew I was friends with Mary Morningstar and the Fortunes, but I just nodded and went straight to the post office, which is around the corner off the main street. There was a small group there too, and I saw that the window was shut and knew Linda Barstow must be getting the ten o'clock mail out.

Linda is a strong, tawny girl with heavy straw-brown hair and yellow lights in the glowing iris of her wide-spaced eyes. She glanced up as I came in and I knew at once that she had heard the news.

"Good morning, Mis' Martha."

"Good morning, Linda. Sorry to be late, but you know—"

"Yes, I know," she said. "Seems strange that our town should have a murder on its hands."

"I don't see why," I snapped. "Where folks are, you're going to find what it is that makes murder, and it don't matter if the folks are in New York or Alder Valley." Just there Linda finished the sorting, opened the window, and was handing out general delivery when I heard a voice say:

"Brade. Captain Courtney Brade." At once everything was right there in the little office with me, most of all Mary Morningstar with her hands in Shane Fortune's, the eyes of them lost in each other's.

I heard Linda tell him there was nothing, then I looked up and he was standing close to the wicket, hat jerked over his eye, smiling at me. He said, not very loud, "You look plum tuckered out, Mis' Martha. You wouldn't come around the corner to the Cozy Cafe and share a pot of coffee, would you?"

I glared at him as best I could, but I *was* that tuckered out it wasn't very convincing, and I knew that I wanted a cup of coffee more than anything in the world.

So without a word I got up and we went to Tommy Parker's Cozy Cafe around the corner, into a booth clear at the back. Brade said, "Lord, I'm hungry! How about some ham and, young man? Mis' Martha, you'll have some ham and, won't you?"

I said, "Ham and what?" and he and Tommy both laughed, Brade saying, "Double it, son," before I could tell him I never ate anything for breakfast but dry toast and coffee and I'd had that hours ago.

Tommy got out of the way fast, maybe knowing I'd stop him if I had the chance, and the next moment I heard the pop of hot grease and there was the most delicious odor of frying ham. I sort of relaxed, leaned my elbows on the table and said, "Well, I'm hungry too, and no mistake."

Brade smiled and settled back. He was nice and comfortable to be around when he was like that, big and easy and relaxed, and you had the feeling that he was equal to anything that might come along. That's a mighty comforting feeling for a woman to have even for a little while, when she's put in so many years fending for herself.

I hadn't realized before how handsome he was. His wasn't the kind of good looks you noticed specially. Rather like Mary's house, just so right and proper that you took it for granted and only felt satisfied to be with him. He was so easy to talk to, always seeming to have so much time, and he had a way of making you feel important and that he was just terribly interested in you and what you were doing.

It didn't seem difficult that morning to believe that he really did want to know a lot about the history of Alder Valley, and the truth about the Indian massacre when the original settlement was wiped out way back in 1768, and if the old Macquarry place on the hill really did date back to the Revolution.

You'd really have thought that he'd come down special to find out how I happened to be post mistress, how much mail went through my office, and if I found it interesting or just did the work to get the money.

Well, that was a subject that I'd thought a lot about, but I'd never told a soul how I felt. With Brade sitting opposite me, sipping coffee and smoking, it was just natural that I should tell him how much the post office meant to me so he wouldn't think my life uninteresting like so many people did.

I had plenty to tell him, too. I gave Marta Flemming the letter from the War Department that told her her Lonnie had been killed at Ypres, and saw her drop before my eyes as if the same bullet that found her boy's heart had traveled straight across the ocean to pierce hers, for she was dead before I could get to her.

And I gave Nell Bronson that letter from Nat Fields and saw her face light up like sunrise as she stood there in her shabby black merino dress and home-made hat, and that night she left her home and her man and her two small children, ran away to join her lover, and no one in Alder Valley had word of her again.

Every month I put the envelope containing a government check into Grandpa Latham's crippled old hands, see his poor, half-blind eyes fill with tears of gratitude because he doesn't have to go to the county farm, and listen again, no matter how busy I am, to his wheezy account of the Battle of the Wilderness.

Just once there had been a letter from Ezra Fortune, who was brother to Amos. It had seemed strange, for at the time Amos was buried there was no word from Ezra. But he had written once to Claribel when Shane was about seventeen, the letter coming from a hospital in Los Angeles, and so, though Claribel never said anything, we figured he had gone there to die, for news of his passing came less than a month later.

Brade asked me questions about Ezra Fortune and I told what I knew, which was little enough, for Ezra had always held a great scorn of Alder Valley and the people there.

I paused just there, thinking I was talking too much and being a bore, but Brade said, "Mis' Martha! What a wonderful life you have," and without my noticing much he signaled Tommy to bring more coffee. After he had gone and the booth curtain was closed Brade said, "You're lucky that you have eyes to see, for through that little window of yours has come and gone the major portion of the joy and sorrow of these folk of Alder Valley. Don't you agree with me?"

I nodded. And then I told him how through that same window had come word from Claribel Fortune in distant Italy that she was going to have a baby, and how old Doc' Wentworth had snorted so loud his glasses fell off and said, "Her! That woman! Have a baby!" Another snort and him glaring at me like I was to blame for everything. "Huh! She can't have a baby. So there!"

And out he had stalked, walking hard on his heels and blowing through his big, quarrelsome nose like the way Mildred, my purebred Jersey, used to when she scented clover in the spring. But Claribel had fooled him, though he didn't live to know it, for he died that same winter of pneumonia, following that trip he made through the blizzard to wait on Tom Foley ten miles in the country. Tom had had nothing worse than a case of lumbago.

Claribel had never married again, though she was so young and pretty and had so much money. Better it might have been if she had, and got a sensible man to handle her fortune for her.

She took it away from Bennet Calder and, though not one of us could tell what she had done with it, she certainly didn't have much left.

Shane had grown up in Alder Valley, and his mother had let her mind get fixed on the notion that the sun couldn't rise unless Shane was around, and developed all sorts of aches and pains to keep him by her. When Mary Morningstar came back she told Claribel something like that, or at least we judged she did, for they had a regular quarrel though they fixed it up and were friends again.

"I suppose that's why Mrs. Fortune wanted to see Mary Dawn this morning," Brade suggested.

"Don't you believe it," I snapped. "She and Mary aren't that close. They're polite and everything, but they really don't like each other. Claribel thinks Mary should have stayed at home and looked after her mother instead of gallivanting all over the world being a singer, and Mary has little use for a woman who faints or goes into hysterics when the meat burns, and has tantrums when a dress doesn't fit properly."

Brade's eyes crinkled in amusement. "Oh you fascinating woman," he said and in some strange way I felt beautiful and mysterious and what Lars calls provocative. I know my thin cheeks flushed that he had put me right in with Mary Morningstar and Claribel Fortune. When he said, "Well, why in Heaven's name then would Claribel insist on seeing Mary?" I just said straight out what I thought: that it had something to do with the death of Pietro Donelli. Brade made odd little marks on the table cloth with his finger nail and said, "Maybe so, maybe so, but tell me, Mis' Martha, Claribel was really ill this morning, wasn't she?"

I told him that never before had I had any real concern for Claribel, though I'd seen her in all sorts of spells, but this morning I'd truly thought she would die.

"Did Mary Dawn go to see her?" he asked, pouring cream in his fourth cup of coffee.

"She promised she would. I left right after Shane came."

"What time did Shane come?" Brade asked, lifting the lid of the sugar bowl.

"About twenty minutes after you left. He and Mary are good friends," I added staring hard at my spoon. "He isn't very happy with Nesta. She's too managing, I think. Shane's a proud lad and he frets because he can't get out and make a living and give Nesta a home of her own. She doesn't mind, and she's taken over the management of Claribel's house completely."

I don't know how much longer I'd have sat there talking like that, with Brade so interested, but suddenly the clock up front began to chime and it was eleven o'clock.

"Good Heavens," I said, starting up. "I must be going. This whole morning I've frittered away, Captain Brade."

He rose too, gray eyes smiling. "Not really frittered, Mis' Martha. You've no idea what an interesting time you've given me."

At the moment I was tremendously set up over that but later, after I'd told him good-by, actually inviting him to dinner Thursday night, well, everything looked quite different.

I sent Linda out to get her lunch. No one came in, and the street was white in the sunlight with Horace, the town dog stretched in the narrow line of shade, snoring peacefully. A few folks drove in from the country in their rusty Fords. Old man Weatherill trudged by on his two canes, his stained Panama on the back of his large, bald head, and I stood listening to the tap, tap, tap of his sticks as he rounded the corner.

He'd come down to get the news as he did every day and had for as far back as I could remember. He just couldn't last *much* longer, as Jane Ruth, his smart, citified daughter-in-law, pointed out on the slightest provocation.

And I realized that when he was gone, and I no longer heard the tap of the sticks, the town would be different in some way, just as every death and every birth made it different, changing the old order for the new. I thought then how nothing remains the same, ever, and how different everything was today from what it had been yesterday, or even that morning when I got up, fixed my breakfast and took my basket to gather wintergreen and tansy.

I hadn't known then that such a person as Pietro Donelli existed, or that he was lying dead on the upper hill road, or that Mary Morningstar had been away from home all night, or could possibly drop in a dead faint when I—

I stopped thinking just there and asked myself just what it was that had made Mary drop in that dreadful 'shot' way. I went carefully over what I had said when she opened the door, recalling how the color drained out of her face, and my own words, "It's that man with the gold ring in his ear who was asking for you—and was murdered—"

Right there, Mary had gone down. Brade hadn't made anything of it, but what did that mean? You couldn't tell what Brade thought from what he said. Then it began to dawn on me what he had meant when he said, "You've no idea what an interesting time you've given me."

Slow, hot color burned my face. I shut my hands hard, and if I hadn't been raised a staunch Methodist I'd have cursed like a drunken sailorman. For I knew that again Brade had tricked me. Tied a bandage around my eyes, put a halter on my neck and led me exactly where he wanted me to go. Fooled me with his interest, his charm, his intentness, into honking like a southbound goose, telling him about everything I knew in complete detail, the history and background of half the people in Alder Valley, especially Mary Morningstar and the Fortunes.

I made a vow then, emphatically and devoutly, that I would never even speak to the man again. Never look at his nice, crinkly gray eyes, listen to his quiet, well-modulated voice, to his casual, friendly questions, never, never, never so long as I should live! Right there I remembered that I had invited him to dinner Thursday night!

I just gave up then and went to work like a sensible, plain woman and cleaned that damned office from top to bottom. It was a sight too, what with the heat of the summer and the rush of mail from extra visitors and all. Dust flew and papers sailed. I made a fire in the pot-bellied stove, not caring how hot it was, and when folks said anything about it I was that snappy they just took their letters and went out.

It was a beastly afternoon. Hot and windy, with dust clouds whirling, a horse whinnying lonesomely, and Horace keeping up a monotonous thumping, busy with his fleas, and when at last I locked the front door and started home, I was dead tired and my left shoulder ached like it does when a change of weather's coming.

I knew it was, too, from the way the wind had soughed all day, and how the leaves drooped, hot and dusty, and the flies kept low to the ground, and old man Weatherill's rooster crowed so late in the afternoon.

I looked down Main street, and there were folks dotted all along, talking endlessly and I knew I couldn't avoid being stopped a dozen times, so I took the back road home.

I do that sometimes. Late evenings in the spring, when the violets are out and the wild grass is like green smoke in the ditches. Or in the autumn when the leaves are changing and crickets sing in the dry, brown fields and there is a big moon, pale as a shadow just beginning to show in the deep blue sky behind the spire of the Congregational church.

The way you go is down past old man Weatherill's place where Ruth Jane and Kelsey, his son, are waiting for him to die so they can do over the house, on to skirt the south side of the cemetery with the tops of the slim, black firs showing above the white gravestones. Then to the right and you'll come up the wide alley back of Evergreen Street.

It's interesting to walk there and see what a different notion you get about people when you look at their back yards. I wasn't caring about that tonight. I only wanted to get home, light my lamp, put on the tea kettle, feed Ratsy, Richard the 7th, my canary, and Evinrude, get a bite for myself and then sit, quiet and not thinking, in my old cane rocker on the front porch, shut in by the red honeysuckle vine.

I walked slowly. Noises reached me: the Wheeler children yelling over in the vacant lot beyond the cemetery and the Dickersons' old red cow bawling as she stood at the pasture bars. The dry grass swished and occasionally a brown leaf drifted down and rustled against my shoulder.

Then a little way ahead was an up-leaping of flame, a fierce crackling, and I saw that Bessie, Claribel's girl, was making a bonfire behind the back fence.

It was nice and bright with Bessie's thick, substantial figure standing out clearly. I went up thinking to ask after Claribel. Bessie squinted at me, face red from the heat, and I saw a big pile of rubbish beside her ready to be burned.

"She ain't so good, Mis' Martha," Bessie said in answer to my question. "She just lies there so limp, and then all of a sudden she begins to moan and cry and we have to get Mr. Shane to give her that quietin' medicine the doc' left."

I sighed. "Did Miss Mary call, Bessie?"

"Yes'm. Her and Mr. Shane come in together soon after lunch. She stayed a time, but, if anything, Miss Claribel was worse after she left. The doc's been twict, but hones', Mis' Martha, he can't do anything."

"No. I guess not," I said dully, eyes on the old gray coat she was flinging to the flames. "What're you doing, Bessie? Getting ready for fall house-cleaning?"

"Figure on startin' first of the week," she said, picking up a rumpled straw hat. "This stuff ain't no good, not even to give to the Helping Hand. Miss Claribel got to worryin' about it this afternoon, and there was no peace until I went through the closets and redded it out."

She picked up a faded blanket. "No use keepin'," she muttered defiantly, and I knew her thrifty soul rebelled at destroying anything. "Miss Nesta's a caution for throwing things away." Viciously she tossed on a slim, bright-figured dress that had Nesta written all over it. "Mr. Shane don't seem to care much," she said, broad face worry-puckered. "He don't seem very happy," she added. "Him and Miss Nesta quarrel somethin' terrible." She glanced at me out of loyal, troubled eyes. "I wouldn't think a man would take offa' woman, the things she says to him."

"What does she say, Bessie?"

Bessie straightened, a roll of old papers in her hand, glanced round guiltily and stepped closer. "She says, why don't he let her buy some decent clothes, take her to N'York, show her the kind of life a girl should have? She says, where is all the money she thought he had and what had he been doing to let his ma' fritter it away?"

My face went hot with fury. "The little snip! I always thought she married him because she figured he had money."

"Yes'm," Bessie agreed tossing on the newspaper and bending for more offerings. "Yes ma'am, she sure did and I'll swear that there marriage ain't gonna last."

"Bessie! What have you there?"

She stopped, thick body bent, hand clutching defensively a pair of slim, high-arched black pumps, the heels, turned toward me, showing like delicate shields.

"Where'd you get those shoes?" I asked, voice thick and husky.

She straightened slowly, staring at them curiously. "Those?" she asked. "Why, them's Miss Claribel's."

"Miss Claribel's, nothing!" I snapped. "Miss Claribel doesn't wear shoes like that. Mary Morningstar is the only woman in town—"

"Yes," Bessie agreed placidly, "I know. Miss Mary give 'em to Miss Claribel a while back, Miss Claribel thinkin' them so pretty. They never fit her proper and I don't believe she wore 'em half a dozen times around the house. So she told me to burn 'em, her not wantin' Miss Mary to know—"

I didn't hear any more. I only saw the lovely shoes illuminated by that leaping fire so everything about them was terribly plain. Shine of the leather, glitter of the tiny steel buckles—stain of red clay half way up the pointed heels, a fragment of dried oak leaf clinging to the left side!

"Yes," I said. "Yes, I understand, Bessie. Miss Claribel wouldn't want anyone to know." I turned away, finding it very dark after facing the fire, then, just like something made me, I took two steps back and stood beside Bessie again. "Let me have them, Bessie. They're so pretty it's a shame to burn them." She hesitated, staring at the pumps, then looked at me slantwise. "Land sakes, Mis' Martha, what you want of 'em? You must take a number—"

"I know what I take," I bit at her. "Suppose I do wear a number nine and a half, don't you suppose I've never *wanted* to wear pretty shoes? Besides, it wouldn't hurt to let me have them, keep them in my closet to look at sometimes."

Bessie stood there like a tall and lusty Fate, holding in her big, red hands threads of destiny in the shape of narrow, high-heeled pumps.

"Miss Claribel will think—" she began.

"Miss Claribel won't know," I reminded her. "If you don't tell her, I won't, and I'll never wear them outside the house."

"No, I guess you wouldn't," Bessie pointed out dispassionately, and swung the pumps gently above the hungry flames.

"Look, Bessie," I coaxed, "I'll give you that wine broadcloth dress you always liked and help you fix it over."

She wet her lips, eyes darting. Surely that night Bessie was tempted with what, for her, were the kingdoms of the earth.

"Maybe it wouldn't do no harm," she said weakly, salving her stinging conscience that only understood loyalty to Claribel.

"The broadcloth's good as new, Bessie," I pointed out shamelessly. "You won't have to spend money for a winter dress, then you can get a permanent like you've wanted for so long."

Her eyes lighted. Involuntarily her hand went to her thin, flat hair and I knew she was visioning herself with waves and ringlets. It was too much. She let the breath out of her deep chest with a mighty gust, thrust the slippers into my hands.

"Take 'em, Mis' Martha, but mind you, if you ever let Miss Claribel know—"

"She won't know," I promised, snatching them before she could change her mind, "and now good night, Bessie."

"Mind you promised to help me fix the broadcloth," she called after me, but I did not answer as I went, stumbling a little along the uneven alley, dry grass rustling around my feet and the crackle of Bessie's fire dying away.

I'd help her fix the wine broadcloth, all right. I stick to my word, once it's given.

CHAPTER FIVE

THE SHOES WERE HOT and heavy against my side. I hurried breath-lessly once I was out of Bessie's sight, anxious to get home and hide the things.

I came in the back way through the old apple orchard, stumbled over Ratsy who always comes to meet me, heard Evinrude's deep bay from the front porch changing to a whine of joy as he recognized my step.

The kitchen felt hot and stuffy. There was the fragrance of the preserves, smell of spices from the open pantry door, then I had the lamp lighted and, paying no attention to Ratsy's yowling, plopped into a chair and looked at those shoes.

What in the name of all that was wonderful did I want with them? Why hadn't I let Bessie burn them? They lay there, one toppled on its sleek side, the other upright, poised, like it was ready to take off, and I stared at them as if they had been alive and ready to bite me.

The muslin curtains swayed gently in the evening breeze, birds twittered sleepily in the big maple. Mary had given them to Claribel because Claribel thought they were pretty. Back of it all would be Claribel's pathetic desire to please Shane. She couldn't have avoided seeing how he admired Mary.

They wouldn't fit well, of course. Claribel had only worn them half a dozen times around the house, then today, when she was so ill, she had insisted on Bessie redding out the closets, burning the rubbish, burning the shoes, so Mary wouldn't know—

"Good Heavens!" I gasped, and yanked off my hat.

So that was why Mary had looked so terrible when Brade mentioned the heel prints. She knew they had been made by her shoes in the only way possible. By Claribel wearing the pair she had given her!

It kept getting clearer and clearer. While Mary was in the hall talking to Nesta she had figured out the story she would tell Brade about how she found the dead man. No wonder she stumbled over where she'd stood. She hadn't been there! She'd lied about it! I remembered her saying desperately, "You've got to believe it, Martha. No one else will, but you must. You must help me make them believe I was there."

I closed my eyes. Why? Fear for Claribel? Loyalty to Claribel? Why, they didn't even like each other! Between them was a deep, intense antagonism. No use pretending any different. Then questions were shouting at my ears: "How did Mary know what Donelli looked like? Why was Donelli seeking her? Where *had* she been all night?"

I lifted one of the pumps. No mistaking that reddish clay stain on the heel. You just didn't find that anywhere but on Alder Hill. The ground around town is all rich, black loam. I stared at the dry fragment of oak leaf clinging to the sole and imagined Claribel stumbling along on that dark path in Mary Morningstar's pumps!

And then, when the pumps were so uncomfortable she couldn't endure them around the house, why had Claribel worn them to climb the hill path? Unless it was to throw the blame onto Mary! Blame for what?

"Oh, Lord," I said, dropped the shoes and gave Ratsy a saucer of cream.

What was I trying to convince myself of? That Claribel Fortune had gone to the hill path last night in the dark, armed with a rifle carrying a silver shamrock on its stock, for the express purpose of murdering an unknown Italian peddler, wearing Mary's pumps to make it look like Mary had been there?

Ridiculous! Claribel would faint at sight of a rifle, be totally incapable of figuring out such an elaborate plan. I had a crazy desire to run to Courtney Brade, put the shoes in his hands, tell him the whole story; puzzles like that were what he was trained to solve.

I picked up the shoes just as a man's voice said through the open window, "Hello, Mis' Martha, may I come in?" and there was Shane Fortune looking like the devil at Mass, black hair rumpled, eyes hot like there were fires behind them.

I put the shoes behind me as I whirled. "Hello, Shane," I said. "What brings you here?" I knew I didn't dare drop them because of the noise they would make. He leaned against the wall and I didn't like the look in his eyes. Right away, I knew that Shane had been drinking.

He said, "Saw your light, decided to come in," and shook himself suddenly like he was cold.

I said, "Sit down, Shane. Let me make you a cup of tea." A silly thing to say, him looking like he needed what Lars calls a shot in the arm, but he crossed over and sat down very hard, leaning forward, hands limp between his knees.

"Okay," he said, "I'm equal to anything."

I didn't like the way he said that, staring at me, me standing there like a ninny backed up to the work table by the sink. I felt all hot and shivery. I thought, "Is this boy in love with Mary Morningstar, and not yet married four months?" remembering that I held Mary's shoes in my cold hands, and that I believed Claribel, his mother, had worn them, for what reason the Lord alone knew, to that dark hill path last night. Suddenly tea and all pleasant things were out of the question. I took a long, slow breath. I said, "Shane, I'm going to do what I've never done with another living soul, invite you to my attic room."

He glanced up. A smile twisted his bitter mouth. "Mis' Martha! I'm honored." He rose unsteadily.

"Get along up," I said. "I'll feed Evinrude and join you."

His eyes clung to my face with a queer desperation; then he said, "Okay, honey," went into the parlor, through the hall, and clattered up the stairs.

I called weakly, "Light the lamp, Shane. I won't be a minute."

I ran to my big knitting basket in the corner, stuffed the shoes in among the bright yarn, straightened, and wiped moisture from my face, then slowly followed Shane across the darkened parlor, up the narrow, straight stairs to enter my own special place.

The attic room isn't very large, the roof sharply peaked, with nice brown beams not quite head high for a tall man. Mat used the room before his accident, always having to stoop a little everywhere but right in the middle.

Shane had the lamp lighted and was standing by the window, shoulders slumped, staring into the thickening twilight over my leafy garden. He turned abruptly when I came in, dropped into the rocker by the desk.

"I'm worried about Claribel," he stated flatly.

I looked down on his rumpled, dark head, the sagging lines of his broad, lean shoulders, noticed how his feet turned in when he relaxed like that.

I couldn't really believe that Shane Fortune had grown up, or that he was any older than when he used to swallow and turn his toes in because he didn't have his arithmetic. I thought no young man less than four months married had a right to look as he did tonight, even if his mother was ill.

I said, "Shane, you worry too much about Claribel. Why don't you take Nesta, go away, live your life."

His head jerked up, deep lines gouged into the firmness of his face. "Mis' Martha, you know I can't do that." He leaned toward me. "Nesta and I had a nasty row," he added, and ran his fingers nervously through his rumpled hair.

I sat down on the other side of the desk. "I'm sorry, Shane, but don't mind it too much. It isn't easy, the first years of marriage. You're both young, in love—"

"That's just it," he interrupted. "We're not in love. We've never—been that." Slow color went over his face and he shook his shoulders violently like he was throwing something off. "Think nothing of it, Martha," he said, low and tired like. "I wouldn't have mentioned it only everything's been so damnable today. We're not used to murder in Alder Valley, I guess."

There it was! I had hoped it wouldn't come up. I said,

"No, Shane, but after all, what effect can the death of an un-known Italian peddler have on us?"

"Martha, you wouldn't think of me as a listener-in to other people's conversations, would you?"

The question dizzied me for a moment, but he didn't let me speak. Shane Fortune was in a state that night, and what he wanted more than anything was just a chance to talk to someone he could trust.

"I brought Mary to see Claribel," he rushed on, "and then went downstairs. Nesta was resting in her room, and maybe half an hour later she came down to where I was listening to the sports' line-up over the radio. She said: 'Shane, do you know where that old kodak album of mine is?' I thought a moment then said, 'Sure, in the up-stairs hall window seat.' 'I guess you're right,' she said and sat down. 'I'm tired as the devil, Shane. Get it for me.' I ran upstairs, couldn't find it right away, kept rooting around, and that was how, without realizing it, I found myself listening to what Claribel and Mary were saying."

I nodded, picturing the window seat right outside his mother's door.

"I heard Claribel's voice first," he went on, "lifted and shrill like it gets when she's terribly upset. She said: 'I swear I didn't mean to do it, Mary. I didn't even realize what I'd done until it was too late. I was that distracted, I can't be blamed for what I did. I couldn't guess—I never thought that he'd—'

"And Mary cut in, low and cool, 'That's always been the trouble with you, Claribel. You do something without thinking, then shirk responsibility by going into hysterics. I can believe you weren't yourself. When have you ever been? But the damage is done and now we've got to make the best of it. Where were you last night when I called around six?'"

Shane paused, frowning at the desk top. "I wanted to clear out, Martha, but somehow I just stayed there on my knees poking through the clutter in the window seat."

"I understand, Shane. Go on."

"I hadn't known that Claribel had been out of the house last night, and when Mary asked her that, there was silence for a time

and then she said: 'I can't tell you where I was. You've no right to
ask.'

"Mary laughed. 'I have a very good right, Claribel. You should
recognize that. I don't care to be accused of murder.' Claribel began to cry terribly, saying a lot of things I couldn't catch and Mary
said: 'Stop it! Your act isn't getting over. I'm giving you a chance
to help straighten out the wretched mess you've made. Where did
you go at six o'clock, after Donelli had been here, and why in God's
name did you arrange to meet him in that forsaken place?'

"Claribel's voice went into a kind of scream, Martha. She said:
'You should know that, Mary Morningstar. You, you, you, of all
people should not ask me why I agreed to meet him; I'd have agreed
to go to hell if he'd asked it.'

"And Mary said, like she didn't care who heard her, 'Why were
you fool enough to give him three hundred and fifty dollars? Didn't
you know that was just opening the door for him? Why didn't you
shoot him here, in your own home, claim he was trying to rob you?
He was, all right. You'd have been perfectly safe.'"

Shane's voice was low and emotionless. I could imagine the
hours he'd put in trying to figure what to do before coming to me.
I'd listened to more than one of his confidences in the past, but
none, God help me, like this one.

He said after a moment, "And now comes the most devilish part,
Martha. I heard a sound, turned, and there was Nesta. She was
smiling and she said: 'Shane dear, I'm so sorry. I found the beastly
album.'

"I got up," Shane told me, "stood there looking at her, and knew
all of a sudden what she'd done. I just took her by the arm, marched
her into her room, and shut the door. She was still smiling. 'Shane,'
she said, 'what ails you?' 'I'll tell you, Nesta,' I said. 'I want to know
why you sent me up here on a fake errand so I couldn't help hearing that conversation between my mother and Mary Morningstar?'
She didn't bat an eye, just said, 'And you *had* to listen, Shane?'

"I said: 'No, I didn't have to listen, Nesta, any more than you
did to what went before, but you knew I would and now you must
tell me what led up to that conversation. You've been in your room

all afternoon, heard everything they said before you sent me here. What was it? I've got to know.'

"She kept on smiling, Martha, with the strangest look in her eyes, then she said, real soft, 'Yes, I did overhear it, Shane. It was just terribly interesting. So many fascinating facts. They explained so much.'"

His voice was thick and breathy. "I lost my head then, Martha. I wanted to—hurt her. Strike her! Choke her! I—I—" that thick voice broke, "wanted to kill her!"

Shane Fortune gave a great sob and dropped his head on his outstretched arms on the old-fashioned desk. I sat very still.

I said inside myself: "Now Martha Berry, this isn't any time to lose your head. You know this boy. You've known him since he was six months old. You knew him before he was born, because you knew his parents and what they were like. You know his temper! That he always worshiped *something* and all the major calamities of his life have been when the object of that worship has proven unworthy. When that happens he goes clear off balance, wants to break something, hurt something; he wants to—kill."

The little blacksmith came out of the old clock to pound on his anvil and I waited until all eight blows had been struck, before I spoke.

"But you didn't, Shane? You didn't hurt Nesta?"

He didn't move, just lay there, head on his arms, and a terrible fear grew on me, and it was as if, with other eyes than mine, I saw into the future.

Then he lifted his head, face gray and tortured. "I didn't hurt Nesta, not after all the things she said to me. About how she thought I was wealthy when she married me; I didn't deserve the name of man for the way I tagged after Claribel. She said there wasn't anything the matter with Claribel, except that she was a weak, selfish coward who clung to me like a leech." He mopped awkwardly at his face. "Remember the leeches, Martha? The things we got on our legs as kids when we went wading in the river?"

I thought then that I could never wholly forgive Nesta Fortune for this horrible comparison she had made about the woman Shane

Fortune had worshiped for so long, because I knew that he would never be able to entirely forget it. I hated Nesta for the brutal truths she had told him, for the fabric of illusion that she had seized with her small, cruel hands and torn in shreds from before his eyes.

"She asked me," he went on dully, "what Claribel had done with the money Amos left, laughed and said I wasn't smart enough to find out. Then she leaned close, Martha, 'Where was Claribel last night, Shane, around six when Mary Morningstar called? Why don't you find out? And why did she meet this greasy Wop on the woods path?'

"I didn't listen to any more," he told me. "I took her by the shoulders, set her out of the way and left. I walked all afternoon, I kept thinking things that I'd tried not to think for as long as I can remember. It was as if a light had been turned on, Martha, I couldn't help seeing." He lifted his hands in an involuntary gesture, pressed the palms against his eyes, let them fall uselessly, sat there staring at them.

"What I saw," he said after a while, "I couldn't face, so I went down to Tom Griswold's bar and took on a shot or two."

Like something made me, I said, "What did you see, Shane?"

Like something made him, he answered me, "That what Nesta said was true. That Claribel has drained the life out of me and that I've allowed it. That I've let myself be flattened and molded into a pillow for her to rest on." His voice was harsh as tin scraped along cement. "That where I longed for strength she gave me weakness. When I wanted courage and pride, she offered me helplessness and shame."

"Not that, Shane," I cried. "No shame where Claribel is concerned."

He came out of the trance then, lifted his head and looked at me with his own, restless, far-visioned eyes. I knew then that never again so long as life lasted would Shane Fortune speak against his mother.

"The shame is mine," he said simply, "that I've lacked courage. You'll not hold it against me, Martha Berry, for the things I've said?"

"I will not, Shane Fortune, for clear thinking and straight speaking are twin virtues in my mind, and no man need feel shame if in his strength he has slowed his journey to help one who is weak. It's only that he must not tarry too long, else his muscles lose their power for striding. Clear vision is yours now and you can see Claribel without a mist before your eyes. What Nesta said was true, in part, only what she did not say is that Claribel clings to you, lad, because of her great love that cannot let you go."

I hated myself for a hypocrite, thinking quite differently.

"I would not go too far," Shane said, eyes looking into illimitable distances there in my shabby, lamp-lighted attic. "I would always come back."

Would he? Or, if once he tasted freedom, could he stay his restless flight this side the grave? Perhaps Claribel sensed that quality in him, knew that in place of the orthodox, matter-of-fact child she should have had, she had borne an eagle.

Shane looked at me again. "Thank you for listening, Mis' Martha. I can't speak of other things now—Nesta and me, this business about the man who was shot. Later, I'll be able to think about it and what Mary meant, and Claribel—those things they said."

I nodded. "You're right, Shane. Don't think of them tonight. Tomorrow, later, we'll see what we can do."

And so he left me, stumbling down the narrow stairs. After a time I went down, fixed a cup of tea, ate a slice of bread and butter. Then I sat for a long time in the shadowed seclusion of my vine-covered porch, rocking gently, Ratsy curled in my lap and at last saw a great silver moon lift behind the spire of the Congregational church, and decided it was time I went to bed.

I stood up, walked to the edge of the porch for one last look at that silver moon, and just then I heard a woman laugh. It went through me like a stab of pain. Nesta Fortune! As if I wouldn't know that bright, tinkling laugh no matter where I heard it. Right on the laugh, came the sound of a man's low voice.

I stepped back into the shadows. It wasn't any of my business if Nesta Fortune chose to stroll the midnight streets of Alder Valley with some man other than her husband, but I had a plain, nosey desire to know who it was.

So I just stood there with Ratsy purring around my ankles and listened to their footsteps drawing closer under the heavy shadows of the maples. Then I realized that I couldn't see who it was and I was that meddlesome I slipped onto the wet grass, walking softly until I reached the tall hedge of yellow roses growing behind the white pickets. That way, even if I couldn't see him, I'd recognize his voice.

My heart was pounding hard and I felt guilty as a chicken-stealing parson, never having done such a thing in my life. It was so still I could hear the blood beating in my body and the sound the little leaves made over my head, under the restless wind.

Nesta's feet tapped lightly on the old, uneven stones, her short skirts made a small swishing noise, the more wonder there being so little of them.

They walked right on past me and though I actually craned my neck, I could not tell who it was she walked beside and then she said, "It's so easy to know that Claribel didn't kill him! She's such a weak sister she couldn't kill a fly."

The man answered quickly, "No, of course she couldn't. Claribel didn't have anything to do with his death."

Bennet Calder! I felt like a simpleton. After all, there was nothing wrong about Nesta's walking with Mr. Calder.

Most of the girls of Alder Valley walked with him some time or other, from the days they ran beside him, rummaging his pockets for candied popcorn, to that hour they slipped a slim, young arm through his and told him they were going to be married.

Then Nesta laughed again as they passed my closed front gate.

"Martha Berry lives there," she said, like he hadn't known it before she was born. "Hateful old witch!"

He said sharply, "Martha Berry is a grand, fine woman, Nesta, and it does not become you to speak ill of her."

I flushed with pleasure and chalked up another mark on the long score I held against Nesta. She laughed with the tinkle of a tiny bell. "Oh, well, I should worry about her, but anyway, Uncle Calder," they all called him that, "I'll tell you something if you promise you won't breathe it." She stopped and I saw the slight gesture she made halting him. "I know who killed Pietro Donelli," she said in a sibilant whisper, and his smothered exclamation was drowned in her laugh. Then they were gone and there was only darkness in the tunnel of the summer night, until from that tunnel a tall, lanky figure detached itself and Lars Knowlton ambled up and leaned across the fence.

"Hello, Mis' Martha," he said with a low chuckle. "How'd you like playing eavesdropper?"

He scared the living heart out of me, appearing like that, and to think that he'd known all the time I was there.

He said, "I saw you cat-footing along and figured you'd scented something good, so I hived up back of the patriarch oak there, and waited. What think you of my lady's latest conquest?"

"Go long with you, Lars," I snapped. "Bennet Calder's old enough to be her, well, yes, her grandfather!"

I could see the scowl on Lars's angular, ugly face. "I don't like him," he said with sudden cold fury and I saw how his hand was clenched on the sharp point of the picket.

"Lars," I said weakly. "Why, Lars, what makes you talk—look like that?"

"Nothing," he mumbled and half turned away, but a crazy thought had hit me. It wasn't so much that Lars didn't like Mr. Calder, it was that Lars did like Nesta Fortune! Much too much for his own good.

Then I saw, as I'd seen so many amazing things that day, a whole train of little incidents, remembered remarks, things I'd seen and heard going back a long way, that should have shown me how Lars felt about Nesta.

"Lars," I said, gentle like, "you're in love with Nesta, aren't you?"

I wouldn't have spoken like that to anyone else, but there was that about Lars—you could say right out what you thought. He shivered and shook the fence with sudden fury. "Yes. Now make what you will of it, Martha Berry.

"I won't make anything of it, Lars," I told him, and knew sudden pity for the boy and the lonely way of his strange, disjointed life. "There's no mortal sin in loving anyone, just so you don't let it get the best of you and make folks unhappy, Lars."

He was silent, staring down the street, then he said, "Don't worry, no one's going to be made unhappy by anything I do. She chose Shane Fortune, who could blame her, and I wish her happiness."

I didn't say anything and, after a moment he said in a different voice, "What do you think of what she said, about knowing who killed Donelli?"

"A play for attention," I said bluntly. "Nesta would say anything to get people interested in her." I stopped, realizing I was speaking unkindly of the girl he loved.

"You're absolutely right, Mis' Martha," he agreed, and I knew Lars was that sort of amazing person who can see things wrong with someone they care for. "Nesta is a born trouble-maker," he went on. "She thrives on stirring up a nest of hornets every chance she gets."

"Yes, and she'll get properly stung some day," I prophesied dourly. "It'd be a great deal more to her credit to be at home than out gallivanting around at midnight—"

"There!" he exulted. "You don't think it's proper for her to be out with old man Calder either."

"Go long with you, Lars! Calder probably spent the evening there, and she's walking a ways with him."

Bennet Calder lived maybe a block and a half beyond my place, being about the same as out in the country since my house was really the last on the street proper.

"I don't care," Lars said sullenly. "If Shane can't take care of his wife—" He paused, looking down at me. "He was out riding with Mary Morningstar today," he stated defiantly.

"What of it?" I asked quietly. "Mary's like his older sister, or his aunt, or something."

Lars snorted. "Okay. And I suppose old man Calder's like Nesta's papa or great-uncle, or something."

"Lars, if you can't do any more than stand there thinking up nasty things to say about people, get along home with you."

I was so tired I suppose my voice shook like I was going to cry. Everything had been so topsy-turvy that memorable day, with all I valued somehow toppled into the dust, and I just couldn't stand any more.

Lars had a queer, intense sense of sympathy. I saw him once on the school ground when he was twelve years old, crying in great, choking sobs because Pete Brandon had broken a meadow lark's wing, and it was flopping pitifully on the ground. Then Lars had gone up to Peter, almost twice his size, and before my astonished eyes just literally beaten the living daylights out of the big, cruel bully, crying like a baby all the time.

He must have caught that tired note in my voice, for suddenly he took my hands in his that were so slim and strong and beautiful.

"Look, Mis' Martha," he said, "let me pay penance for the hateful things I've said." He laughed on the words and I saw his mismated eyes gleaming in the vagrant light through the trees. "You're to name the hardest task you can think of, Mis' Martha, and I'll do it. You know, like the knights of old who went on hazardous missions for their fair ladies." He laughed, holding onto my cold, shaking hands. "Name something you want done, Mis' Martha. Something terribly important."

"Lars," I said, deadly serious, "you find out where Claribel Fortune went when she left the house last night at six o'clock."

His eyes went narrow and sharp as light. His fingers tightened around mine. "Claribel, at six o'clock?" he repeated, and stared hard at me, then abruptly—"I'll do it, Mis' Martha," and like a shadow he was gone, I standing alone, hanging onto the picket fence, wondering why I had made that particular request.

Chapter Six

THEY HAD THE INQUEST next day in the big back room of the Griswold Undertaking Parlors, and I thought that quite appropriate. It didn't take very long, and in its directed efficiency, I thought I recognized Courtney Brade's masterly hand.

There were several folks to identify the dead man, among them Nesta Fortune looking fresh as a new cherry pie in champagne-colored linen with brown trimmings.

Nesta answered the coroner's questions meekly, and it was only in the brief lift of her eyes that you sensed her avid interest. She said that Donelli had come to the house around four-fifteen on the afternoon of the 29th of August. She had answered the door and he had asked for Mary Morningstar. What a ripple went over the room at that. Mary sat, pale and quiet, seemingly undisturbed by the interest she aroused.

"What reason," the coroner asked, "did the man give for wishing to see Miss Morningstar?"

"No reason," Nesta replied. "He just asked if he could see her."

"Go on, Mrs. Fortune."

"I told him that Miss Morningstar did not live there. He knew that, but had been told at her house that she would be at the Fortune residence. I said she was not there, and I did not know when she would be." Nesta paused, letting her bright squirrel eyes flick over the room. "He then asked me if I would buy something, and I let him come in and looked at what he had."

"Did you make a purchase?"

"Yes, some pieces of Italian linen, and a little image."

"Did you hold any particular conversation with the man?"

Nesta smoothed her tan linen lap. "Well, he asked me a great many questions."

"What were they?"

"About people in town, Mary Morningstar, and Mrs. Amos Fortune, my mother-in-law. He saw a photograph on the piano and asked who that was."

"And who was it?"

"My husband, Shane Fortune."

Eyes were popping. Shane was not there, nor was Claribel, who was too ill to be present.

"Then what?"

"That is all, except that my mother-in-law heard us talking and came in. She seemed interested in the linens and, as I had an appointment, I left. When I returned around seven that evening, he had gone."

A few more inconsequential questions, but that was the gist of Nesta's story. Mrs. Amos Fortune's deposition was read. It was short and simple. Claribel had gone into the living room on hearing her daughter-in-law talking to a stranger, found an Italian peddler who carried some exquisite pieces of Italian linens. She had purchased several. This was after Nesta had left for her appointment. The man then made up his pack and departed. That was all there was to it.

Mary Morningstar took the stand and a hush fell, for Mary possesses something of mystery and beauty that instinctively stills voices when she appears.

She gave the same reason she had given Brade as to why Donelli had been seeking her, making it sound convincing. There seemed such an utter gap between the dead Italian peddler and the tall, exquisite woman with the proud, lifted head and quiet hands that it was impossible to believe anything else. She also told how she had stumbled on the body, making a very good story indeed, answering questions simply and in a straightforward manner.

Lars Knowlton and I repeated our stories, corroborated by Brade and Mr. Calder, and that finished the business. The ease and

smoothness with which it was handled, the presentation of surface facts only, convinced me more than ever that Courtney Brade
had engineered it.

What he knew or suspected, the confusing medley of unex-
plained incidents, he kept definitely out of the way. This thing was
merely to comply with the letter of the law, to allow him to peruse
the true facts at his leisure.

I had not the slightest doubt as I looked at him, immaculate
and correct in gray flannels, that peruse them he would, with deadly
persistence and trained accuracy. He seemed entirely different
from the friendly, casual person who had strolled along the hill
path yesterday morning, a rifle in the crook of his arm, the lilt of
the "Kerry Dancers" on his lips. I disliked him more thoroughly
than ever and mentally renewed my determination not to let him
trick me into further gabbing.

Of course, the verdict was "person or persons unknown," but I
had no illusions. The matter wasn't ended. The host of unanswered
questions would somehow have to be taken care of. A bevy of
youngsters milled around the corner, digging bare toes into the
dust, shouting questions that no one answered—Little Billy Summers, and Chick Spandling, and Sydney Makepace, Miss Flora's
skinny nephew, and shabby, homeless Dickie Ball, who is sort of a
town child as Horace is the town dog, with everybody helping to
take care of him, though I think sometimes they do a better job
with Horace than with Dickie.

They parted to let me through and I stopped to talk to them,
always being able to get on with boys. And then along came Lars
and they set up a howl of welcome. Lars is one of them, if he is
twenty-four years old and six feet two. They tag him around like
he was Santa Claus. He goes with them on their hunting and fish-
ing expeditions, teaches them how to make fires and set up a tent.
He grinned now, and waved a hand. "Come on, fellas, let's squan-
der some cash for a flock of cones," and they yelled in glee and
formed round him like a disheveled bodyguard.

He looked at me, eyes bright and concentrated. "See you later,
Mis' Martha. I'm off on that mission you gave me. How about a

token for my spear?" And away they went on the way to Pop Whittlesey's to buy ice cream cones. Yes, Lars is a queer lad.

It was quarter past ten and Linda was standing by the east-bound mail sack when I came in, turning a letter in her hands. She glanced up with quick interest.

"Well, how did it go?" she asked.

"About as I expected."

She continued to look at me, still holding the letter. "They didn't find out who did it," she stated rather than asked.

"Of course not. How could they?"

"I don't know," she admitted, then suddenly, "Mis' Martha, I don't want to stick into this thing, but wasn't there something about a note the dead man carried? From someone in South America?"

I didn't look at her as I straightened my hair before the little mirror. That detail was all over town, like most of the others.

"Yes, Linda. They didn't mention it this morning. It was all very brief and straight to the point."

She said, "What was the man's name? The one who wrote the letter? I've forgotten."

I turned facing her. "Angelo Marquand."

She caught a quick breath, her face suddenly white. "Look," she said faintly, and thrust the envelope into my hands.

It crackled under my fingers. It had writing all over the face, addresses crossed out, forward written in. It had traveled far, that letter, before it found Mary Dawn in quiet, out-of-the-way Alder Valley.

I just stood there staring at it. Linda said, "The foreign stamp— they're always interesting. She's had more than one."

"Yes," I said.

"But the name on the back; I wasn't sure."

I looked at the foreign stamp. I turned the envelope. It said, Return to Angelo Marquand, Bariloche, S. A.

Voices sounded on the other side of the boxes. Keys rattled. A car screeched in the street. I said, "Open the window, Linda. The mail's up, isn't it?"

"Yes, Mis' Martha." She didn't move. I could feel her eyes on my face. She said, "Shall I put it in Mary's box? She comes down for the five o'clock."

I had a vision of Mary coming down for the five o'clock, the crowd that always gathered, Mary opening her box, drawing out the letter from Angelo Marquand.

I said, "No, Linda. I'll take it to her."

She gave a little gasping sigh, opened the window. I didn't have to tell Linda to keep still about the letter. Linda doesn't require reminding on such a point.

I WON'T MAKE any pretense. During the long, hot hours while Linda took her time off I was tempted. Everyone has had, I suppose, such an experience, a certain combination of circumstances that gives you the opportunity of playing God.

I put the letter in a locked drawer in my desk. If Mary dropped in and no one was there, I'd give it to her. Otherwise, I'd take it to her house as soon as Linda returned at three o'clock.

People drifted in and out, to ask for mail, buy stamps, money orders, send packages. Hank Treadwell, the trapper, came in from over on Nodaway Creek to collect his advance fur catalog and bring me news of Starbuck, his pet deer, all but killed by dogs a few days ago. Sooner or later they all talked about the Donelli matter. All but Hank, that is. Hank has little to say at the best. I let them ramble on, saying as little as I could, and all the time I kept thinking:

"Mary knew Angelo Marquand who is, Brade thinks, a prisoner in a South American jail. She must have known him or he wouldn't be writing to her. He knew Pietro Donelli and threatened to kill him. He said he'd hold the thought of death for him many thousand miles away. Donelli was killed here in Alder Valley day before yesterday, and this morning comes a letter to Mary, from Marquand—"

I was alone just then and I unlocked the drawer, examined the post mark on the letter. It had been mailed the 21st of June! Better than three months it had been on its way. Why? Two weeks at the outside should have brought it to Alder Valley, then I studied the forwards, seven of them. That accounted for the time and it showed also that Marquand did not have Mary's present address.

I looked at the one he had written in that fine, slanting hand—

Miss Mary Dawn (her professional name) *c/o*
Sage Rockwell, 72 Fifth Ave.,
New York, N. Y., U. S. A.

Sage Rockwell had been for years manager of Mary's concert tours. I turned that letter a dozen times, as I had turned so many others there in the post office, and then it was that the thought struck me that if I destroyed it—

Resolutely I shut it away and threw myself into work, so angry my hands actually shook. Postmistress of Alder Valley had I been for better than eighteen years and never once had I betrayed my trust.

I worked up a fine fit of indignation at the idea, and then I stopped, stared straight ahead.

"At least you could open it," I argued. "You can do it perfectly; it'd give you tremendous advantage over Courtney Brade who thinks he's so smart. If it should be something incriminating for her, you could burn it."

It went on like that while my fingers flew over the books and I stopped to wait on the window. I told myself I could do a great deal of good by snooping into what didn't concern me, and prying where I had no moral or legal right. I imagined myself reading the letter, burning it, burying forever within the depths of my mind the damning information it contained.

I took it out, held it hard, considering the little Sterno stove on which I sometimes make tea, thinking what steam would do. Then, the Lord be thanked, I came to my senses, slammed the thing into my pocket, put on my hat and watched the clock until Linda came in, right on time as always.

Chapter Seven

MARY WAS IN, black Daisy said, showing her wonderful white teeth in an expansive grin. "In, Mis' Martha, and a'layin' down upstairs."

Mary had heard my voice through the open window and greeted me with a smile of welcome. "Martha! How nice! I'm getting up—"

"You're staying right where you are," I told her grimly, sat down beside the couch where she rested, brown hair in a long, thick braid over her shoulder, a simple dress of sprigged muslin making her look like a small girl.

The room was done in green and silver, and there wasn't much on the walls except one or two delicate etchings in thin, silver frames, a brush of pale green wild grass in the swept hearth.

Mary lay back, hands behind her head, eyes large and dark, face strangely thin. She said, "What brings you, Martha? I know it's something."

"This," I said, and handed her the letter. It had always been that way with Mary and me. Just plain out and out what we had to say to one another.

She looked at the letter, one arm crooked behind her head and she was no longer a little girl in sprigged muslin but an old, tired woman with a gray face and haggard eyes. I tried not to watch that terrible transformation but I could not look away.

"I thought you'd rather have it this way," I faltered, and thanked the Lord that I'd had sense enough to bring it.

"Angelo! It's from Angelo!" She looked at me, eyes blank and sightless. "It can't be," she said. "Angelo couldn't write to me. Angelo is dead!"

"Not when he wrote that, Mary," I heard myself say. "Not the 21st of June."

Her eyes, still wide and unfocused, returned to the letter. She frowned slightly. "Oh!" she said, and again, "Oh! Yes! The 21st of June. No, he wasn't dead then."

"When did he die, Mary?"

"The 12th of August this year."

I thought: "Who is he that she remembers so well the day he died? And what is this letter, from one these weeks in his grave?"

She sat up slowly, tossing aside the thick amber-brown braid. "Give me a cigarette, Martha," she said, and I passed the box to her. After that she opened the letter, fingers steady, cheeks fallen in as though she had been very ill.

I thought: "I won't watch her read it. I'll be damned if I will!" and I turned, staring out through the green silk curtains with their gay festoons of silver maple leaves.

"This is Wednesday," I remembered. "Courtney Brade is coming to supper Thursday evening. I'll not tell him! No matter how clever he is, he'll never find from me that Mary got a letter from Angelo Marquand who died three weeks ago." And then I got what Lars calls a sock on the button.

How did Mary know that Angelo Marquand had died on the 12th of August?

Paper rustled behind me. No other sound. How had Mary known what Donelli looked like? That the ring in his ear was flat? Where had she been the night that he was killed? Mary saying to Claribel, who had worn her shoes, "I don't care to be accused of murder. Why did you give him three hundred and fifty dollars? Why didn't you shoot him here, in your own living room?"

Mary rose. I turned as she crossed to the fireplace, struck a match, held it to the clump of wild grasses, bent and carefully laid the open letter on the flames.

The fire seized it hungrily, lifted it so that it stood straight up and I saw plainly that opening line with the brightness of the fire behind it: *Dear Mary: This is to warn you*—then it curled like a thing in agony, went whirling in fiery tatters up the chimney, and there was Mary with one hand on the mantel, head lowered, looking down at it.

"Dear Mary:" Angelo Marquand had written from South America, "This is to warn you—"

Mary came slowly to the couch, sat down.

"That is the only end possible to a broken, tragic life," she said. And after a moment, "Adios, Angelo Marquand," she whispered, eyes briefly on the flimsy puff of ashes in the grate.

The fragrance of the burned grasses was sweet in the green and silvery room. Hazy sunlight drifted like smoke through the listless curtains. A woodpecker drummed monotonously at the big maple, head a rhythmic scarlet beat against the rich wood.

Mary said: "Nearly thirty years ago, Martha, when I was very young and—lonely, I was living in a small town in southern Italy, because a famous teacher summered there and I thought if I could study with him there would be nothing more to achieve, but that is not the story. I had a room at the old gray villa among the olive trees on the side of the hill above the village."

The scratching of a match made a sharp sound in the silence. She blew a cloud of smoke.

"That was a happy time," she said quietly. "Happy and fearful. I was scarcely twenty-one, a gawky country girl, alone in a strange land. Not," she added, "that Italy was ever really a strange land to me. It was, when I left the boat at Naples, as if I had at last come home."

She paused a moment, then, "You know how it is, Martha, the feeling that sometimes grips you when you first touch the soil of a foreign land, as if something tangible lifts to meet you, reaches up from the very earth and claims you. You know, Martha."

"Yes, Mary, I know," I told her and then wondered at such a ridiculous statement. I did not know, of course. I, plain Martha Berry, who had never touched the soil of a foreign land, who had scarce been outside Alder Valley ten times in my close to fifty-six years. What could I know of the feel of another land than mine?

"I fell ill," Mary said, "and the signora of the gray villa cared for me. It was a fever brought on by too much work, too little food in those years before. She saved my life. When I was strong enough to leave I tried to tell her I had no money, but she only looked at me with great, dark eyes, so luminous in her thin, beautiful face.

"She said: 'Signorina, what I have done for you I would do for anyone who came to me ill and alone. I want no payment in money. I ask of you one favor.'

"She asked me," Mary said, "to help her son, be his friend in that future she felt sure I would have. She knew that his way would be stormy; she feared for him. It seemed little to promise. It is of no moment now, Martha. All I meant to tell you was that the tall, dark-eyed signora who had once been a great lady, and still was in spite of her poverty, was Marianna Marquand, and the son whom she loved better than her life was named Angelo."

She stopped speaking, and I drew myself away from that old gray villa on a slope of hillside in southern Italy, to a small, tree-shaded town in America where, on another hillside, a man had met death.

I said: "And Angelo Marquand died three weeks ago in a South American prison, Mary?"

Her eyes flared wide. "Martha! How did you know?"

I told her of the letter Brade had found on Donelli's body, of his deduction about the address. She relaxed slowly, a pale fear on her face.

"He is clever, Brade. Yes, Martha, Angelo died three weeks ago. The superintendent of the prison notified me because he knew I was Angelo's—friend." Her voice broke on a sob. She covered her working face. "Oh, I did not keep my promise, Martha. I tried but I did not. I should—"

I said sharply, "What could you do, Mary, for this Angelo Marquand?"

Her head lifted. She looked old and unspeakably tired.

"Nothing, Martha. I never could do anything for him, for wild, handsome, devil-possessed Angelo, who had so much of beauty and power and vision, and despair. He was doomed from the beginning! He was sentenced to life imprisonment fifteen years ago for murder. I do not know, I cannot say if he was guilty. Signora Marianna is dead these many years and I am glad. Angelo is dead now—" she shivered in the warm room, "Angelo is dead now—" she repeated and added under her breath, "and I am glad."

It was a strange story, but stranger still that the threads had spun so far: Italy to South America, to Alder Valley dreaming in the summer heat, and that I should in some way be a part of it.

I said after a time, "Mary, who was Donelli?" She roused out of some far contemplation. "Pietro Donelli was a native of that same village. A worthless, low-born boy who sold vegetables at the signora's door. He went out to South America at the same time Angelo did and was in the group accused of the murder of a wealthy rancher. With Angelo, and four others, he went to prison."

I sighed in sheer amazement. "He escaped?"

"No. He was paroled eight years ago. I do not know the details. That is why he was seeking me here, knowing that I had tried to help Angelo, sent money to try and make things easier. He thought to get money from me now on the pretext of helping Angelo, not knowing I had heard of his death. He was a slimy scoundrel. He deserved death."

I took a long breath and plunged. "Claribel? What connection could he have had with Claribel? Why," I figuratively closed my eyes, "should she have given him three hundred and fifty dollars?"

"Claribel is a fool," she said fiercely. "But Martha, I tell you honestly," her eyes met mine squarely, "I do not know, and Claribel will not tell me, why she feared him or why she gave him money."

"Or why she killed him?" I asked, my throat tight.

Mary's face was colorless as linen.

"Did she kill him, Martha?" she asked, eyes on mine.

"Did she, Mary?" I repeated, meeting that glance.

I thought that long look would never end. The tension of it was unendurable, then breath left her on a sharp exhalation.

"Claribel couldn't do it, Martha. No matter how much she might want to, she couldn't kill a man."

It was like she was pleading with me, begging for reassurance.

I said, "I don't know, Mary. I do not have wisdom enough to know what Claribel Fortune might do."

She did not move, still looking at me. Then slowly she nodded.

"You're right, Martha. You have a devilish way of being right. We can't know what Claribel would do."

"Or you," I said, "or any of us."

"Or I, or any of us," she repeated, and after a little while I went, leaving her alone in the green and silver room with her memories of a gray villa in an olive grove on a hillside in southern Italy.

CHAPTER EIGHT

I DID NOT REALIZE how long I had been with Mary until I came out and saw the sun slanting toward a stormy setting. The wind made a lonesome sound in the big trees. Leaves fell thickly round me and the fields had a brown and dusty look.

It was as I turned the corner for the post office that I met Lars Knowlton. "I've finished my mission, Mis' Martha," he said, stepping along beside me.

"Mission?" I repeated blankly.

"Yes. Remember? You gave me a penance to work out."

Suddenly I recalled last night, Lars leaning across my picket fence, Nesta Fortune saying, "I know who killed Donelli."

I stopped, looking up at him. "All right, young man, let's have it. Where did Claribel go that night at six, and how did you find out about it?"

There was high color in his lean, homely face. "I'm a swell detective," he admitted modestly. "I have ways of working things out. Those kids, you know, they get around, they know about folks and—"

"Yes, I understand," I told him, blood pounding my head. "You took those sticky young'uns on a hike and wormed information from them."

"They didn't know it," he explained. "They're a grand lot. We played a game of immigrants going west. Our wagon train was attacked by Indians, our horses killed. We made a barricade of prairie schooners, got one chap out under cover of darkness for relief from the fort, posted guards and sat around an imaginary camp fire, spinning yarns to keep up our spirits. I heard some swell stories."

"Lars Knowlton," I said thinly, "stop gabbing and tell me this minute where Claribel Fortune went that evening."

His face sobered, then the old impish grin was back. "Okay, Mis' Martha, you asked for it. Twenty minutes after Donelli left, she came out of the back door on the double, down the garden path, along the alley, into the back gate of the last house, ran up the path into the back door of that house. That is as far as Dickie Ball, lookout on the good ship 'Pirate's Gold' atop of Fisher's barn, followed her."

I caught his arm. "Lars! You're crazy! So is that little ragamuffin Dickie!"

"Not on your life! Dickie's trained as lookout on a pirate ship; he doesn't make mistakes."

"But, Lars," I said weakly, "the last house—the last house in the block is—mine."

His arm muscles twitched under my hold. His eyes flickered like Ratsy's when he sights a mouse. He stared at me hard for a moment, then he grinned. "Right you are, Mis' Martha. The last house in the block is yours, and the last house is where Claribel went, and don't you dare doubt my information." Then he was gone, striding down the street, hair flopping over his eyes and I stood there looking after him, never so completely bewildered in my life.

During the course of a fairly long life, I have worked out little ways of meeting difficulties. At spring house cleaning, when everything is dumped in the middle of the floor and there seems no way of clearing it, instead of working myself into a state wondering what to do with it, I take care of what I can and the rest goes in the clutter closet. I call it that because it takes care of the clutter until I can figure out what to do with it. That time always comes, and bit by bit the tangle is straightened out, everything finds its place, and I'm not worn to a frazzle.

That was the way it was that evening that Lars Knowlton made his astonishing statement about Claribel, and then walked away so jauntily. I stood in the midst of a tremendous mental clutter, and there certainly wasn't any place, so far as I could see, to put things.

What Lars said didn't make sense, yet I was convinced that Dickie had been right. Just the same I'd been at home all that evening, and Claribel *had not* come, and right there I had to let loose of the problem because I couldn't solve it.

In due time, if I kept calm, I'd sort it out and get it in order. In the meantime, I stopped at the post office just long enough to see that it was closed, then headed home.

It was just as I turned the corner by the Cozy Cafe that I ran straight into Courtney Brade, his arms full of old, dusty papers. He looked a sight, hat laced with dust webs, coat smeared with ink, hands that dirty and grimy he might have been heaving coal.

"Land of Goshen," I said in spite of my resolution not to talk to him again, "what *have* you been doing? House cleaning for Gene Norton at the Citizen office? Needs it all right; he hasn't redded out in thirty years!"

Brade hitched the papers higher, they were all but spilling into the street. "House cleaning wasn't my mission, Mis' Martha," he said, and wrinkled his nose, eyes filling with tears though he wasn't crying. He said, "Good Lord, my nose itches," and wrinkled it again so it looked like Evinrude's when he smells something he doesn't like.

I laughed in spite of myself, and then I just whisked out my handkerchief and rubbed it vigorously, him chuckling and snorting and ending up in a deep down laugh that spilled half the papers into the street.

"Thanks, Mis' Martha," he said, "that was grand," and he bent to gather the scattered sheets.

I helped him, and that's how I saw they went so far back, caught bits of information I'd forgotten these thirty years, saw notices of graduation exercises the last year I taught.

It was queer down there on my knees in the main street of Alder Valley reading those things as I stacked the papers.

He was beside me on the dusty sidewalk and I said, "Lands sake, you must like reading ancient history. Whatever do you hope to find in these sheets?"

He glanced at me sideways, eyes serious. "Is anything ever completely dead and gone, Mis' Martha? Don't the effects of everything we do go on and on, maybe forever?"

That was a queer notion. I stopped stacking and squatted there looking at him. I thought how many things had developed these last few days that seemed to have their beginnings long ago, like Donelli carrying Shane Fortune's picture, how Shane had been born in Italy twenty-four years ago, and Mary's story about how, even further back, she had promised to help a wayward boy, and—

Brade had the papers under one arm now and he rose, lifting me to my feet very carefully like he was afraid I would break. He was smiling though his eyes were grave. "I'm that darned tired," he said, "and hungry. My word!"

I didn't in the least mean to, but there it was. "Come on up to my house," I invited, "I'll fix you something and you can read your old papers to your heart's content."

"Oh, that's tops," he said enthusiastically. "You won't count me out tomorrow night?"

I felt flattered that he'd want to come twice, so away we went by the short cut and in no time there he was, looking entirely too big for my parlor, and not a blessed place to spread those papers.

That was the second time I took a visitor to my upstairs room. I hesitated a moment because it had always been so definitely mine, then I opened the door. "There's a big desk up there," I told him. "It belonged to Mat. He used to spread his blue prints on it."

Brade said, "Thanks. That's nice of you, Mis' Martha," and like a shot he was gone, clattering up those straight, narrow stairs, bending his head, I knew, under the slanting roof. I went after him, lit the lamp, drew the curtains, gave him Mat's old swivel chair.

He stood a moment, looking the place over, then he said real quiet like, "That's Mat, isn't it?" and nodded toward the picture over the fireplace. Before I could speak, not that I wanted to—"And that's you and Mat on your wedding day?" and he stepped closer to the faded photograph I keep back in the corner. I didn't move, and there was that queer achey feeling in my throat, then he turned smiling at me. "What a lovely bride," he said and real quick I went downstairs because I couldn't let Courtney Brade see how my face looked.

I liked the feeling of him being up there in the attic room while I fixed supper. I heard him move the swivel chair into place, heard him whistling softly, and then he was quiet and I didn't hear anything except that now and then the chair creaked as he moved. It was dim in the kitchen but I didn't light the lamp for I didn't want anyone coming in to visit. The wind had risen and it was heavenly cool. It rattled leaves against the windows and set the maples swishing.

I started to make tea, then remembered how Brade had gone for Tommy's coffee, so I put on the big blue pot instead. I sliced down what was left of my Sunday's roast, cut up some cold tomatoes, set out a jar of my own currant jelly, sliced some thick white bread and got the butter out. Then suddenly I got the notion to take the supper upstairs. In less than twenty minutes I had the big wicker tray loaded and was slowly climbing the stairs to the attic room. He heard me coming and opened the door. Yellow lamplight shone on the stairs, and he gave a grunt of surprise when he saw what I carried.

"Hello, what's this? Picnic supper?"

"I thought maybe you'd rather have it up here," I said, and he took the tray from me.

"I'll have it here with pleasure if you'll join me, Mis' Martha."

"I'm going to," I promised. "No, don't move the papers. Run downstairs and wash if you like. I put out towels." I began rolling out my little sewing table, spreading the luncheon cloth, setting out the food.

It was a pleasant meal. The lamp made a wide circle of radiance on the desk, lighted the table beside it. I didn't say much, remembering my determination not to let him trick me into more gabbing. He'd gone through about half the papers, had the rest spread on the desk. I kept wondering what he was searching for, and my curiosity grew until it was hard to keep my eyes from those dusty, yellow pages.

If he noticed my craning, he didn't give any sign. He ate like the food tasted good and he was as hungry as he'd claimed to be.

At last he gave a sigh of satisfaction, leaned back, drew out a long brown pipe, the bowl glistening like watered silk.

He grinned across at me. "Mind?" I shook my head. A pipe is a pleasant thing on an autumn evening and it was a long time since the fragrance of one had filled my house. He chuckled. "You're the answer to a wise man's prayer, Mis' Martha," he said, stuffing tobacco into the bowl. "When his nose itches, you scratch it, when he's hungry you feed him, when he's been fed, you encourage him to light his pipe."

"Courtney Brade," I said real sharp, "you're the beatin'est man I ever saw for handin' out pretty speeches."

He looked at me under drawn dark brows. "When you know me better you won't say that, Mis' Martha. I say what I mean at a time like this, and I say it's a real delight to stretch out here and be myself." Somehow he did sound like he meant it, and he looked so comfortable, long legs stretched out, head thrown back, eyes half closed, smoke of the brown pipe circling lazily.

"You know, Mis' Martha," he said suddenly, "what I told you there on the street about the results of our actions going on forever?"

I nodded, hands hard clenched because I knew he was going back to the one thing that interested him most of all just now.

"Well, it's true. Now look here. We find a man murdered, an unknown Italian peddler, whom it seems no one's ever heard of around here." He paused on that lifted inflection but I shut my lips tight, afraid of what I would say.

"Yet he carries the picture of a young man in this town, Shane Fortune, and his bride. Shane Fortune was born in Italy. His father died in Paris. Pietro Donelli, the dead man, was a prisoner at one time in South America. So was another man, Angelo Marquand. Mary Morningstar was on a concert tour in South America, seven years ago, just a few months after Donelli was released on parole. He comes here looking for her, her heel prints are found near his body, she admits being there, but her story won't hold water."

He placed his pipe between his lips, puffed thoughtfully.

"You see, Mis' Martha," he went on, "all these things are results of incidents set in motion long ago. Why," he asked abruptly, "did Amos Fortune take his young wife to Europe?"

"She was sickly all the time. The doctor thought a sea trip might help and Amos had plenty of money."

"How much money?"

I wet my lips. "Something over half a million."

Brade turned slowly, looking at me. "Huh! Half a million, eh? And yet Mrs. Fortune is anything but wealthy today. It doesn't take twenty-four years to get rid of five hundred thousand dollars, but she's always lived quietly, hasn't she? No extensive travels, lavish entertainment, no wild expenditures?"

I realized that once more Courtney Brade was questioning me, but I felt no particular resentment. I'd brought it on myself. I said, "Claribel has lived those twenty-four years exactly as she lives to-day, with only one girl to do her work, and when Shane was young, a woman to take care of him. She's made two short trips to Califor-nia and it's close to ten years since she's had folks in to dinner. So how she got rid of half a million dollars, I wouldn't know."

He stared hard at me. "Investments?" he hazarded.

"There isn't much privacy in a town like this, Captain Brade. Everyone knew that Amos left his money in good sound stocks and bonds, all except some half dozen fine farms. Merta Dillon, wife of our bank president, talks too much, and I've heard her tell how Claribel's had the bank sell those bonds, get rid of the stocks, one after the other, until they're all gone. All the farms have been sold. As for Claribel investing the money, why, Claribel doesn't know what the word means."

Brade was listening intently, nodding shortly to each of my state-ments. "All right, then," he snapped, "what has she done with it?"

I started like he'd slapped me. "Good heavens," I gasped, "I don't know!"

He grinned amiably. "No, I guess you wouldn't, Mis' Martha. Does anyone in town? What's said about it? What's the specula-tion, the opinions? That's where you're valuable as my aide, folks won't tell me things, but you don't even have to ask—you know."

I flushed at his calling me his aide, but I wasn't going to be tricked again if I could help it. I said, "Captain Brade, it's been one of the topics of interest in Alder Valley for the last fifteen years, but I swear there hasn't been one worthwhile suggestion. No one knows any more than I do. She just turned everything into cash, put the money in the bank and checked it out."

"To whom?"

I blinked and for a moment was terribly confused, then I remembered things I'd heard, gossip at Aid, in the post office.

"The checks were made to herself. Never to anyone else. She'd come to the bank, or send Shane after he got older. They'd give him the money and that was the end of it."

Brade nodded. "About the story I heard from Calder. I thought he might have some idea, having been her lawyer, but he doesn't know. I'd hoped you might have something definite."

"If she'd left Calder to handle the estate," I said, "there'd be some money now."

"Why did she break with Calder?"

"I don't know, but I remember when it happened, all of twenty years ago. I mind well it was after Christmas, one of the coldest Januaries I ever saw. Claribel was stronger then, got around a lot and seemed real happy, having Shane and all. And then one day a man came into the post office looking for her."

I sensed Brade's movement as he leaned forward. "I didn't know him and I don't to this day, but strangers were rarer in Alder Valley then. He was a short, fat, little man with small blue eyes and a big, red-veined nose. He wore a grand broadcloth overcoat with a real astrakhan collar, and carried a brief case and an ebony cane with a gold head. He asked where Mrs. Amos Fortune lived, and when I told him he thanked me and left. The whole town was curious but little good it did them. He landed there about five o'clock in the afternoon and at eleven Charlie Wheeler got a phone call to come up with his hack. He took the stranger down for the twelve-thirty train back to town and that's the last anyone ever heard of him."

"Yes?" Brade rejoiced, in that purring tone. "And how did this bring on the break with Calder, Miss Martha?"

"I don't know," I said sharply, "but after that visit Claribel had her first heart attack. The doctor was called around one o'clock, stayed until morning, and was hard put to it to save her life, yet she had to have her lawyer, in spite of everything. She sent for him—"

"For Calder?"

"Yes. In spite of the cold and how sick she was. Mr. Calder never talked, so no one knows about it, but it soon got around that he wasn't handling her affairs. He didn't seem to be put out and when anyone questioned him he said it was a matter of business, and his client had a right to do as she wished. But from then on Claribel has had nothing to do with him in a business way, though they're friendly enough, and it was a little later that she began drawing big sums from the bank."

Brade's eyes were on fire. I could see that he was longing to wring my neck because I couldn't tell him more about the little man with the gold-headed cane, but he had become a legendary figure in Alder Valley, a man of mystery who appeared out of the storm, stayed a few hours and vanished. And it was a tribute to his powers of concealment that no one in Alder Valley had been able to pick up his trail. They did learn that he had come from the city and returned to it, but that was all. Brade tapped out his pipe and did not speak until it was filled and lighted. Then he leaned back and said very slowly. "Mis' Martha, I'm asking a real favor. I want you to relax, let your mind go back to that coldest January you ever saw. I want you to be there, living every day, every hour, of the days and weeks that followed the visit of the man with the gold-headed cane. I want you to tell me," his voice had a monotonous, almost hypnotic effect, "what strikes you as the most untoward, unusual incident that happened in connection with Claribel Fortune or Bennet Calder."

I was glad he added that last, for that was the winter after Mat died and it had burned into my heart until the chill white mornings, the bitter nights, the short gray days, crunch of steps on the icy walks, screech of frozen branches in the long night hours had become a torturing part of myself, and I had unconsciously woven a thick, dark curtain of forgetfulness, drawn it tight against the aching memory of those lonely months.

Under the quiet insistence of his words, a hand came out, and not my own, to pull that curtain aside. I cried out against the cruel intrusion, but I was helpless; the curtain was drawn and there was everything as if it had never ceased to be.

It was like a room you have locked tightly and not visited for so long you believe you have forgotten its contents, but when the door is opened there it is. Nothing has changed. Everything is exactly as you left it, with maybe a thin gray film of dust; only for me there was no dust to soften the pictures. They stood before me with devastating intensity, so that, for a moment, I did not see the attic room, or Courtney Brade, or hear the wind whooping in the big maple, but instead—

I cried out suddenly and did not know that my hands lifted as if to keep off a blow. "I can't!" I choked. "I can't remember!" It didn't even sound like my own voice, but something thin and pain-filled and far away.

Brade said, "Mis' Martha! I'm sorry," and between my laced fingers I saw his glance go to the picture on the mantel. "Forget what I asked," he added, and laughed a little, like he was in some way ashamed of himself.

My hands dropped. I straightened up, looking at him.

"Bennet Calder wrote to Mary Morningstar," I said. "That answers your questions."

He jerked back and something like a flicker of admiration lighted his gray eyes. "Good work," he said softly. "Good work, Martha Berry. Give me some details, will you?"

I leaned back in my low rocker. "There aren't many, Captain Brade. Bennet Calder came into the post office one evening and asked how much it cost to send a letter to London. I told him and he paid for the stamps, dropped the letter into the box and went out. When I picked it up to put it into the night mail, I saw that it was addressed to Mary Dawn, at a hotel in London."

"And you select that fact as the most unusual in connection with Calder, or Mrs. Fortune, during that period. Why?"

"Because it is the only letter that Bennet Calder ever sent to a foreign address, the first one he had ever written to Mary, and the last, so far as I know."

"It struck you forcibly at the time?"

"Yes. I wondered why he would be writing Mary. He scarcely knew of her existence before she left here."

Brade settled lower in the chair. "Did he receive an answer?"

I sent my mind back along that old trail. "Yes, about three weeks later, from Milan, Italy."

"He never received another from her?"

"Not through my post office."

"How else would he get it?"

"Mr. Calder used to have an office in Croydon, the county seat, thirty-five miles from here. He was there three days a week. He could have received it there, I suppose."

"I see. He could have written her from there too, couldn't he?"

"Of course, but why?"

"I don't know, Mis' Martha," he said impatiently, "really I don't."

Well, maybe he didn't—that is, know exactly why he had asked the questions he had, and insisted on certain points being cleared up. He leaned forward abruptly, picked up a copy of the "Citizen," folded carefully to expose a marked paragraph.

"Read that," he ordered.

The dusty paper crackled under my fingers. The date line was June 28, 1914. The lines Brade had outlined formed a small paragraph in the "News Around Town," the personal column Gene Norton has run for nigh onto forty years, the Lord forgive him. It read:

> Word has reached us of the birth of a son to Mrs. Amos Fortune, on May 10th, at Roleno, Italy. This interesting bit of news came by way of a letter from Claribel, to Miss Nellie Lou Smedley, to whom we are indebted—

I laid the paper down and looked at Brade. His eyes were blurred by that curious, cloudy quality I had noticed before. Before I could speak, he handed me another paper, also folded and marked. Again I glanced at the date line. August 12, 1914. This time the marked portion was in the form of a special news story.

My eyes took it in in one comprehensive flash, picking out the essential facts:

> —a son born to Claribel Fortune—residing in Italy— close to two years. The baby came into the world at the Lady of Mercy Hospital in Rome—May 10th— Mrs. Fortune will return home—

I drew a hand across my eyes. My mind was struggling to recapture incidents, events, of that year of 1914, arrange them coherently. I said, "I don't understand. One account says Shane was born at Roleno, Italy. The other—in Rome."

Brade was watching me intently, exactly the way Ratsy concentrates on a mouse hole, so that even his whiskers point toward it. I could have sworn that Brade's short, clipped mustache quivered faintly.

"There's something wrong," I complained. "Shane, the baby, couldn't have been born twice."

"No," Brade said, "and where, in your opinion, was Shane Fortune born?"

"Why," I said feebly, "I always thought—Claribel said, gave me to understand it was Rome—a hospital."

He touched the old yellow papers. "Yet the first account, written to Miss Nellie Lou Smedley, names the spot as Roleno, Italy. Who is Miss Smedley, Martha?"

"Nellie Lou Smedley was a dear old lady whom we all loved."

"Nellie Lou *was* a dear old lady? She is—?"

"Yes. Miss Nellie Lou died eight years ago come Christmas."

He was silent a moment, considering this, then, "What did you all think about this variation in the reports of Shane Fortune's birth? How did you figure it out?"

I stared at him, deeply puzzled. "Why, we didn't even catch it."

"Yet someone must have noticed it."

I got a sudden flash. "It was 1914! The war! There wasn't anything else talked about, noticed."

"Yes. That explains it, no doubt. And Claribel gave you to understand that the baby was born in Rome? How exact was her attitude on that point?"

I frowned at the roses on the lamp shade. "Claribel is never very exact, Captain Brade. After you've spent an afternoon with her, you can't recall anything definite she's said. She never really told me in so many words: 'Shane was born in the Lady of Mercy hospital in Rome, Italy.' She referred to it indirectly: the long corridors, the pleasant room she had, the nuns in quiet gray, how the bells sounded from the cathedral. She told me—" I hesitated.

"Yes? She told you—?"

"How terrified she was at thought of having a baby yet she was so happy and proud because old Dr. Wentworth had told her she could not have a child."

Brade grunted. "Wrong, wasn't he?"

"Yes. But that's all I have to build up my belief that Shane was born in Rome. As to the other—that town—I don't know anything about it."

"No," Brade said. "You wouldn't. I don't either, really, but it's interesting that both Pietro Donelli and Angelo Marquand were natives of that town!"

I jumped straight out of my chair. Before I knew it, I was standing there, hanging onto the table, and my face must have been as white as the luncheon cloth. I heard myself say: "Mary! Mary Morningstar! That's where she was! Marianna Marquand asked her—" then I got hold of myself. It wasn't until I'd dropped into the chair that I realized that Brade had risen too, was still standing, looking down at me. I wanted to cry out against him, run down the stairs, into the night, anywhere from the dominance of his personality, the insistence of his regard.

He said, "All right, Mis' Martha, let's have it. Mary Morningstar was in Roleno, Italy, was she? She knew Marianna Marquand, mother of Angelo? Marianna asked her—what?"

I couldn't take my eyes from his, but some deeply buried rigidity held me silent, closed my lips like they'd grown together. I'd been shocked into a damaging admission. I didn't have to go on, betray Mary's confidence.

He leaned toward me, smiling. "Look, Mis' Martha, I can't force you to talk. Stick pins into you, roast the soles of your feet with hot irons. There isn't anything I can do except just ask you in the name of decency and loyalty to forget your personal feelings and tell me what you know."

I found words then. I said harshly, "Decency? Loyalty? What's decent about telling what you're pledged not to tell? What's loyal in betraying—"

He shook his head. "See, you've got it all wrong. The decency I'm appealing to is that of order that straightens out unhealthy tangles, clears up muddy backwashes in people's lives. The loyalty I want you to show is to your community, your ideals, that basic cleanness in you that rebels against this thing we call murder, this violent taking of human life which, unless controlled, threatens all of us. That's bigger than loyalty to one person; wider, deeper, higher than any of our little loves and hates and fears." The man's voice was like an organ, low, throbbing, intense, setting every fiber of my being to quivering.

In that moment I saw something about him, something in his own life that spelled tragedy, a bitter victory won only after personal considerations had been eliminated. It set age on him, lined his face with pain, made his hair seem suddenly white instead of just silver, gave to his cloudy gray eyes a strange luminance, and for the first time I wondered what story lay behind the gorgeous moonstone ring he wore.

He sat down very quietly, hands motionless along the arms of the old swivel chair. He didn't say any more. He didn't even look at me. It was like he'd played his last card, appealed to what he thought I was. After that it was up to me. It was, too, and in the little room there was only the hissing of the big lamp, swish of wind-stirred branches, lonely chirping of the crickets in the autumn night.

It was like they were all outside of me and I, alone, stood on a high point somewhere, looking down—seeing people traveling winding roads, lonely, uncertain, stumbling over things that weren't really there, making trouble and discord and tragedy because of their blindness.

A queer way to feel, but I'm glad it came as it did, and that for one breathless moment I could see so clearly.

After a time I sat up slowly, looked straight at him. "I thank you for what you've said, Captain Brade. I'll tell you what I know."

His hand lifted slightly, relaxed. "Thank you, Mis' Martha. It will make it easier for all of us."

As simple as that, my capitulation, his acceptance. Brade was a good winner.

"Before I begin," I said, "will you answer some questions for me?"

"Yes," he agreed without hesitation. "If we're to work together we must be perfectly frank. What do you wish to know?"

"You said earlier in the evening that Pietro Donelli had served time in a South American prison. The other morning you said he *might* have. Do you know definitely now that he has?"

"Yes. Definitely."

"How did you find out?"

He smiled sideways at me. "I'm a member, Mis' Martha, of one of the most efficient crime detection bureaus in the world. I have at my disposal the machinery of that bureau, and through affiliation, the machinery of all the other great law enforcement agencies in every country on the globe. With modern methods of communication not much time is lost. Does that answer your question?"

"Perfectly. The other one, too. As to how you knew that Donelli and Angelo Marquand were natives of Roleno. It's in the south of Italy, isn't it?"

"Yes? How did you know that?"

"Mary Morningstar told me. She went there thirty years ago—" and I told him the story Mary had related that afternoon in her green and silver room, when I took her the letter from Angelo Marquand. I told him everything, all the way through.

He did not seem too disappointed that I had no real knowledge of the contents of that letter beyond those fugitive, fiery lines— "Dear Mary, this is to warn you—"

He said abruptly, "You believed when you saw the heel prints beside Donelli's body that Mary Morningstar had been there, didn't you?"

I smiled without mirth. "I knew it—then."

"Then?" he glanced up swiftly. "You don't believe it now? You're not sure? Explain that, Mis' Martha."

It wasn't easy, but after all I had decided to tell him everything. I said, "I was sure Mary had been there when I saw the prints, because I knew that no one else in Alder Valley wore shoes with heels like that."

He nodded, watching me intently.

"Later," I said making tiny folds in the cloth of my skirt, "I discovered that someone else could have made those prints, because I found that someone else could have worn Mary's shoes."

I leaned back and closed my eyes for Claribel's pretty porcelain face was suddenly there before me.

It isn't easy to say the words that may help to pin an ugly crime on the woman you've known and loved for close to half a lifetime. Loved, for all her weakness, or maybe because of it.

I seemed to see Brade through my closed lids, sitting there so still, looking at me under sharply drawn brows. There wasn't any motion about him any place. He didn't seem even to breathe. Yes, I've seen Ratsy still like that, before a mouse hole. Then Brade said quietly, "Keep going, Mis' Martha. Who, besides Mary Morningstar, could have worn those shoes?"

Well, I got hold of myself then. No use in acting like a skittery schoolgirl when your duty is plain and straight before you. I sat up, ready to answer his questions.

"Claribel Fortune," I said, and told him about Bessie and the trash-burning in the alley. How Mary had given the black pumps to Claribel, how Claribel couldn't wear them except just a few times around the house, they not fitting her, how, for all she was so sick, she'd insisted on Bessie's redding out the closet and burning everything.

"I talked Bessie into giving them to me," I said. "I've—"

"You have them?" He sat forward, not bothering to hide his interest.

"Yes," I admitted, and went downstairs to get them.

He handled them as if they were glass, turning them slowly, studying the stain of red clay on the high heel, touching gently the fragment of oak leaf.

"So Claribel Fortune went to meet Donelli, to pay him blackmail money, wearing Mary's shoes," he said half to himself.

"That's how it looks," I said desperately, "but you know we can't always—"

"I know, Mis' Martha," he said gently, "we can't always depend on appearances. Thank you for telling me. And because of these shoes, you are now convinced that Mary was not telling the truth when she claimed she had been on the hill path that night?"

"I am, Captain Brade. She lied about it to protect Shane!"

"Shane?"

I flinched at that questioning inflection, regretting my unguarded admission.

"Yes," I said doggedly. "Mary wouldn't want Shane to know his—"

"That his mother was involved in this business?"

I nodded, and added quickly, "It was hard to understand how Mary knew so well what Donelli looked like if she hadn't seen his body on the path. The way she described him, I couldn't believe she hadn't seen him, but I understand now. She knew him in Italy, thirty years ago.

"Mary described Donelli to you, Mis' Martha?"

"Yes. The morning of the murder, there at her house. She said that she saw him lying there—his thick lips, heavy dark face, that little flat gold ring in his ear."

Brade said carefully, "Mary described him to you like that?"

"Yes. After you left, when she begged me to believe she'd been on the hill path."

Brade considered the moonstone ring. "Do you suppose that as a boy, thirty years ago, Pietro Donelli wore that same flat gold ring in his ear, Mis' Martha?"

I started. "Why—why, I don't know."

"Neither do I. He may have, except that the condition of the ear lobe indicates that the puncture for the ring was made much later."

"Then—then—" I faltered, "Mary couldn't have known about it from seeing him as a boy."

"I consider it improbable. Even if he wore it then it is unlikely that she could have remembered it, since, according to her story, she only knew him casually."

"Then how did she know?"

He said, "I would offer it as a suggestion that Mary Morningstar has had some vital contact with Donelli in recent years. Something sufficiently important to impress the picture of that flat, gold ring onto her mind."

"But that isn't possible," I protested. "Mary's been here these last seven years. Donelli hasn't."

"No, Donelli hasn't visited her here. Seven years is not such a long time, however. Eight years ago, according to reports I have received, Pietro Donelli was paroled from prison in South America. Something over seven years ago Mary Dawn was appearing in opera in Buenos Aires. During that time she suffered a nervous collapse, was desperately ill, and, as a result, gave up forever the career she had gone to such lengths to achieve."

I said nothing, watching him. "Shortly after Mary Dawn left Buenos Aires, Pietro Donelli was arrested and again returned to prison. The charge which sent him back was blackmail."

"Oh!" I gasped faintly.

"Yes. You remember the line in Marquand's letter found on Donelli's body: 'Silence would earn for you your worthless life, but I know you well enough to realize that you cannot resist the golden lure—'"

"Money, I suppose?"

"I would think so. Remember we found three hundred and fifty dollars in his wallet."

"Claribel gave it to him." And I told him about the conversation Shane had overheard between Claribel and Mary. When I had finished he said, "At least Mary Morningstar accused Claribel of giving it to him. Claribel, I take it, did not deny it."

"She as good as admitted it. When Mary asked her why she had agreed to meet him on the woods path, Claribel said that Mary of all people should know that—that she'd have agreed to go to hell if he'd asked it."

"Which argues," Brade said, "that together, Claribel Fortune and Mary Morningstar share some secret which Donelli has come into possession of, and on account of which Claribel has given him money."

I sighed and leaned back. Brade's clear presentation of things, his swift, concise way of tying known facts into a coherent whole, amazed me. All the more so as the structure he built always remained tentative and capable of being rearranged if it did not stand up of its own strength.

"Marquand said in his letter: 'For what you have stolen from me, for the confidence that you once betrayed—I shall exact death.' Another line, '—this is to say farewell to one whom I was so blind as to call, in an hour of black despair, my friend—' What does that mean to you, Mis' Martha?"

"That at some time when Marquand was in deep trouble he confided in Donelli whom he believed to be his friend, that later Donelli betrayed that confidence because he could not resist the 'golden lure.'"

"Excellent," Brade purred. "My idea exactly. Now tie up Donelli's first parole with Mary's presence in Buenos Aires—"

"She told me," I reminded him, "that Donelli knew of her interest in Angelo, was seeking her here, hoping to get money under pretense of helping Angelo."

Brade glanced at me sharply. "Yes. It is my assumption that Donelli approached Mary in Buenos Aires seven years ago, extracted money from her, in other words, blackmailed her. It is assumption, also, to say that as a result of that incident Mary suffered an illness from which she nearly died, gave up her career, and most clearly remembered Donelli's flat gold ear ring."

"And his greasy hair," I said faintly, "his dark skin."

"Correct. Yet when he comes here seeking Mary Morningstar, it is Claribel Fortune who pays him hush money."

I added another detail.

"And agrees to meet him at that lonely spot on the hill path. I don't see, Captain Brade. It just isn't possible, somehow, that Claribel did that. If you knew her—"

"I had a few minutes' conversation with her this morning."

"Then you can see how frightened she is. Does it seem reasonable to you that she went armed with a rifle to meet this disreputable Italian peddler?"

He leaned toward me quickly. "Yet Mary didn't go. Her story was too obviously untrue. If she didn't; if Claribel didn't; then who did go?"

"The man who shot Donelli! The man who came that morning, wearing tennis sneakers, and stole that gun from under my eyes."

"That man was unquestionably there," Brade agreed, "but so, also, was a woman wearing distinctive high-heeled shoes—"

"Whoever she was," I protested, "Mary or Claribel or God knows who, she may not have shot him. The man may have done that, with that rifle carrying the silver shamrock leaf on its stock."

"The what?" he rapped.

"The shamrock leaf. A small beautiful ornament on the stock."

His voice shook a little. "Why wasn't I told of that? What do you mean withholding information?"

Involuntarily I shrank back. "Why—why—" I stammered, "I don't know. I didn't mean—"

He relaxed. "Take it easy, Martha Berry. Don't let me bully you. I don't mean to, but, oh—damn it—" he rose impatiently, fell to a nervous pacing, "people are so stupid. They mean well, their intentions are excellent, yet they blunder and muddle and lie and cheat all because they don't use the sense God gave them, because their intelligence is so far below—"

Anger was a hot tide surging through me. I stood up. "Keep your opinions to yourself, Courtney Brade," I choked. "Maybe I have blundered, maybe my intelligence is below that of a tree toad, but I'll give you to understand I've lived better than half a century and got along fairly well. Just because I get pulled in on a nasty mess like this, and try to help, first my friends, and then you, is no reason to insult me, and I'd thank you to get out of my house the quickest way you know and not come back."

He stopped square in front of me with my first words, stood there motionless, eyes on my face in that bright, intense regard that was so hard to bear, though I was that plain damned mad it didn't faze me. And now when I was shaking all over, ready to throw something at him, when I felt strong and virtuous, he threw back his head and burst into the most delightfully infectious laugh I ever heard.

"Martha Berry, bless your heart," he said breathlessly. "Why, Martha, that's wonderful! I'd give a month's salary to have that speech made into a phonograph record, listen to it every time I lose patience and get to raving on my favorite subject." And off he went into a gale of laughter, his face all relaxed and twitching with mirth, eyes gay and carefree as a boy's, and I was so amazed I couldn't do anything but watch, and before I knew it, my tight face was jerking and in a moment I was laughing too, and the whole incident seemed too ridiculous for words, and there we stood like two ninnies laughing till our sides ached.

"I didn't mean you, Martha," he managed at last. "I was just speaking generally. This detecting business as you named it, it's a thundering hard grind."

"I know it is," I told him with a huge sigh. "I don't blame you for saying folks haven't the sense God gave a goat."

"Well, you see, Mis' Martha, no one mentioned the silver shamrock on the rifle stock and it struck me hard for—"

Something in his tones sobered me. I said, "Yes? It struck you hard? Why?"

"Just this afternoon," he said, "I saw that gun. I took it from where it was hung over the mantel because it was so handsome, and when I turned it there was a silver shamrock leaf on the stock."

Something cold gripped my heart. "You saw it?"

"Yes. And the important point is—it was hung on the wall so the shamrock leaf wouldn't show."

I felt behind me for the chair. "But who— Where was it?"

"Why, it was—"

There came a furious pounding on the front door, a voice calling shrilly, "Martha Berry! Mis' Martha! Let me in!"

"I found it," Brade said, as if nothing had happened, "in Bennet Calder's study."

Chapter Nine

"Oh, my God!" I whispered, then—"I've got to go. That's Bessie, Claribel Fortune's girl," and I was stumbling down the stairs, groping my way through the dimly lit parlor toward the front door to stop that dreadful pounding and the sound of Bessie's choked, frantic sobs.

Bennet Calder! The gun over the mantel, the shamrock turned toward the wall! Then, just as I reached the hall, something hit me like a bolt of lightning. I stopped dead still and for the life of me I couldn't move. I said in a whisper, "Yes, Bessie! I'm coming." But she didn't hear and went on sobbing, and all the time I was thinking.

"The last house on the street! That's what Lars said. That's what Dickie Ball saw when he was lookout on the pirate ship. The last house on the street, not the last house in the block! The last house in the block is mine, but the last house on the street is Bennet Calder's. That's where Claribel went that night."

And then the Lord gave me back my senses and I opened the door. Poor Bessie all but fell into the room. Her big, homely face was dough-white, tear-stained, her thin, mousy hair straggling, and she stood there blinking in the most foolish way.

I had a desire to shake her hard, for the way my heart was pounding, and the way she had brought me stumbling down the stairs just after Brade told me about the gun.

I snapped, "All right, Bessie, speak up, can't you? Or has the Lord struck you dumb for your sins?"

She whimpered like a homeless kitten. "It's Mis' Claribel, Mis' Martha. She's—she's—" and away she went, blubbering and sobbing and choking, tears pouring over her face.

"Claribel!" I said angrily. "It's always Claribel! Aren't you used to her vapors? Don't you know it's just so folks'll wait on her, especially Shane?"

"It ain't vapors this time," Bessie said. "It ain't so folks'll wait on her—Mr. Shane or anyone. Mis' Claribel—she's dead, and Mr. Shane—he's run away."

A hand fastened round my arm. "Sit here," Brade said, and put me in the chair by the door. "Bessie, take this stool. Now be quiet for a moment, and we'll be better able to help. She died suddenly, Bessie? Was the doctor there?"

I heard his level tones from a long way off, saw him push Bessie down on a silly little stool, saw her broad face, her stringy hair, the dull misery of her eyes, remembered that I'd told her she could get a permanent like she'd always wanted and wondered if poor Bessie Lindstrom would ever want anything again as long as she lived. Then I thought, "Claribel is dead! Claribel! Claribel Fortune!" It didn't seem real to me. For so long Claribel had hovered on the edge of death, and we'd ignored her suffering, been intolerant of her weakness. Now she was gone. Now Claribel had escaped. Claribel Fortune was dead.

And then like the way you throw a switch and a phonograph starts playing, Bessie began to talk. "There wasn't nobody with her. I found her lying on the floor, put her on the bed. There was a cut on her forehead; she didn't open her eyes. She said real faint, 'Shane! Come back!' and I said, 'Yes, Mis' Claribel, I'll get Mr. Shane for you,' but she whispers, 'He won't come back—he's gone— I couldn't keep him—' and then she sat up like she was terrible strong, opened her eyes and cried real loud, 'Shane! Come back!'"

Silence hung thickly in the tiny hall. Brade said, "Yes, Bessie, go on, please."

"That's all," Bessie said. "She died with my arms around her, and I laid her down gentle like and went into the hall, thinking about how many times I'd seen her there and how little her hands were, so she could never hold onto anything. I thought, 'I'll get Mr. Shane. Tell him his mother's dead.' I went to his room. I went all over the house, calling for Shane. I kept calling and calling— and there wasn't anyone to answer, and pretty soon it wasn't me that was calling but Mis' Claribel! Her voice in all the rooms—upstairs, downstairs—louder and louder—calling, Shane! Shane! Come back!—and her lying dead upstairs. I couldn't stand it. That's all! Mr. Shane's gone. Mis' Claribel's dead."

Like Claribel was there, I heard her voice as I had heard it so many times in the last twenty-four years. "If I should lose Shane, if anything should happen to take him away—I'd die, Martha. I couldn't live without Shane." And I thought how her little hands, those small, clinging hands that couldn't really hold onto anything, had clung to mine, and how loosing them was like tearing the tendrils of a vine from a wall where it grew. Shane had been her fine, strong wall to cling to and draw life from. When she was torn from its vitality—

I said, "Nesta? Where's Nesta?"

"I don't know. She isn't there or she'd have heard me." Then her poor, dull face that had only been lighted by love and loyalty for her mistress, crinkled like a piece of oil cloth and she put up her big hard hands to cover it. "She'll never hear me calling again," she whimpered. "Never hear—me—calling."

And it took no great degree of comprehension to know that in those last two sentences she was not thinking of Nesta Fortune.

Brade said, "Come, Bessie, we'll go back with you."

She rose obediently, and we went out into the chill autumn night, where the leaves were rustling around our feet, and the three-quarter moon showed pale and bleak behind the spire of the Congregational church.

We walked slowly, quietly.

Brade said, "Mis' Martha, do you mind running on ahead? I'll come with Bessie."

Bessie walked so heavily, lifting one foot mechanically, putting it down, each step making a hollow, plopping sound on the old worn bricks, that I was glad to get from the weight of them.

But they went with me down the dark tunnel of the tree-shaded street where the sharp points of the firs stood out like tall, exquisite lances against the cloud wrack of the September sky.

I could no more get away from the sound of Bessie's plodding steps than I could put from me the knowledge that Claribel Fortune was dead. That never again would I see her small, porcelain face, her wide, beautiful eyes, her fluttering hands. Never visit her in that bright west bedroom with the mignonette-sprigged curtains and the sweetness of lavender that always clung to it.

The house was big and white under the growing radiance of the moon, a light in the hall, the front door open, a clock ticking loudly some place.

I paused before the door of the west bedroom on the second floor, then turned the handle and went in. It was a beautiful room. In some way it expressed the real Claribel.

I went to the bed. Claribel was quiet at last. Her hair made a golden frame for her little face, the long lashes like shadows on the white cheeks. The blue of her eyes had always seemed to shine through the fragile lids. Her mouth drooped, relaxed and strangely rested.

Whatever had happened had taken her from her bed, stretched her senseless, a bruise on her forehead, blood on her cheek. Bessie had washed it away, but the cut showed.

From somewhere came a low, dull moaning!

I turned slowly. The room was empty, except for Claribel and myself. Everything was in order, exactly as it should be, except that Claribel was dead. Maybe that was as it should be, too. Who was I to say?

The moaning came again. My eyes settled on the closet door, open a tiny crack. I crossed over, jerked it wide. Nesta Fortune lay face down, huddled against the fragrance of Claribel's old-fashioned dresses.

I seized her shoulder. She winced, and jerked away. I said, "Well, come out. No one's holding you!" I had never liked Nesta Cramer.

She shivered, thin shoulders twitching. "Shane!" she sobbed. "Shane!"

I shivered too, remembering Shane's eyes that night in my attic room as he said "I wanted to kill her!"

I heard steps on the porch, Brade and Bessie. Nesta struggled up, squirmed round facing me, eyes wide and black, face white as putty. She fumbled at her throat. I saw the dark stain of a bruise. She touched her cheek where blood stained her mouth.

"What's the matter?" I asked. "What are you doing here?"

The steps were mounting the stairs. The way they came was endless. Nesta pulled herself up by the length of Claribel's shabby broadcloth coat, came into the room as the door opened and Brade entered. A frown twitched his brows when he saw her. He closed the door softly.

"Bessie is stopping outside," he told me, then, "What is the matter, Mrs. Fortune?"

Nesta clutched at her throat, face jerking. "My husband tried to kill me," she said harshly. "He struck me, choked me—I don't remember any more. I came to in that closet." She swayed against the foot of the bed, looking really ill.

Brade said, "Take this chair," and set it beside her.

She collapsed weakly. He drew out a thin flask, uncorked it, handed it to her. "Drink some," he ordered, and without protest she set it to her lips. Then her eyes found the quiet Claribel, flared wide and sightlessly black. She rose, spilling the whisky over the faded pattern of the Wilton rug, staring in hypnotized terror, though I could see little to fear from the small shadow that had been Claribel Fortune. She screamed, sharp and shrill, clinging to the bed—screaming.

Brade caught her shoulders, the force of his grip seeming to lift her from her feet. He said, "Be quiet!" and the words were like a slap in the face.

She stopped screaming. "I'm sorry," she said faintly. "She's dead—Claribel's dead." her face twisted again.

"Yes," Brade rapped. "She's dead. There's nothing to scream about. Sit down."

She sat down, hanging on to the footboard of the bed. "I'm sorry," she said again monotonously. "I'm sorry." Her face crumpled and she began to cry, softly, quite naturally.

Brade drew out a handkerchief, mopped his face. He glanced at me and his eyes held a momentary look of helplessness. "Where'd you find her?" he asked.

I pointed to the closet. He looked inside, closed the door. He went to the bed, bent over Claribel's body, touched briefly the cut on her forehead, laid a hand against her cheek, drew the linen sheet over her face. I was glad he did that.

For a time there was only the sound of Nesta's sobbing. I'd never liked her, but I came close to pity as I saw her thin, narrow shoulders, her lowered head, the twitchings of a muscle in her rouged cheek.

The shrilling of the telephone struck into the silence like a blow! It was standing on the table by the window, an extension from the main instrument downstairs. I was close to it. I looked at Brade. He nodded. I set the receiver against my ear.

I said, "Hello."

Mary Morningstar's broken voice came to me. "Claribel! Claribel!"

It sounded so clearly she might have been in the room. Brade's head lifted. Nesta looked up, dabbing at her cheeks. It was as though Mary stood there, invisible, but vitally present, saying, "Claribel—Claribel!"

I said, "This is Martha. Claribel is—" My throat went tight.

Mary said, "Martha! Where is Shane? He's there, isn't he? Please tell me he's there, Martha?"

"He's not here, Mary. He's gone away."

Her gasp was like a cry. "No, no, not that. He wouldn't run away from anything."

Brade took the receiver. His voice must have been a terrible shock. He said, "Mary Morningstar, Shane Fortune is gone. We don't know where. His mother, Claribel, is dead!"

Nesta began to laugh in a high, shrill crescendo of nerves strained too tightly. "Yes, Claribel's dead, tell her that! Tell Mary that Claribel is dead! Tell her that Shane—her wonderful, wonderful Shane—killed her!"

Brade's hand went out in an involuntary and useless gesture of halting her crazy words. They went through that instrument like stabbing knives. Brade unconsciously lowered the receiver, held it beside him, and that is why Mary Morningstar's words came to us with such intense clarity. More than ever it was as though she was with us.

Mary said, "No, Nesta, that's wrong. Shane didn't kill Claribel. I killed her!"

Brade said quietly into the telephone, "Will you stay where you are, Mary? I'm coming over."

I couldn't catch what she said though I heard her voice, faint, breathless, exhausted. He frowned, then, "Very well. I'll tell her." He replaced the instrument, looked at me. "It's you she wants. You'd better go. Get her story, find out, if you can, what's been going on here tonight."

"I'll tell you!" Nesta said shrilly. "Shane's in love with Mary Morningstar! Crazy about her! He can't think of anyone else. That's why he treats me as he does—why he's come to hate me!"

"Nesta!" I cried, regardless of Brade's angry glance. "That's a sinful thing to say of a boy like Shane—a woman of Mary's age!"

Nesta's bright squirrel eyes flicked my face. Her tight lips parted above white popcorn teeth. "That's what you think, old morality Jane. That shows how much you know. That's what all the trouble was about tonight. Claribel knew. It's what tore her heart all these weeks. Tonight when Shane told me he was leaving me, going away, I ran to Claribel. I shouldn't have, but I was out of my senses. To be deserted four months after my marriage—and all for that woman!"

"Exactly what did Shane say?" Brade's curt tones cut into her rising hysteria.

She relaxed a little, looking at him under thick stiff lashes. "That he was sick of Alder Valley—I could go to the devil. A sweet story, me knowing it was because he couldn't face his friends with that other woman. Oh, he threw a sop to me, said I could have all the money his Uncle Ezra left him."

"What's that?" I rapped. "His Uncle Ezra left Shane money? I never knew—"

"Isn't that too bad," she mocked. "Poor Martha! A personal matter in Alder Valley that old nosey-bones isn't wise to."

"We'll forget personalities, if you please, Mrs. Fortune," Brade said "What about this money? I'm asking and not because I'm nosey."

She looked at him. Nesta was like that. She couldn't see a man without letting her bright, consuming eyes go over him in that slow, fiery way. She settled her thin shoulders, brushed at her tumbled hair, smiled.

"No, Captain Brade, I'll be glad to discuss it with you."

"That's fine," Brade said lazily, the faintest trace of a smile beneath his mustache. "Now suppose we start our discussion, just the two of us."

She wriggled her slim body. "Martha must go. I won't talk before Martha. I don't like Martha."

"Well, that's mutual, my girl," I snapped, "and if anyone killed Claribel Fortune, you did with your lying and snooping, the way you drove Shane out of his wits nagging at him."

She rose, hanging onto the bed. "I could scratch your hateful old maid face for that," she said hoarsely. "You who never had a real man, but only that paralyzed—"

"Nesta!" Brade said, and like he had struck her, she cowered back, head lowered, sobbing. He looked at me.

"Go on, Martha. I'll handle this," and I went blindly from the room, downstairs and into the night with such black hate in my heart that the blood was frozen; I could not breathe, there was darkness before my eyes and I know not how I went.

Chapter Ten

My steps sounded muffled and dull on the stones. Tree limbs brushed my face, jerked my hair loose to tumble down my back. But I scarcely noticed for I went under the lash of a terrible fear that burned out hate for Nesta and left me only an unthinking automaton, motivated by terror.

For Mary! Shane! I could not rationalize such destructive emotions as had been let loose in peaceful Alder Valley since Pietro Donelli died. Shane in love with Mary! I turned sick at memory of Nesta saying it. The way she said it made it all wrong. The way I had sensed it that morning Mary rose to meet him, as naturally as a flower turns toward light, that way he came to her, taking her hands, looking into her eyes, they not knowing I was there—that was right. In that there was no wrong.

I stopped, chilled by the long, lonesome howling of a dog, stood staring at Mary's tall grilled gate. Beyond, in the moon-checkered garden, Sandra was grieving with her long, beautiful muzzle toward the stars.

It went through me in undulating waves of sound that set me shivering and I cowered, staring at the house where light burned dimly in the lower windows, a door banged dully, and a slim, white dog mourned with muzzle lifted.

Then I roused, went up the path, not to be panicked by a dog's howling. I called to her once and the ungodly howling stopped. I heard her moving over beyond the marigolds, but she would not come. I went up the steps into the hall. The silence of the house was like a thick, cold weight.

I said, "Mary!" my voice small and brittle. "Mary!" I called, but only echoes answered from shadowed walls, and dusky corners.

I went into the living room. It was almost like seeing Mary, so was it stamped with her personality; a book face down beside her favorite chair, a cigarette crushed out beside it, a cigar half smoked on the mantel's edge. Well, at any rate, Mary didn't smoke cigars.

I studied the charred band. El Centro! My lips shut hard. Mr. Calder! His special brand. Mr. Calder had been here. When? I touched the cigar. Cold as clay. The long shell of ash crumbled under my fingers, then on the divan in the corner I saw the worn suede glove.

Gloves have a heart-breaking way of suggesting the wearer. It lay there upturned, lines creased like the palm that had filled it, fingers curled, a seam ripped, a grease stain around the clasp. Shane Fortune! It was as if he had spoken to me! Shane's driving glove. Shane had been here!

I dropped the glove, looking at the silent room. Where was Mary? Black Daisy? Then I remembered that Daisy had gone to her sister for a brief vacation.

I went upstairs, snapping on lights. The house was empty as a bird's nest, chilled with November sleet; Mary was gone, and in the garden Sandra mourned again in low, whimpering monotone.

I looked at the telephone, decided against phoning Brade, went downstairs, outside. Sandra was silent now. The garden lay like a delicate pattern of black lace picked out with silver. And suddenly fear was back and I ran, gravel crunching under my feet. I stumbled just as I reached the swinging gate, staggered through and plumped hard against a tall man!

I screamed, he caught my shoulder and I heard Lars Knowlton's voice say, "Mis' Martha! Where're you going like the devil was on your coat tail?"

I hung onto him, feeling his strong skinny arm round my shoulders, the swift, dangerous beat of his heart, the violent trembling that shook him. It was good to hang onto someone just then, even if that someone was most as bad upset as I.

I said, "I'm going— Oh, I don't know. I came to find Mary. It's Claribel. Claribel's—"

He squeezed my shoulders. "Yes, Martha, Claribel's free at last. Claribel knows now that there's no cause for fear."

I could feel his voice in his deep chest like the throb of a motor, going round and over me like strong, vitalizing currents of electricity and I was suddenly still there beside him. The night and the wind, the pale moon behind the black church spire, the dog mourning in the deserted garden, no longer held terror for me. Grief for Claribel, hatred for Nesta, fear for Shane and Mary, all of it ebbed, leaving me quiet.

I drew a deep slow breath, pushed back tumbled hair, looked up at Lars. He grinned, his long, homely face partially revealed in the shifting moonlight. He looked older that night, and there was something in his eyes that made my heart ache.

He said, "Everything better now, Mis' Martha?"

"Yes, Lars, better. I came to find Mary. She phoned Claribel's, asking for Shane. She—she isn't here."

"No," he said gravely. "Mary's gone."

"Gone? She asked me to come. Why should she go?"

"She's gone to find Shane, Martha. After she talked to you, she couldn't wait. After she heard Nesta say Shane had killed—"

"Claribel? Yes, I was there."

"Well, Mary couldn't wait after that, Martha. She asked me to tell you that she'd be back. She hoped to catch up with Shane—he drives like the devil."

"He went in his car?" I remembered the forgotten driving glove on the divan.

"Yes, and it's a demon for speed, but she had to try. She didn't want him running away."

"Not with his mother dead," I said weakly.

"Shane didn't know that. Mary told me. He had a terrible row with Nesta."

"Shane told Nesta he was leaving her," I stammered. "He said she could go to the devil. He was going away with Mary."

"Shane said that?" Lars's sharp tones stilled me.

"So Nesta says."

His hand bit into my arm. "Nesta must be wrong," he said gently, and I remembered that he loved her and wondered why a man like Lars Knowlton should waste himself on Nesta Cramer. "Mary told me that Shane came here. He'd been drinking."

"Yes, he struck Nesta, choked her, shut her in the closet."

He frowned. "So?" he asked in that queer, gentle tone. Then astonishingly he laughed. "Don't much blame him," he said as if to himself. "At any rate, Shane came to Mary, told her he— Oh, I don't know what he told her."

"Lars Knowlton, you're lying and you never did that well. Now tell me exactly what Shane said to Mary."

He was silent and I wondered why tonight Lars seemed so much older. He said, "You're right, Mis' Martha, I was lying. I'm sorry. I can't tell you what Shane said to Mary. Mary told me because she was so distracted she had to tell someone and I happened along."

"Happened? What brought you here, Lars?"

His lips went hard. "I was following Bennet Calder."

"Oh! So that's it!"

"Yes," he said, and stopped.

I leaned against the tall iron gate watching him as best I could in the uncertain light. I knew there was no use urging Lars when he looked like that. If he wanted to tell what he had on his mind, well and good. Otherwise—

"I don't like Calder, Mis' Martha. I've never liked him since I was a gangly, barefooted kid and he was going to have me sent to the reformatory for stealing corn from old man Watson."

"Did you steal it, Lars?" I asked, stifling hysterical laughter.

It was such a muddle, a crazy-quilt jumble of past and present, of cross currents in the lives of all these friends of mine. Shane's flight, Claribel's tragic death, Nesta's hatred, Mary's inexplicable actions, a pair of slender high-heeled pumps, an ugly little Buddha, a silver shamrock, a dead man with a scattered pack on the hill path—

and here was Lars prating of a twenty-year grudge against Bennet Calder over a passel of corn! Yet somehow all these tumbled fragments were necessary parts of the whole. All of them I sensed would eventually form a clear, coherent pattern, guided by the deft slender fingers of Captain Courtney Brade. I heard Lars saying:

"You're thundering right I stole that corn. I was hungry and there wasn't anything to eat except what poor Granny Sears had to have. I was too young to get work. No one paid any attention, seemed to think we were human—" His harsh voice caught, his lips closed like a trap. He turned away quickly. "Anyway, that's why I've never liked old man Calder, and these last days I've tried hard to remember that kid hate, keep it from making me see crooked."

"These last days!" That phrase jerked me from the dreary years when crazy old Granny Sears lived on her stingy little farm south of town, with only a ragged, shock-haired orphan boy to care for her, and none of us likely could measure by any personal standard just how dreary and heart-breaking those years had been for Lars Knowlton.

"These last days?" I asked uncertainly. "And have you kept from seeing things crooked, Lars, where Bennet Calder is concerned?"

"I wonder? He was on the woods path that night Donelli was killed."

"Lars! You're sure?"

He stared at me curiously. "I got a job yesterday, Mis' Martha, worked half a day helping Milly Slocum clean house."

"Whose house, Lars?"

"Bennet Calder's," he said, and again shut his mouth like a trap.

I nodded. Milly Slocum would be doing the fall house cleaning for Mr. Calder about now.

"Calder wasn't there," Lars continued. "I quit washing windows long enough to sneak into his closet and find a pair of old shoes. I went to the woods path, fitted 'em into the dried impressions leading from the spot where Donelli was shot to the point where the gun was dropped beside Tan Top."

That gun! Brade had said, "Why wasn't I told? I held that same gun in my hands yesterday."

"You're sure, Lars?" I asked again. "Shoe prints are a lot alike, aren't they?"

He snorted indignantly. "Scarcely. Those soles had diamonds in the treads. The heels went in the impressions like a hand in a glove, the round blunt toes—all was perfect. No mistake, Mis' Martha, take my word for it."

I had to. Lars had a genius for accuracy.

It was on my trembling lips to mention the gun Brade had found, then I remembered that Brade had told me that he was expecting me to keep it in confidence.

I said, "Have you told Captain Brade, Lars?"

"Not yet. I've more investigating to do."

I was suddenly afraid for him. "Lars! It isn't sensible. It's not your job. Brade—he's the law— he's paid to do things like that. It's Brade's job!"

There was smothered laughter in his voice. "Dear Mis' Martha, you're kind to be concerned about me. Don't worry. It is my job. Mine alone! What it means to me, proving that Bennet Calder shot that Wop, no one'll ever know, no one, understand?" Then, as Lars so frequently does, he started off down the street, so immersed in his own thoughts that he forgot I was there.

He went striding off, muttering under his breath, carrying on a perfectly sensible, entirely logical conversation with himself, as I had heard him do so many times, as others had heard him do and named him crazy as a coot.

I looked at his tall, ungainly form disappearing in the darkness and wondered at how long he had hugged that childish hate of Bennet Calder to his lonely heart.

I returned to the Fortunes. Lights were blazing. Dr. Sloan's Ford stood in the drive. I saw people in the big front parlor, knew there was nothing for me to do. I turned away and a man said, "Oh, Mis' Martha," and there was Brade, lounging on a bench under the shadow of the syringas. I sat down beside him. He said, "Mary's gone, isn't she?"

"Yes, how did you know?"

"Oh, one of those female undertakers saw her drive out of town in a whirl of dust. Where's she headed?"

"After Shane."

He grunted softly. I told him about seeing Lars, what he had said about Shane's coming to Mary, how Lars wouldn't tell me what Shane had said to her, insisting it was her story.

I deliberately withheld that amazing bit of news about Mr. Calder's shoe, giving myself no reason for it then, but hugging it to me in a queer secret way, though I knew I was doing wrong in not being honest with him.

I asked him what he'd learned from Nesta. Little, apparently, beyond what she had indicated while I was there. "Except," Brade added, "the hundred thousand dollars left young Fortune by his uncle Ezra."

"Yes?" I asked eagerly. "What about that?"

It was simple. Ezra Fortune, alone, with only a few months to live, remembered his older brother and his family. He wrote to Claribel, advising her to get in touch with a lawyer in New York, she finding that Ezra had left a hundred thousand in her care for Shane when he was twenty-one.

"But he's twenty-four now," I objected. "He didn't get it. Why, he had to work part of his way through college."

"Yes, that is the curious part. The money never appeared here, never appeared anywhere, though Nesta said Claribel admitted it was in a bank in New York in her name."

"But why?" I gasped, remembering Claribel's devotion to the boy. "Why should Claribel hold back Shane's money? Claribel wasn't like that. She never hung onto money," my voice broke. "Claribel never hung onto anything."

"That's what Nesta wants to know," Brade admitted dryly. "I gather she all but held a gun at poor Claribel's head to get the story a month or so ago, after Claribel had accidentally hinted at it. All she could learn was that the money was there. Not a penny of it had been spent. Shane would get it—"

"When?"

"Nesta enjoys acting," Brade commented irrelevantly, "but she actually forgot to act when she went into a fit of hysterics and told me Claribel said Shane would get it when *someone* died."

"Someone?" I echoed dully.

"Yes. That was the term, and nothing Nesta could do would bring more. Claribel just said when someone died she would give Shane the money, adding it was useless to do it before because he, Shane, couldn't keep it."

"Oh, good Lord," I said angrily. "Why don't folks say what they mean?"

Then I remembered Claribel, so frail and quiet in her wide bed, the pitiful lines of her little, porcelain face, and I was sorry, understanding that it is not given us to know a great deal, at best, about those we live with through the years.

Brade nodded. "Money in the Fortune family seems to be clothed in mystery. The problem of what became of the money Amos left his wife is still unsolved. The answer to why Claribel practiced this deception with her son's heritage—"

He paused there, sat quiet for a time, then he said, "Let's not think any more about it tonight. Go home now and get some sleep. Tomorrow won't be easy."

I rose. "Good night, Captain Brade," I said, and gave him my hand.

"Good night, Martha Berry," he replied gravely, and shook my hand firmly.

Then I left, and I swear when I started home I had the best intentions in the world of going straight there.

Chapter Eleven

I WAS JUST GOING to go to my small cottage, to my orderly bedroom, undress, put on my nightgown, lie down on my smooth, good bed and go to sleep, leaving in the hands of an unseen providence the events that the morning would bring.

As I reached my own gate, I heard heavy steps approaching and into the quivering patch of moonlight came Bennet Calder, walking slowly, white head bent, shoulders hunched, using his cane as if he really needed it.

I stopped, and in that action my good intentions vanished. Mr. Calder stopped too. He towered over me, and I heard the harsh sound of his breathing. Standing there like that I saw that he was an old man, and that, in some way I did not fully understand, he was very tired.

I said, "Good evening, Mr. Calder."

"Good evening, Mis' Martha. You have been to the Fortunes'?"

"Yes. Claribel is dead."

"I know. Sloan phoned me." He struck gently at the head of a drooping wild daisy. "Claribel!" he said, pronouncing the beautiful name slowly. "Little Claribel Fortune. She has been a long time dying."

"You were going to the house?"

"No. I was just strolling before going to bed. Will you join me?"

I said, "I'll be glad to," stepped beside him as he turned and started back along the way he had come. It was so quiet that night Claribel Fortune died. I have seen so many nights in Alder Valley but I do not recall one with that same quality of stillness. Yet there was movement. Wind in the trees. Grass stirring. Clouds in a swift silent rush across the black sky.

Calder walked slowly, something in the way he put his feet down reminding me of Bessie's plodding steps. The open fields between my house and his looked bleached and white under the September moon. They had a dusty smell, and presently I would see them flat and smooth under the snow—until April came and the black earth stirred and reached toward life again.

Mr. Calder said, "What caused Claribel's death, Mis' Martha?"

"Shane left. She could not live without Shane."

"No. Claribel would not live if Shane left her." Then after a moment, "Why did Shane decide so suddenly to leave?"

"You know as well as I, Mr. Calder. Shane has been like a man prisoned since his marriage. Nesta—"

"Yes," he interrupted, "Nesta would be a disturbing influence."

Then the craziest impulse came on me. "Mr. Calder," I said, "do you know anything about the hundred thousand dollars that Ezra Fortune left to Shane in Claribel's care?"

He stopped so suddenly I thought he had dropped beside me. I turned, seeing him standing there in half light and shadow, his handsome, florid face white as the moonlight, his eyes strange and blank. He lifted a hand, rubbed it across his doming brow.

"Ezra Fortune," he muttered thickly. "A hundred thousand dollars!"

I was suddenly ashamed of my carelessness. "Yes," I stammered, "forget I spoke about it, please. I didn't mean—I shouldn't have—"

"Why, it's preposterous," he choked. "Claribel is, was absolutely exhausted financially. I haven't handled her affairs for a long time, but I know that, just as everyone knows it. Why just the other evening she came to me, came here, begging a loan of three hundred and fifty—"

He checked his startled flow of words and for just a moment I missed the significance of what he said, then I remembered "She went down the alley," Lars had reported, "and into the last house." And I remembered the bills that flowed over Brade's hands from

Donelli's wallet, and Mary saying angrily to Claribel, "Why did you give him three hundred and fifty dollars?"

I said, "Mr. Calder, you know why Claribel met that Italian peddler on the woods path, don't you? You were there, you—"

Oh, I was a mouthing fool that night! And I had worried about safety for Lars! Mr. Calder's hand came out, big and broad with long strong fingers, like hooks, and fastened around my arm. He said, "Mis' Martha, come into the house. There are some things I'd like to talk over with you."

I hadn't realized that we had reached his place, as I had never realized how lonely it was, this grand house that Bennet Calder had purchased twenty-five years ago, built into a splendid mansion, furnished with the richest, most expensive things he could get, living in it all that time entirely alone.

I opened my lips to protest, tried to find energy to jerk from his grasp, but I was paralyzed. He marched me through the gate, up the walk between the carefully tended flower beds, across the wide porch, into the silence and utter aloneness of his big living room.

The waxed floor shone like a mirror. The walls were fresh swept, every expensive canvas in place, every rug just so. I'd always known that Mr. Calder had a fine house. Long ago I ceased to speculate or wonder if he'd ever bring a bride into this lovely place.

I knew what most everyone did, that long ago when Bennet Calder came to town, a big, clumsy fellow, and set himself up to practice law, no one had taken him very seriously or thought to see him get far. He was desperately poor but he wasn't ashamed of his poverty, and just went ahead half-soling his own shoes, patching his own pants, actually cutting his hair in his shabby office over Cunningham's general store. I remembered all this as I stood before his grand fireplace, saw how splendid the room was and how much it must have cost.

I remembered, too, the summer Lucy Grether came to visit her Aunt Lizzie, how Bennet Calder took one look at her and from that moment lived for her alone. It was an old story now, but at the time everyone knew about it and laughed, and made a lot of it.

For the poor shabby wight actually thought he could marry Lucy Grether, and she wasn't above leading him on, narrowing her pretty, tip-tilted eyes at him over her spangled fan summer nights when they met at an ice-cream sociable. She even went riding with him a few times behind the bay team from Tom Hawkins' livery stable, and then, when he asked her to marry him—

Well! Pretty Lucy Grether just ups and told Bennet Calder how she wouldn't be seen in public with anyone who looked so funny or wore such shabby clothes, except that she got a big laugh out of it. How, when she married, it was going to be a man with money, and not a poor, cut-at-the-seat-of-the pants lawyer who lacked the price of an ice cream soda on a hot Sunday.

It all came back to me that September night, and I realized how Calder had become a different person from that time on, living for one purpose only—money and fine possessions. I dropped into a chair by the massive walnut table. I'd known it all along, of course, but I'd never thought much about it, and I daresay that Calder himself had lost sight of that terrible incentive, and him never looking at another woman.

Not that he so devotedly loved Lucy Grether, I'm sure, but that she gave a terribly destroying blow to his pride, and he only lived to try and heal the wound.

Then, with my head awhirl, I wondered where he had made his money. It wasn't written that a country lawyer could do so well. But I knew that however he'd managed it, it had been just to prove to Lucy Grether, who married a no-count traveling salesman and was poor as dirt all her life, exactly what he could do.

He snapped off the hall light, marched straight to the walnut table, laid his stick across it, sat down opposite and folded his hands across his middle.

"Mis' Martha," he said, looking at me from pale blue eyes, "I want you to tell me exactly what you know about this money Ezra Fortune left to Shane in Claribel's care."

I squared back and folded my hands across *my* middle. I looked at him and said, "Mr. Calder, I won't tell you one thing more than I've already said. First because I don't know any more, and second, because it's not your business, or mine."

He wet his lips. Breeze from the open window lifted his white hair, laid it down gently on his smooth pink scalp. He sat there for a time looking at me, and I sat there looking back. I'd known Bennet Calder for better than thirty years and I didn't mean to be bluffed. I heartily wished I'd gone home as I'd intended, but since I'd made a fool of myself, I meant to hold my own against all comers.

He said at last, "What made you think I knew why Claribel went to the woods to meet the peddler?"

"You loaned her the money she gave him. She'd have told you— You must have known—"

"You're trying to say I wouldn't have loaned her money without knowing why she wanted it?" he inquired, and when I nodded he smiled and shook his head. "After all I've known Claribel Fortune a long time. I was a friend of her husband's. Would I have refused her money she needed so desperately?"

I caught at that last word. "Why did she need it so—desperately?"

He pressed his fingertips together carefully. "Assuming that I knew, I am too good a lawyer to pass out information indiscriminately. If a woman whom I liked and admired came to me in such a state—"

"What kind of a state?" I asked so quickly that he said before thought:

"Claribel was frantic, incoherent—" then he stopped, frowned impatiently. "How did you know she came here?" he demanded.

"She was seen," I said, then shut my lips firmly.

"Very well, let it go at that. It was broad daylight, but even assuming that I loaned her the money, how does that put me on the woods path that night?"

My heart flopped. "Because those were your shoe prints," I said, not very clearly, "and because—because—" my tongue stuck to the roof of my mouth like it does when I try to eat peanut butter.

"Yes, Mis' Martha—because—?"

"Because it was *your* gun that Lars Knowlton found by the Tan Top Rock, and it's hanging this minute upside down or something over the mantel in your study."

Out in the hall a deep-toned clock struck twice. Mr. Calder did not speak until the echoes had died. "Knowlton figured out the

print, I suppose," he said gently, "and that policeman, Brade, probably snooped around yesterday and decided about the gun. I
shouldn't have taken him in there."

"No, and it'd have been better to just hang the gun up properly
for then Captain Brade wouldn't have wondered about it."

He nodded, as if recognizing my remark as quite reasonable.
"Well, if I was there, as seems to be proven by my shoe prints, which
I take it someone has verified, if my gun has been unquestionably
identified—"

"There are ways," I interrupted, heart pounding, "to tell about
the bullet, know for sure if it came from your gun."

He smiled. "Yes, the science of ballistics is rather conclusive.
So if I was there, if the bullet that killed Donelli came from my
gun—well, it looks as if I might have shot the man, doesn't it?"

"You did shoot him!" I heard myself say, in a strong clear voice.

His eyes were pale fire, burning into mine as he leaned across
the table. "Martha Berry," he said, "if you were a jury of one trying
me on the charge of murdering Pietro Donelli, whom I never saw
until I looked at his dead body, you would convict me entirely on
circumstantial evidence."

I didn't deny it.

"All right, Martha," Mr. Calder said, "you sit nice and easy and
I'll tell you what did happen that night."

I didn't sit easy, and my tight lips did not relax.

"Claribel came here about six," he told me. "I loaned her the
money after I was unable to persuade her against paying blackmail, which is always foolish. She let it slip in her hysteria that she
was going to meet Donelli on the woods path at eleven that night.
At the time I discounted that, feeling that Claribel was too timid."

He turned the heavy stick carefully, smoothing it with his long,
strong fingers. "After she had gone," he continued, "I realized that
she might, considering her motive, do just what she said she would.
So, Mis' Martha, I went to the woods path also, approaching from
the west, coming on to the clearing through the elderberry thicket
from Tan Top."

He paused and I could not speak or move, only sit there listening.

"When I reached the clearing," he said, "there was no sound, and I was not as careful as I should have been. I made a slight noise as I approached. Immediately there was movement, a woman's startled gasp, a choked exclamation; for just an instant a flashlight showed."

He laid down the stick, leaned back. His face looked old and haggard. "I saw her bending over something on the ground. I know now she was rummaging through the pack. My coming frightened her and she was gone, scarcely making a sound as she went through the dark woods. I had seen just enough in that flash of light to know that a man lay—"

"Yes?" I urged. "What did you do?"

"I shot on my flash, saw Donelli lying dead on the ground, and beside him my own rifle with the silver shamrock insignia!"

"Good Lord!" I said faintly.

He smiled without mirth. "I believed for a moment that it was— hallucination." He mopped frankly at his face. "Then I came to myself. I didn't stop to examine anything. I picked up that gun and—"

"Ran like the devil, stumbled, fell, almost broke your neck, and lost the gun!"

"Yes," he said eagerly. "Yes, that's right."

"But why," I asked reasonably, "didn't you go back for it? Why wait until daylight to sneak through the bushes—"

"Because," he interrupted, "someone was coming toward me through the woods."

My heart did a definite flip flop. I sensed him lying there, breathless, shaken with that scene in the clearing, the desperate flight, the heavy fall, conscious of the night and the woods.

"My flashlight was broken," he said. "It was very dark. The gun could not have been found without a real search. I got up, away from the place."

I asked suddenly, "It was Claribel, wasn't it? Claribel stumbling along in the dark?"

"I believe so. At the time I did not question too closely. I put in the remainder of that wretched night trying to decide what to do about the gun. By daylight I was past intelligent thought. I only wanted to get it. You can imagine— When I found it was nowhere around I kept hunting, heard voices in the clearing, saw the gun beyond the bushes—"

Suddenly it was all too much. "Just a moment, Mr. Calder. You tell me that you saw Claribel bending over the body of Donelli, that she ran when she heard you, that you found your gun beside his body, that Claribel returned, prowling through the woods—"

"Yes, that is how it was. I am convinced now that it was Claribel I heard."

"But Claribel! She'd be afraid. She was always so frightened."

"Fear is sometimes the strongest incentive to action," he said grimly.

I knew that he was right. "But, how did she look? Did she seem—?"

"I only caught the flash of her face, heard her startled exclamation," he said, and stared at me curiously. I stared back. A startling idea had struck me.

"Then," I asked, "how do you know it was Claribel?"

He frowned. "Of course it was Claribel. She told me she was meeting Donelli there. Besides," he wet his lips, "who else could it have been?"

I held myself steady. No time to jump at conclusions.

"Also," Calder said slowly, "Claribel stole my gun!"

That brought me up. "Claribel—did—what?"

"No one else could have done it, Mis' Martha. The gun was over the mantel during her visit. It's always there. If it were missing I should know it at once."

"You tell me," I demanded angrily, "that Claribel left this house carrying that weapon and you didn't even see it? That she took it without your knowing?"

"She did the last, not the first. I left her alone in the study for a few minutes, then called her into the living room, finished my transaction—"

"Gave her the money she asked?"

"Yes. She left immediately and I did not go into the study again that evening. The next time I saw the gun it was beside Donelli's body. I conclude that she unhooked the gun, dropped it through the screen which can be opened from inside, picked it up on her way home. No other explanation is possible. No one else was here that night. I was in this room until I left for the hill. She took it."

My mind did one of its unreasonable feats of gymnastics. "Mr. Calder," I said, "never mind how I know, but Nesta Fortune said she knew who killed Donelli. Whom did she name?"

He blinked in swift surprise. "Mary Morningstar," he said.

I put my hand across my eyes to shut out the light, knowing how tired I was. Why was I such a fool as to be meddling in other people's affairs?

I said, "I'll be going now, Mr. Calder. It's been a long day."

I rose, steadying myself by the edge of the table. Just to go home, stretch flat on my bed, close my eyes—

He said something but I didn't answer. I went into the hall. He was beside me, asking me something, something about that money Ezra Fortune left. I was so tired of questions, of asking them and answering them.

I passed slowly down the steps, out the front gate, and heard the big door of Bennet Calder's house close behind me. I went home and into my cool, fresh bedroom.

I got out my best nightgown, the one of fine nainsook with the embroidered yoke, and the row of tatting around the wristbands. I brushed my long hair very carefully, braided it and threw back the covers of my bed.

I stretched out flat, closed my eyes, breathed long and deep. I slipped at once into complete unconsciousness.

Chapter Twelve

I WAKENED TO THE SOUND of Evinrude's bark, savage and startling in the stillness before dawn, heard it change to a low rumble of friendliness, heard him galloping down the path; steps were approaching my door, quick, purposeful, intent.

I got up, put on my slippers, kimono, went into the dim hall. It was quarter past four. The morning world was misty and dew-drenched, birds riotous, as I opened the door. Evinrude was lolloping along the path, alternately growling uncertainly and barking welcome. Evinrude has a sure sense for friends, but after all, Courtney Brade had only been there once.

He was bareheaded, his hair seeming more deeply silver than usual, his face lined and tired. He said, without preamble or apology, "Has Mary Morningstar been here?"

"Not that I know of, Captain Brade."

He turned, narrowing his eyes at the lighting garden. "I hoped she might have come."

"What's happened to Mary?"

He glanced at me. "Nothing to Mary," he said quietly. "There was an accident. Shane Fortune's in the hospital over at Mansford."

I drew my plaid kimono closer. "Is he bad hurt?"

Brade patted Evinrude's smooth head absently. "I'm afraid so, Mis' Martha. Crashed into a culvert, drunk I guess. Mary Morningstar was there."

"How did she happen to be there?" I asked, then, "Oh yes, he was trying to get away."

"Yes. Mary couldn't get him out of the wreck alone, so she walked to a farm house for help, took him in her car to the hospital. They phoned twenty minutes ago. He's unconscious, an operation may be necessary. They wanted to get in touch with his family."

"Why did you think Mary was here?"

"They said she'd left, believed her headed toward Alder Valley. I thought she might have come to you."

He lifted his head. In the still morning air came the sound of a deep-throated motor. Brade said under his breath, "There she is now!" and stepped into the shadow of the bridal wreath bush beside the path, just as Mary's long gray coupe rounded the corner, slid down the street, panted to a halt outside my gate.

Mary got out slowly, closed the door, turned toward the gate.

I thought, "Brade doesn't want her to know he's here. He thinks she might not come in."

Evinrude recognized her, went bounding down to meet her.

She was a tall, muffled figure in the strengthening light, walking slowly, mechanically, like a woman in deep sleep. I was so helpless watching Mary Morningstar coming up my garden path, the chrysanthemums brushing her skirt.

I went to her, put out my hands. She looked at me, tried to smile. I saw the ghost of it in her sunken, black-shadowed eyes, but her white, dead face would not respond.

I said, "Come in, Mary."

She put her hands in mine, allowed me to lead her inside. I saw then why she looked so strange. Her hair was white! I stood motionless staring at it. I'd heard about hair turning white in a few hours. I'd never believed it! Then I saw that Mary's hair was powdered with dust, her slim shoulders seemed to droop under the weight of it, her brown silk dress was bleached with it. She was like a woman slowly turning to dust before my eyes. Suddenly I could endure it no longer, her standing there, the dust so white on her hair.

Brade stood in the doorway. Mary did not seem to see him. I said, "Come, Mary," and took her up to the attic room, wishing in some way to hide her, shield her from curious eyes that would feed on her disintegration.

I heard Brade's steps behind me. I thought, "I wouldn't have his job. I'd hate to be always prying into people's hearts and lives."

Mary hadn't spoken. She sat where I indicated. I didn't know what to do. Brade pushed me gently aside, extended his open cigarette case, said casually, "Smoke?"

She obeyed the suggestion mechanically, drew smoke into her lungs. Her face relaxed a little. She looked up, straight at Brade. Her eyes were so deeply shadowed, so remote, so far from us.

She said, "Thank you, Captain Brade," and I sat down heavily. It had seemed that I would never hear Mary's voice again. My hands were cold and shaking. It's always cold before dawn in September.

I heard a horse's hooves clopping in the dusty street outside, and knew that old Pete McGregor was going the rounds with his milk. I thought of the time he had agreed to take Mary to the railroad when she ran away, and her being only seventeen.

He had always been so proud of his part in helping her. He used to save every newspaper clipping he could see about her, show them at every opportunity. "See," he would say, "the bonnie lassie! She owes a bit of her fame to old Pete, to just plain old Pete McGregor and his milk wagon."

The plodding hooves died away and there was silence around us, Mary sitting there, staring straight ahead, holding the smoking cigarette between her slim, soiled fingers. I couldn't speak. It was not for me to speak in that moment. Mary had come to me. Mary had to say why she had come.

She spoke without moving or looking up. She said, "Shane is near death, Martha!"

For all I'd heard the news from Brade, Mary's words were a terrible blow. I said helplessly, "Shane? Shane—Fortune?"

"No," Brade said from the wall where he leaned, "Not Shane Fortune, Mis' Martha," and paused, voice lifted in a curious questioning way, so that I felt it might fall at any moment and bring destruction with it.

Mary's head lifted slowly. She looked at him. Her face did not change. She said, "No, not Shane Fortune, Martha. Shane Marquand, my son!"

It didn't make sense at first. I didn't feel anything. I just sat there in my nice nainsook nightgown with the embroidered yoke, under my decent plaid kimono, and there wasn't anything that I could feel or think.

Then tears were running down my cheeks, pouring like rain over my thin, bony face. They were hot and seemed somehow dry; they kept raining down. They seeped into my mouth and I tasted them, hot and salty, dry, dry as ashes, against my tongue.

Mary said, "Don't cry, Martha," though I did not know that she had seen. She said, "For all the selfishness and wickedness of my life, Martha, I have paid this night," and lifted slim, dusty hands, brought them down slowly and hid from us her thin, tired face.

Brade spoke so quietly that his voice did not jar on the silence.

"You married Angelo Marquand when you were very young, Mary Morningstar?"

She did not lift her head. "Yes, just past twenty. I was there in Roleno, studying. I lived at his mother's house. He was young, too, we were going to— We made plans—"

"He had a fine voice?"

"No. He played the violin. He should have been— Angelo had the genius—"

"For one of the great violinists?" Brade questioned, and I was dumb before this strange thing.

"Yes," Mary said, and let her hands drop to her lap.

"This is Angelo?" he asked, and held a small photograph toward her.

She looked at it a long time. "Yes, Angelo, as I knew him twenty-six years ago in Italy. Not the Angelo I saw—" Her hands went swift and fierce against her throat.

"Seven years ago in Bariloche Prison in South America?"

She cried out at that, begging mercy from too much pain, but Courtney Brade knew no mercy. He laid the picture on the table, sat down on a low stool not far from her. I picked up the photograph. I could not see clearly, leaned nearer the light. The pictured face gradually formed before me. I said, because I could not help it, "This is not Angelo. It's Shane!"

"Yes," Brade said, "the likeness is remarkable. That's how I knew."

"Where did you get this picture?"

"Donelli carried it in his pocket. Put the cigarette here, Mary Morningstar," he said, and held an ash tray under her hand. Obediently she let the charred cylinder drop. "Why," he asked, "did you give the baby to Claribel Fortune?"

Mary said clearly, "Because, God forgive me, I did not want anything holding me back. I wanted to be a great singer."

"And Claribel wanted a baby?"

"Beyond anything. She spoke of adopting a child and the inspiration came. She could have mine when it was born, if she would swear never to tell."

"So neither of you bothered about legal adoption? Isn't that right?"

"It is. We were so young and ignorant. I never thought to want—my child. She believed if there was no record he would be in some way more particularly hers."

"Your husband? He agreed?"

Her long hands clenched. "He did not know. He was so tempestuous, so driven. He could not stay long in one place."

I thought of Shane's far-visioned eyes, of his saying, "I would not go far. I would always come back."

"There was no peace between us, ever." Mary said faintly. "He had gone away. He was always going away. I did not tell him about the baby—I thought I hated him."

"Where was Shane born?"

"In the house of Marianna Marquand, my mother-in-law in Roleno. She was a wonderful woman. She knew that each of us must go his appointed way. When Claribel took the baby, three days old, Marianna pretended to believe what I told her. That my friend, Mrs. Fortune, who was wealthy would give wonderful care to the child until I was strong enough to reclaim him."

"And when you failed to do this?" Brade prompted.

Mary's fine hands clenched as memory laid raw those distant years. "Marianna broke her silence, told Angelo on her death-bed of his son."

"She must have realized the danger in that, for Shane," Brade suggested.

"The Marquands were deeply religious people, Captain Brade. She knew her own flesh and blood. Once given, Angelo would never break the promise to forever allow the boy to work out his own destiny."

"And he confirmed that trust?"

"Yes. Poor Angelo! There was but once, years later, that he wrote me, telling me of that pledge to his mother, and begging news of the boy's whereabouts, his welfare. I believed him and felt I had no right to refuse."

There came silence again, the riotous clamor of birds in the big maple. "There is one woman living in Roleno who remembers the birth of Marianna Marquand's grandson," Brade told her, "an old serving woman."

"Lucina! Yes, Lucina would remember. Marianna told me the day I left that it was a long road that led to understanding—and I would travel it all the way." Again the slim, dusty hands went over the ravaged face. "I have traveled it," Mary Morningstar whispered, "all the way!"

"The first step toward understanding came seven years ago when you saw Angelo in Bariloche Prison?" Brade asked.

"Oh no, far back of that. Six years after Shane's birth I was in London. I bought a paper from a ragged boy one winter night. Something about his eyes, his hair—" Her voice caught. "I thought of Angelo and our son."

Brade nodded as if something had been cleared in his mind. He stared hard at the brightening window for a moment. "You attempted to regain Shane? You sent someone, a lawyer perhaps, a small, fat man with an astrakhan collar on his coat, a gold-headed cane, to Alder Valley?" Brade waited for her to answer.

She lifted her head, looking at him. For the first time, I believe, she realized how amazing his knowledge appeared to be.

"Yes. I sent Arno Ernst out from New York. He was a good man and my friend. I could trust him. I thought all I had to do was to tell Claribel I had changed my mind and would like to have my son." Her white face twitched in a faint smile.

"Yes," Brade said, "you might think that. You were very much engrossed in yourself in those years, weren't you, Mary Morningstar?"

She did not flinch from his dispassionate appraisal. "Completely. I did not see that I had done anything wrong, or that there was injustice in demanding the child from Claribel. Arno's letter was a terrific blow. I was frantic. I began thinking what I could do. I knew there was no legal adoption. I considered court action—"

"And then," Brade said swiftly, as if his mind had leaped over many obstructions straight to a given point, "Bennet Calder wrote to you?"

She nodded. "Claribel had called him in. He was her lawyer. In her frenzy she put the whole story in his hands, begging his help. He helped her. He wrote me a long letter. It was a masterly composition. He made me see what an ugly thing it would be if I insisted on dragging it into court, what a wrong would be done the child."

"How?" I demanded.

She looked at me from shadowed eyes. "He said the boy would grow up with the knowledge that his mother had given him away as you would a—puppy or a kitten. That it would have been kinder to have drowned him at birth—as you would a puppy or a kitten."

We were silent for a time. Then she said, "I learned something in those days. I came to see more clearly. I saw that whatever you do, always you abide by the results of that action. I saw that it was wrong to try and take Shane from Claribel. So, I gave him up, for good."

"And Angelo?" Brade questioned.

"Angelo? Yes, that influenced my decision. He had gone a sad way. He'd been in prison. He lost hold of everything after I divorced him. I did not want Shane to know, as he grew up."

"You thought it was kinder that Shane should believe that Amos Fortune was his father?"

"That is right. I wrote to Bennet Calder. I told him that I would never try to take Shane from Claribel."

Brade stroked his chin thoughtfully. "That being the case," he asked slowly, "why did Claribel pay practically her entire fortune into Calder's hands during these last nineteen years?"

I sat up with a gasp. So that was where Claribel's money had gone. That was why Bennet Calder could maintain such a home for his loneliness and devotion to an old hurt.

"It's simple," Mary said, "when you consider Claribel and how frightened and helpless and impractical she was. Calder simply deceived her. He did not tell her of my decision. Instead he made her believe that only through his cleverness and intervention could I be restrained from taking the matter into court and undoubtedly winning my claim to the boy she thought of as her son. He built such an edifice of terror for her that she would not ever speak to me of Shane after I came back, and though she took the management of her affairs from Calder, she paid him huge sums as long as her money lasted. I had suspected that, but only confirmed it the last day I talked to her."

"And I suppose," Brade said, as if speaking entirely to himself, "that is why Claribel kept the knowledge of Shane's inheritance to herself, waiting for Calder to die!"

"Good heavens," I said, "that's it, of course. She told Nesta Shane would get the money when *someone* died."

"Yes. Naturally, Nesta couldn't guess who as she knew nothing of Calder's real character. Claribel thought, in her terror, that if Calder knew of that money he would take it as he'd taken hers. He held over her always the threat of disclosing to Shane his true parentage."

Brade lighted a cigarette, inhaled deeply. "I got considerable of this from Calder when I dropped in on him a little time after you left, Mis' Martha. He was pretty well shaken. He's an old man. It was not too hard. What I could not get from his was the reason for the blackmail. In that, Calder was loyal to Claribel. He would not tell me why she paid him."

It was on the tip of my tongue to ask him how he had found out about Shane, but I bit back the question.

Brade finished his cigarette, lighted another. He said, glancing at me, "Mis' Martha, I'm famished for coffee. Any suggestions?"

I said, "Yes, a most practical one," and went down stairs leaving them alone. I put the pot on, covered the tray with a white linen cloth, set on dishes, silverware, made slices of thin, crisp toast, got out a jar of orange marmalade. I also took time while the coffee was cooking to get into a decent garb and brush my hair. I gave Ratsy his morning cream, Evinrude a bone, removed the cover from Richard's cage, gave him fresh water and heard him burst into joyous, tumbling song. The wild canaries in the fruit trees answered him, and the world was suddenly alive with yellow sunlight and the sound of many birds singing.

There had been so many mornings that I had done those very same simple acts in just the same way, but this morning would be forever set aside in my mind as one that was wholly and totally different. I tried to think of Shane as Mary's son, and it was not difficult, after I had uprooted the idea that he was Claribel's son. Mary didn't show in his face, only his dark restless father. There was Mary in the way he stood, though, the way I had said when he was young that he had wings on his heels.

Then it came over me suddenly that Shane might die. That maybe he was dead now and pain was so thick in my heart that I could not breathe. I had a moment of blind resentment, when I thought there just couldn't be anything or anyone wiser than us poor stumbling humans, or how could such a thing be?

Then I got hold of myself and went slowly toward the stairs, remembering that always we make our own lives, that no one ever can hurt us or destroy us—but only ourselves.

"Shane can do what he will about it," I thought. "It's just up to Shane. If he lives he can make what's happened into something fine, or that which is ugly and distorted and of no value."

Mary had stretched out on the old red sofa, a cigarette in her fingers. Brade stood by the window, looking out into the green depths of the maple tree. Neither moved when I came in. They didn't seem to hear me or know I was there. I put the tray on the sewing table, began to fill the cups.

Mary said, like she was just going on with what she had been saying, "—that is why I shall never sing again, after seeing what Angelo had become, that time I visited him in prison."

"You felt," Brade asked, not turning his head, "that you were in some way to blame? Because you had gone your own way? Divorced him?"

She sat up. "In some way to blame?" she echoed, "I was all to blame. If I had been wiser, more patient, we might have made our life successful; Angelo might have played the way he should. I ruined him—I killed him, not the fever that ended his life. I killed Claribel, and I killed Donelli, no matter whose finger pressed the trigger. I—have likely killed my son!"

I set the coffee pot down with a clatter. "Stop it!" I cried. "Stop talking like that! You've no right to take so much to yourself, Mary Morningstar. No one can make anything out of anyone, for good or bad. No one but himself! Angelo Marquand didn't have to drink and steal and maybe murder, and get in prison, just because you left him. If you did wrong that was your wrong and you would pay for it. He didn't have to ruin himself just to spite you!"

I stopped, trembling and frightened for what I had said. Brade had turned and was watching me, his eyes narrowed to hard, bright slits. Mary sat there, head up, eyes on my face, like she'd never seen me before. The cigarette dropped from her fingers, she not noticing.

She said, "Martha! Do you think that could be true?" and slumped suddenly on the sofa, sobs shaking her, tears trickling between dusty fingers.

Brade glanced at me, nodded briefly, and picked up the cigarette that was scorching the rug. "Thank you, Mis' Martha," he said and took a cup of coffee. I felt somehow that he was not thanking me for the drink.

I was shaking all over and the coffee burned my lips. I broke a piece of toast but it was tasteless. I laid it down, went to Mary, put my arms around her.

"Mary," I said, "please run downstairs and wash your face. I do declare you're a sight. All that dust and tears! You look worse than a ten-year-old with measles."

Folks are queer. You wouldn't have thought Mary would care how she looked with all that had happened, but I couldn't have said anything that would have snapped her back like that.

She stopped crying, felt her wet face, looked at her hands, glanced sidewise at Brade with his back to us, drinking coffee. She continued to sob gently, but she got up, looking guilty, and headed for the door.

"There's powder on my dresser," I called and dropped into a chair.

Brade said, "Think I'll take up plumbing, Mis' Martha. It's honest, clean work and the worst you can get is a complaint about a leaky water pipe."

He picked up a piece of toast. "I was right in some of my conclusions," he told me. "You know we were talking, when was it—last night here in this room?"

Last night! I just looked at him.

"Donelli, out on parole, approached Mary in Buenos Aires seven years ago, gave her the lowdown on Angelo who had been his cell mate. He collected handsomely and then, well, she couldn't stand it—had to go and see for herself." He reached for a second piece of toast.

"She visited Angelo and the sight of him set her off so she just cracked up in big way." Brade frowned at the toast. "His hands seemed to impress her particularly. She mentioned his fingers and the violin. Years of hard labor in a prison camp wouldn't help the touch on a violin string, at that."

I said, "How did Donelli know—" then remembered that he had been cell mate to Angelo.

Brade followed my thoughts. "Donelli got Angelo's story one time when Angelo was very sick, enough of it to pry the rest loose when Angelo was beginning to recover. He stole the picture and a letter Mary had written her former husband, which he had kept all these years. It was," Brade explained carefully, "the one she wrote in answer to Angelo's plea for news of his son."

Broken lines from Angelo's letter found on Donelli's body came to me. "For what you stole from me—for the confidence you have once betrayed—" That would be the time Pietro sought Mary out and collected money. "—silence would earn for you your worthless life—you cannot resist the golden lure—to say farewell to one I called my friend—always I hold in mind—in my lifetime of darkness—the thought of death—"

A pathetic, futile sort of letter, written by a man who was helpless to prevent the thing that he had unintentionally set into motion. I said abruptly, "What was in Angelo's letter to Mary? Did she tell you that?"

"Yes. He wrote that Donelli had headed for the States, to warn her against him. His letter came too late."

I looked up straight into his eyes, "Captain Brade, all this is very interesting and important—but do you know we haven't yet found out who murdered Donelli?"

Very carefully he placed his empty cup on the table. He said, "Yes, Mis' Martha, I'm not forgetting that." He picked up a napkin, absently touched his mouth, laid it down. "I believe I can say with confidence, however, that before the morning is much older, the murderer of Pietro Donelli will, of his own accord, walk into this room."

I sat up so suddenly my neck cracked.

Brade laughed, not very loud. "I didn't mean to be melodramatic. It's just that I had a very busy night. I can't give you details now, but the way the lines are laid, there isn't much question. The murderer will come."

Steps sounded on the stairs. I sagged back into my chair. It was Mary. She had done wonders with herself. I never ceased to be amazed at her recuperative powers, at the way some inner vitality seemed to surge up at the slightest opportunity, filling her with an almost inextinguishable buoyancy.

The dust was gone from her lovely hair. Her face was fresh and, though pale and worn, it seemed to me just then beautiful beyond words. Her dress was brushed, even her tall-heeled oxfords gleamed.

She flashed me a smile of gratitude as she sank down on the lounge. "I could do with some coffee, now," she said. "Thanks, Martha. That helped a lot."

Brade served her. Mary would always have a man to wait on her, I thought, knowing something not far from jealousy with memory of my own life that had been so hard and giving.

"Martha has reminded me of a very important point," Brade remarked, passing the cream. "I wonder if it has occurred to you, Mary Morningstar?"

She glanced at him swiftly. "You mean we still don't know who shot Donelli?"

"Correct," he said, returning the sugar bowl to the table. "Or," he asked carefully, "do you know?"

She stared at her cup for a long moment. "Claribel Fortune," she said at last, very low.

He sat down, crossing long legs. "Claribel told you this?"

Her eyes lifted, met his, dropped. "I believed that Claribel had shot him when you told me about the heel prints—"

He interrupted, "Where were you really, that night he was killed?"

"I told you the whole truth, except that I did not go near the hill path. I just drove all night."

"Why?"

She said slowly, "My maid told me on my return, shortly after six, about Donelli's visit, but did not explain that she had sent him to Fortunes'. Daisy was not with me on that South American trip so Donelli's face meant nothing to her. You can imagine what that news did to me. I had to get away! It did not occur to me that Donelli would go to Claribel. I only thought of his seeking me, that if I could keep away until I could figure something—"

"Then you told me you were on the woods path after I mentioned the heel prints. You insisted you were there because you didn't want Shane to know?"

"Yes. I couldn't let him believe his mother would be implicated in a sordid killing."

"No," Brade said, "you couldn't do that." Then after a moment, "Shane knows you are his mother? You told him last night?"

"No, Captain Brade, I did not tell him. Nesta told him!"

"Nesta!" I repeated blankly.

"Yes. She forced the facts from Claribel. She had become suspicious. She is that kind—always prying."

"That's right," Brade added. "Nesta did tell Shane the truth last night in a fit of temper. Naturally it hit him pretty hard. He stormed into Claribel's room. When Nesta tried to interfere," Brade smiled briefly, "well, Shane used her pretty roughly."

"He told me he slapped her," Mary said, "choked her."

"He did not, however," Brade pointed out, "shut her in the closet."

I looked my amazement.

"He left the house," Brade explained, "and Claribel tried to run after him. She fell, struck her head, and Nesta, hearing Bessie coming, hid in the closet where she just naturally passed out for a time."

"She would," I accused vindictively. "That's like Nesta, to run and hide, leaving Claribel—"

I stopped myself and went no further.

Brade looked at me curiously. "It is not always easy to follow the workings of a mind like Nesta Fortune's. She has a tremendous sense of the dramatic, a passion for climaxes. She was so angry and frightened at what she had roused that she wanted to make her position as secure as possible by building up Shane's brutality to her. She did not, I am sure, realize that Claribel Fortune was so near death. Not," he added, "that she could have done anything about it."

I wondered bleakly just then who had really killed Claribel. Shane? Because he left her? Nesta? Because she had motivated that leaving? Mary? Because years ago she had given her baby to Claribel? I looked at Brade, remembering his saying: "I'm not a judge. I do not pass on the motives behind murder!"

He stood by the window, looking down through the leafy tangle of the maple tree toward the road and the gate and the path bordered with chrysanthemums.

He turned slowly. "Miss Morningstar," he asked, "when Shane came to you last night did he carry anything? Have anything in his hands?"

She shook her head. "Nothing but his gloves. After he had gone, I found one on the divan."

Brade nodded, strolled across, picked up a small brown dispatch case from the corner. I had not noticed it before. He sorted through the conglomerate mass of its contents, selected a letter, turned toward Mary.

"I suppose there's no question but what you wrote this to Marquand?"

She took it, glanced briefly at the contents, returned it.

"It's the one I wrote fifteen years ago, in answer to the one from Angelo, begging for news of our son." Her head lifted suddenly. "Where did you get it, Captain Brade?"

"It was in Donelli's pack. The murderer stole it."

Like a clear picture came the scene that Mr. Calder had made me see. A woman glimpsed in the momentary light of a flash bending over something on the ground—a dead man and a rifled pack.

"If Donelli told Claribel about these proofs he had," I began, and could say no more.

"He did," Mary stated. "She couldn't enumerate them but she mentioned a letter, pictures."

"Did she," Brade asked calmly, returning the letter to the case, "intimate that she had them in her possession when you talked to her?"

Mary did not speak for a time. Her hands were clenched tightly in her lap. She stared unseeingly at the tip of her brown oxford, then gradually her hands relaxed. "Claribel is dead," she said faintly, "We must not judge her. She told me that afternoon I went to see her, the day the murder was discovered, that she—had the proofs."

"Did she say where she got them?"

"She did not say, Captain Brade."

"Where did you believe she had got them?"

"I thought that Claribel had met Donelli on the woods path, given him the money, and then—shot him!"

Brade snapped the case shut. I could not take my eyes from it. It was a handsome thing of fine brown leather, with two slim straps holding it, a stout handle at the top. Two small metallic buttons on the flap snapped into corresponding sockets set into the body of the bag. I had seen it somewhere, and not in Brade's hands. I had seen someone in Alder Valley carrying it, not too long ago.

He set it on the table, tilted against the massive old inkwell. He said, "Miss Morningstar, when you talked with Mrs. Fortune, did you mention the oddity of her wearing your shoes?"

"Naturally," Mary smiled rather hopelessly. "It was like trying to get sense out of a very young child. She repeated and contradicted herself, gave half a dozen ridiculous reasons. She thought she'd feel taller in my shoes, couldn't find hers—things like that. Then she began crying, Claribel's ultimate refuge, and admitted that she didn't know why she'd done it. She didn't know whose shoes they were—whether she had on shoes or not. She did admit that they'd worn a devilish blister on her left heel. That she'd had the doctor dress it that morning."

"Yes," Brade purred, looking inexpressibly happy, "an ill-fitting shoe may well produce a blister. Did you believe her?"

"No," Mary said sharply. "I thought she'd literally hidden herself in my shoes. I was furious!" She shrugged wearily. "What difference does it make now?"

"It might make considerable," Brade reminded her. "We have not, you know, discovered definitely who murdered Donelli."

Mary's head snapped up. Her eyes were suddenly frightened.

"No, we have not discovered that."

Brade said, picking up the dispatch case, "I am convinced that this belongs to the murderer!"

I choked back a startled gasp. Suddenly the innocent brown case held a terrible significance. I could not look away from it as Brade turned it slowly. Where had I seen it? Whose was it? Why, in heaven's name, did he feel sure that it belonged to the murderer?

The morning light coming through the tangle of vines over the dormer window touched the bag with sudden brilliance so that each small detail stood out sharply. I cried, "The button! That little button—"

Brade's glance met mine with startling force. "You remember? Good! Now look!"

He fished something from a pocket, held his hand toward me, and once again I saw a palm extended holding a small round object of dull metal. That little bronze-gold button, its surface engraved with a beautiful 'g' in old English script. I could not stir as realization came. That button, or whatever it was, had been found under the dead man's hand by Lars Knowlton. I remembered how he had snatched it up, how for a moment I had thought he would refuse to give it to Brade, how white and dazed he looked, how he insisted angrily that he had never seen it before, and I so sure that he had. I remembered Bennet Calder's stubborn insistence that it was off a glove.

Brade said, "Now! Get this!" He turned the bag, so the two small buttons on the flap were toward me. "Observe," he said softly, and I saw then that the snaps did not match. That on the right was the duplicate of the one Brade held, the other the same size, but cheaper, shinier, and not engraved.

He said, "The button in my hand was obviously torn from this bag in a struggle, presumably between Donelli and his killer. You can see where the leather was broken and mended when the new snap was set in place. The bag has been repaired. There is little question but that the button found under Donelli's hand came from this case."

I could only nod. If Brade knew the owner of the bag—

His quiet voice broke into my speculation. "This case is manufactured by a firm famous for fine leather baggage. It is known as the 'Grosvenor.' This line is not sold in Alder Valley, but one merchant can supply a customer's wants through special order." He paused, considering the bag affectionately. "In my opinion, this case was used by the murderer as the most natural, and what he considered the safest, place of concealment."

"Concealment of what?" I asked.

"Those things which were taken from the body of the murdered man," Brade said, and at that moment I heard steps crunching on the gravel path below.

Chapter Thirteen

"Before the morning is much older," Brade had said, "the murderer of Pietro Donelli will walk into this room!"

"Where?" I asked weakly, "did you get that case, Captain Brade?"

He said sharply, "So you know whose it is, Mis' Martha?"

I tried hard to tell him. I did know. I'd seen it! In someone's hands. Seen hands closed around it, holding it. Whose hands? What kind of hands? It belonged to a man surely. It looked like a man. A doctor? A lawyer?

"Mr. Calder is your caller, Mis' Martha," Brade said quickly. "Will you suggest that he come up here?" It was not a request. It was an order. I rose heavily, went to the stairs, descended slowly, steadying myself by the wall, feeling its lumps and areas of smoothness beneath my cold fingers.

Mr. Calder looked very tired. There were heavy lines in his normally pink face. It was still pink, but there was a static look to it, as if life had gone out and only the semblance remained.

I leaned against the door, looking up at him. I said, "Good morning, Mr. Calder, what brings you here so early?"

He seemed to have difficulty in speaking. "I came to ask, suggest— We're friends of long standing, Martha Berry. What we discussed last night, about me being on the hill path—"

I opened the door. "Come in. I have a pot of coffee."

He mopped his face. "Yes, I should like coffee, Martha," he glanced around rather helplessly.

"It's upstairs," I told him, and he went ahead of me across my neat little parlor, hesitated at the open stairs door, began mounting heavily.

I was just behind him when he stopped, saw first Mary Morningstar, then Courtney Brade. I heard the breath go out of him. His big shoulders slumped. He steadied himself by a sudden hold on the door.

Brade said, "Come in, Calder. I've been hoping you'd drop round."

Brade had such a way of making everything seem casual and matter-of-fact. He sounded then as if he had just been hoping that Mr. Calder would come by so he could ask him to clear up a point on the last world series—something like that.

Mr. Calder said, "Yes, yes, of course," and went into the room. Mary smiled at him, and the way Mary has of smiling at times might make a man forget less important things, like being suspected of murder.

Mr. Calder sat down by the table. I poured coffee for him. Brade still lounged by the window. He said, "You gave me a good deal of help at our conference this morning, Calder, but there were one or two points you failed to clear up."

Mr. Calder stirred his coffee mechanically, sunken eyes on Brade's face. He said thickly, "Yes, of course. Anything I can do—"

"Fine," Brade applauded. "Now, why, exactly, did Mrs. Fortune take the management of her affairs from you?"

Calder blinked and took a great gulp of coffee. "She was angry," he said huskily, "at what she considered exorbitant charges for my services."

"In other words, your blackmail," Brade suggested amiably. "She couldn't get out of paying it, but she could refuse to allow you to act as her official representative."

"She considered my charges exorbitant," Calder insisted stubbornly, and Mary laughed, suddenly and unexpectedly.

"She was justified in that, I think, Mr. Calder. Claribel paid you a thousand dollars a month for practically as long as her money lasted."

His lined, sagging face flushed angrily. "What my fee was I consider my own affair," he said stiffly.

"It was your affair, if you could get Claribel to meet it," Mary told him ruthlessly. "You collected a neat sum from me, also, at the time of our isolated correspondence, on the grounds of keeping Claribel from going to court and attempting to gain legal title, so to speak, to my son."

Calder's cup clattered to the table. He started forward, but Mary only smiled at him. "It's no use now. The income's stopped from that source. You can't hope to collect from Shane's inheritance." She stopped as steps sounded in the parlor and a voice called, "Mis' Martha? Martha Berry, you up there?"

Brade's eyes flicked, raced toward the door. He nodded and I said, "Yes, Lars, I'm here. Come up!" We were motionless while he clattered up the stairs, burst into the room, stopped like someone had smacked him hard between the eyes.

"Oh," he said on a quickly drawn breath, "a party, eh?" and slouched in, his head all but touching the raftered ceiling, his shock hair tumbling into his sunken, red-rimmed eyes, a growth of dark beard staining his thin cheeks.

Brade said, "Well, Knowlton, how'd it go? Unearth the information I wanted?"

Lars lifted a big, grimy hand, brushed hair from his eyes.

"Yeah," he said breathily, and folded up like a patent dress hanger to sit on the floor, long legs encircled by gaunt, corded arms.

"That's fine," Brade commented softly. "I'd be glad to get your report. Knowlton," he added, not looking at any of us, but just at Lars, "very kindly agreed to locate the owner of a certain piece of property, since proof of its ownership will definitely settle the identity of the murderer of Pietro Donelli."

He lifted the dispatch case, turning it slowly. "Who," he asked, "does this belong to, Knowlton?"

Mr. Calder sat forward like a spring had been released, face a cold pasty gray, sweat gleaming at his temples. His hands came out, dropped helplessly.

Lars said, "It belongs to Bennet Calder! Charlie Cunningham, at the Main Street Drug Store is willing and ready to make a sworn statement to that effect. Last June 21st he ordered the case special for Calder."

Ratsy would pick just that moment to stroll in, a huge black cricket in his mouth, the thing kicking feebly, entangled in his cannibalistic whiskers. In he stalked, waving his handsome striped tail, said meow in a deep, triumphant tone, and jumped into my lap. I gave him a swift boost in the general direction of any place but where he was. He landed softly, retired into the hall, looked at me reproachfully.

Brade said, "Calder, eh?" and fingered the case lovingly. "That's correct, isn't it, Calder? You did buy the case at the Main Street Drug Store last June 21st, didn't you?"

Mr. Calder tried to speak. His plump jowls quivered, his eyes were strained until I thought they would pop out. He said, "Yes, yes, I—I bought the case, but I bought it to give—"

Lars Knowlton threw back his disheveled head and laughed. "Oh, forget it, old man," he choked. "Don't try to stall us along. Maybe you did buy the case to give to someone, but you kept it yourself. Everyone in town's seen you carrying it. I've seen it under your arm, in your hand a dozen times. So's Mis' Martha. Right, Mis' Martha? You've seen it in Calder's hand when he came after the five o'clock? You remember how his fingers curled round it like he couldn't chance dropping it, like—"

He went on like that, building up such a clear picture of Bennet Calder standing before the window with that brown leather case in his hands that I could have sworn that I'd seen him like that a hundred times. I knew I'd seen it in someone's hands. I wanted to be sure; to tell the truth. I said uncertainly, "Let me think, Lars. Don't talk so fast."

Brade spoke from where he stood by the window. "Another caller, Mis' Martha," and I gave a sigh of gratitude. I believed then that it was his way of giving me time to get hold of myself so I might answer accurately. I went into the hall.

Nesta was halfway across the parlor when I reached the stair foot. She said, a bit breathlessly, "Is Lars here? Lars Knowlton?"

I nodded, knowing my eyes unfriendly, my lips hard. I had never liked Nesta Cramer from the time she was a small, ringleted, avid-eyed child, old with knowledge far beyond her meager years.

"I want to see him," she said, "at once! It's important."

I stepped aside, and she ran past me and up the stairs with a whiff of expensive perfume, a swish of her short tweed skirt.

She looked fresh and manicured, her hair tightly curled, bright spots of rouge on her thin cheeks, a batik scarf around her bruised throat. Little Claribel Fortune was dead. Shane bound in a darkness that might only lift with death. Mary Morningstar—well, we were all in ruin that morning and Nesta knew the facts. She came twittering and rustling in her brightness, and I wondered if anything, anything at all, would ever really touch her, if it was within the compass of her limited awareness to even dimly sense another's heartbreak.

I climbed the stairs wearily. It seemed to me then that I had been climbing those same stairs endlessly for hours and hours.

"Oh, Lars," Nesta called in her thin, bright treble. "It's Nesta. I've lost my—" A moment's startled silence, then—

"Well!" The hand that had fluttered toward her throat steadied into a casual gesture. "Excuse *me!* Conference of war, or something, Captain Brade?" She went slowly toward him, slim hips swaying, "or just one of Martha's coffee fights?" Her sharp eyes, searching every face, denied the lightness of her tones, settled on Lars hunched on the floor. A smile flicked her lips. Her lids lowered over those bright squirrel eyes.

Lars's lean body had stiffened. His somber glance held hers momentarily, alive with something I could not read. He started to rise. Brade's casual tones delayed the action.

"You were saying, Mrs. Fortune, you had lost something?"

Nesta's slim body was like a lance. One hand curled hard and tight into a meager fold of the tweed skirt. She said, "Oh, nothing much. Just my dispatch case, sort of a pocketbook, you know." Her laugh was sharp and clear like a cleft in green ice. "I cashed a check yesterday and missed the case shortly after I got home. I got out of the car with my arms full of bundles, must have dropped it."

She was catching the electric stillness in the room. Her face was so white just then that the round patches of rouge stood out like bloodstains. She said, in sudden breathlessness, "Mrs. Chambers told me Lars stopped by asking for me, sat whittling on the fence, waiting. I thought he might have seen—" Her words trailed off as her darting eyes settled on the case beyond the stack of magazines on the table.

"Oh!" she said, hand at her throat, then, with an impatient exclamation she pounced on it exactly like Ratsy does on a cricket, whirled, eyes black with defiance. "Someone might have told me," she accused, crimson-tipped fingers curling round the tightly fastened straps in a gesture I was suddenly recognizing.

Brade's smile was deceptively somnolent. He said, "A practical bag. Scarcely a vanity—"

"No, but it's a wedding present from Uncle Calder, useful too. Holds my household accounts, appointment list—everything."

"Yes," Brade agreed slowly, "it would carry everything. Even the letter and picture taken from Donelli after you shot him that night on the woods path!"

Bennet Calder gave a dull groan, covered his face. Lars rose awkwardly, white as dust. I was motionless, fingers twisting painfully into the stuff of my skirt. Mary Morningstar sat erect, wide, suffering eyes on Nesta's face.

Nesta took one quick step backward. She looked old then, haggard, spent, but back of her bleakness was a slowly growing, fiercely raging fire of anger. She said thickly, "Do I understand—fully?"

"I think you do," Brade assured her gravely, "only too well. That blister on your left heel, Mrs. Fortune. The doctor asked you about it at the house this morning. He'd dressed it for you earlier. Tight pumps with extremely high heels would make such a thing, eh?"

Nesta's smoldering eyes met his. "A very intelligent conclusion, Captain Brade," she said, and looked at Lars. He winced visibly as if she had struck him. "It's useless now I suppose to deny that I met Donelli that night in the woods. I don't deny it. I'd have admitted it any time you asked. I'd have been a fool to offer the information."

"Likely," Brade agreed. "You went in Claribel's place? Because she was so—?"

"Completely addled with terror I knew she'd fumble the whole business."

"And what," Brade inquired, "was the whole business, Mrs. Fortune?"

She said, lips curled back from prominent white teeth, "We wanted, Claribel and I, to save Shane's inheritance for him. The money his Uncle Ezra left him. Donelli—he could have ruined that; he could prove that Shane wasn't Amos Fortune's son, had never been legally adopted." Her glance went fiercely over the motionless group, rested longest on Mary. Beneath that cruel regard Mary's eyes closed momentarily, then her head lifted and she looked straight at Nesta.

"Go on," she said very low, "you're not telling anything that's news, Nesta."

"Okay," Nesta said. "It's up to you, my dear. That's the bare truth. I knew Claribel wasn't up to it. I took the money Donelli demanded as payment for the proofs, the gun Claribel had taken from Uncle Calder. I didn't expect trouble, but I wasn't taking chances. I met Donelli," she recited in a harsh, flat voice, "gave him the money—and then—"

Suddenly she was crouching there, shoulders hunched, head sheltered by an uplifted arm, her voice thick with remembered terror.

"He wouldn't give me the proofs," she chattered. "He laughed at me, said he was glad I had come. He seized me. His hands were big and strong—and—"

"You shot him with the gun Claribel had stolen from Calder." It was a quiet statement from Brade, rather than a question.

Nesta sagged to a chair, sobbing jerkily. Lars spoke in a smothered voice, his homely rugged face lifting pleadingly to Nesta.

"You thought I turned in the dispatch case, spilled everything, Nesta, but you're wrong. Brade found it. I thought perhaps—" his head sagged slowly and he covered his face with his hands.

Oh, Lars, Lars. All of your stifled love for the girl lay quivering at our feet then—your valiant effort to save her at the expense of the man you hated. Scarcely knowing how I got there, I was beside him holding him tight, hugging him hard.

Brade's face was granite hard as he continued, ignoring the interruption, "You shot Donelli, Mrs. Fortune, when he failed to give you the proofs, keep his part of the bargain. There is no question about your ownership of the bag. I found the man who repaired it for you. You probably intended to kill the Italian when you went out armed with the rifle, wearing Mary Morningstar's shoes." He shrugged. "I'm a detective, not a lawyer. Your suggestion of a struggle argues attempted assault. Perhaps you can make it stick with the jury, convince them that you killed in self-defense."

"You—you think I could?" she quavered, lifting a strained, ravaged face, and with those simple words made her confession.

Chapter Fourteen

THE TELEPHONE RANG just then and, creature of habit that I am, I rose, stumbled out of the room and down the stairs. It was for Mary Morningstar, from the hospital.

She was standing, white-faced, eager, when I came back. Her eyes clung to mine with a terrible intensity. "Shane?" she whispered. "He is—?"

"Out of the coma, Mary, seems much better." I took a deep breath. The morning seemed suddenly very bright. "He's calling for his mother," I said, and she gave one glad cry, filled with the pent-up longing, the suffering and frustration of many empty years, and, pushing past me, flew down the stairs.

AFTERWORD
Secrets and Lies: Mothers and Sons in Katherine Wolffe's *Tall Man Walking* and *The Attic Room*

Curtis Evans

SPOILER WARNING: Major plot spoilers to both *Tall Man Walking* and *The Attic Room* are given in this afterword. For the sake of their own enjoyment, readers are urged to finish both novels before even glancing at this afterword.

Two of Marian Gallagher Scott's three "Katherine Wolffe" mysteries, *Tall Man Walking* (1936) and *The Attic Room* (1942), are narrated by single women in their fifties who reside in New England villages where murder has struck, intimately impacting these women's closest social circles. In both novels the male detective figures—psychiatrist Kenneth Borden in *Tall Man Walking* and policeman Courtney Brade in *The Attic Room*—discover the culprits of the crimes primarily by probing the minds of these two highly respectable women, prompting them unconsciously to reveal hidden truths about themselves and others. In *Tall Man Walking* the surprise revelation that so impressed contemporary reviewers of the novel is that the narrator, spinster Laure Hosmer, herself is the murderer, while in *The Attic Room* the killer more conventionally is the individual whom the narrator, widow Martha

Berry, most dislikes. Yet both narrators are alike in that during the course of events in the novels they are repeatedly forced to acknowledge shocking secrets about the people residing in their seemingly placid villages.

The shocking secrets in both *Tall Man Walking* and *The Attic Room* concern mothers and "their" sons. In *Tall Man Walking* Laure Hosmer's obsessive devotion to David Kaye, the man she raised for five years when he was a young boy, provokes her to murder his intended bride, Wiletta Owen, in order to prevent that designing woman from, she believes (with considerable justification, it must be admitted), effectively destroying her beloved David's life. In *The Attic Room*, Martha Berry learns that her dear friend, retired opera singer Mary Morningstar, is in fact the birth mother of Shane Fortune and that Shane's supposed birth mother, Claribel Fortune, was involved in the murder of Pietro Donelli, a man possessing knowledge of Shane's true nativity who had come to their village with blackmail in mind. (In the event the murder was actually carried out by Claribel's viciously determined daughter-in-law, Nesta Fortune.)

Although Marian Gallagher Scott was happily wed for twenty-six years, her marriage lasting from 1917 until her death at the age of fifty in 1943, she and her husband, fellow circuit Chautauqua performer Earl W. Scott, appear never to have had any children. In *Tall Man Walking* Laure Hosmer's obsessive devotion to a child ultimately leads to her committing three murders. As Kenneth Borden explains to Dr. Marcus Wayne near the end of the novel, to the younger Laure Hosmer a man was "important for only one thing. To give her children. For that she loves him, until the children come. Then his importance vanishes. The children are all that count. The man is pushed aside. He lives outside her world of reality, which is composed entirely of her devotion, her abnormal absorption in her children. . . . All [Miss Laure's] real ability, and she has plenty of it, all the energies of her mind, were transformed through hungry necessity into love for David." Similarly, in *The Attic Room* the pathologically needy Claribel Fortune's obsessive dependence on the adopted son she falsely presented to the village as her birth child sets in motion a chain of circum-stances that culminates in murder. In these two novels was Marian Scott justifying her own life choices: her evident prioritizing of her spouse and her careers in circuit Chautauqua and crime writing over having children? We may never know, but the question lends interest to the consideration of these two mystery novels.

COACHWHIP PUBLICATIONS

COACHWHIPBOOKS.COM

VULTURES
IN THE SKY
A HUGH RENNERT MYSTERY

TODD DOWNING

Vultures in the Sky, by Todd Downing
Introduction by Curtis Evans
ISBN 978-1-61646-149-2

COACHWHIP PUBLICATIONS

NOW AVAILABLE

There is No Return, by Anita Blackmon
Introduction by Curtis Evans
ISBN 978-1-61646-223-9

COACHWHIP PUBLICATIONS

COACHWHIPBOOKS.COM

Murder in Style, by Emma Lou Fetta
Introduction by Curtis Evans
ISBN 978-1-61646-232-1

Murder of the Honest Broker, by Willoughby Sharp
Introduction by Curtis Evans
ISBN 978-1-61646-211-6

COACHWHIP PUBLICATIONS

COACHWHIPBOOKS.COM

Murder Ends the Song, by Alfred Meyers
Introduction by Curtis Evans
ISBN 978-1-61646-298-7

www.ingramcontent.com/pod-product-compliance
Lightning Source LLC
Chambersburg PA
CBHW020534020726
47494CB00006B/1762